BREAD
AND
BUTTERMILK

HELEN PAYTON

BREAD
AND
BUTTERMILK

Disclaimer

The story of 'Bread and Buttermilk' is fictitious as are all names and characters portrayed in the book; Carreg-y-Bedd is a fictional village. However, the incidents in the narrative take place against the backdrop of actual places in Wales.

No identification with actual persons (living or deceased) is intended or should be inferred. The exception are those public figures mentioned by name, such as Lloyd George.

The fictional events in the book are merged with genuine local and global historical events.

The following are a matter of historical fact:

Mr. E. W. Lovegrove was headmaster of Ruthin School from 1913-1930.

Hugh Vaughan and Margaret Roberts of Mwrog Street, Ruthin, lost three sons in the Great War: John in October 1917, Stephen in April 1918 and Christmas in September 1918.

Charles Edward Boxer was killed on 14th May 1884 when his horses bolted, causing his trap to overturn and pitch him out on to the road between Bontuchel and Cyffylliog.

The War Diary of 8th April 1916 for the 2nd Battalion of the Royal Welch Fusiliers states that three craters were captured and, 'A good trench was dug, linking up the craters with our front line. The idea was to close on an enemy sap in the Cambrin section and scupper or capture the garrison'.

The War Diary of the 9th Battalion of the Royal Welch Fusiliers for 22nd/23rd March 1918 states that near Morchies, in Northern France, '6 prisoners and one Machine Gun were captured by the 9th RWF by patrols'.

Dedication

A gwaedd y bechgyn lond y gwynt,
A'u gwaed yn gymysg efo'r glaw.

Their cries of anguish fill the wind,
Their blood is mingled with the rain.

Hedd Wyn 1917

Eternal God, whose strength raised up our Lord Jesus Christ from the dead, uphold, we pray thee, the ancient valour of the Royal Welch Fusiliers, that we may ever endure hardship after his example, and may rise with him to shine as the sun in thy Kingdom, through the same Jesus Christ our Lord.

Amen

Collect of the Royal Welch Fusiliers

Dramatis Personae

The Tudors: Cwyn-y-Gwynt

    Emyr Tudor: a farmer

    Mali Tudor: his wife

    Bethan Tudor: their older daughter

    Tŵm Tudor: their oldest son

    Caron Tudor: their younger daughter

    Brad Tudor: their second son

    Sion Tudor: their youngest son

    Nain (Eira Reece): Mali Tudor's mother

The Parrys: Y Betws

    Thomas Parry: a farmhand; killed in WW1

    Ruth Parry: his wife

    Gwyn Parry: their son

The Griffiths: Tan-y-Graig

    Howell Griffiths: a farmer

    Olwen Griffiths: his wife

    Ebrill Davies: their older daughter; widow of Harri

    Catrin Sturrock: their younger daughter; married to Charles Sturrock

    Evan Griffiths: their son; killed in WW1

The Bowens: Ffynnon Ddu

    Gwilym Bowen: a farmer; ex-soldier WW1

    Nia Bowen: his wife

The Philpins: Yr Efail

    Weyland Philpin: a blacksmith/farrier

    Nerys Philpin: his wife

    Dee Philpin: his daughter

The Morgans: Hendreforgan; better known as Lane End

    Griff Morgan: farm labourer and part-time gamekeeper

    Beti Morgan: his wife

    Cadoc Morgan: their older son; farm labourer; ex-soldier WW1

    Gethin Morgan: their younger son; farm labourer; ex-soldier WW1

    Bronwyn Morgan: their daughter

The Craddocks: Bryn-y-Castell

    Sir Edward Craddock: estate owner

    Lady Eleanor Craddock: his wife

    Harriet Craddock: their daughter

Alice Craddock: their daughter

Humphrey Craddock: their son

The Gypsies: God's Country

Moses: Romany gypsy; skilled in farming

Grizell: his wife, sister to Valentina

Abram: their son

Esmeralda: their daughter

Solomon: Grizell's brother-in-law

Valentina: his wife, sister to Grizell

Silvaina: their daughter

Matthew: their son

Seraphina: the matriarch, a widow, mother of Grizell and Valentina.

Carreg-y-Bedd: the village

Richard Owen: the doctor. Tŷ Faenor

Daniel Ellis: the minister. Tŷ Capel

Roland Pugh: the schoolteacher

Ynys Môn: Anglesey

Dr. William Owen: Richard Owen's father

Huw Owen: Richard Owen's younger brother

Aberporth

Mair Pritchard: cousin of the Tudors

Dr. Bartlett: GP

Hannah: Post Office

Villagers in Carreg-y-Bedd

See Appendix 2

Author's Note

'Bread and Buttermilk' is the Romany name for Denbighshire.
The chapter headings are the Romany names for the months of the year.

Chapters

Month of the Rain

The morning that the body, which had once been Gwyn Parry, floated to the surface of Pwll Berw was the same Sunday the Gypsies arrived in Carreg-y-Bedd. It was the special Sabbath so there was no-one to see the corpse emerge through the weed, which clung to the head in green, feathery strands. One arm reached out, gently nudging the donkey grey sedge growing on the banks of the pool. Spiky rushes, their blades pointing skywards, nestled in between the knees; two stray water snails clung to the sodden wool shirt. A dragonfly hovered, taking advantage of the weak sunshine, oblivious to the unfolding story beneath its wings.

The three caravans drew up just before dinner time on the common land which bordered the Ebenezer chapel on one side and the 'Lamb and Lion' tavern on the other. Favouring the holy flank for the caravans but tethering the horses on unholy territory, it seemed the Gypsies were settling in. Soon a wisp of smoke could be seen eddying upwards from a camp fire. Urchins began carrying water from the village pump.

Abram could just hear the strains of *'Christ the Lord is risen today'* as he strode over to help his sister who was struggling to give the horses a well-earned drink. They had been travelling for days through Snowdonia and Hiraethog after passing much of the winter on the Llŷn, near the coast. The Gypsies would not come as a surprise in Carreg-y-Bedd since they usually spent spring and summer in the village. Neither would they be unwelcome, bringing with them as they did, unique talents much valued by the community.

Abram was restless, poised at the age of limitless possibilities. Ahead of him lay his journeys, his horses, his music and his women. He was impatient for his adventures to begin. Revelling in his lithe athleticism, he vaulted over the hindquarters on to the back of Sal, a rather portly piebald who took no notice of the intrusion whatsoever.

A shout from Moses prevented Abram from enjoying a canter round the green. "Leave thet pony alone. She's done enough fer today. Come an' 'elp wi' settin' up. I need 'nother pair of 'ands fer t' bender. Get some 'azel branches from t' wood. Tek young Matthew wi' yer an' show 'im what's what. It's about time 'e learnt. An' don't forget yer knife."

It was enough. His Da was not to be disobeyed. Abram called to Matthew and the pair set off, Abram none too pleased about being accompanied by his young cousin. It would make the task that much longer, especially since he had to instruct him.

Inside Ebenezer, Tŵm Tudor closed his hymn book. He had tried and failed to focus on the message of the sermon which, for once, was uplifting, a welcome relief from the usual oppressive weight of sin. Tŵm, musing rather than praying, could not rid himself of the nagging unease which had been an unwelcome lodger for the past three years. God had allowed Gwyn to return from France but not Evan. Tŵm tried to rationalise that fact. Millions of fathers, sons and brothers had not returned from the war. It wasn't just Evan. Many had been obscenely mutilated and Evan would have despised a deformity; not in others but certainly in himself. Better dead than broken, whether physically, or worse, mentally. But somehow the logic didn't help. He still struggled to handle the reality that Evan's God had deserted him.

Gwyn had opened up to Tŵm about his time at the Front on only a couple of occasions but for the most part it was as though he had detonated a wall of slate to block the tunnel of his memory. Tŵm had found out more about the war from going to a lantern lecture in Denbigh Town Hall than he ever had from Gwyn. In 1918 with both his friends at the Front and minimal news in the 'Denbighshire Free Press', Tŵm had found the search for more information less than easy. To find out what his friends were living through, he gleaned his knowledge from a combination of listening to the lectures and poring over national newspapers. Hearing news of a local hero, he had been with his Tad, Emyr, to watch the mayor present a young Ruthin soldier with the Military Medal and a gold watch for bravery in the field.

"We must go to applaud him Tad," he'd said. "The paper said he's in the 9th Battalion of the Royal Welch. That's the same one as Evan and Gwyn."

The day after Gwyn's homecoming at the end of June 1919, he had visited Evan's Mam and Tad to tell them of Evan's courage, his fortitude, his gallantry; to share some memories and some tears. Since then, Tŵm could only recall Gwyn once allowing a glimpse into his ordeal, praising Evan's heroism and loyalty. Tŵm, with the tactless curiosity of youth had asked Gwyn all manner of questions at first but quickly learnt that all he would get in reply was, "Better not go there. Let the dead stay dead." Allusion to the fighting often resulted in Gwyn becoming even more withdrawn. Always reserved, he now verged on taciturn. Spending much of his time in the chapel, Gwyn was prominent at every service as well as attending Bible reading and prayer groups. Tŵm supposed Gwyn found comfort in God's arms after the horrors of France. It was more than unusual then, on this Easter Day, to see Gwyn's mother, Ruth, solitary in a side pew.

Gwyn and Evan had been friends since their first day in school. Three years later when Tŵm arrived, in all his stocky seriousness, the older boys, attracted to an intelligence beyond his years, had 'adopted' him. He, in turn, relished the glory of being friends with the big boys, the 'bechgyn mawr'.

The final Amen drifted upwards. At the door the minister waited to pass on his Easter tidings.

'Well-chosen hymns, Mr. Ellis.' Emyr Tudor always felt the need to make a comment on the service.

"Thank you, Mr. Tudor. I'm glad you enjoyed them."

Mali Tudor interrupted. "It's not a case of enjoyment Mr. Ellis; the proper hymns nourish the soul."

"Quite. That's what I meant." Daniel Ellis was more than a little discomfited. Mali Tudor always made him feel like a gauche youth. He wondered whether she singled him out for special treatment or whether she made everyone feel inadequate.

The congregation clustered around Ebenezer's open oak doors. Since it was Easter Day, socialising for a short time was obligatory. Mali, aware of the celebratory joint of lamb awaiting her attention, would have preferred to return home. Social exchanges with the neighbours she viewed as irksome. But duty was duty and Mali Tudor was not one to shirk it. Feeling obliged, she stopped to speak to Ruth Parry.

Only Mali could turn commiseration into a massaging of misfortune. "A hard day for you Ruth I know. It must bring back memories."

"I try not to think like that, Mali. Instead, I thank the good Lord for saving my son."

Mali was not to be deterred from her satisfying excursion into someone else's misery. "Yes, but it must still bring it all back to you. It was Holy Week you got the news about Thomas wasn't it?"

"Yes, Maundy Thursday 1916. Six years ago, now. Gwyn was nearly seventeen."

"It's hard to lose a provider but at least you have the comfort of knowing that he died for King and Country."

Two of the younger children, bored with grown up conversation had wandered off across the road in the direction of Pwll Berw, collecting some stones on the way to skim across the surface. The pool lay still as the silent voice that had been mentioned in chapel that morning.

"Don't you get your Sunday best wet and muddy now." Their Mam had spotted them out of the corner of an eye, while she was admiring a particularly fetching straw hat adorned with canary yellow flowers. "And stay away from the edge. You know how deep it is."

"I'll keep an eye on them," Tŵm offered.

Intent on counting bounces, the lads did not spot what lay in the water. Tŵm, standing by them, sensed rather than saw, that something was amiss. He edged closer. The weed-strangled body danced gently into his consciousness. Realisation took only a few seconds; significance a little longer. Instinctively, Tŵm knew whose remains were bobbing like a fishing float on the surface of Pwll Berw. Keeping the unspeakable firmly in his sights, Tŵm triggered his mind into action. He grabbed both protesting boys by the back of their shirts and led them away back to the crowd outside the chapel. Emyr's face changed as his son whispered in his ear. Determined to prevent panic, he asked men from the congregation to form an impromptu cordon. Women and children, kept decently away from the spectacle, were ordered to wait by the chapel entrance.

Forcing himself to walk with a measured pace, Tŵm accompanied Emyr back to Pwll Berw. He felt strangely distanced as though he were watching himself perform the necessary actions.

Emyr took charge. "Tŵm, help me. He may still be alive." Heaving the body out by its shoulders, they rolled it over as they hauled it out on to the safety of the bank. Tŵm, who had never seen death, looked into the face of his friend who had seen too much and knew that his father was simply voicing what he felt he must.

Men from the chapel carried Gwyn to the doctor's house, laid him gently on the bed in the surgery and covered the body with a white sheet. Richard Owen was not there. He had been called out to a difficult confinement early that morning.

"Tad, we can't leave him alone." Tŵm's quiet certainty was evident in his voice.

"We'll sit with him until Dr. Owen returns." Emyr wondered how exactly his son had developed this quiet air of authority at such a young age so that even his father accepted rather than argued.

"If you don't mind being alone for a while Tŵm, I'll go back to the pool and see if there's any clue as to what happened."

Tŵm nodded. "I think I'd like some time alone with him Tad. You go."

He sat in silence across the room from the shrouded figure that had once been his friend. In later years Tŵm could not say with any certainty what had been his thoughts during the three hours before the doctor's return. A few memories lingered. The thrusting reality that two out of the three friends were now gone; the overwhelming anxiety about how the widowed Ruth would cope with the loss of her only child, just a few short years after losing her husband; the anger he felt at himself for craving the roast lamb dinner waiting for him at home; but above all the uneasiness about what Gwyn had told him had happened the previous Thursday evening.

When Emyr returned, he shook his head at Tŵm's enquiring look. "Nothing. Nothing to be seen. Just plenty of footprints in the wet ground and a few broken plants but they're likely to be from us pulling Gwyn out of the water."

When Emyr and Tŵm finally arrived back at Cwyn-y-Gwynt, late afternoon, it was to find that there was no lamb dinner after all. Mali was still at Ruth Parry's house. Bethan, as elder sister, taking over her mother's role, had made them some cheese sandwiches, helped by Nain.

"We didn't know what time you'd be back," they said by way of a reason when the men queried the lack of sustenance.

"Has the doctor returned?" asked Bethan.

"Yes. We waited until he reappeared, explained to him what had happened and left him to examine..." Emyr, realising that his youngest son, Sîon, was there, stopped in mid- flow, then added, "Not now Bethan. Later. Sîon is listening."

Bethan looked at her little brother. "I can send Sîon to feed the chickens."

"No, we'll get all the jobs done first and talk later."

Since it was the Sabbath, it was only a question of feeding the animals. Often, after dinner they would return to chapel. Today was not normal. It was the first time Tŵm could ever remember services being cancelled. Even during the war, they continued as usual. But today Daniel Ellis had decided God would wish him to stay with Ruth Parry.

Later that evening when Mali had eventually arrived back and Sîon, in bed, was safely hidden away from any hint of infamy, the Tudor family sat around the rectangular kitchen table that was the hub of family life, used as it was for preparing and eating meals, for gossip and, as now, for serious debate.

No-one seemed prepared to open the conversation. In the silence, the tick of the long case clock seemed louder than usual. An ember dropped from the fire into the grate.

Emyr began. "Mali, how is Ruth?"

"How do you expect her to be? Shocked, disbelieving. But Ruth is Ruth.

Refusing to cry and saying that it is 'God's will'. She looks as though she has aged twenty years in one afternoon but her faith is keeping her going."

Caron's chair creaked. She had little space since her chair backed on to the oak dresser. Adorned as it was with lusterware and blue and white china, she had to be careful not to knock a cup or a jug off the hooks. She tried to sit very still, staring fixedly at the maxim proudly displayed on the wall opposite her:

Christ is the Head of this house;
the Unseen Guest at every meal;
the Silent Listener to every conversation.

Caron wondered whether Christ would be listening to this conversation and whether, if he were, he would help Ruth in her suffering. She knew that Mam might send her away. At nearly eighteen, this was the first time she had been present for an important conversation. Her brother Brad scowled. He did not approve of her female presence she knew. He thought of important issues as male business even though he was a year younger than her. Twm smiled at her reassuringly. At least *he* would not want her to be sent upstairs.

"What time did the doctor get back?" Mali asked.

"About three I think." Emyr looked at his son inquiringly. Twm nodded his agreement.

"Did he say anything?"

"Just that he would ask Idwal Edwards from the village to ride into Ruthin and tell the police what had happened as the body would have to be taken away for a post mortem. He hadn't examined Gwyn when we left but it's obvious that he died from drowning. It's just an accident I'm sure."

"It's a terrible tragedy. I knew there would be a death in that family. Ruth Parry had a crow down the chimney last week." Emyr looked a little startled. Nain had not said anything much since his return. He had almost forgotten she was there.

"Superstitious nonsense Mam!" Mali sounded very sure of herself. "God giveth and God taketh away. If there is anyone who can endure this, then that person is Ruth Parry."

"Even so," Nain went on. "To have both her husband and her son in the grave before her is more than any woman should have to bear. She is all alone in the world now."

Mali leapt on her mother at once. "You are never alone when Jesus is with you, as you well know."

"Yes, but Jesus isn't going to put his arms round her at night and chop the firewood during the day, is he?"

"Mam, that is positively blasphemous."

Nain, unperturbed, continued. "It's not blasphemous. It's just a fact. She more than struggled when Gwyn was away at the Front. If you remember, you used to send Twm to help out. After Gwyn was discharged, he took over all the heavy jobs. I don't know how she'll manage now."

"She's not the first woman to have to manage alone," replied Mali, "and she won't be the last. Not all women are lucky enough to have men to look after them, even more so after the war." She stretched out her legs to warm them in front of the fire. It was her favourite position, evidenced by her fire-scorched skin, which closely resembled corned beef.

"That may be so Mali," Emyr intervened. "But your Mam's right. Ruth is going to find it difficult alone."

Caron could feel her anger rising at her mother's attitude but knew better than to say anything. She would only be sent to her room if she argued. Yes, Mali had gone back home with Ruth but only out of duty and mainly for the sake of appearance. Caron could imagine the gossips now. "Mali Tudor went back with her. Such a good person she is. Always ready to help when she's needed." Yet as Caron knew from her own experience, genuine sympathy lay well beyond the realm of Mali's practical help.

Later when Caron and Brad had gone to bed and Nain had followed, Emyr tried to voice the unspeakable.

"What if...?"

Mali jumped in to stop him. "Don't say it. I'm sure it wasn't."

"Wasn't what?" asked Bethan. Missing the point, she asked, "Do you think he was murdered?"

"In Carreg-y-Bedd? Don't be ridiculous. This is Wales, not Liverpool. And your Tad didn't mean that. He meant the death might've been self-inflicted." Mali was indignant.

"Well, something strange must've happened," Bethan replied.

"I'm sure it was just a tragic accident," Mali went on.

Emyr tried again. "It could've been an accident but... well it's difficult to see how he could have fallen into Pwll Berw. Everyone in the district knows how dangerous it is. Gwyn knew that as well as anybody."

"See," said Bethan triumphantly. "Someone might have pushed him."

Emyr had been acutely aware of Twm's silence during the conversation so his son's first words made quite an impact. Ashen-faced, Twm's first direct contact with death had left him unable to think clearly. "Gwyn couldn't swim. He was scared of water."

Emyr, looking at his son, realised that he had had enough for one day. "No point in speculating. We need to wait for the doctor to tell us what happened. It's been a long day. I think we should all get some sleep."

Tŵm thought sleep would be impossible but shock and exhaustion worked their magic and he slept soundly until Mali called him early the next morning.

After the stock was fed and the cows milked, breakfast was a subdued affair. Over porridge and oat cakes, Mali declared her intention of collecting some rhubarb to take over to Ruth. "I'll make her a bara brith as well," she announced. It would also allow her to be in the right place at the right time if any news emerged from the infirmary. "I do feel responsible for her," she told Emyr. "After all, Thomas and Gwyn did work for us."

Leaving Bethan and Caron in charge of yesterday's lamb dinner and with strict orders to heat the bread oven, Mali left about ten. Tŵm knew that tragedy would not disturb the sowing of barley scheduled for every day that week. Human adversity could not be allowed to interrupt Nature's cycle.

Tŵm didn't mind. In fact, he welcomed the mechanical task that awaited him. He could put his energy into physical rather than mental effort. Re-ordering his fragmented thoughts would be as impossible as restoring the shattered ice on the winter water troughs. As Tŵm took handfuls of seed from the straw lip to broadcast over the land, Emyr controlled the cob's pace with the drill. They worked in perfect harmony, instinctively aware of each other's rhythm.

Back in Carreg-y-Bedd, Moses, setting up camp, had watched the Easter drama unfold with much curiosity. Realising quite quickly that a death was involved, he stayed well away feeling, as an outsider, he was not entitled to intervene in village affairs. He was more than stern with the children when they wanted to run over to see why a crowd was gathering and when Abram finally returned with the hazel, Moses told him that it was his job to make sure the younger ones did not go near the pool.

"T'ere may be signs t'ere of what 'appened," he said to his son. "Thet water's dangerous fer t' little ones. Springs feed into it from t' bottom. Even in a drought t'ere's always water fer t' 'orses. One yeer a sheep fell in, struggled an' then dis'ppeared. Pwll Berw's not only deep, it 'as t'ick mud like quicksand near t' bottom. T' ground underneath is like a sponge. It draws t'ings into 't."

The families concentrated instead on building the two benders with a balk in the middle. Since they intended to stay a while, the tents would give them extra space while the covering of the balk would protect the fire against the elements. Though Easter was not early that year, there was still time for some late frosts and heavy rain. Once the curved rods were securely fixed into the ridge pole, Moses, Solomon and Abram wired overlapped blankets firmly in place. When it was finished, the women, Grizell and Valentine, spread out a heap of straw on the ground, covered it with a bright red rug and piled up extra blankets at one end. With Abram and three other children, the extra room would mean the caravans were less cramped.

Easter Monday was unusually quiet in Carreg-y-Bedd. The football match against Clocaenog was cancelled as a mark of respect but the competition for the best decorated Easter egg, organised by Lady Eleanor Craddock, did take place as usual. Bryn-y-Castell was far enough away from Ruth Parry's cottage for the sound of the children's laughter not to reach her. Every child had spent a lot of time decorating the eggs so Lady Craddock thought it best not to disappoint them. "It would be such a shame for them not to have a winner. They've spent so long using onions, vinegar, oak bark and even beetroot juice to dye their eggs and then they've painted on their patterns. I think it's better to take their minds off what happened yesterday so this year I'll hide hard boiled eggs in the garden for them to find and give a special prize to the child who finds the most. That should keep them occupied for most of the afternoon."

While the children of Carreg-y-Bedd were searching through the shrubbery and peering down into the ha-ha, Ruth Parry could enjoy some peace and quiet. Deluged with visitors, she had rid herself of Mali Tudor saying, "I know everyone is being very kind but I really do need some time alone to think and pray."

"You know Ruth that I'm not far away. If you need anything at all then just send one of the village children to get me. And you make sure you eat that bara brith I brought. It won't do you any good to starve yourself."

Left alone, Ruth did as she said she would and prayed. She had a tendency to speak to the Lord as though he were drinking tea in the parlour with her. "God, please look after Gwyn for me until it is my turn to pass. Please make sure he meets up with his father because I know he will look after him. And

Jesus please help me to bear my suffering as you did yours. Amen."

A while later she climbed the stairs to Gwyn's room. His bedroom was tiny, stuffed under the eaves. She sat down on the bed and looked about her. His drawings were everywhere, pinned up all over the walls and the beams. There he was laughing with Twˆm and Evan the day they caught a trout in the river. She recalled when he won the school prize for Art. It was unusual for him to draw a building, though he had the skill. Not interested in landscapes or still life, Gwyn's pictures were nearly always peopled with the inhabitants of Carreg-y-Bedd. The winning picture of the school, with its thick, grey stone walls and thatched roof, now hung in the headmaster's room. Ruth looked closely at a drawing of Gwyn being presented with the prize by Lady Craddock. Gwyn himself was often central in his drawings. His pictures were his pictorial autobiography.

Ruth smiled at his first efforts. Gwyn had begun to wield a pencil when little more than a baby. Next to his bed were his portraits, labelled 'Mam' and 'Tad,' produced when he was about four. Even though the childish scribbles lacked his later sophistication, his talent was obvious even then. Ruth gazed into her own eyes and then into those of Thomas. Gwyn had been so proud of his father. She saw that Gwyn had pinned the British War Medal on to the picture itself. A big man in every sense of the word, big built, big hearted, generous to a fault, Ruth couldn't imagine how Thomas would ever have brought himself to fire upon the enemy. But he knew his duty and his duty was to fight the Hun. Not waiting for conscription and knowing God was on the side of the King, he had joined up soon after war was declared.

"I know there are those in the chapel who say they'd prefer to be shot rather than enlist but I think they're misguided. Pacifism is all very well but if we turn the other cheek we'll be overrun by the Germans. Lloyd George himself has told us that we should rescue poor, little, peaceful Belgium from the barbarism and brutal bullying of the Boche. Wales is a little country just like Belgium. The 'mailed fist' he spoke about may well strike us next. Powerful speech it was. No wonder it was printed in the papers. Certainly convinced me. He said enlisting was a great opportunity to defend honour, duty and liberty. It was nothing less than a call to arms and I'm going to answer that call."

There was never any question of which regiment he would join. The oldest infantry regiment in Wales, with a reputation for outstanding gallantry: The Royal Welch Fusiliers. Thomas' grandfather and his great-uncle had fought in the Crimea; his father in the Third Ashanti War. Thomas had been the first of his line not to join up as a youth. From a child, he had loved the land. Never happier than helping Emyr Tudor with lambing, hay-making or harvesting, Thomas had opted for a farming life in Carreg-y-Bedd. A man of few needs, he was more than content with his wife, his son and tilling the soil.

Later, a while after Thomas had sworn allegiance to George V and been sent for training, Ruth and Gwyn had watched the 3rd battalion march through Wrexham on St. David's Day with bearskins, scarlet tunics, white leather gloves and sword belts, golden buttons and braid that glinted in the hard, cold sunlight. The drummers and the fifers, as part of the regimental band, played 'Men of Harlech,' the sound reverberating from the Victorian buildings, while the Goat Major escorted the regimental goat, resplendent with gilded horns and a silver headplate. Clad in an embroidered khaki coat, the goat escorted the battalion through the crowded streets. The mêlée of colour, the beat of the footfalls, the stirring music brought an emotional lump to Ruth's throat. Pride suffused her soul.

"Tad told me that the goat is actually an officer of the regiment, not a mascot," she explained to her son.

"What do you think his name is Mam?"

Ruth laughed. "Billy, I expect."

Moving to her own bedroom, Ruth pulled open a drawer and lifted out a bundle of letters tied with a narrow black ribbon. It had been a while since she had read them. Spreading them out on the patchwork counterpane, she searched until she found the one she had in mind.

December 30th 1914
Basingstoke

My dearest Ruth

I hope that this letter finds you and Gwyn both well. I am going on fine though naturally I miss you both and hope to have some leave before I quit the country for foreign parts.

I began training in Wrexham but have now been moved here to Basingstoke. I'm learning how to use the weapons of war but I shan't bore you with the details. It's not a matter for women.

I haven't been given a uniform as yet. The war took everyone by surprise and they're busily making us the right clothes for the battlefield. For the moment I'm wearing blue serge overalls. My only complaint is that I feel the cold and hope the new khaki will put an end to that.

Well, those who said the war would be over by Christmas have been proven wrong. I wonder how much longer it will last. Not that long I don't suppose. Once we get more troops over in France, we'll soon send the Boche packing.

I'm sorry I wasn't able to get home for Christmas. None of us have had any leave as yet except for my pal Rob. His mother died suddenly and he was allowed to go to the funeral. I hope to get some leave though before I go over the Channel.

I hope you and Gwyn enjoyed the Yuletide services and the carols. I recall how the three of us used to gaze at the stars in a clear sky on a frosty Christmas Eve after going to chapel. You always used to tell Gwyn to look for the special star that meant Jesus was on his way.

Your parcel landed with me on Christmas Eve and real glad of it I was, particularly the plum cake and the fruit gums. That was a tidy bit of money you sent me too. You should have kept more for you and Gwyn. The 15 shillings the army sends you is not much to live on.

Joining the RWF was of course the right decision. I have mates here from Ruthin, Wrexham and Cerrigydrudion, though some have been transferred from the 2nd to another battalion, the 4th, I think.

Morale is excellent. We're all excited though apprehensive. It's a great adventure and a great cause.

It's likely that we'll have many weeks of training. We need to be fit as well as knowing how to handle ourselves when we have to fight.

Give my love to Gwyn. Tell him that, while I'm away, he's the man of the family and I know that he'll look after you.

Don't worry about me. I am in the pink, enjoying the army food (though of course it isn't as good as your home cooking!) and the splendid companions.

All my love
Thomas

Ruth smiled. So typical of Thomas. He loved them both but was not overly sentimental. Not for her the love letters that some wives would have received. And she would not have wanted them because they would not be true of Thomas. Despite the seeming lack of sensibility, Thomas' strength of feeling lay within every word. If necessary, she knew he would have given his life for his family. Well, in a sense he did, she reminded herself.

Thomas had eventually been granted the hoped for leave in October 1915. A precious few days when life returned to normal. He'd not talked about the fighting at all, simply telling her, "I had several weeks more training when I got to France and then was put in a unit digging supply and communication trenches. I think they thought I'd be good at digging being a farmer! Of course, I've taken my turn on the Front line but you don't need to know about that. I just want to forget it for a few days. I'm just thankful that Gwyn isn't old enough to be there. I hope the war will be over soon so that he doesn't have to go."

Once he'd had a bath and changed his clothes Thomas spent his time cycling round Carreg-y-Bedd, exploring old haunts and visiting friends. "I just want to remind myself how beautiful it all is," he'd said. The three of them had taken the train to Chester for a day out, walking round the walls and taking a trip on the river; a golden memory to be held close for ever.

Ruth shuddered as she remembered washing Thomas' filthy, grey flannel shirt. It had practically walked to the sink itself. She'd had to pour disinfectant in the water. The rags that had once been underwear were past rescuing and she had to buy new.

Parting for a second time was worse than when Thomas joined up. Then there had been excitement; a sense of adventure. This time Thomas had seemed resigned, stoical. Hugging them, he hadn't wanted to let go.

She was glad now that Thomas hadn't lived to see this day. He would have found it almost impossible to bear his son being taken before him. She hadn't imagined that she would ever be grateful for the official notification. She picked that up now.

No. Cas W 13487   Army Form B. 104-82

(If replying, please
quote above No.)

Record Office

Madam

It is my painful duty to inform you that a report has been received from the War Office notifying the death of:

(No.) *13487* (Rank) *Private*
(Name) *Thomas Elwyn Parry*
(Regiment) ROYAL WELCH FUSILIERS
which occurred *in the field France.*
on the *8.4.16*

The report is to the effect that he *was Killed in Action*

By his Majesty's command I am to forward the enclosed message of sympathy from Their Gracious Majesties the King and Queen. I am at the same time to express the regret of the Army Council at the soldier's death on his Country's service.

I am to add that any information that may be received as to the soldier's burial will be communicated to you in due course. A separate leaflet dealing more fully with this subject is enclosed.

	I am
Mrs. T. Parry	*Madam*
Y Betws	Your Obedient Servant
Carreg-y-Bedd	*MCShelley*
Ruthin	*Officer in Charge of Records*

A couple of days before the letter arrived, Ruth had received a letter from 'my pal Rob'. When it arrived, she had been puzzled by the strange writing on the envelope. Since she hadn't yet received the official missive, the shock had been immense. Rob had explained that it was a tradition amongst the soldiers for a friend's letter to break the news first. That way 'Killed in Action' at least had some explanation.

Thomas, in Rob's words, had 'died instantly'.

He had written, '*We were in countryside near* ██████████████ *That morning we heard a cuckoo and spotted a German soldier shooting at a hare. Earlier that week we'd been digging communication trenches to link some captured craters with the front line. Then on 8th April Thomas volunteered for a raid. Though I'm not allowed to give you information about that, what I can say is that it was a daring one and that Thomas displayed conspicuous gallantry and determination in the face of strong enemy resistance and heavy fire. He was a magnificent example of courage and devotion to duty. The only comfort I can give you is that he did not suffer. He was shot through the head and died instantly.*'

Ruth hoped that this last line was true. At the time she hadn't doubted it. In the years that had passed, however, she had heard tales from soldiers who had returned. Cadoc Morgan, glorying in notoriety, had volunteered information that she would rather not have known. "I were fightin' in a trench alongside a lad called Alf from Manchester. Only nineteen 'e were. Told me 'is Mam and 'is sisters was fillin' shells in a munitions fact'ry. We'd jus' bin given the order to 'man the fire step' and Alf were quicker than the rest of us. That's why 'e bought it. A shell burst straight in front of us an' the shrapnel scattered like hailstones strikin' a tin can. Alf's leg were blown clean off. Stretcher'd away 'e was. I 'eard later that gangrene set in. It took 'im two weeks to die."

But Rob had said of Thomas, 'he did not suffer'. Ruth clung on to that like survivors from the Titanic clung to the lifeboats.

At least Thomas was killed before the Somme and Passchendaele, the terrible battles she had heard about. She just hoped Rob had told her the truth. She did not doubt that he would try to protect her if Thomas had endured a long, agonising death, as so many did. If she had been a soldier writing to a grieving wife then she would have done just the same.

With Rob's letter came a photo of the three of them. They had it taken just before he joined up. She rather wished it had been buried with his body. Thomas had a grave somewhere in France. The army had told her that Thomas' final resting place was Cambrin Cemetery and she had the letter carefully stored away. Dying as he did, at least he was properly laid to rest. How lucky she was, she thought to herself. At least he wasn't missing like so many others, buried where they had fallen with unknown comrades in an unknown grave. To find solace, their loved ones could only visit the Unknown Soldier in Westminster Abbey. She and Gwyn had intended to go to France together to find Thomas' grave, once they'd saved enough money. She doubted now that she would go on her own.

After his return to France, Thomas had written a few times. Short letters just assuring her that he was well and she had no need to worry. His last letter was longer. It was this she found hardest to read.

March 1916   *Somewhere in France*

My dearest Ruth

Please don't worry about me. I know you must have been reading newspaper reports about casualties but there has been little fighting going on here for a while. We think there's something coming off soon though so it's likely to get a bit more lively. A few men have been wounded by artillery fire but I promise you I am safe and feel strong and healthy.

The countryside in France is very different from home. It is so flat here compared with the hills and mountains of North Wales. It keeps me going to think about the few days we had together last October when the trees were blazing gold, yellow and orange. There has been very little sun here. Everything is grey: grey sky, grey houses, grey trees, even the grass is grey, not at all like the green of Wales. They don't have hedgerows as we do. Fancy that! But they do have spring. Behind the front lines there are anemones flowering, violets emerging and I heard a lark only yesterday. If I were working at Cwyn-y-Gwynt, I would already be well into the sowing. When I think of Carreg, my hiraeth is overwhelming; I ache for the sounds and scents of home.

I am looking forward to the warmer weather. Though we have thick woollen uniforms and greatcoats, it has still been very cold. A few of the men have had 'flu but I've been fortunate and have escaped it.

Life's got a routine here but it can be boring. We have a few days on the front line, then some time on the support line and then a week's rest from soldierly duties. I have to admit it's a relief to get away from the Front. As we move around there's a lot of foot slogging, carrying the heavy kit that you saw when I came home. You wouldn't believe what I have hanging off my body. I'm sure it weighs as much as I do! There's my pack, smoke helmet, rifle, ammunition and that's just the start.

We keep up our spirits by singing. 'Keep the Home Fires Burning' is a real favourite. Then during our 'rest' week we still work hard strengthening bridges, improving roads and so on, though we do have some free time to watch boxing matches and play football. I'm pleased to say that so far, our battalion is unbeaten! On rare occasions we have performances with magicians, singers and joke tellers. These all help to raise our spirits. St. David's Day was not forgotten either. We woke to the sound of bugles, enjoyed a rendition of 'Mae Hen Wlad Fy Nhadau' and all wore a leek in our caps. We had to parade without a goat though as our battalion doesn't have one here in France.

We are indeed fortunate to have a regimental chaplain with us so I can receive Holy Communion on a Sunday morning. It provides me with the courage and fortitude I need to face possible danger and it's a great comfort to feel that God is as active here in France as he is in the hills of Wales.

We had an inspection a couple of weeks ago. The General was good enough to stop and speak to me. I was tickled pink! He asked me where I was from and on hearing I was from a tiny village near Ruthin he said, "What a lucky man you are!" I responded, "I am doubly lucky sir because I have a wife and son of whom I am so very proud." He replied," I expect they are proud of you too." I felt honoured that he had singled me out like that.

I'm looking forward to receiving some more letters and if you could send me an extra couple of toothbrushes (one for cleaning my gun!) and some chocolates, they would be most welcome. Strawberry jam would be nice too. We do have jam if we're lucky but it's always plum and apple, never strawberry. Our main diet is bully beef and hard biscuits though we do get eggs, beans, cheese and bread and butter. Well, they call it butter but it's more like axle grease! Mustn't grouse though; they do us well enough.

God willing, I will have some more leave soon and will be able to spend a few days at home. I'm sure I must be due some soon. Tell Gwyn that he must do the heavy work for you Ruth. I don't want you carrying the water or the coal or digging the potatoes. He's a good strong boy and must do all that for you. Of course, I miss you both very much. I carry your pictures with me at all times. More importantly, I carry your love in my heart.

God bless you both
All my love Thomas

The final sentence was extraordinary for Thomas. Ruth had never known him say anything of that kind, even when they were courting. She couldn't recall him even asking to marry her. He had mumbled something about 'speaking to her father' and that was that. Reading between the lines, he had been more troubled than he cared to admit, Ruth thought. But that was typical too. He would not have wanted his family to worry about him.

Taking a tour through such bitter-sweet memories took its toll on Ruth. Exhaustion took over. She had not slept since Gwyn had been found. Giving in for once, she lay on Thomas' side of the bed and fell asleep.

She was awoken the next morning by a knocking on the door. Still slightly dazed she went to answer it, pinning up strands of hair as she walked downstairs.

"Dr. Owen, I'm so sorry. I fell asleep early yesterday evening. I haven't had chance to prepare myself for the day. What time is it?"

"It's ten o'clock and please don't worry Mrs. Parry, I'm sure you needed the rest. I have come to offer you my sincere condolences. Please may I come in? I do also need to speak with you about an important matter."

Ruth ushered the doctor into the parlour. "May I offer you a cup of tea?"

"Yes please but only if you have one with me." Looking at her, Richard Owen was aware that Ruth was in need of sustenance and thought that she was more likely to partake of it if he accepted her hospitality. Once Ruth had brought the tea with a slice of Mali's bara brith, he ensured that she ate by declaring that he hoped she would share bread with him since he did not like to eat alone. It was the first food that had passed Ruth's lips since Sunday and she was surprised how it cleared her head. She had been feeling slightly dizzy. To be fair to Mali Tudor, it was an excellent bara brith.

Ruth opened the conversation. "The minister was so kind to me yesterday. He stayed for over two hours. I could see that he was personally affected by..." She paused and then, with a catch in her voice, continued, "by what had happened. He spoke very highly about Gwyn and his devotion to God. Said he didn't know how he was going to manage without Gwyn's devoted service to the chapel, especially in the prayer and reading meetings and with the singing festival."

"Mr. Ellis is right. You can be very proud of Gwyn, Mrs. Parry. Gwyn was loyal to his country and to his chapel, a hard worker and a fine son. You couldn't have asked for more."

"I couldn't doctor. God gave me the best son any woman could have asked for. I must be grateful for that and not question God's will. Not that it won't be hard to be without him but I am fortunate to have help and comfort from the chapel members."

The chapel community at its best, thought Richard. Though often frustrated by, what he considered to be, its narrow teachings, he had to concede that when one of its own people was in need, it offered strong, caring arms.

He decided he could prevaricate no longer.

"Mrs. Parry, you are aware of course that there has to be a post mortem?" He was unsure whether she knew. On his return home he had been more than shocked to discover that Gwyn Parry's body lay on his surgery bed. Normally he spent his time delivering babies, treating measles or stitching up cuts on the farms. He had never had to deal with a suspicious death before and in Carreg-y-Bedd he could hardly have expected to. He had told Emyr Tudor of the necessity for a post mortem but whether this fact had been passed on to Ruth through Mali he did not know. He was rather hoping that it had so that he did not need to be the bearer of what would be yet another blow. If he had known Mali Tudor rather better than he did, he would not have had to either speculate or indeed underestimate her. Mali had thought it her duty to mention it to Ruth within a few minutes of handing over the bara brith.

"After all," she said to Emyr later, "someone had to do it and it was better that it came from a friend."

Before then, Ruth hadn't given a thought to the circumstances of Gwyn's death. The fact of his death was enough to take in. Even Mali hadn't ventured to explore other possibilities but this was more to do with ignorance of procedures than sensitivity.

"Would you like me to explain what will happen? I think it is important that you understand."

Ruth nodded.

"Gwyn's body has been taken to the infirmary in Denbigh. There he will be examined and the coroner will make a judgement about how and why he died." She did not need to know much more than that, he thought.

"Why does that have to happen? Can't he be allowed to rest in peace?"

"I'm afraid not." Richard was gentle. "If the cause of death is unclear then there has to be a post mortem. The law demands it." He looked at her face. It was a mask. He could not ascertain her thoughts. "Mrs. Parry, you need to know too. Uncertainty is a terrible thing."

For the first time Ruth looked him directly in the eyes. He was humbled by her dignity.

"Dr. Owen, I am certain that my son, like my husband, is with God. That is all I need to know. How he got there is not important to me. There are many exits from our earthly existence but only two destinations."

Impressed by her simple piety, Richard decided, as Emyr had decided earlier that week, not to voice his main concern. Now was clearly not the time. He took another tack. "The post mortem is taking place today. When the results are finalised one of the coroner's officers will want to speak with you. This will undoubtedly be within the next few days."

Ruth appeared not to hear him. "I must speak to the minister about the funeral service."

"Mrs. Parry, I'm sorry but you cannot organise the funeral until the coroner releases the body. He will not release Gwyn until he determines the cause of death. Neither can the death be registered."

Ruth did not reply.

Richard tried again. "Once everything is settled, would you like me to take you to Denbigh in my pony and trap? You will need to go to the infirmary and it would be best if you had someone with you." He found himself unable to broach the subject of identification of the body. One step at a time, he said to himself.

"That would be very kind doctor but I don't want to trouble you. I can get the train from Ruthin. There are three every morning and I can walk to the station."

Richard was quick to reply. "Nonsense, I wouldn't hear of it. It would take you a couple of hours to walk there. I could, of course, take you to Ruthin station but as I said before I don't think it's at all wise to go to the hospital on your own. In any case, it's easier to go directly to Denbigh down the back lanes than it is to drive to Ruthin and take the train."

Ruth gave in. She could see the sense of the doctor's words.

On the same day, Emyr Tudor had waited some time for Moses to arrive. He had been pleased to see that the Gypsies had arrived in the village. One of his Shire horses, Delilah, had been out of action for a couple of weeks and she was badly needed. He had managed so far by substituting Cariad to work with Samson. It had been a problem.

"Damn silly horse and damn silly name," he muttered to himself. He looked round anxiously as if expecting Mali to heap wrath upon him for his oaths. When the new foal had been born, Caron had only been eleven. She had been thrilled with the new arrival.

"She's just a darling," she had announced. "She must be called Cariad."

Any name less appropriate would have been difficult to find. Normally the Shires were gentle giants but Cariad had an attitude. A serious attitude. Though handling had improved her, she had taken twice the usual length of time to break to harness. She did not work well with Samson largely because she felt she should be in charge. Driving the plough felt to Emyr as though he was driving two separate horses rather than a team. He wanted Delilah back in harness as soon as possible. But Delilah had an abscess on the top of her off side leg that simply wouldn't heal. A puncture wound he was convinced. Probably hawthorn. Delilah had a bad habit of wading into the hedges to nibble the young shoots. He had poulticed it regularly but though it was draining, the hole simply wouldn't heal. Emyr did not want to call in the vet, Samuel Davis. This was not solely because, as Mali often said, he charged "the most outrageous fees." Cariad was so intractable that Emyr was prepared to pay a big bill to get Delilah back on her feet but he knew that Moses was a magician with horses and so he was prepared to wait a short while until the Gypsies arrived for their annual stay.

Moses was non-committal as usual. "Just leave 'er wi' me. I've brought what I need. Come back in 'alf a nower."

Moses never allowed an audience. Gypsy remedies stayed with the Gypsies. From across the yard, Emyr watched surreptitiously. Moses had with him a mixture of plants, both leaves and roots, and what looked to be puffball fungus. The only ones Emyr recognised were black poplar buds and the slightly hairy leaves of comfrey. Moses began to grind up the mixture with a pestle in a wooden bowl. He then added an oily substance and took this into the stable. Some while later he reappeared, called to Emyr and returned to Delilah. Emyr joined him. The concoction had been smeared on to the sore. A not unpleasant but pungent smell hung in the air.

"'er leg'll be better wit'in t'ree days," Moses stated. "I wouldn't work 'er fer a week t'ough. Give 'er time t' 'eal prop'ly."

Emyr nodded. "How much do I owe you?"

"Do yer 'ave a sack o' 'tatoes at all?"

"I'll drop them off for you at the camp," Emyr told him.

Emyr watched as Moses left, mounted bareback on a piebald horse that only wore a rope halter. Moses had a gift, there was no doubt about that.

The Thursday after Easter Richard Owen knocked, for the second time that week, on Ruth Parry's door. He had come to give her the post mortem results.

Once again, he was shown into the parlour. Richard noticed the scent of polish; Ruth had been cleaning the room ready to receive Gwyn's body. After she had brought him his tea, she sat on a hard chair opposite him, rather than sharing the couch. Richard cleared his throat.

"I had hoped to bring you some answers Mrs. Parry but I'm afraid I am unable to do so."

Ruth looked at him enquiringly.

"The results of the post mortem are inconclusive. Gwyn died of drowning, that at least is certain, but there are other questions that cannot be so easily answered."

Ruth still did not speak.

Richard continued. "An inquest will take place in due course but at the moment Gwyn's death is still being treated as unexplained."

His voice softened. "Mrs. Parry, I'm sorry but I will have to ask you to come to identify the body. You are the next of kin."

This prompted a response.

"Doctor." She hesitated.

"Yes."

"Will he... will he be... well, spoilt?"

Momentarily, Richard was unsure what she meant. Then he realised.

"No, Ruth. Please don't worry about that. He will look the same as he always did. A post mortem is carried out with great reverence."

Richard was not even aware that in his concern for Gwyn's mother, he had used Ruth's Christian name. He was sure that Gwyn would have been carefully restored after the examination. The coroner was always punctilious about protecting the relatives from the grim reality of the procedures.

"I will make the arrangements with the coroner today and then come to collect you at nine o'clock in the morning. Is that convenient for you?"

Ruth knew that the question was mere politeness. She had no choice but to conform with the official regulations.

It wasn't until the next day that Ruth started to ask a few questions. They had travelled in silence, Richard holding the traces lightly in his hands. He kept his eyes fixed firmly on Dandy's plump, dappled rump as they trotted briskly towards Denbigh. As they neared Llanrhaeadr, Ruth stuck up a conversation of sorts. It seemed she at last wanted some answers before they reached the hospital.

Ruth was tentative. "Doctor, if it's certain that Gwyn drowned then why was the result inconclusive?"

Richard was cautious. "Though Gwyn died by drowning, Mrs. Parry, it isn't clear why he was in the pool in the first place. Gwyn was a sensible lad. Though it's possible, it isn't that likely that he fell in." He had to ask the question. "He didn't drink did he?"

The question was a mistake. Ruth was affronted.

"Doctor, Gwyn was a God-fearing young man. I'm a member of the Temperance Union. Gwyn would not allow a drop of the demon drink to pass his lips."

Richard chose to ignore the anger in her voice and pressed on. There were things she needed to know before they reached the hospital.

"Well, in that case, it isn't likely that he fell in Pwll Berw then is it? So he may have been pushed."

This time Ruth's shock was palpable. "In Carreg-y-Bedd?"

"Violence can happen anywhere Mrs. Parry. Even in Carreg-y-Bedd."

"I am aware, doctor, that the devil's ensnarements can reach anyone, anywhere." Ruth was still stiff with disapproval. She had still not forgiven Richard his original question. "However, Gwyn had no enemies. Who would want to hurt him?"

"That I don't know, Mrs. Parry, "but the possibility does have to be considered." He pressed on. "There's something else you should know..."

"What's that?" Ruth interrupted, her anxiety causing her to overlook her usual impeccable manners.

"Well, another reason for the coroner's decision is that Gwyn had suffered a blow on the head. In addition, there was some unexplained bruising on his body, particularly around the face, neck and shoulder area."

Ruth was astonished. "Why didn't you tell me this before?" she asked.

"I thought it better not to give you all the information at once," Richard answered. "You have had so many shocks to bear."

"But what does it all mean?" Ruth was clearly at a loss.

"It means we are not sure what happened to Gwyn. He may have been hurt or dazed or both before he entered the water. He may have hit his head after he fell in the pool but that would not explain the other bruising. It's all rather a mystery I'm afraid."

Later that morning, Ruth sat next to Gwyn's body. After the formal identification, she had asked for some time alone with him. Richard had wanted to stay with her but she had refused and, though concerned, he had to respect her wishes. She was dry-eyed. He had not seen her cry once and wondered whether she cried alone at night or whether her faith did not allow her even that indulgence.

Looking at her son's frosted countenance, she noticed the bluish tinge to his eyelids, his long, curled eyelashes, that his lips were slightly parted as if in the act of completing a last sentence. She took his hand and stroked the long, artistic fingers so different from his father's practical working hands.

When she emerged from the room, still fully in control, the coroner's assistant handed her an envelope. "Gwyn's effects," he told her.

She nodded but did not attempt to open it. That would come later. "May I organise the funeral now?" she asked.

"Of course." Ruth was grateful for his professionalism. She had not realised before how formal, practical procedures suffocated emotion, nor how necessary that was. She wondered if that was their purpose.

Gwyn came home after the week-end. He lay in the parlour awaiting his visitors. The village came to pay their respects. All except Twm.

"I have said my farewells," he told Caron. "Tad and I were with him on the day he passed."

Gwyn was laid to rest in the chapel graveyard on an inappropriately, sunny spring day, later that week. The Gypsies, still camped next to Ebenezer, could hear the service as clearly as if they were inside the chapel itself:

'Now the labourer's task is o'er:
Now the battle-day is past;'

As the words of the hymns and prayers emanated from the building, Moses made the children sit quietly in the caravans rather than allowing them to play outside as usual.

"Such a shame he couldn't be buried next to his father," Mali said to Ruth by way of comfort, as the coffin was lowered into the ground.

Hawthorn Month

It was dawn on Calan Mai. Caron cantered Jac past the embers of last night's bonfire and on up the long, gentle hill of Cae Hir that reached towards the forest. On her bedroom window sill was the cup she had filled with the cowslips and birch twigs she had collected the previous afternoon. Wedged underneath the brass horse's head that adorned the front door, was a branch of carefully placed hawthorn. Caron knew that she would be in trouble if it were discovered but this was unlikely since only the back door, that led directly into the slate flagged kitchen, was ever used.

Mali Tudor disapproved of, what she termed, "pagan ritual." But after Sunday School the previous day, Caron, seated on the rag rug and leaning back against Nain's knee, had learned what used to happen when Nain's Mam was just a slip of a lass.

"My Mam, Sara, your Hen Nain, looked forward to Mayday every year. I well remember her telling me about it. In those days the outside of the house would be decorated with hawthorn. Only the outside mind; hawthorn indoors attracts bad luck. Draws the fairies in, it does. Inside the house you want cowslips, rowan and birch. Nothing better to lure in the young men than those. In my view, all gardens should have a rowan in any case. A rowan clothed in berries protects against evil spirits. Like a sentry on guard, it is." She paused. "Married women search out the cowslips. You know what they say, 'Gather a cowslip in May; Find a babe on the way'."

Caron glanced out of the window to check that Mali was still in the garden planting potatoes. She would not be amused at the rhyme. Mali was out of view but the next minute she came into the kitchen, her hands wet with soil.

Nain continued despite her daughter's presence. "On the day itself all the young men would go from house to house dancing and singing to celebrate the start of summer. Bedwyr, your Hen Taid, dressed up and played The Fool. Me Mam used to say that he acted the fool all the time; he didn't need to wait for Mayday. It used to make him so cross. He would say, 'A man has to have real talent to clown around, entertaining rich and poor. You should be proud of me!' He told me that all the lads wore white breeches hung with white ribbons, white smocks and straw hats and waved handkerchiefs while they danced. And then there was the Cadi of course, with his blacked-out face."

Mali rubbed her hands together to rid herself of the worst of the soil.

"Mali, you're getting dirt all over the clean kitchen floor." Nain wasn't going to miss the chance to triumph over her daughter. It didn't happen often.

Mali looked discomfited. She went on the attack.

"I just heard you mention the Cadi, Mam. Caron doesn't need to know about that."

"Oh, don't talk your nonsense," Nain dismissed her.

"What's the Cadi?" asked Caron.

"The Cadi was a man dressed up as a woman," Nain replied.

Mali interrupted, "It's unnatural, that's what it is. A man pretending to be what he's not. Have you ever heard of such a thing?"

"It was only a bit of fun Mali. No harm in it." She turned to Caron. "The Cadi looked backwards to winter and forwards to summer. It's a shame all the old traditions have disappeared."

Mali was not to be so easily dismissed. "You can't tell me there's no harm in men dressing up as women. No good will come of it. In any case, we do still uphold tradition. You know very well that we welcomed in May with a bonfire at the chapel last night. That was a proper celebration with hymns as well. As for some other customs, well we're all better off without men taking leave of their senses."

Nain ignored her daughter. She was thinking aloud now. "The Cadi collected money from everyone."

Mali went in for the kill. "Begging! That's all it was. Begging! What did they do with the money anyway? I hope they gave it to the poor?"

"No. Mam said they spent it on beer."

"Well, there you are then. It was the work of the devil. Don't be filling her head with all that nonsense. Caron, go and collect some eggs. I need some for supper."

Nain decided not to hear her daughter. She was in full flow now. "Mam told me that May Eve was a night when spirits were abroad. Just like Nos Calan Gaeaf, All Hallows. But on that night, you can find out who you're going to marry!"

"Mam, will you stop filling Caron's head with such nonsense. I won't have it. You never know where it'll lead."

"Shhh child. There's no harm." Nain was the only one who called Mali, 'child.' It was less a term of endearment; more a reproof.

"I thank God that the world has moved on from pagan superstition. Caron, you enjoyed the bonfire, didn't you? God-fearing singing not godless dancing."

Caron nodded. She had found the chapel bonfire celebration more than a little dull but she did not wish further wrath to be heaped on her head. Least said, soonest mended, was the safest approach with Mali.

Later when Mali was back in the vegetable garden, this time planting peas and beans, Caron asked, "Nain, how can I find out who I will marry?"

"Well, what you do is take an apple and then, starting at the top, peel it round and round in one long piece. It's a bit tricky, mind. You have to be careful and have patience. You might need a few apples because if the peel breaks it won't work. Then when you have the whole skin in one piece, you throw it over your left shoulder. It will drop into the shape of a letter and that letter will be the initial of your husband's given name." Nain stopped for a moment. "Oh yes, it's coming back to me now. There's something else you can do too. You can cut an apple into sections and push a knife through them. Sit in front of a mirror and hold the knife over your left shoulder. The face of your husband will rise up in the mirror."

Caron shuddered. "Sounds a bit scary."

"No. More exciting than scary." Nain was never a one to lack courage, Caron thought. She hoped she'd inherited her Nain's staunch spirit.

The rituals seemed to involve a lot of apples. Caron idly wondered just how she was going to smuggle apples into her bedroom the next October. Once the apples were picked, they were laid out in rows on newspaper in the attics, eaters on the 'Denbighshire Free Press' and cookers on the 'North Wales Times'. 'Y Gymraes' was reserved for pears. The apples and pears had to last all winter. None of the children were allowed to take one as they were only doled out at meals. Mali always knew if any had been taken. Caron was convinced she counted them.

Smouldering wisps of mist dissipated into the air as Caron urged Jac faster. She flew the length of Cae Glas Uchaf, enjoying the crispness of the early morning air. Reining Jac in to a walk, she allowed him to relax as she made her way up the track that led to the forest. Before long, arching branches shaded the path and trees thickened on each side of her. She could hear rustlings in the undergrowth as nocturnal creatures scuttled away to the safety of their burrows. A red squirrel leapt from a leafy bough making Jac shy sideways. She stroked his neck to calm him, then pressed forward. She knew exactly where she was going and it was not long before she reached her destination. One year, picking primroses for Mothering Sunday, she had found the perfect refuge. It was a clearing, well off the main path that led to a quarry. The sound of trickling water had led her to it. A natural spring bubbled up over some limestone rocks, keeping the earth moist. It then fell away into a clear, deep pool fed by more underground streams. It was a haven for all her favourite flowers: primroses, cowslips, bluebells and later, red campion. The trees wrapped themselves round the circular clearing, as though protecting its secluded beauty.

Dismounting rather awkwardly due to the fullness of her khaki-coloured woollen skirt, Caron tied Jac to a tree with the lead rope she always tied round her waist. Jac, enjoying the break, took his fill from the spring and then cropped idly at the grass. Caron had asked Mali if she could wear a pair of trousers just as the Land Army girls at the Griffiths' farm had done. It had caused a storm. Mali had been enraged. "Trousers! Trousers! What is the world coming to? Of course you can't. You're not a boy!"

Caron had argued. "But I've seen pictures of ladies in London wearing trousers at parties. Dee showed them to me. She has magazines."

"Nerys Philpin should have more sense than let her daughter read such rubbish." Mali was adamant. "Decadence, I call it. Sheer decadence!"

Caron hadn't raised the topic again. She recognised a futile cause.

Since the age of ten, Caron had followed the annual ritual, learnt at her Nain's knee. By the time she was three, she knew the rhyme by rote.

'*The fair maid who, the first of May,*
Goes to the fields at break of day,
And washes in dew from the hawthorn tree,
Will ever after handsome be.'

Not for her the quick dash that some of her friends, like Dee and Mari, made to the nearest field to catch the dew before the sun rose. Here, in the forest, the blossoming hawthorn grew thick and plentiful. She drank a cool draught from the spring, then drew down white blossom, shook the dew into her hand and then gently stroked its silkiness over her already flawless skin. In just ten days she would be eighteen; she wanted to be at her most beautiful for her special day.

A low laugh interrupted her reverie. "Yer don' need t' dew t' give yer beauty. Yer 'ave 't in 'bundance." He said it as a fact with no trace of flattery or pretence.

She turned. A young man of about Tŵm's age was laughing at her. She blushed red with embarrassment, her anguish quickly turning to anger. "How dare you spy on me!"

"I weren't spyin'. I was 'ere when yer arrived."

"I didn't see you."

He shrugged. "What's yer cob called?"

"Jac."

He ran his hands over the horse's back and legs. "Good, strong quarters. 'ave yer 'ad 'im long?"

"Yes. He was born on the farm." Caron found the praise of Jac easier to take than the compliment to herself. She too admired Jac's strength and speed.

"Yer ride 'im bareback." Again, it was a statement.

"Yes, mostly. He's in harness most of the time." Caron didn't want to admit the real reason for riding Jac without a saddle. Tŵm always used one. But without riding clothes and in her skirt and boots, bareback was a lot more comfortable. She liked it better anyway. She felt closer to the horse.

"What's yer name?"

"Caron. And yours?"

"Abram."

Back in Carreg-y-Bedd Ruth Parry had risen early as always. She still hadn't opened the envelope that had been given to her at the hospital. It lay in wait on the dark oak table in the parlour. Ruth was a firm believer in there being a time for everything and the time for viewing the contents of Gwyn's pockets had not seemed right until now. After the funeral tea, presided over by Mali Tudor, "Don't you worry about a thing. I'll organise it all," Ruth had felt the need for a few days' quiet contemplation and worship before tackling any practicalities. The previous day she had attended the services on the Sabbath, just as usual. After she had tidied away her breakfast dishes, she sat on a hard, upright chair in the parlour and fingered the envelope. It just did not seem fitting to open it in the kitchen. Taking a knife that she had brought through with her, she sliced open the top with precision. She did not want Gwyn's possessions to be marred in any way. Carefully she shook out the contents on to a sheet of white paper she had laid out for the purpose.

Before her lay Gwyn's final effects. Ruth fingered them one by one. The water had affected their condition. First of all, a pencil stub, slightly chewed. She smiled. She couldn't ever recall Gwyn being without a pencil in his pocket. Next, a silver threepenny bit, a piece of string, a small, white button with thread attached and a penknife. She turned the button over in her fingers. Just an ordinary shirt button. She hadn't realised that Gwyn had lost one. She was normally so careful about making sure his clothes were in a good state of repair. "A missing button is so slovenly," she remembered Mali saying to her one day. "Shows a woman's not looking after her family properly." Ruth could only agree.

She looked again at Gwyn's possessions. Not much to show for a life well lived she thought. Still, she had his legacy upstairs in his room. She intended to sort his drawings into chronological order so that she had a record of his passing years. Making her way to the kitchen, she found an empty tea box, carefully installed Gwyn's effects in their new home and took it upstairs to his room.

A policeman arrived to question Tŵm and Emyr late one morning.

"Don't they realise we have work to do?" Mali asked no-one in particular. She ushered the portly sergeant, who had arrived by bicycle, puffing and red faced, into the parlour and went off to find Emyr and Tŵm.

The sergeant was surly, his temper not improved by his exertions. He proffered a hand, "Alun Edwards," he announced by way of introduction. "I have a report to write for the coroner, so if you could just answer my questions, I'll be off and out of your way."

Emyr explained that he'd been alerted by Tŵm as to what he had seen in the pool. "My first thought was to pull Gwyn out of the water," he said. "I wanted to make sure there were no signs of life and then remove him from sight. I knew that the chapel congregation was watching, there were children there and that his mother was a part of that congregation."

The sergeant nodded his understanding and turned to Tŵm. "I hear that the dead lad was a friend of yours. Is that so?"

"Yes, it is."

"And he worked for you?" he asked Emyr.

"He did."

"So when did you last see him?"

"Saturday 15th April it was. Easter Saturday. He worked here all day as usual. Then he left for home. I never saw him again."

"Did you see your friend again? Did you meet him that Saturday night?" the sergeant continued, turning to Twm.

"No, I didn't. I was here all night with my family. I didn't go out."

"That's quite right, sergeant. None of us went out on Saturday evening. My wife was cooking in preparation for Easter Sunday."

"So, you can throw no light on what happened?" the sergeant asked.

Emyr answered for both of them. "None at all, sadly. It's a mystery."

The policeman looked at Twm. "Would you say he was in sound mind? He'd fought at the Front, hadn't he? Had that affected him? There've been cases where…"

Twm interrupted. "Yes, he'd fought in France but I'm sure he wouldn't have done what you're suggesting. He was happy enough. He had a job with us, his mother to look after and the chapel was important to him. He helped the minister a lot. He would never have harmed himself; he would consider it a sin. And he'd know how upset his mother would be if anything happened to him. She'd already lost her husband in the war. Gwyn wouldn't want to cause her more pain."

Alun Edwards was briskly practical. "If you're right, then the question is, did he fall or was he pushed?"

Twm shrugged his shoulders. "I wish I knew."

"Well, I'll write my report and we'll leave it to the coroner. Glad I haven't got his job. Don't know how he's going to work this one out."

Without further formality, the Sergeant sighed and reluctantly clambered back on to his transportation. He had several steep hills to face.

Caron and Abram sat idly swinging their bare feet in the welling spring water. Caron was enjoying the delicious sensation of the icy water trickling against her skin. She was also enjoying Abram's company. He was so different from the boys she knew from chapel or school. For one thing he seemed older. When she asked, he told her that he was nineteen. So, he was the same age as Aled Owen and Dafydd Roberts. But he didn't behave like them. Aled was painfully shy. Caron had only asked him what was the Bible text for Sunday School and he had blushed to the roots of his spiky fair hair and mumbled that he didn't know. Dafydd, by contrast, knew it all. Caron had heard him hold forth on Lloyd George's hatred of General Haig, the dates the Welsh rugby team won the Triple Crown and the new treatment for liver rot epidemic in sheep. He was destined to become a deacon in the chapel. It was only a matter of time.

She looked across at Abram. Already a man, he was built like the oak, growing strong and tall, that towered over the barn at Cwyn-y-Gwynt. His bare forearms, thick with dark hair, displayed muscles standing proud prepared, it seemed, to burst forth at the mere prospect of a challenge, while sinews sprang taut against his bark brown skin. Dark shadow betrayed an already coarse beard; strength lay in every contour of jaw and browbone. But it wasn't solely his appearance that set him apart. At ease with himself, Caron had never encountered such confidence. Fully relaxed, he struck up a conversation.

"D' yer like ridin'?" Caron was unused to being looked at so directly. Nevertheless, she met his gaze. His eyes were as dark and fathomless as Pwll Berw.

"I love it," she pronounced. "I love it more than anything."

He didn't ask her why. He knew why. "It's t' same fer me. Gallopin' t'rough t' wind an' rain, yer become part storm, part horse. In t' end yer can't tell which is which."

She nodded her agreement. No-one had understood before. "Jac's speed makes me forget who I am. I become a cry in the wind."

Abram did not laugh at her fancy. "We can go ridin' one day, if yer like. I can tek yer t' parts of t' forest which yer don' yet know."

"I would like that." As the words were uttered Caron realised that meeting Abram again may be well-nigh impossible. She had known immediately that Abram was one of the Romanies who were staying in the village. His clothes marked him out: the worn, ribbed trousers; the splash of scarlet that was the knotted scarf; the chain of burnished gold round his neck.

Emyr and Mali did not dislike the Gypsies. But it would never have crossed their minds to socialise with them. In any case Caron would not have been allowed out alone with someone of the opposite sex even if he were a member of the chapel congregation. To ask if she could go riding in the forest alone with Abram was unthinkable. Even to ask the question would result in days of persecution. It also meant admitting that she had been alone with him already. The fact that their meeting was accidental would make no difference.

Abram voiced her thoughts. "Yer'd be allowed?"

She flushed. It was uncanny how he seemed to know what she was thinking. "No, I'm sure not. But I ride alone all the time, especially in the summer and once my jobs are done. As long as Jac isn't needed for work, I can take him out. Tad says it keeps him sweet."

"'e's right. 'orses need t' play just as we do. It's no fun pullin' a trap all t' time. T'ey was born t' be free."

"Jac loves to gallop free as much as I do," Caron agreed.

"When'll yer ride next?" Abram asked.

"I don't know; maybe a week Saturday. Jac will be needed over the next few days."

"T'en I'll wait 'ere fer yer, early, soon after sunrise. If yer don't come I'll wait t' next Sat'day. I mus' go now." He left immediately, striding easily down an unworn path to the side of the spring. Within seconds he had disappeared. She could not even hear the rustle of a leaf, the snap of a twig. Looking round it almost seemed that she had dreamt his presence.

From the kitchen window Tŵm saw Caron return from her ride. She was later than expected. Emyr would have a few words to say to her if Jac was sweaty and tired. Caron had only been permitted to take Jac out under the strict instruction that he was not to be worn out and that he was back well before Mali wanted to use the trap. Tŵm slipped outside and walked over to the stable. He found his sister rubbing down a steaming Jac. With practised ease, Tŵm dampened some hay in a bucket, fashioned two loops, twisted them alternately, tucked away the bits and stamped on the end product. The resulting hard, plaited wisp fitted snugly into his hand. He began to expertly massage Jac, at the same time as helping him to dry off. Caron smiled at him gratefully.

"You'll be in trouble if Tad sees him in this state," Tŵm muttered, rather unnecessarily.

"I know. It was such a beautiful morning and I forgot the time. When I noticed how high the sun was in the sky, I had to race home." Caron was apologetic.

"I'll do this. You take out his bucket. He mustn't drink cold water while he's still hot. He'll go down with colic. Go and get some warm water from the boiler and mix both together until his drink is warm. He must be thirsty."

Caron looked horrified. "Mam'll see me. What will I say?"

"Just tell her that I asked for some water. You don't need to tell her why."

Later that morning, Tŵm sat on a tree stump bordering the edge of the forest. Today was unusual. He had been sent out with a hunk of bread, a lump of cheese and a Cox Cymraeg and ordered to check the ewes out on the ffridd, the lower hilltop fields which bore more grass than the mountain slopes. During the war the Tudors had cut down the number of sheep and ploughed some of the ffridd to produce much needed corn to feed the nation but now they could increase their flock once more. Some of the lambs were over a month old and were enjoying the spring sunshine. He watched as one butted its twin out of the way in its quest for milk. Most of them wouldn't be on the farm for long. They would soon be on their way to market in Corwen. He whistled to Jono who came at once to lie at his feet.

Tŵm had a lot on his mind. It wasn't often that he had chance to sit and work matters out but today gave him that opportunity. He had many acres of hillside to cover so need not be back for hours. Rational as always, he compartmentalised his worries before dissecting them: Gwyn's death; Ruth Parry's grief; Brad's jealousy; how to achieve his secretly nurtured ambitions. It was typical that he left his own dreams until last. Gwyn loomed over everything. Tŵm knew he should tell the police what had happened the Thursday before Gwyn's death but despite being fully aware of where his duty lay, he was equally sure that he would stay silent. His loyalty to his friend came first. It was strange that he was even less capable of letting Gwyn down when he was dead than when he was alive. Deeply protective of Ruth, Gwyn would expect Tŵm to do everything he could to save her from more pain. Looking back on the sergeant's visit, Tŵm couldn't believe he had been let off the hook. He hadn't been asked any questions about Gwyn's bruises.

He thought back to when Gwyn returned from France in June 1919. Tŵm had wanted to know what it was really like to be at the Front. Of course, he'd read all the newspaper reports about the last German offensive but that wasn't the same as speaking to someone who was actually there, who had fought against von Ludendorff's waves of storm troopers, who had survived the shelling, the artillery fire, the gas. Tŵm knew that he wouldn't have felt driven to join up even if he'd been old enough. He wouldn't have been a conchie though. He would have gone to France if he'd been conscripted.

It wasn't so much that Tŵm was unwilling to defend his country. Far from it. Tŵm knew where his duty lay. But he was more concerned with saving human life than taking it. He liked nothing better than to spend an afternoon with Dr. Owen. Richard Owen had got to know Tŵm well during the winter and summer of 1919 when Carreg-y-Bedd, like many other places, was badly affected by the influenza epidemic. Gwyn had been fortunate to escape it. The graveyards of church and chapel bore testimony to the severity of the outbreak. Rebecca Johnson, who was with child at the time, was the first casualty, closely followed by two other young married women, Elen

Roberts and Rose Williams. Rose's four-year-old daughter died shortly after her mother. By the summer of 1920 the village had lost two young men, four mothers and three children to the virus as well as Abigail Phillips who was ninety-four and had survived the births of eleven children and the deaths of two husbands. The old people simply did not call in the doctor soon enough, preferring to rely on traditional concoctions involving rhubarb, treacle and vinegar. With not so much to do on the farm as in the summer months and the doctor in dire need of help, Tŵm, with a reputation for academic success, was happy to provide assistance. He filed records, wrote letters, balanced the accounts, ordered and collected medicines, sterilised instruments, carried messages and even drove the trap when the doctor was simply exhausted. Richard Owen came to rely on him. "You have a good head on you Tŵm. You read and write exceptionally well; your number work is accurate and you are totally dependable." Tŵm consumed the books that Richard lent to him. Gray's 'Anatomy of the Human Body' and Osler's 'The Principles and Practice of Medicine' became familiar friends.

Tŵm blossomed under the doctor's praise. In elementary school he had always been top of the class in every subject. Certificates for the annual prizes, Scripture, Mental Arithmetic, Writing, Science, were displayed in the room he shared with Brad and Siôn, as Mali's incentive to the younger boys to follow Tŵm's example. At thirteen, as one of the few boys to win an exhibition to Ruthin School, Mali and Emyr had allowed him to go even though he was needed on the farm. As Mali said to Ruth, "When you have a son as clever as mine, you can't hold him back. He's quick with figures and that will be useful when he takes over the farm. Brad can take some time off school. He's never going to amount to anything with sums and writing. Takes after his father."

The war changed Tŵm's future as it did for so many others. During the conflict farm labourers were hard to find and food was essential for the war effort. When Thomas Parry joined up, Emyr took on Gwyn in his place. Gwyn had left school the year before and had supplemented the Parry income with casual jobs on local farms. Though not a natural farmer like his Tad, he was pleased nevertheless to have gained full time employment with the Tudors. His Mam needed the money. Emyr found Gwyn frustrating. "The lad tries hard and I can't accuse him of being work-shy but he's clumsy and slow." Nevertheless, Emyr believed it was his duty to do what he could to help Thomas' family so he persevered with Gwyn, patiently explaining tasks over and over again when Gwyn had forgotten the quantities of feed or how to stack the hay. "Has his head in the clouds," he told Tŵm. "Just doesn't concentrate."

But despite Gwyn's shortcomings, when Gwyn and Evan were called up in the summer of 1917, Emyr simply couldn't manage. Brad, though learning fast, was only eleven and was still in school. There was no alternative. Tŵm, owing twin loyalties to family and country, was forced to leave full time academia.

To Tŵm, sowing and ploughing were poor substitutes for full time reading and studying. The headmaster of Ruthin School, Mr. Lovegrove, recognising his talents, gave him special dispensation. He allowed Tŵm to attend school when Emyr could manage without him and to study at home when he couldn't. "Our Ruthinian boys have a proud tradition of fulfilling their duty to King and Country, whether in military service or in other ways," he told Tŵm. "Your duty at this moment is to help provide food for the nation. You are a clever boy and a hard working one. I'm sure you'll still manage to pass your examinations."

Mr. Lovegrove was proven right. Tŵm kept up with his studies despite all his difficulties. It had not been easy. Many an evening, he had fallen asleep over his books after a hard day of fencing or harvesting but his determination had carried him through. Helped by the tutors at the school who recognised both his ability and his commitment, he managed to more than keep up with his peers. "English, French and Divinity I find quite easy," he told Emyr, "but Science and Mathematics are my favourite subjects. Greek and Latin, I find hard but I will have to persevere. I've got to reach the standard in all of them."

Once Gwyn returned from the Front and came back to work at Cwyn-y-Gwnt, Tŵm's life became a little easier. He was able to return to school full-time and finally passed the new Higher School Certificate with flying colours.

Carreg-y-Bedd had lost nine strong young lads in the war: five in France, one in Mesopotamia, two in Gaza and one in Palestine. On his return Gwilym Bowen spent many months seated in the farm kitchen, speaking only when spoken to and hurling an occasional expletive at the fire that his wife, Nia, lit each morning. John Pritchard had returned in late 1917 but minus one leg below the left knee; he and Gwilym Bowen had fought at Passchendaele. It was John who informed the populace of the village that Gwilym had been buried up to the neck after a shell burst on the trench parapet. "Poor Gwil.

His front teeth were knocked out but that wasn't the worst of it. He was unconscious for three days and woke up in a hospital bed in Boulogne. By all accounts he was a wreck. Legs rigid, convulsions, sweating. They sent him from there to Edinburgh. Electric shock treatment, I think. But they couldn't mend him. Better than he was, but still a right mess I reckon. If you ask me, he'll never be right now. Rather lose me leg than me mind."

Some soldiers did return in one piece. Attracted by the King's Shilling and hearty meals, Cadoc and Gethin Morgan had joined up rather late in proceedings. Gethin, had announced their departure from Carreg-y-Bedd with, "Goin' for the real gud food an' a reg'lar pay packet. Too gud to miss i'nit?"

They both arrived back, more or less unscathed despite having been in the thick of it. Gethin though had lost the third finger from his left hand. "Copped a shot didna I. I were takin' a risk. Popped me 'ead above the parapet to take a dekko. Lucky it were only me 'and. Could've been me 'ead."

Gwyn had sniffed in disgust when he heard this, saying to Twm, "More like a Blighty wound if you ask me."

"What do you mean?"

"Happened a lot. Tommies in the trench who were shit scared would raise a hand in the hopes of getting shot."

Twm, baffled, asked, "Why on earth would they do that?" Shocked at hearing Gwyn swear, he put it down to strong feeling.

"Because they'd be sent to the Dressing Station and, if bad enough, then back home to recover in hospital. It gave them time away from the front line. Some got court martialled for it, if the officers suspected they'd done it on purpose. Gethin must've had a good explanation. He always was a slippery customer."

"But it's not fair on the others!" Twm was incredulous.

"No, it's not. That's why I didn't do it. I understand shit scared. I was too. But I couldn't do that. It wouldn't be right."

Unlike Gwyn, Cadoc and Gethin did not find comfort in returning to the chapel. "I'll niver set foot in it agin. Not after wot I've seen," Gethin announced in the 'Lamb and Lion', a Woodbine, as usual, hanging from his bottom lip.

After Gwyn returned to live with Ruth, he went back to his former job at Cwyn-y-Gwynt. As before, he did not really enjoy it. But it was work and it was in Carreg-y-Bedd. It was unthinkable to leave his Mam now his Tad was gone. Emyr still bemoaned the fact that, "Gwyn doesn't take after Thomas. He doesn't have his strength, his knowledge or his way with animals. I have to tell him everything and even then, he doesn't remember it." But Emyr took care only to speak to Tŵm and not to complain about Gwyn to Mali. He felt honour bound to keep the lad after what had happened to his father. Gwyn was nowhere near as good a worker as Brad who, now fourteen, had left school to work on Cwyn-y-Gwynt. Sturdy and keen, he could do twice Gwyn's work in half the time.

"I don't know why you keep him on Tad. We could easily manage without him now I'm not in school anymore."

Emyr, not wanting to admit his reasons to Brad replied, "An extra pair of hands is always useful Brad, especially at busy times such as lambing and harvesting."

Brad was all practical logic. "Then just hire him when we need him. There's no need for him to be here all the time."

But Emyr stood firm and Gwyn continued to turn up for breakfast at the farm every day except the Sabbath.

After Tŵm had gained his certificates, he had plucked up the courage to speak to Emyr and Mali. Nain was in her chair in the corner of the kitchen, mending a tear in Brad's trousers.

Typically, he came straight to the point. "Mam, Tad, I want to be a doctor. I could go to Liverpool; it has an excellent medical school."

Mali's response was swift. "Tŵm it's out of the question. Medical training is expensive and I suppose you expect us to pay. And Liverpool! It's a den of iniquity. Everybody knows that. Even more importantly, as you well know, Cwyn-y-Gwynt will be yours one day."

"Mam, you and Tad could always leave the farm to Bethan. She's the oldest."

"Now you're being absurd Tŵm. Bethan couldn't run the farm."

"She might get married Mam."

Mali was shocked at the suggestion. "I'm not having a stranger run my farm Tŵm. Anyway, I have other plans for Bethan. Cousin Enid and I have already talked about it. She'd be a good match for her son, Trefor. Pen Rhiw Bach has one hundred and fifty acres."

Tŵm, unaware of female family machinations, was taken aback. He'd had no idea that plans were afoot for Bethan's future. "But it's in Llanrwst Mam. That's a long way."

"It's not that far Tŵm."

"Does Bethan know? Is she happy about it?"

"Of course, she knows. Bethan can see the sense of it. It's the best thing for her. Anyway, she'll do as she's told. She's a good girl."

Tŵm tried a different tack. "But I don't want to farm. And you've got Brad. He's so good at it. Much better than me and he loves it too."

"Tŵm, Cwyn-y-Gwynt needs both you and Brad especially with the extra land we bought last year. Siôn's too young to be much use yet and your Tad's getting on. He won't be able to work such long hours soon. Farming's hard work. It takes its toll. It wore out my Tad. He passed on far too soon."

Nain dabbed at her eyes. "I miss my Eifion every day."

Emyr resisted Mali's portents of doom. "Don't write me off just yet, Mali. I'm not that decrepit."

Though aware that it took Emyr longer to complete chores than in the past, Tŵm felt honour bound to support him. "Mam there's no better farmer in Carreg than Tad. And he's as strong as a Shire horse."

Mali was adamant. "That may be so Tŵm but no-one can go on forever and we have to be realistic. I wouldn't have let you accept that Exhibition if I'd known it was going to cause all this trouble."

Emyr objected. "Now, now Mali. That was a real achievement for Tŵm. I was proud of him and so were you. I remember you telling Ruth Parry how clever he was." Emyr well remembered how Mali had basked in reflected glory.

Tŵm was horrified. "Oh, Mam you didn't did you? It might've made her feel bad. Gwyn didn't do that well in school."

Mali dismissed Tŵm's comment with, "I'm sure not Tŵm. Ruth was just pleased for you." She continued, "I didn't stand in the way of your education Tŵm because I thought you'd use what you'd learnt to expand the farm. Nowadays a farmer needs a good business head if he's going to succeed. You're right that Brad's a good worker but he hasn't got your brain."

Nain intervened, "Mali, don't stand in the lad's way. Medicine's an honourable profession."

"Mam, don't interfere. It's nothing to do with you."

Mali's tart comment angered the normally unruffled Nain. "How can you say that Mali? Can I remind you that Cwyn-y-Gwynt belongs to me! It'll only become yours and Emyr's when I pass on!"

Tŵm was dumbfounded. He'd never considered ownership of the farm. "I didn't know that. I thought the farm belonged to Mam and Tad!"

A furious Mali turned to Nain. "Mam that's private family business. Tŵm didn't need to know. Tŵm, don't you dare discuss this with your brothers and sisters."

"Well, he knows now." Nain was unperturbed at Mali's wrath. "Twm, it's because I was an only child like your Mam. Your Hen Taid and Hen Nain Maddock lost a son at birth and a daughter at five years old. Gwyneth her name was. Died of diphtheria she did. Then I came along. They never liked to talk about her. I found her birth and death certificates after they died."

Mali, needled both by Twm's announcement and Nain's revelation, took out her ill humour on her husband. "You were more than fortunate to marry me, weren't you Emyr? You got me and a farm."

Emyr sighed. "Yes, Mali, so you've often told me." He took a risk and supported Nain. "Your Mam's right. Medicine is a vocation. A doctor has status in society and we shouldn't stand in the lad's way if that's what he wants."

Mali's face, suffused with red, revealed her feelings. She was furious at being contradicted. Emyr recognised the signs. He became placatory. "Your Mam feels strongly about this Twm so let's just wait and see what happens. We don't need to rush into it and decide now."

So Twm went back to working on the land and two years later he was still there. Mali used every chance she could to drive home her point. "Twm, Brad's not old enough to have that kind of responsibility," and, "You're stronger and more experienced than Brad and Gwyn," and, "Your Tad relies on you, you know. Remember he's not getting any younger."

The presence of Brad and Gwyn had at least meant that Twm could be spared in the winter months and at less busy times to give some small relief to the doctor. Richard Owen had more than appreciated Twm's efforts and was happy to encourage his ambition. "It makes my life so much easier to have an assistant," he told Twm, "and if you do apply for medical school, what you've learnt will stand you in good stead." Twm had told him how Mali and Emyr had responded to him voicing his wishes. The doctor's response was, "Give it time Twm, give it time. Let your Mam get used to the idea." But time was passing and Twm felt all the frustration of impatient youth.

Mali kept the extra money Twm earned from working with Richard Owen, "for a rainy day." She stored it inside a flour sack which she kept inside the butter churn in the cool slate benched dairy. This was not the most convenient of places since it had to be removed every time she wanted to make butter but as she pointed out, "No-one would think of looking there."

Twm's reverie was interrupted by a shout. He looked up and saw Brad approaching. "Slacking are you?"

"No, just eating my sandwich." Twm was accustomed to Brad's not so thinly veiled criticism. He was well aware that it stemmed from jealousy and had long ago decided that ignoring it would cause least trouble.

"Tad said you'd need my help," Brad announced. "We've got such a large flock this year." Twm was torn between annoyance at losing his precious thinking time and relief that the job would not take as long. The lambing was going well that spring and Emyr was hoping for a decent profit when he took them to market. But profit was dependent on fine, healthy lambs. Any problem needed to be spotted early. A few lambs had succumbed to dysentery so droppings needed to be looked at. Emyr had particularly asked them to check for foot rot and abscesses since it had been a wet spring.

Brad, as usual, tried to take charge. "No need to check for scab. They've all been dipped."

"I do know." Twm was indignant. "I was there."

"Just making sure." Brad was unapologetic. Twm watched his brother as he whistled to Jono, expertly eyed each lamb and worked with the dog to pen the suspect lambs. He was in his element, sensing instinctively which lambs required a closer inspection. Twm too knew exactly what to do but his approach was more tenacious than intuitive. Brad was simply a natural farmer, born to move in partnership with the seasons like seaweed on a wave. For Brad, Cwyn-y- Gwynt was a joy; for Twm, it was a burden. Twm wished, not for the first time, that Brad had been the eldest son.

Once the lambs were safely penned, Brad turned to Twm. "Have you heard the news? Mam was telling Tad just as I left."

"What's that?"

"Gwyn. The results of the post mortem are out. Ruth Parry told Mam."

Twm waited, not wanting to give Brad the satisfaction of indicating even the slightest curiosity. Brad would tell him soon enough.

"He drowned."

"Tell me something I don't know." Uncharacteristically savage, Twm did not want to discuss Gwyn with Brad. It felt disloyal, like crows picking over a dead lamb.

Brad flushed. "There's going to be an inquest."

"When?"

"In a few weeks. I don't know the date."

Twm's unease grew. He had seen for himself the gash on Gwyn's head when he had sat with him in the surgery. Drowning was not the full story. He was sure of that.

The two Tudor boys made their way back to the farmhouse in silence. Brad would return with Emyr to examine each selected lamb but Twm had promised to check the doctor's medical supplies. Some stocks were running low and needed to be ordered. Richard Owen had particularly asked him to ensure that bandages of all sizes were in stock. Farmers managed to keep him busy with cuts caused by scythes, wire and all manner of rusty metal. The doctor himself wasn't there. He was visiting his family back in Anglesey. Talk was that he had a sweetheart there. Tŵm wondered idly whether a possible doctor's wife would mean that his services would no longer be required.

Caron's 'special day' turned out to be rather a disappointment. "I don't know what I expected to happen," she confided dejectedly to Tŵm. "It's just that when I was a little girl, I always wanted to be eighteen. It seemed so glamorous somehow. But I don't feel any different at all. All I got as presents were some sheets and towels for my bottom drawer. Mam said I should start collecting linen just like Bethan. It was just a normal day except we had a plum cake at supper."

Tŵm tried his best to console her. "Come on Caron. Cheer up. You know Mam and Tad don't make much of birthdays."

"Dee Philpin always has a special tea. Her Nain and Taid and her aunts and uncles come for the afternoon and they take her presents. Last year she had chocolates, a scarf and new boots."

"Your friend Dee is an only child," replied Tŵm. "Her Mam and Tad spoil her. I'm sure Mam and Tad'll give us more of a celebration when we come of age. They did for Bethan. I met relatives I didn't know I had."

"Yes, I suppose so," agreed Caron.

A few days after their conversation, Tŵm was feeding the calves when he heard the unusual sound of a motor car entering the yard. It was unseasonably warm and Tŵm wiped his sweaty hands on a sack as he emerged from the bing, the feeding passage that saved him from the head butting of excited youngsters. He found Richard Owen beaming with pride.

"Come and look at my new acquisition Tŵm. It's a Chevrolet. I bought it from Williams of Denbigh." He stroked the windshield with pleasure. "Splendid, isn't it?"

"It certainly is," Tŵm replied, walking all round it. "Why did you choose a Chevrolet?"

"I looked at Fords in the Sun Garage, Llangollen but I thought this was better built and more comfortable. It was less money too."

"I didn't know you were thinking of buying a car. It's grand." Tŵm added.

"When I took Ruth Parry to Denbigh in the trap, it made me think. It took a good hour each way and we were lucky it wasn't raining. This," he patted the car again, "will do up to 45 mph though I doubt I'd drive it that fast. I can put the hood up and it'll keep me dry. No more soaking clothes or cold hands and feet and no pony to feed. Young Idwal Edwards looks after Dandy for me, as you know, but if I'm called out at night, I have to harness up myself and then rub the pony down and give him hay when I get back. This car will make my life much easier. And it'll be better for my patients too. I can get to them much more quickly when I'm needed."

Twm nodded. He could see the sense in what the doctor said.

By this time, they had an audience. Siôn was in school and Emyr and Brad were out checking for holes in the hedges. Sheep had been escaping and getting out on to the lane. However, Mali, Bethan, Caron and Nain all came out to see what all the excitement was about.

Mali was unimpressed. "You'll hurt yourself in that thing doctor. Motor cars are a danger to life and limb if you ask me. And they scare the horses. I was reading in the paper that someone was in court for speeding last week. Doing 45mph he was. Can you believe it? 45 mph! Fined him £50 they did. And he thoroughly deserved it. Reckless he was. Served him right. Could've killed someone."

The doctor was unperturbed. "You don't need to worry Mrs. Tudor. I'm going to drive carefully."

Nain supported him. "Mali, you need to move with the times. There's always been accidents on the roads, even with horses. I remember when Charles Boxer, Fachlwyd Hall, was killed near Bontuchel. Must be nearly forty years ago now. His horses bolted, the trap couldn't take the corner, it overturned and he was pitched out. They carried him into the blacksmith's house in Pentre but he died within a few minutes. Internal injuries they reckoned. Such a kind man he was too. Gave such a lot to the poor and needy."

Caron and Bethan excitedly opened doors, peered inside and inspected the identification plates.

"Are the seats leather doctor?" Caron asked.

"Yes, Caron, they are. And they're very comfortable. Do you want to try sitting in it? You too Bethan."

Caron climbed into the driver's seat leaving the passenger side for Bethan.

"Now don't touch anything, Caron," Mali told her.

"It's alright Mrs. Tudor. The engine isn't working now. You play all you like with it Caron. It's quite safe."

Caron flashed him a grateful look as she turned the steering wheel and pressed the foot pedals. "What are the dials for doctor?"

Richard Owen pointed them out to her. "That one's shows how fast I'm going and that one tells me how much oil I've got in the engine. I haven't got time to show you more of the car now Caron but I will call and show you it again, I promise."

Bethan came in with, "It must've cost a lot of money."

Mali frowned at her. "Now Bethan you know it's not good manners to ask about the prices of things."

Richard Owen laughed. "She's right. It was a lot of money. But worth it I believe. And all you've got to do is look the price up in Williams' advert in the 'Denbighshire Free Press'. It was £250."

Mali pursed her lips in disapproval. "That's a small fortune! All I can say is you doctors must earn a lot of money!"

Richard couldn't let that go. "We earn every penny of what we get Mrs. Tudor. I'm often up all night with patients and the car means I can get to them faster. It will save lives."

"That's as may be. But it's still a lot of money."

Richard shrugged. "Money isn't everything Mrs. Tudor. The war has taught us that. Now come on Tŵm, get ready. You're coming for a ride in my new car!"

"Really?" Tŵm's excitement was evident in his voice.

"Yes, really. I have to go over to the Bowens. Thought you might like to come with me. You could prove useful. There's been some kind of accident out there. Nia Bowen sent the farmhand to get me."

"I'll just get cleaned up and I'll be there."

Within a few minutes, the doctor had cranked up the car and they were on their way, rattling along at a fair old pace.

Tŵm, enjoying the sensation of speed, watched as the doctor accelerated and changed gear. "How do you know what to do?" he asked.

"They gave me a lesson in the garage. I soon picked it up. Nothing to it really."

"How fast are we going?"

The doctor looked at the speed. Thirty-five mph. I'd better slow up a bit. There's often loose sheep on this road."

He'd no sooner spoken than he rounded a bend to see four sheep wandering across the lane. Richard applied the brakes but it took a while to stop. "That's why you can't drive too fast," he told Tŵm, "but it is a temptation. It's good fun. I'll have to teach you how to do it. Would you like that?"

"I certainly would," Twm replied. "Thank you. Doctor, what's happened to Gwilym Bowen?"

"Apparently he was trying to mend a dung cart and managed to slice off the top of his thumb. I'm going to need those bandages you were sorting for me. When we get there, I want you to scrub your hands thoroughly and then pass me what I need. I may have to suture the wound. You know what instruments I will need. Tetanus is always a danger too."

Twm, changing the subject, tentatively raised the topic of Gwyn's post mortem. He was unsure whether Richard was allowed to tell him the results. "Did the post mortem reveal anything else other than the fact that Gwyn had drowned?"

"Not really. You know of course that he had a blow on the head because you saw it."

"Did he have any other bruises or marks on him?" Twm asked.

Richard looked at Twm quizzically. "What makes you ask that?"

Twm was uncharacteristically hesitant. "I th… th… thought I saw bruises on his chin and neck when I was sitting with him in your surgery but I wasn't sure because he had a blueish tinge anyway."

Richard relaxed. "Yes, the coroner did find bruising around the jaw, neck and shoulders. I don't suppose you know anything about how that happened do you?"

Twm prevaricated. "How would I know? Would it have happened when he fell in the pool?"

"Unlikely," Richard replied. "Gwyn must have bruised himself while he was still alive."

Twm looked at the doctor questioningly.

"I fail to see how several bruises could have resulted from falling into water," Richard went on, "if that is indeed what happened. Bodies don't normally bruise after death. How could he bruise himself when he was under water? No, in my judgement Gwyn suffered those bruises before he entered the water and probably a day or two before his death rather than on the actual day. Those plum-coloured bruises had clearly had time to come out. You must've seen him between Thursday and Saturday. He would've been working on the farm."

Twm cleared his throat. "Well yes I did. We went out shooting rabbits early Thursday morning."

"And did you see any bruises on him then?"

Twm heaved a sigh of relief. He could honestly answer, "No, he was fine.

It was a warm day so he had an open neck. I would've seen any marks on him."

The doctor pursued his enquiries. "What time did you get back?"

"About eleven."

Richard raised his eyebrows.

"Yes, I know that's a long time to hunt rabbits. But Tad said he could manage without us for a few hours and the warm sun had drawn them out. In time we had a brace each to fill the pots. Then we moved on to another colony rather than take from the same one. We didn't rush back. Just sat by the river for a while with a hunk of cheese and some bread."

"Well one thing's certain," Richard replied, "those bruises didn't make themselves. The police have asked Ruth whether she saw them I'm sure. They've already spoken to me about them, wanting my professional opinion. Have the police spoken to you yet?"

"Yes, they came to ask Tad and me some questions since we were witnesses."

"I thought they might. They were complaining to me about possible evidence being trampled all over by well-meaning but thoughtless villagers."

Though Twm was well aware of Gwilym's 'strangeness' he was still shocked when they walked into the farm kitchen. Gwilym, only twenty-seven, looked older than Emyr. He didn't look at his visitors, keeping his gaze fixed on the flags. He gripped the arm of his chair tightly with his good hand so that white knuckles stared out against the mellowness of the oak. He said nothing.

"I don't quite know what he did doctor." Nia was apologetic. "He was doing something with the dung cart. It was Wyn, our labourer, who called me when he saw the blood. I sent him to get you straight away when I saw how much blood he was losing. I've bound it up as best I can."

Richard removed the piece of blood-soaked butter muslin that had been wrapped tightly around Gwilym's thumb. Immediately blood gushed from the wound.

"This will need suturing I'm afraid. The important thing is to keep it clean. Can you get me some hot water please? Twm get my instruments ready."

"I boiled the kettle on the fire in case you needed it, so I'll just pour some hot water in a bowl," Nia went on.

"Not too hot," Richard interrupted.

"No, it'll be fine," answered Nia. "It's been standing a while."

"Twm, pass me the iodine." Richard was as professional as always.

Gwilym held out his hand like a dog offering a paw. Not once did he so much as glance at the doctor's face or at what was happening to his thumb. Once Richard had swabbed the wound clean, he sterilised it with iodine.

"Useful stuff this," he observed to Tŵm. "In the hospitals on the Front they used it to reduce the incidence of gas gangrene. Burns when you put it on though." Despite what Richard Owen had said, there was no reaction from Gwilym. He didn't even wince.

Tŵm threaded the gut through a curved needle and passed it to Richard. That must really hurt thought Tŵm but again Gwilym did not utter a sound. Disconcertingly though, the right corner of Gwilym's mouth pulled itself upwards in a nervous tic, giving him the strange semblance of a grimacing smile on one side of his face; the other side remained in its frozen stare.

"Tidy that," Richard congratulated himself. Once the task was complete, Gwilym did not thank him or acknowledge in any way that the doctor had sorted out a problem for him.

Nia, flushing to the roots of her dark hair, spoke for him. "He's very grateful aren't you Gwil?" If only he would nod, thought Tŵm. Then at least, Nia would feel a little more comfortable. But Gwilym didn't nod. He simply transferred his gaze from the floor to his bandaged thumb.

"I know he is," said Richard cheerfully. "Well, Gwilym, there'll be no more repairs for you for a while. You mustn't use that thumb until it's completely healed."

"I'll make sure he doesn't doctor. We don't want you hurting yourself again do we Gwil?"

She's speaking to him like Tad speaks to Siôn, thought Tŵm.

Tŵm remembered Gwilym singing in chapel just before he went to France. His resonant, bass voice gave strength to the somewhat sparse choir, decimated by men going off to war. Chapel success at the annual singing festival, the Cymanfa Ganu, was in part due to Gwilym. He had married Nia just before he left. "I'll be back in no time," he had consoled his new bride. Vigorous, strong, he was looking forward to the adventure of war. "Won't take us long to whip the Hun, don't you worry." He had returned to the village once during his training and that was to bury his father. Staying just long enough to make sure he could retain the tenancy of his father's tyddyn, he had been one of the few who returned at the end of war with even his limbs intact. If only his senses had been whole as well, thought Tŵm.

Before they left, Nia Bowen brought Gwilym out to see the motor car. Gwilym stared at it, then polished a head lamp gently with his sleeve but said nothing. "I think he likes it," Nia said.

Then, as he had done at Cwyn-y-Gwynt, the doctor cranked it up. The engine fired into life. As it did so Gwilym dived behind the low stone wall that separated the garden from the stack yard clutching his head in his hands.

"Damn it. I should've had more sense," Richard swore. "I should've known a sudden, loud noise could frighten him."

Nia was reassuring. "Don't you worry doctor, he's often like this. You get on and I'll see to him."

On the way back to Carreg-y-Bedd, Twm asked Richard, "Will Mr. Bowen get better?"

"I just don't know," replied the doctor. "Love and safety can work wonders but it's been a few years now. There's been some improvement but he's a long way to go yet. He doesn't talk most of the time because when he does, he stammers badly. Trauma locks itself into the body and then manifests itself in all sorts of ways."

"Can't something else be done?"

"Well, some doctors are using electric shock treatment but, in my view, not enough is known about the long-term effects. I believe it was tried on Gwilym at one stage before he came back here."

"I can see why Mrs. Bowen doesn't take him out much. People would stare at his face." Twm's concern was evident in his tone. "His eyes are blank and one eyelid droops. Then there's his mouth twitching."

"It's a nervous tic. It doesn't always happen but of course it was stressful having his thumb stitched. Yes, I can understand why Nia Bowen keeps him on the farm. She shouldn't be embarrassed but she is and she doesn't know how to deal with the situations that arise. Gwilym gets more anxious when he's out and that makes it worse."

"What do you mean doctor?"

"I believe he doesn't feel safe. He worries about possible threats. On the rare occasions I have seen him in the village he's constantly looking around him. He was exposed to constant danger so he still perceives it to be there. Like today. The sudden noise of the car."

Twm was keen to understand more. "He doesn't seem to be aware of what's going on around him."

"But maybe he's all too aware of what goes on in his own head. It's hard for Nia. He's not the man she married. He's able to do jobs on the farm but she can't have a proper conversation with him. You could say he's a work horse rather than a husband. Work is less frightening for him than thinking."

"Can't you help?"

"I'm not a specialist in war trauma. As to how to help men like Gwilym, well, research is in its infancy. There are too many destroyed men and too few doctors."

"Doctor Owen, why didn't you join the army as a doctor and treat wounded soldiers?"

Richard Owen shifted uneasily in his seat. "You've touched a raw nerve there Tŵm."

Tŵm's response was rapid. "I'm sorry. Forget I asked."

"No, no, Tŵm. It's fine. I do feel guilty when people ask me because it makes me feel as though they think I should've enlisted. But I didn't train as a surgeon and it was surgeons that were needed more than anything else. There were hospitals here in Britain of course but again I didn't have the skills to re-build jaws or graft skin. I suppose I could've trained but, to be honest Tŵm, I gain my satisfaction from looking after ordinary people living ordinary lives. It wouldn't do for every medical man to dash off to tend the wounded. Civilians need doctors too, even during a war. I enjoy the relationships that you build up over the years in a country practice. In a hospital, doctors treat patients who, once recovered, they're unlikely to see again. Here I live the family stories with the people themselves: the marriages, the deaths, the new babies, the tragedies and the triumphs. Some may see my choice as an easy way out, as an escape from the horrors of the battlefields but we're not all born to be war heroes. There's a place for each of us and mine's right here in Carreg-y-Bedd."

Over the next few days Tŵm thought a lot about Gwilym Bowen. All the soldiers he knew had returned as different men from those who went out. When Gwyn came back from France, he was certainly not the same Gwyn who had left with Evan all those years ago. But change was not the right word. What the right word was, or even whether there was a right word, Tŵm simply didn't know. Gwyn was still there with his shorn hair, his whitewashed features and his expert pencil strokes. But he seemed somehow faded. His personality was reduced to a flat image rather than a real flesh and blood person. It wasn't so much that he was quieter than he had been before. Gwyn had always been quiet, preferring to speak through his pictures rather than words. It was more that his reserves of energy were no longer accessible. Though still so young, he was embers rather than bonfire.

It had all been so different when they were in school together. Then Gwyn was up for most things. True he had been a follower rather than a leader but where Evan went, Gwyn had been sure to follow.

"Tŵm, Tŵm." Evan, spoke conspiratorially.

"What?"

"The Morgan boys are up to something."

"How do you know?"

"I heard them talking at playtime. They were planning something to be sure. Let's follow them and see what they're doing."

Tŵm cautiously asked, "Is that a good idea Evan? We can't let them see us. They'll beat us up again."

Tŵm had vivid memories of his last encounter with Cadoc Morgan. They had been in the school playground, the girls playing hopscotch and the boys fighting with carefully prepared conkers, dipped in vinegar, baked in the oven and threaded through with string. They had collected pockets full of new conkers on the way to school. That morning most of Tŵm's friends had been still kicking over the horse chestnut leaves hoping to find the elusive treasure of a satisfyingly obese conker, when the ringing of the school hand bell had dragged them away. They couldn't be late for prayers.

Just before playtime found them chanting:

'Three feet in a yard,
Twenty-two yards in a chain,
Ten chains in a furlong,
Eight furlongs in a mile'

Mr. Pugh cuffed Gethin Morgan across the ear for saying 'twenty' and missing out the 'two'.

Once they were let loose into the freedom of the school yard, it all started with an argument over ownership of a conker. The conker lay on the ground, just outside the door into the school cloakroom, glowing like burnished copper in the autumn sunshine.

"It's mine," stated Cadoc Morgan flatly as he picked it up.

"No, it's not," replied Tŵm. "It's just fallen out of my pocket. I found it this morning under the tree by the chapel."

"Liar!"

This was too much for Tŵm whose natural sense of justice was now under attack. "It's mine. Give it back."

"No. If ya wan' it, ya'll 'ave t' take it." Cadoc clenched his left fist tightly round the conker. Tŵm clenched his jaw just as tightly.

"Nobody's going to call me a liar and 'specially not you Cadoc Morgan."

Tŵm grabbed at Cadoc's fist, trying to retrieve the precious conker. At the same time Cadoc threw a punch with his free hand directly into Tŵm's ear. It knocked him off balance. The next minute Tŵm was flat on the ground with Cadoc kneeling astride him as though he was drenching a ewe. Tŵm was conscious of blood dripping down his bare knees. Cadoc directed short punches into Tŵm's cheek with his free hand. The other one still clutched the conker.

By the time Mr. Pugh came to see why there was such a commotion outside the school door, Gwyn and Evan were doing their best to pull Cadoc off Tŵm while Gethin Morgan had launched himself onto Evan's back. Gwyn was shouting, "Leave him alone, leave him alone."

"The place for a rugby scrum is on the playing field." Mr Pugh's sinister tone scythed through the screaming boys. "I want to see all five of you inside now."

They knew what was coming. Mr. Pugh unhooked the cane that hung at the ready next to his desk. He slid it to and fro through his hands, savouring the cool smoothness of the glossy surface.

"It were Tŵm Tudor's fault," sniffled Gethin Morgan. "'e started it."

"No, he didn't," Evan was indignant. "Cadoc started it. He stole Tŵm's conker."

"Where is this conker?" Mr. Pugh never raised his voice. It cut, clean as a blade, through the silence.

Cadoc slowly opened his hand.

"Give it to me." Slowly Mr. Pugh took the conker and placed it carefully on the floor in front of them. They watched as he slowly placed his heel over it and ground it into tiny shards.

"There is now no conker to fight over," he announced. "I will not have fighting in Carreg-y-Bedd school. And since there is no agreement about who started it, you can all have the same punishment."

Tŵm objected. "But Gwyn, Evan and Gethin were not part of it. They were trying to stop us." Tŵm's sense of honour extended even to Gethin Morgan.

"What I saw was a heap of boys. I haven't got the time or the inclination to sort this out. I want all of you to put out your left hands. We don't want you not to be able to write do we?"

"But Sir, I write with my left hand." Evan held out his right hand in front of him. Whether writing on his slate or in the silvered sand, Evan's writing slanted backwards.

"No-one, Evan Griffiths, writes with their left hand. Is that clear?" To emphasise his point, he brought the cane down on the long desk they all shared. Tŵm could feel the vibration running along its length.

Six strokes of the cane were the usual punishment for what Mr. Pugh considered a severe crime. Two strokes were meted out for more minor offences such as, 'eight sevens are sixty-three' or writing, 'buter'. Tŵm had never suffered the cane for such offences. In contrast the Morgans were hardened to almost daily thrashings for failing mental arithmetic tests.

That afternoon Tŵm, sitting on his left hand to quell the throbbing, watched Evan struggling to write the story of Noah's Ark with his right hand. By the end of the afternoon, he had suffered two further strokes for illegible handwriting.

Lying in bed that night Tŵm tried to assess which part of him hurt the most. On balance, he came to the conclusion that his left ear won the grim contest. It not only stung as though someone was holding a nettle against it, it also buzzed as though a wasp was suffering its death throes deep within his brain.

He had returned home with a rapidly swelling left eye, a bloodied nose, a crimson ear and tingling fingers. His appearance had certainly not been welcomed by Mali who had added to the painful parts of Tŵm's anatomy with a strapping for fighting in school and for coming home with a torn jacket. "Spare the rod and spoil the child," was her firm answer when Nain objected. "I've got to mend that tear now. As if I haven't got enough to do."

Though the bruises had long since faded, the memory was still vivid. Hence Tŵm's objections to Evan's plan. Delving into the Morgans' affairs was not a good idea, Tŵm was sure. But Evan was adamant. "We need to pay them back for getting us caned that day."

"We'll just get into trouble again," Tŵm replied. He sighed resignedly. There was no stopping Evan once he had decided on a course of action. Gwyn, listening to the exchange, offered no comment. He simply followed on behind as Evan tracked the Morgans. Even Evan was wary, Tŵm noticed. He kept well back as the Morgan brothers disappeared around the corner of the chapel. The Morgans were clearly on a mission. They moved fast and it was all Evan could do to keep them in his sights.

Carreg-y-Bedd was not the sort of village that clustered in a picturesque kind of way around a village green. Ebenezer, the 'Lamb and Lion' and the twelfth century church jockeyed for position amid patches of land that had been in common use for as long as anyone could remember. Opposite the chapel, Pwll Berw lay in wait, its malevolent gaze staring back at anyone who ventured across the rough tussocks that lay between it and the road. Tŵm had never even seen any boys fishing in it. They much preferred the friendlier ponds that could be found on several local farms.

To find the cottages of Carreg-y-Bedd a visitor had to venture down two lanes that bent like a dog leg behind the church. After the smithy, where Tŵm took Samson and Delilah to be shod by Weyland Philpin, the post office came as a surprise. It did not advertise itself as somewhere to bring letters. It was well hidden within Jane Turner's converted parlour and only those in the know were able to buy a postal order or National Savings Certificates. In contrast the village shop displayed itself as such by standing hardware on the lane outside. Many a time a bucket had gone flying or a broom stale diverted into a hedge when a trap wheel had passed too close for safety. The shop doubled as a cobbler's, with the repair room out the back. John Hughes kept the villagers' boots weatherproof while his wife, Rhian, weighed out cheese, wrapped foodstuffs and sold sundry items. The only other trading place was that of the butcher, Maldwyn Price. It lay behind a rusting corrugated iron shed. Monday was Killing Day. During a hot summer the stench of blood clung to the nostrils of those who were unlucky enough to dwell in Heol Isaf rather than Heol Uchaf. Beyond the string of cottages, the two lanes merged into one. There the imposing residences, which housed Carreg-y-Bedd's more esteemed residents, surveyed their surroundings from higher ground, their windows providing clear views across to Moel Famau and Moel Arthur. One of them, Tŷ Faenor, where Richard Owen lived, was familiar territory to Tŵm. The Morgans however showed no interest in it and carried on at a brisk pace.

"This'll mean I'm late home," Tŵm hissed at Evan. Mali was none too pleased with latecomers when she had spent hours 'slaving' over a hot hearth to cook the supper. They were likely to stay hungry until the next morning.

"Shhh." Evan did not raise his eyes from the bobbing caps way in front of them. "They must be going to Tŷ Celyn. There's nowhere else left."

Tŵm's spirits sank. Tŷ Celyn lay well past the other houses. It had fallen into disrepair. No-one had lived in it since the Boyle family had failed to return from a trip to Liverpool to visit relatives. It had been a tragedy. Two parents and two children all dead in a rail crash. Tŵm remembered Mali and Emyr talking about it.

"These cities are so unsafe," Mali announced. "You never know what's going to happen next. Such dirty, unhealthy places too. People always coughing and no wonder with the thick fogs they get. Not like the fresh air of Wales."

"A whole family gone just like that." Emyr's voice was heavy with sadness. "Those poor children. You knew them didn't you Tŵm?"

"Yes, a bit. They were younger than me." Tŵm remembered a tow-headed, freckled boy and a small, rather grubby girl who constantly sucked her thumb.

"They should never have moved there," Nain interrupted. "No good ever came of living in Tŷ Celyn."

"So, it was their own fault they were killed then?" Emyr's tone was gently teasing.

"Oh, you can mock, Emyr Tudor, but you explain to me why tragedy has struck every family to live in that house."

"Coincidence." Mali's tone brooked no argument.

Evan's guess proved to be right. The Morgans turned into Tŷ Celyn. They had to heave the rotting, wooden gate upwards to open it.

"What can they be going to do?" muttered Evan. "There's nothing there."

The Morgan brothers seemed to know exactly where they were going. They made their way round to the back of the house, pulled open a window to the side of the back door and disappeared.

"Now what?" asked Gwyn.

"We follow them in. I bet they're up to no good."

"No way." Tŵm was firm. "I'm not getting trapped in there with the Morgan brothers. There's nobody else around here."

"There are three of us and two of them," Evan ventured.

"No."

"Well, let's wait and see what happens then."

The three of them crouched low behind a holly bush in the shrubbery that bordered the unkempt lawn. It wasn't long before the shape of a head appeared in an upstairs window. This was followed by some creaking noises and a series of muffled thuds.

"Sounds like they're moving something around the room," Evan whispered.

Gwyn shifted position. "Ow!"

"Shhh. What's the matter?" Evan was cross at what he perceived to be unnecessary noise.

"Holly leaf down my shorts. Sorry. Let's move along a bit."

Shuffling down to move behind a laurel, they could all see that both Cadoc and Gethin were in full view. Framed in the grimy pane, the Morgans could be seen bending over something, heads close together. After ten minutes or so, Tŵm had had enough.

"Look Evan, I really have to get back. We can't see what they're doing anyway." Tŵm was becoming progressively more anxious.

Gwyn stepped in. "You go Tŵm. It'll take you much longer to get home than us. I'll stay with Evan."

Tŵm flashed him a look of gratitude. "Be careful both of you. Don't tangle with the Morgans. See you tomorrow." He sidled out from behind the shrubbery, taking care not to catch his jacket on an ill-placed branch. The last thing he wanted was another thrashing. Within seconds, moving at a fast trot, he had disappeared down the lane.

Gwyn and Evan did not have long to wait. The Morgan brothers soon emerged through the same window heaving a sack after them. Giving a quick glance both ways, presumably to check the coast was clear, they too vanished round a corner.

The temptation was too much. Levering the same window was easy and within a very few minutes Evan and Gwyn were inside. The house had a strange smell. Dust, damp and an unidentifiable pungent scent rather like that left by a fox that had plundered a henhouse. Gwyn did not like it one bit but not to be outdone, he followed Evan up the stairs. Evan opened and closed doors trying to find the room where he had last seen the Morgans. "This is it, I'm sure," he announced. "The window overlooks the shrub border."

Both boys leaned on the sill. Below them they could see the laurel which had provided them with such good cover. Beyond that was Bryn-y-Castell divided by the wall that separated the village from the estate grounds. They turned round to check out the room.

"There's nothing here," said Evan in a disappointed tone. He had not known what he had expected to find but he had at least thought they would find something there.

"Well, they were carrying a sack so I expect that they have taken away whatever was here. I don't see how we are going to find out what they were doing now."

"Whatever it was," replied Evan, "they must have hidden it here before."

Gwyn nodded. "S'pose so. Let's get out of here. That smell is even stronger in here. It's making me feel si..."

He stopped mid-word and clutched Evan's arm. Slowly he lifted his left foot. There was a slight noise rather like that of a rubber boot squelching in mud. Looking down they saw a seeping stain which had stuck to the sole of Gwyn's boot.

It was blood.

Summer Month

Caron's flowering bloomed late in early June. It had been weeks since her chance encounter with Abram but it had been impossible to ride out on either the Saturday week that she had suggested or for the two Saturdays after that. It was a busy time with castrating and ear tagging of the lambs combined with repairing walls and cleaning out barns. Jac had been needed for drawing the sled while Samson and Delilah were dealing with the second harrowing. The dry May had provided perfect conditions for the harrow but Emyr decided some fields needed doing again. "Aerates the soil and we'll get better grass growth," he told Brad.

So when Caron eventually ventured abroad, she had no real hope of meeting Abram. The mist hovered low amidst the trees as she trotted Jac towards the clearing. The primroses were long gone but the heavy scents of damp moss and wild garlic rose to greet her as she neared the spring. It was already warm though the air had not yet lost its crispness. Slipping down easily from Jac's sturdy back, she led him towards the water. Leaning against the trunk, she unlaced her boots, tugging with frustration at a particularly resistant knot. Mali did not buy new laces when old ones could be reknotted. Freed from constraint at last, Caron slid her feet into the chilly water then kicked them up and down, splashing like a baby in a bath.

"I never doubted but thet yer'd come, t'ough it's later rather t'an sooner."

This time Caron did not turn round. His deep, resonant tone was enough. "Abram!"

"I've waited 'ere fer yer fer t' past t'ree Sat'days. But I knew Jac'd be needed on t' farm so it'd be unlikely thet yer could come."

He had pre-empted her words yet again, removing the need for her apology.

"That's Brân over t'ere. Me Da paid fifteen guineas fer 'im at Appleby las' yeer." He pointed towards a handsome cob who was wearing only a bridle. "'e should be a match fer Jac!"

Abram spoke the truth. Brân was a match for Jac. He stood a good hand higher, an attractively marked skewbald, with a powerful chest and silky feathers falling over his hooves. Unusually his mane and tail were pure chestnut. His neck arched as he caught sight of Jac.

"'e's showin' off. 'e's still an entire. Da 'opes t' breed some fine foals from 'im. D' yer wan' t' race?"

Caron pulled on her boots, lacing hastily, rather than accurately. Abram chose a well grassed over track that eventually took them out of the forest, past a stone cairn and on to the open moorland that led gently upwards to the low summit that was Foel Goch.

"T'is way t'ere are no tree roots t' trip up t' 'orses. First to t' rock shaped like an otter's 'ead." He pointed into the distance. Caron calculated it was about half a mile. "Would yer like an 'ead start?"

Caron blushed crimson with anger. "I would not. That would be unfair."

Abram laughed. A long low laugh that seemed to ripple through his body. "Fine, let's go." He kicked Brân in the sides and was off, hooves thundering on the damp ground. Jac sprang into action, afraid he was going to be left behind. Caron wound her fingers through his wiry mane and urged him faster, surrendering to the rhythm of Jac's galloping stride and the rush of misty air. There was no way of dodging the clods of earth thrown up by Brân. She soon realised that Jac was going to be no match for the Gypsy stallion. But no-one had told Jac that. Undaunted, he manfully strove to keep pace. His heroic efforts were rewarded with reaching the rock only a short distance behind Brân.

Abram spoke first. "'e 'as a great 'eart, yer Jac."

Caron regarded him with relief. She hated losing at anything but Abram had made it easy for her; instead of gloating, he had admired Jac.

Her loyalty to Jac came to the fore. "He's smaller than Brân."

Allowing the horses to regain their wind, they led them to the top of the hill. With the countryside now emerging from the mist, a panoramic palette swept out before them. In the far distance, the smoke grey blur of the Clwydians, then as the mountains gave way to stone walled slopes, the land changed from smudged sepia shadows to khaki patchwork before giving way to squadrons of oaks, ash and birch marching up the hillsides.

Abram indicated downwards. "Look, thet's where we galloped up. We've come a fair way."

His arm swept upwards as he gestured back towards the mountains. Referring to them as if they were familiar companions, he continued, "Thet'n be Moel Arthur. See t' 'ill fort on 'is summit, a good place t' find milkwort. Thet'n wi' t' broken tower on 'is 'ead be Moel Famau. We collect brambleberries over thet way late in 'edgehog Month. Over t'ere's t' bare 'ead of Moel y Plas where lower down, t' ground is t'ick wi' bilberries late Corn

Month. Can yer see thet narrow green line, snakin' up an' t'en right over t' top? Thet's t' ancient Offa's Dyke path. Looks 'zactly like t' partin' in me Uncle Jim's 'air. Yer can walk from t'ere t' Llangollen, Chirk, Welshpool an' t'en right down t' South Wales if yer wan' to."

Caron viewed the mountains with new eyes. She had walked up Moel Famau shortly after the war ended. It had been a chapel summer outing with bread, cheese, Welsh cakes, and raisins to eat after the climb. But to Caron, one mountain was very much like another, especially from a distance. She was startled by Abram's intimate knowledge of each one. He spoke about them as though they were close friends.

Abram changed the subject. "Let's go back down t' f'rest. T'ere's somethin' I wan' t' show yer."

"What Abram? What?"

"It's a secret. Yer'll 'ave t' wait an' see."

He gave her a leg up on to Jac, vaulted on Brân and led the way down the slope, back into the forest. Before long he turned left into the trees.

"This can't be right Abram. There's no track here."

"Trus' me Caron. I know where I'm goin'."

He twisted in and out, between ivy covered trunks, rotted stumps and tangled undergrowth, the horses' hooves muffled by the soft debris of last winter's leaves. After about ten minutes, he slipped noiselessly from Brân's back.

"We'll leave t' 'orses 'ere. We need t' be silent." Pulling the reins over Brân's head he simply left them trailing.

"Aren't you going to tie him up?"

"No, 'e doesn't need tetherin'. 'e knows not to move."

Caron did not have the same confidence in Jac. She looped his reins over a branch, praying that he didn't break his bridle. She narrowed her eyes to search for Abram who had already vanished into a tangle of saplings, deadwood, docks and ferns. Carefully, she made her way after him. A twig snapped. He stopped, turned and whispered, "Shhh." Trying not to make a sound she followed. Abram seemed to be able to move in complete silence. Caron, though slight, felt clumsy in comparison. Abram held up a hand. She stopped. He disappeared into a hazel coppice, emerging with a small wooden box held in his hand.

"Me Da made t' box. Shhh. Don't fright'n 'im!"

"What is it?"

Putting the box on the floor, Abram knelt down and lifted the lid. He reached inside. Caron knelt down beside him. Cupping his right hand over his left, he opened up a gap wide enough for her to see. Inside the nest of Abram's hands was a creature that Caron recognised as a mouse but it wasn't like any mouse she had ever seen before. This one was round, plump and golden. He was curled into a ball with his tail wrapped protectively around him like a shawl.

"Oh, how lovely he is!"

"'e's a dormouse. Not many people 'ave seen one. T'ey live in t' forest, sleepin' most of t' time. I 'id a lot of boxes before a dormouse made 'is bed in one."

"How did you know where to put them?"

"They love 'azel so I looked fer chewed 'azel nuts in dark places away from t' main tracks."

Caron stroked his soft fur, running her hand from his head to tail.

"We mus' put 'im back." Abram replaced the lid and vanished again round the tree.

When he returned, he asked, "Can yer find yer way 'ome?"

Caron shook her head. She realised that she had no idea where she was. Abram smiled. "I'll get yer back to t' right path. Jac'll be missed."

"Will we meet again soon?" Caron tried not to allow the anxiety she felt to creep into her voice.

"Whenever yer can get away."

"How will you know that I'm in the forest?"

"I'll know."

Suddenly Abram grabbed her arm. "Stay still," he whispered. He pointed between two gnarled trunks that lay to the left of them. At first Caron couldn't see anything in the dimness of the undergrowth. Then there was a movement. A young fox, head held high, trotted into full view. Abram gave a low whistle. The fox stood stock still. Abram whistled again, longer and lower. Then he uttered a high-pitched bark, part warble, part low scream.

He held up his hand to Caron. "Stay 'ere." It was a command not a request. Caron was conscious of a certain breathlessness. She realised she was trying to breathe quietly as she watched Abram move forward, it seemed to her, silently. The fox's eyes fixed on the movement, vibrant with curiosity. At any moment, Caron knew, the fox would spin round. She would see a glimpse of the white tip of his brush and he would be gone.

She waited. To her bewilderment, the fox lay down. His eyes continued to watch Abram as he approached. Abram knelt down by the creature's head. Extending his hand, he stroked the fox under the chin, as Caron did with the farmyard cats. Caron could hear him talking to the fox in a low crooning voice but she was not near enough to be able to hear the words.

Abram turned his head towards her. "Come. 'e will stay still now thet I'm wi' 'im."

Caron crept forward. Abram gestured to her and she knelt beside him. "Stroke 'im. 'e'll allow it." The fox trembled at her touch but did not move. "I call 'im Kit. We know each other well don' we Kit? Kit, t'is is Caron." The fox rested his head on Abram's knee. "It were late Corn Month nearly a yeer ago when we first met. It were just after dawn and t' 'unt were out cubbin'. I saw t' cubs scatter an' t'is one ran in me direction. T'en I saw 'im 'ide under a fallen tree, rigid wi' fear. 'is attention were all on t' 'ounds so 'e didn't 'ear me approach downwind. I picked 'im up and 'eld 'im close.

"Didn't he fight?"

"Not really. Struggled a bit but I soon calmed 'im." Caron had already seen Abram's calming effect on animals. She was sure very few people could have quietened a terrified, wild fox.

"Fortun'tely I were near water. I strode mid-torrent an' walked upstream, t'en made me way out on t' opposite bank. T' 'ounds lost 'is scent. 'is brothers and sisters was not so lucky. I took 'im back wi' me an' raised 'im. When 'e were grown I let 'im run free, at first a few 'ours at a time. In t' Month of the Snow 'e met a vixen an' returned t' live in t' forest. 'e 'as cubs of 'is own now."

Abram removed his hand from Kit. "We mus' go. Time's runnin' on."

Within a short time, they were back in the clearing. "Yer know where yer are now." Again, he gave her a leg up on to Jac. Caron was keenly aware of his touch on her bare leg. No-one outside the family had ever touched her skin before. It was a strangely pleasurable sensation. Vaulting on Brân again, he waved his hand at her and was gone.

June was a busy month on the farm. Once Whit Sunday and the Eisteddfod events of Whit Monday were over, sheep shearing took priority but additionally manure had to be carted and crops weeded. On the lower ground there were fences to mend and on the higher ground stone walls to repair. Tŵm did not enjoy the heavy physical work of heaving stones into place. At least he didn't have to do the shearing itself but, with Brad and Tad, he did have to bring sheep down from the uplands, where they had been taken after grazing the ffridd. Not an easy task, though Jono was a huge help. Once the flock was penned near the stack yard, Tŵm's and Brad's job was to catch unruly sheep and carry them in to the shearers. This was back-breaking, exhausting work. Again, and again, under the hot sun, Tŵm would chase each ewe, use Jono's expert manoeuvring to corner her, clutch the woollen coat with fingers burrowed deep and hands thick with grease and then heave her across to the long, narrow benches in the shed. No matter how much effort he put in, Brad would always manage to haul in more than him. "Come on, come on Tŵm, Brad's way ahead of you," would ring in his ears. Even Siôn helped. Young though he was, he was quite capable of rolling up each fleece into a bundle. Caron and Bethan did the same. It took three of them to keep up with the shearers. Keen to get the job done, the men clipped on relentlessly. As each sheep was freed, Emyr would clip its hooves, slice its ear, splash the Cwyn-y-Gwynt russet mark on the mid-rib, and then let it loose.

In contrast to Tŵm, Caron loved the shearing days. Shearing was a real occasion. All the farmers pulled together to make sure that everyone got their wool to market. That year Emyr had been allocated the final Friday and Saturday in June. Eight neighbours turned up to lend a hand. The weather was unfortunate. After a cool, changeable month, the days were very warm. Mali and Nain were kept busy supplying water to replenish that lost from the sweat running in rivulets down the men's faces and arms. Caron, rolling fleeces, breathed in the stench of damp blankets. She loved to watch the shearers, especially Marc, who won all the competitions. Short, stocky, and darkly, low browed, he would grasp the ewe with bulging arms, the colour of old leather, turning her belly up. Vulnerable, she gave in immediately. Gleaming with sweat, looking as if he had been polished with saddle soap, he would raise the blades and start with a strip down the belly. Within minutes a pure white sheep emerged from the thick, grubby casing. Caron never tired of this resurrection. She thought it must be a wonderful release for the sheep to shed their dirty, heavy coats and run clean and free through the summer grass. Not that she was allowed to watch for long. Mali saw to that. "I'm not having you lazing around while everybody else is working."

To Caron, best of all was the final day's celebration. As soon as the last sheep ran off to join its fellows, Mali, Nain and Bethan started to bring out the food while the men horsed around. Marc started it by ducking Brad in the water trough. Dylan Jenkins snatched a bucket of water and threw it over Marc. It took Emyr to stop the mayhem. "Hey, hey, don't waste the water. It all has to be carried you know." The shearers stood there, dripping water that pooled in soggy puddles round their feet. A cheer went up as Mali, Bethan and Nain appeared carrying plates of food which they laid out on the shearing benches in the shed. The men fell on ham, cheese, bread, cakes, griddle scones, bowls of early wild strawberries and cream fresh that morning with water and pots of tea to quench their thirst. Nain had suggested beer or cider but Mali had denounced this idea as 'devil's broth.' At Cwyn-y-Gwynt the men would drink soft Welsh water, just as they did for the harvest celebrations.

A short time after the food had been consumed, Caron heard the unmistakeable sound of hooves on the farm track. She wondered who her father had asked to entertain the shearers. The previous year it had been Will Edwards, the story-teller who held them spellbound with tales of white stags, jumping giants, hooded monks and sleeping kings. Looking up she saw Moses ride into the yard, on a piebald pony, carrying a case on his back. Following him was a distinctive skewbald that, with a start, she recognised. It was Brân. She did not dare to even glance at his rider.

An hour later the party was in full swing. Moses was an expert on the fiddle, the lilting airs of 'Merch Megan' and 'Llwyn Onn' carrying well beyond the confines of the farm. What Caron hadn't expected was Abram's rich baritone voice as an accompaniment. Suddenly Moses changed the mood of the music and the jaunty 'Jenny Jones' caused Marc to push back the benches, take Bethan's hand and start dancing round the barn. Caron noticed how uncomfortable Bethan looked, only allowing the tips of her fingers to brush Marc's hand. Well, he does smell of sheep, Caron thought to herself. She still hadn't felt able to look at Abram but now, with Bethan and Marc stepping it out in front of her no-one was taking any interest in what she was doing. Tapping her foot, she glanced over to the fiddler but Abram was no longer by his father's side.

A voice to her left explained why. "Dance."

Just as when Abram told her to stay still while he moved towards Kit, it was a command not a request. Unthinkingly, Caron followed him. Two or three steps later the music stopped.

Mali was speaking to Moses. "We don't need to dance," Caron heard her say. "A hymn I think would be more suitable to give thanks to the Almighty for the wealth of wool we have gathered today. Obediently Moses started to play, 'Guide me O thou Great Jehovah.' Abram gave Caron a quick look of regret, dropped her hand and moved alongside his father to start singing again.

Later that evening Mali was in full flow as Emyr opened up the case to wind up the clock. However late, it was a task that could not be forgotten. Woe betide the sinner who did the winding on God's Day.

"And as for you two, making a spectacle of yourselves like that. Bethan you know quite well that Marc Benyon is a churchgoer and as such is unfit to dance with a Tudor." She spat out 'churchgoer' as though it was a form of abuse. "Dancing indeed! Carousing has no place in a god-fearing family." She turned her anger towards Caron. "As for you, young lady, well words fail me."

It would be the first time they had, thought Caron, but I wish they would.

"A Gypsy! A Gypsy! You touched a dirty Gypsy. You were going to dance with a Gypsy lad!"

"He wasn't dirty. He was much cleaner and less smelly than Marc and the other shearers."

The movement was too swift for Caron to be able to avoid it. She felt the sharp slap across her left cheek before she even sensed the movement.

"Don't you dare contradict me like that! Go to your room."

Caron refused to allow Mali the satisfaction of tears. Without a word she obeyed the instruction.

Lying in bed Caron thought back to the evening's events. It had been sober fun; controlled, within strict limits. Dancing was a step too far, a step beyond the chapel boundaries. After Mali's intervention, the farmers had sung a few more hymns and listened sleepily to a few melodies from Moses. Emyr's thanks followed them home.

The next morning was the Sabbath. Emyr, Brad and Twm milked, watered and fed the stock and came in to share porridge with the rest of the family. Sunday best meant just that. The men greased the boots while the women dressed. Since it was fine summer weather, Nain was coming too. In the winter she often stayed in the warmth of the Cwyn-y-Gwynt kitchen but felt she had to explain seasonal absences to the minister. Every time she saw him, she would say, "As you know Mr. Ellis, my bronchitis prevents me from coming to chapel when it's cold and wet. After all I'm not as young as I used to be. It's not that I don't want to come. When I have to stay at home, I read the Bible there instead." Caron smiled every time she heard this. One bitterly cold winter day, when she had a nasty cough, she had stayed home with Nain, who had dosed her with onion juice and blackberry vinegar. The Bible had not made an appearance. Instead, Nain had drawn her chair up to the fire, stirred up the logs with a poker and played Ludo with Caron.

On this summer Sabbath, the kitchen at Cwyn-y-Gwynt was hotter than outside. The shearing had prevented Mali from preparing for chapel the night before, as she usually did, so Sunday morning saw her with an iron ready for pressing clothes, after heating it on the range. Caron donned her grey flannel dress, pushed on her unadorned, straw bonnet and wished, not for the first time, that it wasn't so warm. At least the journey in the trap provided a welcome breeze though poor Jac was sweated up by the time they got to the chapel.

Ebenezer lay in wait for her, squatting, like a wildcat about to pounce.

Caron stood and watched as Emyr led Jac over to Moses, and saw to it that Jac was tethered in the shade and given some water. Intent on catching a glimpse of Abram and not realising that Mali and the rest of the family had already entered the chapel, she was startled when Emyr nudged her. "Get a move on. We can't keep God waiting."

"I was just checking that Jac was alright."

"No need. Moses knows what he's doing."

Her final glance revealed there was no sign of anyone except Moses and a couple of grubby children.

Caron proceeded upstairs to join Mali and Bethan in the pew they always occupied right at the front of the gallery. She could see her father and brothers down below. Caron knelt, greeting her God. Strange that Bethan isn't here yet she thought. Her sister had decided not to come with them in the trap. "It's so lovely today, I think I'll walk," she had said, leaving early. They hadn't passed her on the way so Caron expected her to be there before them. Just before the preaching meeting started, Bethan slipped in beside her.

"Where've you been?" Caron whispered, earning a glare from Mali.

Bethan shook her head, put her finger to her lips and knelt to pray.

A short time later Caron was shifting uneasily on the hard benches of the chapel. Ebenezer felt both alien and comfortingly familiar. Unease won the battle as the minister announced the text for the day: '*I John. 2: 15-17. For all that is in the world, the lust of the flesh and the lust of the eyes and the pride of life, is of the Father but is of the world. And the world passes away and the lust of it; but he who does the will of God abides for ever.*'

The apostle's words echoed above her head into the soaring void of Ebenezer's roof. Just thirty minutes previously she had been guilty of 'lust of the eyes.' The penetrating voice of the preacher, Daniel Ellis, rose as he relished a further text. '*But I say, walk by the Spirit, and do not gratify the desires of the flesh. Galatians 5: 16.*' There was to be no respite it seemed. '*The works of the flesh are plain: 'immorality, impurity, licentiousness... party spirit, envy, drunkenness, carousing and the like.*'

It seemed last night's 'party spirit' had only added to her damnation though Mali had prevented the carousing before it had barely started.

'Especially those who indulge in the lust of defiling passion.' Thrusting out 'lust' as an expletive, Daniel Ellis lingered over 'defiling', elongating the sound. Caron's isolation from the rest of the congregation increased with her growing sense of sin. Had she already indulged in defiling passion? She wasn't sure but she had been alone with a man and, according to the strict rules of Mali and her chapel, that was not allowed. Not only that but she had been alone with him in a remote place. Abram had touched her bare skin. It had made her feel something she didn't understand, a stirring that she hadn't felt before. To add to her wickedness, she had kept it all secret. Told nobody. Not even Twm. She was used to sharing all her thoughts with Twm.

'Jude Chapter 8. Just as Sodom and Gomorrah and the surrounding cities, which likewise acted immorally and indulged in unnatural lust, serve as an example by undergoing a punishment of eternal fire.'

The minister savoured 'unnatural' rolling the 'r' round his tongue. Was she unnatural to feel as she did? She would be castigated. There was no doubt about that. God would not let her get away with such behaviour. What could she do? She could not see a way out of her dilemma. To admit to the sin was out of the question. Mali's venom would know no bounds. She would have to endure the eternal fire whilst here on earth. She preferred the threat of hellfire. At least that wasn't imminent or so she hoped. She could imagine her Mam now. "How could you? How could you? Bringing shame upon the family. You're nothing but a cheap tart."

'The sinful Adamic nature that uncontrollably longs to sin; totally corrupt and evil; the inheritance of the sin of Adam; that part of man that is intrinsically sinful; the lower and base nature of man with which he is born that is inclined only to do evil and no good...'

Caron fought to prevent images of Abram flashing like a silent movie across her mind. Adam, Abram, Adam, Abram reverberated in her head keeping time with the pounding of her heart. She could feel the sinful touch of his hand on her leg as he helped her mount Jac, the brush of his fingers on hers in the shearing shed the previous night. It seemed to her that the deacons in front, ensconced in the Sêt Fawr, the Big Seat, were staring at her, significantly, like a jury in a court. She felt exposed, transparent. Did they know what she was thinking? She knew well that a sinful thought was just as bad as a sinful deed. Were her sins and wickedness indeed 'manifold'. She repeated the words of the Confession, *'We do earnestly repent, and are heartily sorry for these our misdoings,'* again and again in her head to make sure God heard. Later her over-enthusiastic, *'Have mercy upon us,'* caused Mali's wrath to be heaped upon her for, "Drawing attention to us like that."

'Forgive us all that is past,' brought a further problem. Because it wasn't past. It was only just beginning. She knew that. Just as she knew that she was helpless to prevent it. Even before chapel she couldn't prevent her eyes from searching for him. How could she be more sinful than that?

'Those who do such things shall not inherit the earth.' The minister thankfully brought the sermon to a close. Those who *were* going to inherit the earth stood up to sing Hymn 224 and Caron copied them.

'How many a soul with guilt oppressed
Has learned to hear the joyful sound
In that sweet tale of sin confessed,
The Father's love, the lost and found!

How many a child of sin and shame
Has refuge found from guilty fears
Through her, who to the Saviour came
With costly ointments and with tears!'

Even the hymn was a torment. Was that what she was? A child of sin and shame? Guilt was the burden she carried. But would her confession to God help? Would He take pity on her? She thought not. Mercy was only heaped on those who were truly repentant. Try as she might she couldn't bring herself to feel true remorse. 'Refuge' seemed particularly unlikely given that she wasn't sorry she had met Abram. The first time was an accident but the second, she well knew, was by design.

Emerging into the bright sunshine, she was startled when the minister approached Bethan, "Are you able to start this Tuesday evening?"

Bethan flushed. "Yes. That will be quite convenient. What time?"

"Seven o'clock."

Bethan nodded her agreement. Caron looked at her sister enquiringly.

"I offered to help with the rehearsals for the Eisteddfod. I called to see Mr. Ellis since I arrived early for chapel this morning."

"So that's where you were. I wondered why you were late. Why do you want to do that?" Caron's view was that too much time was spent on chapel activities as it was. She much preferred to walk in the forest, ride Jac or press wild flowers.

"I am happy to serve God in any way I can." Bethan compressed her thin lips into a tight line and turned to acknowledge Howell and Olwen Griffiths. Their attendance at chapel had been erratic since they lost Evan.

"How are you Mr. and Mrs. Griffiths? Nice to see you here. And how are Ebrill and Catrin?"

"Not too bad at all Bethan thank you. Ebrill and the children are fine. We don't see much of Catrin now she and Charles are living in Liverpool."

"It must be hard for you on the farm without Evan to help."

A shadow passed over Howell Griffith's face. "It is but we manage."

As the Tudors walked over to Moses who was waiting by the trap, having harnessed up Jac again, Mali turned to Emyr. "The Griffiths' may be able to manage Tan-y-Graig now but they won't be able to in another ten years. It would have been different of course if Evan had lived. Or if Ebrill's Harri, had survived the war. Either of them could have taken over the tenancy. When the time comes perhaps Sir Edward will let us have the land."

"The time hasn't come yet Mali."

"Well, no, but it doesn't do any harm to plan for the future. We have three sons, remember."

"Many people don't even have one anymore." Emyr's discomfiture was evident.

"Well, quite. That's what I meant."

"We're fortunate indeed that our sons were too young to fight. I don't want to benefit from the misfortune of others." Emyr spoke quietly, looking round to check that no-one could hear.

Mali had no such compunction. "Nonsense Emyr, don't be so ridiculous. We didn't cause the war. It's our duty to do the best we can for our sons. With Twm running Cwyn-y-Gwynt, helped by Brad and Sîon, we can easily farm more acreage."

As Emyr ushered them all into the trap, Caron could not resist a sinful glance over her shoulder. There was still no sign of Abram.

Early Tuesday evening Bethan left for the Eisteddfod practice as arranged. She prided herself on her ability to read and play music with precision. Her voice, though not strong, was tuneful. She would be an asset to the potential competitors. Bethan had thought the minister would have been more pleased at her offer of help. After all, Alis Phillips, who had played the organ for more years than anyone could remember had been forced to stop. Crippled with arthritis, her hands resembled the bark of the ancient holly trees which grew round Tŷ Celyn, lumpy and disfigured as they were. Her knees would no longer carry her as far as the chapel. The minister visited her now so that she could partake in the sacrament. One of the elders had volunteered to play the hymns in the chapel but his farm work prevented any further commitment to the Eisteddfod.

However, Daniel Ellis seemed strangely reluctant to take her on. His eyes shifted from her gaze. "Two or three other people have indicated an interest," he told her.

She had been forced to put herself forward more strongly. "The more teachers there are, the more chance our chapel will have. Who else has offered to help?"

The minister's hesitant reply revealed that offers had been received from Gareth Bevan and Dewi Rogers. Gareth did not surprise her. He was a fervent supporter of the Eisteddfod and had been awarded the Chair at fifteen years old for his harp solo. However, Dewi came as a shock. He was a fine musician, no doubt about that. Young though he was, he could make his violin speak to the audience. As a choir member, he was unsurpassed, his boyish, fine soprano maturing into a countertenor that could still hit a clear high F. Yet she could not see how Dewi would be able to coach the village's aspiring competitors to success. He may be able to make a violin give voice but, painfully shy, he barely volunteered a word himself. If someone spoke to him, his pale face flushed to the roots of his wispy, mouse coloured hair. Still, it was not for her to decide.

The bell outside the front door rang loudly. "Excuse me a moment Miss Tudor."

While the minister was out of the room, Bethan had the chance to look round. The room was clearly part study, part library. A large but plain desk dominated the room. It was impressively tidy. A sheaf of papers, covered in elongated copperplate handwriting, was lined up with edges exactly straight. His sermon probably, Bethan thought to herself. A glass inkwell was positioned next to a pen and paper knife. A copy of the Bible, a prayer book and a hymn book were stacked neatly, according to size, on the left-hand side of the leather-bound blotter. She turned her attention to the bookshelves lining the room. It seemed that Mr. Ellis had an interest in geography for alongside theological tomes were books on exploration, especially to the New World. What was more unexpected were the poems of Byron, Shelley and Keats rubbing shoulders with novels by Maugham, Wodehouse, Lawrence and, shockingly, Wilde's 'The Picture of Dorian Gray.' Startled, Bethan put the inclusion of such horrors as being down to the fact that the minister was an intellectual who must have an insight into evil in order to combat it. Such books would never have been allowed to cross the threshold of Cwyn-y-Gwynt. She was pleased to see suitable periodicals such as 'Y Gwyliedydd Newydd' filed on a bottom shelf, correctly classified in date order.

The minister returned to find her still examining the magazines. He raised his eyebrows. Flustered she felt the need to apologise. "I hope you don't mind but I haven't read the latest copy."

"Would you like to borrow it?"

"Thank you but no. Once Tad has read his copy, he will pass it on to me."

"I am pleased to find that you are a devout follower of its writings."

"I am indeed."

She gave him a slight smile. She wished he were more attractive. Daniel Ellis was a slight, angular man, lacking in musculature, with mouse brown hair and pale Celtic skin. A shame he was so ordinary but in every other way he was ideal. Bethan was aware that her choices of a partner were limited to say the least. She had been analysing possibilities for over two years. Basically, she didn't have much of a choice. Her Mam and Tad would have to approve the match. With three healthy brothers, she was unlikely to inherit anything at all, whether it be land or money. Mam had already suggested that she visit her cousins in Llanrwst. Bethan knew exactly what Mali and Enid, were planning. Her cousin Trefor was just twenty-one. Married to the land, he was the eldest son and so a perfect choice. He was a little younger than her but that wouldn't matter. What was important was keeping the land in the family. In the Tudor family, acreage was only ever acquired, never sold. More sacred than hallowed ground, it represented security, stability and permanence. Trefor had been fortunate to escape the worst of the war. He had started army training but the war had finished before he could be sent over to France. It was not that Bethan particularly minded marrying Trefor. If she had to, well she had to. But she would much prefer to stay in Carreg-y-Bedd. She felt safe there. Secure. She knew everybody and they knew her. Llanrwst seemed a long way away from her home, family and friends and by all accounts it was subject to flooding.

Now that Evan was gone, she had to be practical. His crooked smile had always brought a lightness to her step, a smile to her eyes. In chapel, his strong baritone had reached those parts of her that she kept strictly under control. But it was now over four years since the news had come through. 'Killed in Action. March 23rd 1918. Morchies. France.' Better not to know how he died. Gwyn hadn't said and she hadn't asked. He'd been brave. That was evident as he'd been awarded a medal. She just knew that the path of her life had changed when Howell and Olwen Griffiths received their telegram. For all of them the heaviest burden was the lack of consecration. No grave to visit in Carreg-y-Bedd. Just a space where someone had been. It shouldn't be like that. There should be prayers, a funeral oration, hymns. Something suitable like at Gwyn's funeral, '*Now the labourer's task is o'er; Now the battle day is past.*' If Evan had died at home he would have been wrapped in the embrace of the chapel. There would have been a procession from Tan-y-Graig, bowed heads, family bearers, handshakes, words of solace, prayers at the graveside, the thud of earth on the coffin. As it was, Evan lay somewhere under the turf of France. So far away from home. She had no chance of ever going there. She wouldn't know how. All that she could hope was that he had received a Christian burial. That the right words had been said. That he had reached his God.

Not that Evan had ever indicated that he favoured her but she was sure that would only have been a matter of time. He teased her certainly but then he teased everyone. She had called at Tan-y-Graig once with Twm. Evan was milking a cow. Hearing them arrive he called to them from the byre. Always the prankster, as they entered, he twisted up the teat and squirted them with warm milk. Bethan gasped. The sticky mass was in her hair, her eyes and dripping down her good, black blouse.

"Evan, how could you?"

"Not objecting to the milk of human kindness are you Bethan?" He gave her a skew-whiff look from underneath the hair flopping as usual over his forehead.

Twm laughed. "He's got you there, Bethan."

No-one else had ever treated her with such disrespect but she loved it. Evan was different. He had a courage about him that had as much to do with attitude of mind as physical bravery. She would often gasp at the way he spoke to the elders in Sunday School. He was never rude but always challenging. "How can everything be pre-destined if we have free will to choose our path?" he asked a deacon.

"Though you have free will, God knows how you are going to act. He is all seeing," came the answer.

"That doesn't make sense," retorted Evan. "God can't have it both ways."

"Evan Griffiths, that is positively blasphemous. I will speak to your father later."

Bethan couldn't remember which elder it was but he was extremely angry. "You will have to keep an eye on your Evan," he told Howell Griffiths later. "He has the seeds of the devil in him."

Yet Evan had turned out to be a fine young man. "Too handsome for his own good," Mali often said sourly when he came to help Twm with some muck spreading. But he was not afraid of hard work, he was a more than loyal friend to Twm and Gwyn, was always ready to help anyone and knew his duty to King and Country. When Bethan knew he was joining up, she had determined to wait secretly for his return, perplexing Mali by rejecting any suggestions for other appropriate suitors.

"If anyone is going to do well in life, it will be Evan Griffiths," Bethan had heard her father often say. "He can charm the birds off the trees."

He had certainly charmed her, she thought. And he was a good man. A member, though not a stalwart of the chapel, he lived the Ten Commandments in a way superior to the deacons, always looking after his family, his neighbours, his friends. It was just his irreverent, wicked sense of humour that enraged the righteous.

But Evan was gone.

Now, if she were to escape Trefor, the only course of action was to set her cap at the minister. He was single, came from a decent family, his father was a well-known preacher, his three sisters all firmly established with families of their own; most importantly he had status in the community.

Daniel Ellis was not showing any interest in her that was true. But time would take care of that she was sure. She couldn't think of any other woman in the village who would be as suitable as her. Mam and Tad could not make any objections to her marrying a man of the cloth. She would be able to stay where she felt safe and she would be marrying a good, God-fearing man who shared her views on how life should be lived.

The object of her desire, unaware that he had been singled out for special treatment, failed to behave appropriately. He ushered her out of the front door, reminding her that the meeting would begin shortly.

Bethan was even more disappointed to find that Daniel Ellis was not actually at her first Eisteddfod practice. That day he had been called to administer the sacrament to a chapel member who was in danger of dying unforgiven. Without complaining, Bethan listened to recitations from the scriptures, as Gareth Bevan deemed her too inexperienced to coach the musicians. "You have to start somewhere. They're practising Isaiah 53 Verses 1-6."

The date of the inquest into Gwyn's death had been set for July. Twm could not rid himself of a sense of unease. The date, July 28th, was like a parasite infestation lurking under his skin. Like the sheep he had to learn to live with it. The more he tried to push it to the back of his mind, the more it came to the fore. Monotonous, tedious farm work did not help. It left far too much space for mental activity. As a result, taking Jac to the smithy in Carreg-y-Bedd came as a welcome relief.

"How long will he be Mr. Philpin? I need to do a few errands," Twm asked, leading Jac in.

"About an hour. Don't worry if you come back later than that. I'll tie him up in the yard."

Twm was on a mission. A few minutes later he was knocking on the door of Ruth Parry's cottage.

"Twm. How nice to see you."

"May I come in Mrs. Parry?"

She opened the door wide and showed him into the kitchen where she was in the midst of baking bread. "I'll make you a drink Twm."

"Thank you. I've brought you some fresh eggs. Mam sent them specially as we've got too many and she didn't want them wasted." Twm was aware he had to be careful that Ruth did not offer to pay. "I've also come to see if you have any jobs that need doing."

"Oh, Twm that is so kind of you. I'm sure you have enough to do for your Tad."

"No, really Mrs. Parry, you would be helping me out. I have to wait while one of our horses is shod. I hate sitting around."

"Well in that case, there are one or two..." Ruth's relief was evident in her voice.

Two hours later, Twm had chopped wood for the fire, dug up new potatoes, weeded the small vegetable patch and brushed out the coal house ready for the winter delivery. He was glad of the newly baked bread, thick with jam, offered to him when he eventually came in.

"Thank you Twm. That's such a big help. Gwyn used to..." Her voice tailed off.

"I know," Twm replied, "I know."

"Mrs. Parry, I don't want to interfere but will you be OK for..." Twm hesitated. This was a sensitive topic, not normally spoken about, especially by a young lad to an adult woman.

Ruth rescued him. "If you mean will I be able to manage for money Twm, then yes I will. I've put a bit by over the years and I have my war widow pension, though it's little enough. And now I have a job which I'll start after the inquest. That'll give me a decent mourning period as well."

"Job, Mrs. Parry?"

"I'm going to be working at Bryn-y-Castell. Just for two days a week. Lady Craddock called with her labradors in tow and offered me a job as a housemaid. She said she needed someone else as one of her girls, Siân, left to go to the home training centre in Wrexham. After twelve weeks of training, she can apply for a job anywhere. Lady Craddock told me she doubts that Siân will get better pay but she was determined to go as she sees London as far more exciting than Carreg-y-Bedd. Then Lady Craddock added that it was much harder to get staff than it used to be before the war because girls are saying they want proper jobs not housework. They don't want to live in either. So, she said, if I agreed to help out, I'd be doing her a favour."

Tŵm smiled inwardly. Clearly, he was not the only one to recognise Ruth's unbending pride.

"Tŵm, I've been meaning to ask you whether you would like something of Gwyn's. The two of you were always such good friends."

"Oh, no, Mrs. Parry. You must keep everything for you."

"I have my memories, Tŵm. That's all I need but I have plenty of Gwyn's things in any case. I am sure that Gwyn would like you to have something."

"Then thank you. I would be honoured."

Ruth led him upstairs to the room where Gwyn, Tŵm and Evan had so often sat on the bed together planning fishing trips or a visit to Denbigh. Tŵm was uneasy. It felt wrong to enter Gwyn's private space. He stooped slightly, his body having to bend forward under the eaves.

"Sit down on the bed Tŵm. You'll be more comfortable."

Tŵm did as Ruth asked. Ruth opened the panelled closet to reveal a pile of boxes. She lifted them out. Perched on top of them lay a brown leather hymn book. Ruth picked it up and opened it. "Look, Tŵm, it's inscribed."

Tŵm leant over. '*To Gwyn Parry. May God's grace be with you. Daniel Ellis,*' he read.

"So good of the minister," Ruth carried on. "Gwyn's faith had always been a part of his life as you know but when he returned from the war it became more important than anything else. He told me that the only reason he survived was because he kept his faith under fire. Just after he came back home, he said that he'd had to do things that no man should ever have to do and he hoped God would forgive him. But he didn't say any more after that. He didn't like to talk much about the war. Well, I'm sure you know that Tŵm. He needed the chapel to help him heal and I believe it did. Mr. Ellis helped a lot. Such a good man he is. He seemed to understand that Gwyn needed time to forgive himself. He gave the book to Gwyn as a present last Christmas. It must've been expensive too. It's real leather. Such a kind man."

Tŵm gave her the agreement she wanted. "I'm sure the chapel brought Gwyn a lot of comfort Mrs. Parry."

"It did Tŵm, it did. As it does to us all. Gwyn was so devout you know. Just like his father. Thomas taught him to say his prayers every night before bed. And he never failed to do that. Even in the field of battle. He told me that. Proud of it he was. And when he came back, he did the same thing every evening. We read the Bible together and then said our prayers. Then of course he attended all the chapel prayer meetings." Ruth reached for a tea box. "This is very special."

Tŵm looked at her enquiringly.

Ruth opened the lid. "These are what Gwyn had in his pocket when he..." She paused. "When he passed into God's arms."

Tŵm surveyed the contents, conscious of a growing disappointment. He was hoping for enlightenment, a clue as to what had happened. But the items were unsurprising. Gwyn, he knew, was never without a pencil and used string to help with perspective. All farmhands carried penknives. They were invaluable. Threepence was nothing out of the ordinary and if a button came loose then anyone would stuff it in a pocket.

Not knowing what to say to Ruth, Tŵm made do with, "Not much there, Mrs. Parry."

"No. The only one I don't understand is the button. When I saw it, I was cross with myself for not having noticed he'd lost one and sewn it on for him. But I checked the shirt he was wearing when he... well, when he was... in the water and it wasn't missing a button. So, I checked his other shirt and that didn't have a missing button either. There's probably a simple explanation though. Perhaps he just found it on the floor one day and picked it up thinking it would come in useful."

"That's likely to be the case," Tŵm agreed. "Shame though that there wasn't anything else."

"There wasn't likely to be, was there Tŵm? After all what happened wasn't suspicious. Gwyn must simply have slipped and fallen in."

Again, Tŵm nodded. The last thing he wanted to do was upset Ruth Parry. But the situation was odd. Why was Gwyn there in the first place? He decided to risk a question.

"Didn't you think it strange Mrs. Parry that Gwyn wasn't here in the house on the morning of Easter Sunday?"

"The police asked me that Tŵm but not really. Gwyn often went out sketching early on a Sunday with it being his free day so I just thought that was what he'd done. He would've wanted to capture the morning light."

"But surely he was going to go to chapel?"

"Yes of course, especially since it was Easter Sunday. I did think he might come back home to change before chapel but when he didn't, I thought he'd join me there. He did have a tendency to lose track of time when he was sketching. I just hoped he'd remembered to put tidy clothes on. Then I was a little worried when he didn't turn up but I couldn't leave the service, especially on such a special day. God asks for the best of manners." Ruth smiled at him as she went on, "I've had plenty of time to sort all Gwyn's things," she said. "I thought you might like something of his to remember him by. One of his pictures perhaps but you can choose."

"I will never forget Gwyn Mrs. Parry. He was my closest friend but I would like something of his to keep. That's very thoughtful of you."

Tŵm did not like to riffle through Gwyn's possessions. It seemed disrespectful especially with Ruth looking on. He spent only a short time on each box, trying hard not to disturb the arrangement of the contents: a christening gown, razor, marbles, school books, pencils, charcoal, boys' treasures – a fish hook, white pebbles, some used sealing wax – a couple of photographs, a pack of well-thumbed playing cards and, of course, numerous sketches. One box was devoted to Gwyn's army possessions: an army issue pocket Bible, dog tags, three dried up poppies and a few letters tied up with a piece of string. On top of the last box lay a battered brass bugle decorated with an eagle.

Ruth picked it up. "Gwyn found this on the battlefield. He thought it was German but his officer told him it was Russian. Gwyn said that when the Germans attacked on the day Evan was killed, there had been reinforcements moved in from the Eastern Front. So, it seems it made its way from Russia, to Germany, to France and now to Wales. He said the poppies were for his Tad and for Evan."

"But there are three." Tŵm was bemused.

"Now the third can be for Gwyn," Ruth offered. "Perhaps he had a premonition that he was going to join them."

Tŵm resisted the impulse to say that he didn't believe in premonitions. He changed the subject.

"Did Gwyn send you many letters when he was away fighting?" asked Tŵm.

"No, he didn't. You know Gwyn… knew," she corrected herself. "Not one for words, was he? Either spoken or written." She smiled. "His pencil was his voice."

"But he wrote some?" He indicated the letters.

"Of course. I have his letters in my room. He didn't say much though. I suppose he didn't want to worry me. Those letters over there are the ones I wrote to him and I found them in the pocket of his uniform. That's why they're so dog–eared."

Tŵm turned to look at the sketches again. "I think I would like one of Gwyn's pictures to keep, Mrs. Parry. Like you said, they were his voice. Did he bring sketches back from the war?"

Ruth frowned. "That's the one thing I don't understand Tŵm. I can't find them. He did bring back some drawings. Told me he smuggled some out in his leggings. He said there were others but they were spoilt during the battles. Got wet, muddy and torn. But then after he came back, he drew a lot of war pictures from memory. Said it was easy as he could not forget what had happened."

"What did he draw?"

"I don't know. I didn't see either the ones he brought back or the new ones. He said pictures of the battlefield were not for me to see. I didn't argue as his attitude reminded me of his father. Thomas didn't tell me much about the fighting in his letters either."

"So where do you think they could be?"

"I've searched everywhere but they're not in the house. I think he must've destroyed them. I don't know why he'd do that though. As a child, he always kept all his drawings. Each one was precious to him. He called them his frozen moments."

"I'd like one of those moments from when we were children together. That's how I want to remember him."

"Well, there are lots of those. You have a look through and choose what you want. Take your time. I must go to bring my washing in off the line."

Left alone, Tŵm, watching through the window, could see Ruth lowering the clothes prop before he spread out Gwyn's pictures all over the bed and floor. They laid their childhood bare. What was remarkable about them was the way in which Gwyn had captured not only their likenesses but their personalities. Even if you didn't know Evan you could read the mischievousness in his features. The sketches showed the three of them racing out of school in the afternoon, sitting in chapel in their Sunday best, throwing stones in the river, climbing trees in the forest, hurling snowballs at each other. Tŵm picked up a couple to look at more closely. What were they doing? The three of them seemed to be squatting underneath a bush. Evan was looking upwards, Gwyn had his hand on Evan's shoulder as though he was restraining him and Tŵm was edging away. Then there was another one of Gwyn and Evan together in a bare room looking down at what looked like a puddle of water on the floor.

Then Tŵm remembered. Of course. Tŷ Celyn. When they had followed the Morgans that day after school. He had gone home leaving Gwyn and Evan to explore the house by themselves. And the puddle wasn't water; it was blood. He remembered the conversation at school the next morning.

He had shuddered. "You were crazy to go in there. They could've come back."

Evan, relishing the drama, had reached his own conclusion. "They must've murdered someone, hidden the body in Tŷ Celyn, then cut it up into little bits and put it in the sack."

Gwyn looked horrified. "Not even the Morgans would do that," he retorted.

Tŵm joined in. "Gwyn's right." He drew on logic to support his case. "Anyway, no-one's disappeared."

Evan was not to be deterred. "You never know. Maybe one of the Boyle kids was left in the house and the Morgans found him."

Tŵm smiled as he recalled the memory. Evan was always the one for adventure. The three of them had spent a considerable amount of time following the Morgans around largely because of Evan's hunch that they were "up to no good." In the end he had been proven right though not quite in the way he had expected. One mid-November evening there was a real chill in the air. The nights were drawing in so by the time school finished it was already dusk. The three friends had been stalking the Morgan brothers for two weeks since their initial excursion into the shrubbery of Tŷ Celyn. Most evenings they found themselves simply trailing along towards the Morgans' smallholding down Lane End. Once it had seemed that Cadoc and Gethin had been going towards Tŷ Celyn. But Gwyn had been seen. Unused to such subterfuge, he simply hadn't been careful enough. The Morgan brothers had spotted him darting behind the oak tree by the smithy, Yr Efail. They turned round immediately and raced back for a confrontation.

"Was ya spyin' on us Gwyn Parry? Why're ya an' ya two pals 'ere? Shouldn't ya be on yar way back to yar Mam and Tad?"

Evan answered for Gwyn. "He's not spying on you Cadoc Morgan. Why would any of us be interested in what you're doing?"

"So why're ya 'ere then?"

"Our errands are nothing to do with you." Evan was quick to reply.

Tŵm tried to smooth things over. "Just get on your way, Cadoc. We want nothing to do with you."

"Wantin' 'nother pastin' are ya Tŵm Tudor?"

"I didn't say that but I'm ready if you are."

The fight was stopped by the appearance of Weyland Philpin. "Hello boys. What can I do for you?" Tŵm, sensing an escape route, led the others into the smithy, asking a question about welding a metal gate, to cover his tracks.

After that episode they were a lot more careful. They suspected that the Morgans had gone on to Tŷ Celyn that night but they had not dared to follow.

On a Saturday later that same month they got their chance. Thomas Parry was building a chicken coop with Gwyn. Tŵm and Evan had offered to help thinking that it sounded fun. In case they didn't finish until late, Tŵm was to stay the night there, sharing Gwyn's bed head to toe. They were also likely to be offered some of Ruth Parry's apple pie. The Parrys had two fine Bramleys overhanging the hedge at the side of their garden. Thomas was always catching children on their way home from school picking good apples from the overhanging branches. "I don't mind them having the windfalls from the grass verge," he would say, "but they shouldn't be stealing from the trees."

The coop was finished by three. The boys wolfed down pie and milk.

"Can Gwyn come out to play in the woods now?" Evan asked.

"Yes, Evan," replied Thomas. "You've all worked hard. You go off and make a den or whatever it is you want to do. It'll be dark soon so don't be too late."

As the three of them wandered down into the village, idly kicking stones as they went, Evan spotted Gethin Morgan outside the 'Lamb and Lion'. He grabbed Tŵm's arm, pulling him into the chapel graveyard.

Gwyn followed. "What's going on?"

"Gethin Morgan's ahead of us. They must be going up to the house again."

Tŵm heaved a sigh. He just knew Evan wasn't going to give up and wherever Evan went, Gwyn would follow.

"We know where they're going so all we need to do is give them time to get there. Then they won't see us."

Tŵm knew it was not worth arguing. If they didn't go, Evan would go by himself and then who knows what would happen.

As a result, thirty minutes later, they found themselves in the very same shrubbery that had concealed them so well the previous time. It was soon apparent that things were afoot in the same room as before. Thumping and thudding noises echoed in the growing darkness.

"They're dragging sacks around again." Evan was confident he knew what was happening.

Tŵm was sarcastic. "Must've found themselves another body then."

Shortly afterwards the Morgan brothers appeared, both carrying a loaded sack and disappeared into the darkness.

Evan took charge. "Let's follow them. We need to find out what's in the sacks."

Darkness had descended on Carreg-y-Bedd, its welcome cover concealing them from any possibility of being seen. They didn't need to worry about losing the Morgans. They could hear them breathing heavily as they struggled with the sacks on their backs. Cottages materialised as they neared the village. Shadows slunk past the post office.

Evan couldn't resist a whisper. "They've disappeared."

"They can't have. There's no bends in the lane yet." Tŵm was adamant.

Evan replied, "Well they must've gone into one of the cottages." They crept forward. No-one wanted to risk facing the Morgans again. As they stopped outside the post office, they could hear voices and the clink of coins a little further ahead.

"They're in Mr. Price's yard." Tŵm hissed rather too loudly.

"Shhh." Gwyn feared for their safety if the Morgans became aware of their presence.

Crouching behind the wall that encircled the cobbled slaughter yard, they could now hear the conversation. A transaction was taking place. As they heard Maldwyn Price bidding the Morgan boys farewell, they moved further up the lane round the corner, through the gate and round the back of the chapel. The protective hand of God had never been more useful. Giving the Morgans time to remove themselves from the vicinity, not one of them spoke for a good while. Then Tŵm, not realising he had been holding his breath, took a lungful of air before starting with, "I told you it was nothing to do with murder."

"Well, it was sort of..." Evan was reluctant to admit his error.

Tŵm relented. "I s'pose so. And it's still against the law. Constable Lewis will be very interested."

"Are we going to tell him?" Evan was eager for revenge. He had not forgotten his painful thrashing from Mr. Pugh.

"We need to think what to do? We don't want the Morgans to know it was us."

"But they're stealing." Evan was indignant.

"Well, yes. But how do we prove it? It's our word against theirs. Anyway, what are we going to say? That they sold rabbits to Mr. Price? That'll get him into trouble as well. He paid them four shillings for two sackfuls. That's a lot of money."

"I don't understand," Gwyn interrupted. Mr. Price can't hang them in the shop if they're off the Estate."

"He'll sell them under the counter or at the back door," said Evan authoritatively. He had often heard his Tad speak about Mr. Price's dubious trading methods. "I'll bet the Morgans sell pheasants to him in the winter."

"But why were the rabbits in Tŷ Celyn?" Gwyn was still puzzled.

"I've been thinking about that," replied Tŵm. "They must store them there. Cadoc and Gethin can't have been out poaching by themselves. Mr. Morgan must've gone out to trap or shoot them. He wouldn't stand out as someone who was trespassing because he sometimes does casual work on the estate; I know he was coppicing a short time ago. He wouldn't want to risk being caught with rabbits by the gamekeeper. Tŷ Celyn's just on the edge of the woods so it's a perfect hiding place. Then he can send Cadoc and Gethin to get them and sell them. The gamekeeper's not going to be watching out for schoolboys."

Tŵm looked at Gwyn's sketch again. The memory was as clear as if it were yesterday. To anyone else, it just looked as though three boys were playing in the bushes in the grounds of a big house but to Tŵm it had real significance. 'A frozen moment,' Gwyn had called it. Tŵm smiled. It was true in more ways than one. He had a vivid memory of how chilly it had been that night. He took the picture downstairs. "This is the one I would like Mrs. Parry, if that's alright with you."

Ruth nodded her agreement.

"I must go and collect Jac from Mr. Philpin. He will've enjoyed his rest."

Tŵm pinned up Gwyn's depiction of the three of them on his bedroom wall that night. They had in the end decided not to tell the constable. An official visit by the constable to the Morgan's house carried the possibility of the three friends being found out as the ones who had ratted on them.

But Tŵm himself had been to see the gamekeeper, Sam Lloyd. He hadn't told his friends, believing that the fewer people who knew about his secret conversation, the more likely it was that the Morgan family would not find out who had shopped them in. One dark November night Griff Morgan was caught red-handed on the Estate with several brace of pheasant, a fine hare, longnets and a silenced 410 shotgun. Two months later he was sentenced to a spell in prison and a hefty fine.

"See," Tŵm had told Gwyn and Evan. "As Mam says, God moves in mysterious ways."

Hay Month

Since the sheep shearing Caron had not seen Abram. Despite her best intentions, her eyes had instinctively searched for him every time she had attended chapel. But there had been no sign. Children had been playing on the common; his brothers and sisters she supposed. She speculated that he was doing some chores for Moses, was inside the caravan or cantering Brân along some bridle path. He had probably forgotten about her anyway, she reasoned. But she couldn't forget about him. Goodness knows she'd tried. She'd tried very hard. But he filled her head. She knew full well how she *should* behave. She knew what her family expected and what her God expected. And it didn't include secret meetings with a young man in the forest, however handsome he happened to be. She remembered the words from that chapel service only too well: 'the lust of defiling passion'. Was that what she felt? Defiling passion. Was her soul being stained by whatever she felt for Abram? After the searching heat of the deacons' gaze, she had determined never to see Abram again. She might not be able to stop herself thinking about him but she could certainly stop herself from meeting him.

Her resolution lasted until the Saturday after the service. Tŵm seemed to have been using Jac constantly, either for work on the farm or for riding out on errands. She had been kept busy by Mali, the endless round of cooking, washing and cleaning added to considerably by constant tending of the summer vegetable garden. Her hands were rough with weeding and scrubbing the soil from under her nails. There couldn't possibly be any harm in riding out into the forest, she told herself. There's nothing wrong with riding a horse and enjoying the summer weather. It would be unfair on Jac not to take him for a gallop. He'd been working so hard all week. Abram wouldn't be likely to be there, she convinced herself. It had been three weeks since she'd seen him and he wouldn't be expecting her to be in the forest as they hadn't arranged to meet. She decided, just to be safe, not to go near the clearing. Then she definitely wouldn't see him. Neither would she have done anything wrong.

Keeping to her resolution she rode a different way. Taking the lane that wound eventually towards Clocaenog, after about a mile she turned right up a green lane, forded a shallow stream and then enjoyed a long canter, giving Jac a loose rein to climb a steep bank before reaching the outskirts of the forest itself. She chose a rutted track that she knew would eventually wind its way to Tan-y-Graig. From there she could take a narrow path overhung with trees which would take her back to the boundary of Cwyn-y-Gwynt. She could then gallop back across the fields. Jac would love that. But for the time being Jac had to be content with walking. Sure-footed though he was, he had to negotiate tree roots which snaked their way across the path. Checking the ground and concentrating on holding up Jac's head to support him if he tripped, Caron was taken unawares when Jac stopped and nickered, blowing gently down his nostrils. She looked up. There in front of her stood Brân. Jac had recognised him. Abram stood alongside with his arm thrown over his neck, his fingers playing with Brân's mane. Caron, disconcerted, said nothing. She had done her best. It wasn't her fault. It was fate.

"Shall we go to t' clearin'? We can talk t'ere."

Caron followed him. His spell was such that resistance did not cross her mind. Abram tied up the two horses and led her to the pool. They took off their boots and slipped their feet into the cool, silky water.

Abram waited a few moments. "'Tis a long time since we spoke."

Caron nodded.

"I liked our dance; short t'ough 'twas."

He began to stroke her hair. "Yer 'air. 'tis beautiful. Like t' russet leaves of autumn. Yet yer eyes are t' colour of new leaves in spring." He ran his hand through Caron's untamed mane of deep curls much as he had with Brân's. It had the opposite effect. Brân found it soothing; Caron found it thrilling. She shivered.

"Are yer cold? Sun's not up yet." Abram put his arm round her shoulders.

Involuntarily, Caron leaned against the rough cotton that covered his shoulder. She knew she should feel scared. She was in a remote place with, what many would term, a stranger. This was wrong. She knew that. It was more than wrong. It was wicked. So why did she feel oddly secure, drawn towards Abram in a way that was alien to her.

"I 'ave somethin' for yer." Abram unfurled Caron's fingers and held her left hand, palm upwards. Then he put his hand in his pocket. Keeping the object hidden in his fist, he dropped it into Caron's outstretched palm.

"Oh, what is it?"

"It's a rush ring. I plaited it meself. I 'ope it fits. Yer fingers are so tiny."

"How clever of you Abram! It's lovely."

Abram, laughed at her evident pleasure as he slipped the ring onto her wedding finger. "It's no' much but 'tis symbolic."

Caron reddened. Abram ran his hands down her body and she reacted.

"'ey, don't tremble. Yer 'ave no need t' fear me."

As his lips met hers, Caron no longer thought about sin. She raised her arms round his neck, felt the growth of his hedgehog stubble against her skin, closed her eyes and gave herself to the moment. It was a long moment, achingly pleasurable. Her body rippled with joy.

That same morning, while Caron was in the fresh air of the forest, Tŵm had risen early too. A strip of cloth, tied across his face, protected his mouth and nose from the thick dust that was swirling round the hay loft. Emyr and Brad were similarly masked. The three of them were forking the remainder of last year's hay from one end of the loft to the other where it could be easily thrown out of the open, round hole down into the stack yard. It wouldn't be used until November when the hay for the cattle and sheep would be pitch forked out onto a trailer ready for carting to the fields. Emyr preferred to use old hay first, leaving the richer, new hay for the bitter months of winter.

"This'll leave plenty of space for the new hay we bring in." Emyr's voice was muffled under the mask of an old scarf.

When they all emerged, their bare arms were streaked with grime, their faces black and their hair full of grass seeds and bits of hay. Mali was firm. "You can all clean up before you come in for breakfast." She pointed towards the water butt at the end of the barn.

Tŵm stripped to the waist, filled up an old wooden pail put there for the purpose, leaned forward and tipped it over his head. Rubbing the dirt from his hands and arms, he looked towards Brad. "You next."

Brad nodded. "Fill it for me."

After rinsing himself again, Tŵm slowly tipped fresh water over Brad. As he did so, he saw Caron leading Jac into the stable. He walked over to her, drying himself on the flannel shirt he had just shaken to get rid of the hay seeds.

"That's better," he said to her as she untacked. "I'm less itchy. Put Jac out in the field. Let him have a rest today and tomorrow. He'll be working hard enough when we get the hay in. Did you have a good ride while we were working our fingers to the bone?"

"I'll help next week in the fields." Caron sounded defensive.

"It's fine. I didn't expect you to help in the loft. It's not a job for a girl. I was just teasing you."

Tŵm was vaguely surprised. It wasn't like Caron to take offence. She hadn't been quite herself lately he thought. Quieter than usual especially at meals. He was used to Caron chattering away and Mali constantly telling her to be quiet. It was Bethan who barely spoke. Always shy as a child, Bethan had become even more reserved in the years since the war. Of course, he hadn't really paid much attention to Caron of late. He'd had too many worries of his own. Feeling slightly guilty, he went over to her. She didn't look that well he thought.

"Are you OK?" he said to her. "Your face is very pink. Did you fall off Jac? You're not hurt, are you?"

A flush of red suffused Caron's face. "I'm fine. Just hot. The weather's close and there's a wind getting up. Perhaps we're in for some thunder. Storms always give me a headache."

"I do hope you're not right." Tŵm sounded anxious. "We want some hot sun on the hay for the next few days."

The fates seemed to favour Caron's story, for that afternoon a clap of thunder heralded a downpour. The rain fell in rods, bouncing off ground too hard and dry for it to soak in, splashing wet mud all over walls and doors.

"It seems you were right," Tŵm said to her that evening after supper.

"What was she right about?" Nain asked, leaning back in the oak rocking chair.

"The storm. Caron sensed it this morning."

"Caron, you must have something of the witch in you," Nain said. "It's not everyone who can foretell the weather."

"Nonsense, Mam. Most country people can smell a storm in the air. Caron's nothing special." Mali turned to her daughter. "Have you got your clothes ready for chapel in the morning? Boots polished? Books ready? You're always on the last minute. I don't want you making us late. Nain and I need to get to Carreg early in the morning."

Emyr looked at his wife enquiringly.

"I thought we might call on Ruth Parry before the service. Take her some baby carrots and broad beans. We have plenty."

"Isn't the inquest going to be held soon?" Nain asked

Tŵm and Brad spoke in unison. "July 28th."

Nain looked a little startled.

"He was my friend," Tŵm said by way of explanation. "I'm bound to be interested."

"Had you remembered the date?" Emyr asked his wife.

"I may have heard it," she prevaricated. "I thought I might offer to go with Ruth. She will be in need of a friend."

Emyr nodded. "I didn't realise you were such a close friend of hers."

"I wouldn't say close, exactly. But I have been taking her some food and staying for a chat. I think she's glad of my company. Poor soul."

"Mam, if you're going to the inquest with Mrs. Parry then I could take you in the trap if you like," Tŵm offered. "I'd like to be there anyway. What about you Tad? The day he died, we stayed with Gwyn until the doctor got back. Don't you want to know what happened?"

Emyr was firm. "It's not a party Tŵm. Ruth Parry won't want the whole neighbourhood there gawping. I can wait to hear the verdict."

"Where's the inquest being held Tad?" Tŵm asked.

"It'll be in the village I expect, near to where the death occurred. That's what usually happens. They need to find somewhere with enough room to hold all the people involved. So, it could be in the chapel or even in the 'Lamb and Lion'."

Mali was horrified. "In the 'Lamb and Lion'! That wouldn't be a suitable place at all."

"Well, it does have a big enough room," Emyr ventured. "They hold all sorts of events there."

"Ruth Parry won't go over the doorstep. That's for sure." Having made her point, Mali turned her attention again to Caron. "I thought I told you to get everything ready for chapel."

Caron hesitated. "I thought I might not go."

An intake of breath heralded the onslaught. "Not go!" Mali hissed out the words through clenched teeth. "Not go!"

"I am eighteen Mam. I can decide for myself."

"Decide for yourself! Decide for yourself! I can't believe what I'm hearing. While you live under my roof, you will do as I say. And why would you not want to go to chapel? It is God's day and you will respect it."

Tears sprang to Caron's eyes. Her revolution was short-lived. Tŵm sitting next to her, grasped her hand under the table and squeezed it.

Nain intervened, trying to smooth over matters. "I'm coming too Caron. I'd like to have your company."

Mali was still in full flow. "You get your things ready for chapel this minute my girl. And don't let me hear any such nonsense ever again. And after you've done that you can wash the pots and clear up the kitchen all by yourself as a punishment for being so wicked."

Later that afternoon while Mali and Nain were knitting winter jerseys in the cool of the parlour, Tŵm came in to the kitchen. He had been out to check on some young heifers who had a tendency to push against the fence next to the lane. Caron, left alone, was still tidying up. She was scrubbing the table as Tŵm came in.

"Why did you do it?" he asked her.

They had always had an understanding. She did not need to ask him what he meant.

"Because I'm not good enough to go to chapel."

Tŵm stared at his sister. Whatever he had expected, it had not been that. However, Caron had always told him the truth. She had no reason to lie to him.

"Not good enough?" He laughed. "Goodness I sound like Mam, repeating your words like that! What on earth do you mean?"

Caron looked directly into Tŵm's eyes, green gazing into hazel. "I'm not a good person Tŵm. I have bad thoughts."

Though he thought it ridiculous, Tŵm didn't laugh. She was too serious for that. "Caron, you are the sweetest, kindest person I know. Everybody has bad thoughts at times, that's just normal. It means you're a human being. I have bad thoughts. I wanted to punch Cadoc Morgan the other day."

"But you didn't, did you?"

"Well, no, that's what I mean. It was just a thought. It didn't translate into a deed. Now come here and give me a hug." Tŵm put his arms round her. Then he stepped back and tried to lighten her mood. "Anyway, if you think you're a sinner then you'd best go to chapel. That's what it's for, to ask God's forgiveness."

His attempt at humour didn't work.

"Do you think so?" Caron sounded just as serious. "If I go to ask for forgiveness then God will have mercy on my wickedness?"

"I'm sure your God loves you a great deal. I'm also sure that whatever it is you think you've done, it's nowhere near as bad as you say."

Caron looked unconvinced.

"Caron, look, Mam will never allow you to stay at home and not go to chapel. You will have to do as she says. So, don't worry about it anymore. Just go to chapel. Make your life easy not difficult." Tŵm's logic was inescapable.

Caron nodded.

The next morning, she rode to chapel in the trap as usual.

As Tŵm checked whether the hay was ready for cutting, his thoughts dwelt on Gwyn's inquest and the Morgans. He wished he could forget Cadoc and Gethin for a while but they kept intruding. They were 'a bad lot' as Mali often said but would they seriously go to the most extreme lengths and what reasons could they possibly have?

After a week of showers, the fine weather had returned. Early spring rain had led to a rich crop of grass. There had been a few thundery showers the previous week but that had only helped the growth. There would be plenty of hay this year to last the Cwyn-y-Gwynt stock through the winter months.

"I'll take Jac, ride round and sort out the dates with the other farms," Tŵm said to Emyr.

"Go into Carreg and ask Moses if he can come to give extra help," Emyr told him. "We need to get it in before the end of next week. We can't carry hay on a Sunday."

There would be no chance of helping Dr. Owen for a while Tŵm knew. The hay always came first. It took him most of the morning to organise when their hay would be fitted into the Carreg cycle so by the time he rode up to the Gypsy camp it was nearing noon.

Moses was sitting on the step of the caravan repairing a leather headpiece from a bridle. He looked up as Tŵm dismounted and led Jac across the green.

"'nother fine day Moses."

Moses nodded. "What can I do fer you?"

"Tad sent me to see if you could give us a hand with the hay."

"D'yer want Abram too?"

"Abram?"

"Me son. 'e sang at t' shearin'."

Tŵm, thinking back, realised that Abram would be an asset. Tall, built like the cob he rode, he would provide much needed strength to the harvest team.

"Oh, yes, the more people we have the better. Could you both come Monday if the weather holds?"

Moses grunted his agreement. "Bad news t'ey are." He inclined his head.

Tŵm, surprised at the change of tack, looked towards the direction Moses had indicated. Cadoc and Gethin Morgan were on their way out of the 'Lamb and Lion'. They strode purposefully towards Moses and Tŵm.

"I think you're right there Moses," Tŵm answered as they approached.

"'ey there." Cadoc attempted a smile.

Moses did not return the greeting. Cadoc, forced into speaking again, resumed with, "We wanna get our 'ay in quick as we can."

Moses remained silent.

Gethin intervened, removing his Woodbine first. "We're offrin' ya some work."

"Come t' pay me 'ave yer? Fer thet fencin' round yer yard." Moses asked, unaffected by the Morgan brothers' attempt at civility.

"Tell ya wot, we'll add it on to wot we pay ya for the 'ay. That a'right?" A grimace, restricted only to his mouth, accompanied Cadoc's last two words.

"I'll not be accommodatin' yer."

It took a moment for the Morgan brothers to realise they had been refused. Gethin scowled. Tŵm tried to defuse the situation. "Moses can't," he explained. I've just hired him to help with our hay."

"Moses, Moses..." Cadoc's voice dripped with sarcasm. "Didna think the fancy Tudors'd be on first name terms with gyppos."

Tŵm moved forwards. He felt Moses' restraining hand on his arm. "Not worth 't. Leave well alone."

"Want wot we used to give ya in school, do ya, Tŵm Tudor?" Cadoc sneered. "'member we're trained soldiers now. Could give ya an 'ell of a beatin'."

Tŵm held Cadoc's gaze. "I would've thought you'd had enough of fighting, Cadoc."

"Me? No. Ya can never 'ave 'nuff of fightin'. Ya should see wot I've seen. 'ands blown clean off, legs too, lads coughin' up their lungs, guts 'angin' out..."

"Shut up Cadoc, cau dy geg." Tŵm was firm.

As Cadoc opened his mouth to start again, Moses shouted to Abram, who Tŵm had not realised was in the caravan.

"Abram, just give me an 'and. T'ese two're jus' leavin'." Father and son stood shoulder to shoulder alongside Tŵm. Moses, even taller than his son, was built like a brick privy.

Gethin pulled at his brother's sleeve. "C'mon Cad. Let's go."

Reluctantly Cadoc turned away. He spat at Tŵm's feet. "'nother time Tŵm Tudor; 'nother time."

Moses waited until they were out of earshot. "Crooked as a ram's 'orn," he commented. "Monday then." Tŵm nodded, mounted Jac and rode back towards Cwyn-y-Gwynt.

Skirting a stray rake that had fallen down outside the shop, he trotted on until he passed the last of the village cottages. Suddenly Jac snorted and shied sideways. Tŵm was startled. It was most unlike Jac to behave like an in-season mare.

"Stop messing Jac. What's the matter?" Jac blew down his nostrils and sidled into a privet hedge in front of one of the cottages.

Tŵm soon found out. Jac had clearly heard something. As he rounded the bend, he found the Morgans standing in the centre of the road. Tŵm slowed. He could hardly ride through them.

Cadoc raised his hands causing Jac to throw up his head.

"Stop it Cadoc. You're frightening my horse. What do you want?"

"I wanna word with ya, Tŵm Tudor."

Tŵm did not feel too threatened since he had the advantage of being on Jac. He could at least look down upon the Morgans. He also knew he could turn Jac round and ride the other way.

"Well, blocking the road isn't the right way to go about it. What do you want?"

"Cadoc wants t' speak t' ya so I said I'd 'elp 'im make ya pay attention." Gethin removed his cigarette, the better to sneer at Tŵm. In doing so he exposed the tips of teeth, pointed like ice shards and yellowed with nicotine. He certainly didn't have his brother's natural advantages. He moved his hand upwards to take hold of both the reins, just behind the bit.

Tŵm reacted at once. "Let him go!"

"No way. Gerroff the 'orse." Gethin tightened his grip. Jac, resisting the pressure, tried to throw up his head.

"You needn't think I'm going to do what you say Gethin Morgan."

"Don't think ya've got a choice." Cadoc was taking charge.

Despite his bravado, Tŵm was conscious of a dart of fear. He knew he was no match for even one Morgan let alone two. He raised his riding whip and struck down hard on Gethin's forearm. Gethin, taken unawares, relinquished his grip. Tŵm snatched the opportunity. He reined back Jac as swiftly as he could, then span him round and began to canter. After a few strides he stopped. What was he thinking? He couldn't flee from the Morgans. That would store up even more trouble for the future. Anyway, he was curious. What did they want with him?

He reined in, turned Jac to face the Morgans, who had chased after him, walked forward and stood square in the middle of the lane. Keen to prevent Gethin grabbing his bridle again, he took care this time to stand several yards away. "Don't come any nearer," he warned them, "or I'll gallop off and you won't have chance to have that word with me."

Cadoc stopped, restraining Gethin by placing his arm across him. Gethin was clutching his elbow. He spat out his Woodbine, shouting, "Ya'll pay for tha' Tŵm Tudor. Don't think I won't get me own back, 'cos I will."

Twm ignored him. Cadoc ignored him too. Looking directly at Twm, he said, "Y' know wot we want."

"I have no idea." Twm was not going to give them the satisfaction of a positive response.

Forced to voice his concerns, Cadoc was uncharacteristically careful. "Ya 'aven't said anythin' 'ave ya Twm Tudor? T' that doctor ya so thick with or t' the police?"

"'bout what?"

"Ya know wot. Ya canna tell me that ya friend didna tell ya wot 'appened. I weren't born yesterday."

Twm did know what. He flushed hot, sick with turmoil. What he really wanted to do was to ask questions, lots of questions. However, he had a strong feeling that Cadoc Morgan wouldn't answer any of them.

"Ya'd betta not or it'll be the worse for ya. I dunna think ya 'ave or the coppers'd 'ave bin roun' to us. Wise move."

"I don't have to do what you say, Cadoc." Twm hoped that he sounded more confident than he actually felt. It wouldn't do to give the Morgans the upper hand.

"Ya just better say nuffin' that's all. That'd be better for ev'ryone. Includin' ya dead friend an' ya friend's mam."

"Just stay away from me Cadoc. And you Gethin. Don't you start threatening me. Because it won't work."

"Oh, it won't work," mimicked Cadoc. "I'm willin' t' bet it will work. Ya wouldn't wan' that pretty little sister of yours to get damaged, would ya?"

Twm felt a current of fear. "You stay away from my sister. Don't you hurt Caron. This has nothing to do with her."

"I wouldna 'urt 'er," Cadoc leered. "She might like wot I've got in mind... "

"Don't you dare go anywhere near her, Cadoc or you'll have me to answer to." Twm hoped his bravado hid his terror at what Cadoc was implying. "Now step aside and leave me alone."

To Twm's surprise Cadoc pulled Gethin into the verge. However, he had to have the last word.

"Jus' ya 'member wot I said," he flung at Twm as Jac trotted past.

Twm had plenty to occupy his thoughts as he made his way back to Cwyn-y-Gwynt.

On the Monday morning the Tudor family rose as dawn broke. Hay making was a big event. Within an hour all the helpers were there, paid labourers and local farmers alike.

"You'll be there on Friday to help me won't you Tŵm?" asked Howell Griffiths.

"Of course, I will," Tŵm reassured him. "Let's hope the dry weather lasts. After those few hot days we had, it's been cool for July but as long as the rain stays away..."

"T'ink we've got a few days o' dry weather yet," Moses joined in, looking up at the sky.

By noon they were well on the way to a high yielding harvest. It always surprised Caron how quickly the hay was cut with the horse drawn mower that the Tudors had bought jointly with Howell Griffiths, Gwilym Bowen and a couple of other neighbours. By the next year she wondered whether they would have that tractor Emyr was keen on buying and the work would be finished even more quickly. When Caron arrived with bread, cheese, ham and jugs of water, the hay was already in straight, neat swathes in the two fields near to the farm. Needing to carry baskets, she took the trap to the labourers working at a distance from the farmhouse. Some of these, working on higher land, still preferred to use their scythes, finding it easier on the steeper gradients. Their practised, effortless strokes rasped through the stems like a hot knife through butter. Moses and Abram worked rhythmically as one, only stopping to straighten aching backs at the end of each section, their boundaries invisible to everyone but them.

That morning, suspecting that Abram might be there, Caron had asked Tŵm, "How many have you hired?"

Tŵm, startled at her unexpected interest, replied, "Only four. With Howell Griffiths and Gwilym Bowen coming plus a couple of other farmers, we don't need as many as last year."

"Who did you ask?"

Tŵm, still a little surprised at this investigation, answered, "A couple of lads from the village and two of the Gypsies."

Caron didn't dare ask which Gypsies, since Tŵm wouldn't expect her to know them personally. She knew that Moses, in all probability, would be there so thought it was possible that Abram would be as well. She wasn't sure if she wanted him to be there or not. She was fearful of not seeing him but scared of how she would react if she did.

Mali had insisted that Caron take the food out to the men. She preferred Bethan's quiet efficiency in the kitchen to Caron's rather haphazard approach. "You're too much of a dreamer," she said to her daughter. "I don't know where you get it from. You certainly don't take after my side of the family."

Caron, on hearing this, thought that her Mam was likely wrong. In her view, her Nain had fanciful tendencies which Mali either chose to ignore or attacked ferociously depending what mood she was in. Certainly, Mali was right that she didn't inherit her Tad's practicality. A man of routine, work on the farm ruled his life. Hard graft was punctuated only by Sunday chapel visits, attendance at christenings, weddings and funerals and visits to the local country shows. Caron had to admit Mali was right about the dreaming. Being sent on errands suited Caron. It gave her time to think. Though sociable, her introspection needed nourishment. Long walks, rides on Jac and taking messages all allowed her mind a loose rein.

The men were working where the land began to sweep gently upwards and was too steep to use the mower. Abram was indeed cutting hay. She had recognised him when she was way back by Pen-coed, the cottage occupied by Howell Griffiths' widowed mother. It was something in the turn of his shoulder, the line of his back, the way he held the scythe. She knew it was him. Unsure how to react, when she arrived, she took care to first go over to Dylan Jenkins and Merfyn Kendrick, the village helpers. They often did odd jobs for Emyr and greeted her with friendly waves. She set out the food and waited for them to make their way over to her. It didn't take long. They were hungry and thirsty. It took slightly more time for Moses and Abram to walk over from the far side of the hill. Moses greeted her with thanks for her journey. Though she did not look at Abram, focussing her attention on dividing up the cheese with the knife Mali had provided for her, she was keenly aware of his presence. Flustered she dropped the knife. A hand picked it up and offered it to her. She looked up directly into Abram's eyes.

"Thank you," she murmured.

She jumped nervously as Moses spoke to her, entirely forgetting the existence of anyone else in her proximity. "Yer brot'er or yer Tad comin' up 'ere?"

"I don't know but I should think so," Caron replied.

"We'll be gettin' on back t' work."

Reluctantly Dylan and Merfyn retrieved their tools. They had been hoping for a longer rest but could hardly sit and watch if Moses and Abram were already scything.

As she loaded the jugs back into the trap, Caron watched, fascinated by their skill. The hay didn't lie in tidy lines as it did when the machine cut it but the whole process was so much more peaceful. She sat on the seat of the trap for a moment, the sweet scents of warm horse and newly cut hay hot in her nostrils, the beat of her heart keeping perfect time with the swish of the scythe. I'm going to remember this moment for ever, she thought. I'm eighteen and I'm in love.

Gwyn's inquest loomed. Richard Owen, well aware of Ruth's abhorrence of public houses, had managed to persuade the authorities that the chapel was a more suitable venue. Like Mali, he didn't think she could be persuaded to cross the threshold of the 'Lamb and Lion'.

It had taken four days to move the hay from field to barn, the sleds bringing it in from the far pasture; Samson and Delilah pulling the cart in from the fields nearer to the farm. They had been lucky with the weather. The rain had stayed away until the hay lofts were full to the rafters.

As the last load was safely stored away, Emyr inhaled deeply. "There's nothing like the smell of sweet meadow hay," he said to Brad and Twm. "The cattle are going to do well this winter. Before the end of the month, we'll need to collect the bracken for winter bedding and then, whether winter brings snow, wind or rain, we'll be well prepared."

Twm was glad to be busy, his anxiety deepening as the inquest neared. Working hard was a good antidote to worrying about what he would be asked and what he would answer. Along with Emyr, he and Brad spent days cutting, carting and storing bracken. Jac was needed almost every day, leaving Caron with no hope of riding. Then just as with the hay, Emyr called in help for the sheep dipping. He wanted to avoid flystrike at all costs. On the day itself, Jono helped them pen all the sheep, then Howell Griffiths was the first to arrive, closely followed by Idris Jones, Gwilym Bowen and Cadog Roberts. Twm knew he was in for a hard day; they all were. It was heavy work. Brad and Twm manhandled each sheep through into the trough while Emyr, Idris, Gwilym and Cadog made sure every single one was completely submerged in the disinfectant. Caron watched as the sheep shook themselves dry and waited for her to open the gate that led to freedom.

A threatening sky heralded the day of the inquest itself. Ebenezer had been taken over for the occasion with the coroner, pathologist, police sergeant and clerk seated in the Sêt Fawr. With its inbuilt air of solemnity, along with its banisters and carved oak spindles separating the good from the great, the chapel provided the ideal backdrop for such formal proceedings.

Richard Owen collected Ruth at ten before walking with her to the chapel. She had refused Mali's offer to accompany her, saying, "I don't want to put you out. I have agreed to go with Dr. Owen. Since he has to go as a witness, he thought it best that he looked after me as well." Even Mali couldn't argue with what she perceived as medical advice. Later though she grumbled to Emyr about that, "interfering doctor poking his nose in everywhere. I blame him for Twm wanting to be a doctor. He must've encouraged him."

Twm had received a summons to attend the court as a witness. Mali, already aggrieved at not being able to accompany Ruth, had immediately offered to go with her son. She was thwarted a second time by Emyr who came in for breakfast slightly later than Twm and opened an envelope to find that he too had a summons. "Twm and I will go together," he said firmly. There is no need for you to be there Mali. It isn't a charabanc outing." His uncharacteristic firmness silenced even Mali.

Twm had been shocked by the summons. Knowing nothing of the procedures, he had assumed that his witness statement made to the police in the week after Gwyn's death plus the questioning from the sergeant would have been the end of the affair. The gnawing anxiety that he had become accustomed to over the previous three months grew in ferocity in the weeks before the inquest. How could he have thought that he could ever get away with keeping silent? It had been madness. But what could he possibly do about the situation now? If he told the full truth in the inquest, he would be asked why he hadn't spoken up before. He wasn't sure what would happen to him but he knew it was a serious offence to lie to the police. Not that he had lied. He just hadn't told the full truth. Of course, he told himself, he would have had to if the sergeant had asked him the right questions but that hadn't happened. Nevertheless, he was sure that withholding information from the police would count as an offence when something as serious as a death was involved. A criminal record didn't bear thinking about. It might even mean going to prison. His family would disown him. Not only would it bring shame on the family but it would almost certainly mean that his dream of becoming a doctor would be dashed. His motives had been good ones but did the end justify the means?

Even when Twm arrived at the inquest he still had not decided what to say. One look at Ruth Parry's face made the decision for him. He had been right after all. His first loyalty lay with his friend. He had to do what Gwyn would have wanted him to do. And Gwyn would not have wanted him to cause further distress to Ruth. He would have wanted her protected.

Ruth walked into the inquest, upright, proud, refusing even to hold on to the arm offered to her by Richard Owen. She looked straight ahead, acknowledging no-one. The doctor sat to her left in the front pew facing the coroner. Seeing Emyr and Tŵm seated a few rows back, he indicated to them to sit alongside him. Emyr did as he was asked, leaving Tŵm no alternative but to follow.

"As witnesses you need to be at the front," the doctor said to them.

They all sat in silence. Nobody knows what to say, Tŵm thought and it's better to say nothing than to upset someone. He looked round and recognised Daniel Ellis, Howell and Olwen Griffiths, Sir Edward and Lady Craddock, Constable Robert Lewis, Alun Edwards, the sergeant who had questioned him and other villagers from Carreg-y-Bedd. With only a couple of minutes to go he heard the heavy door creak open behind him and glanced round. Cadoc Morgan crept in and seated himself at the back. Tŵm felt himself go hot and clammy. Cadoc hadn't just come because of curiosity. He had come to watch him. He was sure of that. His train of thought was interrupted by the arrival of the coroner.

The coroner began by greeting them and expressing condolences to Ruth Parry who sat quite still, her gloved hands folded in her lap. He went on to establish the facts of the case, Gwyn's personal details, his contribution to King and Country during the war, the date and place of his death, 16th April 1922 and where his body was found, Pwll Berw, Carreg-y-Bedd. Next the coroner read out the results of the post mortem. The cause of death was asphyxiation by drowning. However, the pathologist could not be totally certain whether Gwyn Parry was conscious or unconscious when his body entered the water because he had also suffered a blow to the head. In addition, the body had significant bruising across the shoulder, neck and chest.

Tŵm glanced across at Ruth Parry. She was rigid; her face expressionless.

The pathologist began with an explanation of how drowning occurs. "Submersion is followed by a struggle to survive. Within a short time, the individual becomes exhausted and drowning begins. Once this process starts, the individual holds his breath until enough carbon dioxide accumulates to stimulate respiration. This results in inhalation of water which causes coughing and vomiting. Loss of consciousness and convulsions follow rapidly. Finally, there is respiratory and heart failure."

When questioned further by the coroner, the pathologist continued with, "It's almost impossible to say exactly what happened. There was a cerebral contusion which had caused a number of haemorrhages. In layman's terms,

Gwyn Parry's head was bleeding. The blow could have occurred before he entered into the water or his head may have come into contact with a rock or a tree trunk as he fell into the pool."

"Could he have tripped over, hit his head and then fallen into the pool?"

"It's certainly possible."

"Could he have been intoxicated?"

"Again, it's possible."

Ruth clenched her hands together so that her knuckles whitened.

"Is it feasible that he was struck over the head by a person or persons unknown and then fell or was pushed into the water?"

"Yes, it's feasible..."

The questions continued.

"Does the fact that the wound had been bleeding help to indicate whether the blow occurred before or after the body was submerged?" asked the coroner.

The pathologist gave a technical explanation. "Well, if the body had entered the water immediately after the blow, then the wound would have bled but it wouldn't have bled much and not for very long. You see once the pressure in the blood vessels drops enough to be equal to the air pressure outside the body, the bleeding stops, since with the heart no longer pumping there's no force behind it. So, the amount of blood would be minimal."

The coroner asked for further clarification. "Let me get this straight doctor. If Gwyn Parry had been hit over the head, then fell or was pushed into the water, it is likely that there would not have been much bleeding, whereas if he had been hit over the head and not fallen into the water then it is likely that there would have been a lot more blood?"

"Broadly speaking yes," answered the pathologist, "but of course we can't know how much bleeding there actually was, since we don't know whether he received the blow on his head before or after he fell into the water."

"Is either a clear possibility?" the coroner asked.

"Yes."

The investigation moved on to explore possible explanations for the bruising.

"The situation is less murky here," the pathologist told the court. "Though we don't know how Gwyn Parry became badly bruised, I would say that in my professional judgement, the body was bruised quite some time before it entered the water. I do not believe that Gwyn Parry suffered the bruising just before entering the pool. If that had been the case, the bruises would not have been as clearly evident on the skin as they were."

Tŵm shifted uncomfortably in his seat.

"Is it even remotely possible then that the bruising happened once he was in the pool?" asked the coroner.

"No, I would say not. Victims of drowning do, at times, bruise or rupture muscles in the bodily areas where Gwyn Parry had bruising. These are the consequence of struggling violently to try to survive. However, if this had been the case, the bruising would tend to focus on the muscle bundles. The bruising on Gwyn Parry's body was random, more superficial and did not follow any such pattern. It is therefore extremely unlikely that the body was bruised after it entered the water. Bruises are blood, from broken capillaries, that seeps into surrounding tissues and accumulates in the fat under the skin. The bruises on the body were dark in colour so enough time had elapsed for the bruising to emerge. However, they were inflicted only a short time before death. They certainly were not old bruises which would have had a paler, more yellow hue."

The coroner was not prepared to let this go. "Could you put a more accurate timescale on when they are likely to have occurred?"

"I cannot say for sure but it is likely from the colouration of the bruises that it was in the previous two or three days."

"So, the bruising and the head wound may not be connected and indeed the bruising may well have no connection at all with the drowning?"

"Exactly so. The bruises may have been caused by an accident, such as a fall from a horse. They may be marks of violence, inflicted by another person but it's impossible to say. If the latter is the case then that same person may also have inflicted the head wound at a later time or another individual entirely could have done so. Of course, this is pure speculation. I am just listing the possibilities."

"There seem to be a lot of unanswered questions in this case," the coroner announced as much to himself as to the assembled courtroom.

Tŵm had not realised the significance of the floating body until the pathologist began to reply to the coroner's questions about the likely time the body entered the water.

The pathologist explained, "A dead body will sink when placed in water. However, after the gases of decomposition build up in the chest and abdomen, the body will inflate and rise like a hydrogen-filled balloon to the surface. In time, with further decomposition, the body cavities eventually rupture, the gas escapes and the corpse will sink for good."

"How long does it take for the body to come to the surface?"

"That very much depends on the depth and temperature of the water. In

April, in a pool of this kind, I would estimate two to three days."

"But we know that Gwyn Parry was alive on Saturday 15th April."

"That is true. But after several hours, corpses will also sometimes float to the surface if air becomes trapped in their clothing. Though April, it was still chilly. Gwyn Parry was wearing trousers, a shirt, a waistcoat and a coat so there were plenty of places for air to be trapped. Becoming entangled with the weeds in the pond may too have prevented Mr. Parry from sinking to the bottom. In all likelihood the waters closed over Gwyn Parry some time on Saturday evening."

"You can't be more specific?"

"It is difficult to categorically state the length of time but I would estimate between twelve and fifteen hours from the pooling of the blood in the head and neck. Rigor mortis had set in and there were other indications too." The pathologist looked at the coroner and then at Ruth Parry.

"I don't think there is any need for more physical details to be divulged in open court," the coroner announced. "I am sure all relevant information will be in your report. We just need the estimated time of death. From what you say that narrows it down to between nine o'clock and midnight on Saturday evening of 16th April."

"That is correct."

The coroner moved on to ask, "Were there any other indications of whether Gwyn Parry was conscious when he entered the water?"

"The post mortem examination did find a fine, white froth or foam in the airways. Dr. Owen's report on his initial examination of the body illustrated that he also found the same foam exuding from the mouth and nostrils. It usually indicates that the victim was conscious at the time of submersion."

The coroner sighed. "Are you telling me now that Gwyn Parry was definitely conscious when he fell or was pushed into the pool?"

The pathologist paused, then answered, "I would not use the word definitely. I think the balance of probability points towards Gwyn Parry being alive when he entered the water especially when one considers that the lungs were over-inflated and heavy with fluid. This indicates active inspiration of air and water; that is drowning by drawing water into the lungs. Such an appearance cannot be reproduced by the passive flooding of the lungs with water which would happen if the body was unconscious when it entered the water."

"Were there any further indications that would help us reach a conclusion?" asked the coroner.

"During the post mortem some water, silt, weed and other foreign matter was found in the airways and in the stomach," the pathologist replied.

"Wouldn't that be usual with any drowning?"

"Yes it would, but it is again significant because large quantities of water and debris strongly suggest immersion during life, whereas absence of water would suggest very rapid drowning or death prior to submersion."

"And in this case?"

"In this case once again the evidence is not completely conclusive. The stomach wasn't empty but neither was there a large quantity of water; there was just some water in the stomach."

The coroner spoke again. "So, to sum all this up, was the cause of death drowning or a blow on the head or both? And once again was the victim conscious when he entered the water?"

The pathologist prevaricated. "What I can say is that the blow on the head did not in itself kill Gwyn Parry. It was a severe blow but his skull was not fractured. However, whether the blow occurred before or after he entered the water, it almost certainly contributed to his death. The blow may have been the reason why the victim fell into the water. Alternatively, he could have fallen or been pushed in and then hit his head and been unable to get out. The severe blow to the head could have disoriented him so he may have been semi-conscious when the water closed over his body. I would say once more that the weight of evidence suggests that Gwyn Parry was conscious when he went into the pool but I cannot be completely certain."

"Could he have jumped in himself and hit his head?" the coroner asked.

"Yes, that's possible too. He could have thrown himself in and hit his head on a submerged object. Whatever the reason for the submersion, the result would be the same."

Emyr and Twm were called to give evidence concerning the finding and recovery of the body. Their evidence was identical. Twm had found the body floating face down at the edge of the pool, partially covered by pond weed. He had informed his father. They, with others helping, had then carried the body to Dr. Owen's surgery, laid Gwyn on the bed there and waited for the doctor's return.

Emyr explained to the court, "We dragged Gwyn out of the water to check for any signs of life. Then once we realised there was no hope, we thought it more dignified to hide the body away. After all no-one wants a spectacle. And we had his mother to consider. She was in the chapel congregation."

The coroner nodded to indicate his understanding.

Twm was asked, "Did you notice the gash on his head?"

"I did."

"He was your friend was he not?" asked the coroner.

"He was."

"Could he swim?"

"No. Gwyn was frightened of water. I learnt to swim in the river and so did several of my friends but we could never persuade Gwyn to come in. He hated the water."

"Did your friend Gwyn Parry ever drink alcohol?"

"No, never. I have never known him even think of taking a drink. He didn't ever go in the 'Lamb and Lion'. He held true to Christian principles, was a committed member of the chapel and believed alcohol was sinful." Twm was pleased to have the chance to defend his friend and comfort Ruth at the same time.

"The witness statement from Bryn Powell, the landlord of the 'Lamb and Lion', confirms that Gwyn Parry was not there on the Saturday evening of 15th April and indeed had never entered his premises," the coroner commented. "I think we can discount intoxication as a factor in his death."

The coroner progressed to questioning Ruth Parry about Gwyn's movements the night before his death. As always, she was composed and calm.

"We ate our meal about five," she said. "Then I prepared food for the next day. I don't like to work on the Sabbath. Gwyn did some jobs for me, dug up some vegetables, planted some seeds, did some weeding."

"Did he do or say anything unusual?" asked the coroner.

"No. In my mind I have gone back over that evening time and time again but I can't think of anything. Gwyn was not a talkative boy. He just did his chores as normal. Then he said he wanted to sort some of his sketches and went to bed quite early, about half past eight, I think."

"You can't be sure?"

"No. I had no reason to look at the timepiece. But it couldn't have been much earlier than that because Gwyn wouldn't have had time to do his jobs."

"So, he must have left the house at some point?"

"I suppose he must have. But I wasn't aware that he had."

"Could he leave the house without you knowing?"

"Not if I were downstairs. But I went to bed just after Gwyn. I like to read the Bible every night before I go to sleep. I read Luke's account of the Easter story, I seem to remember. So uplifting. The cottage has a small landing at the top of the stairs and the two bedrooms open separately off that. He could have gone downstairs without me hearing him."

Or, thought Twm, he could have gone the other way. Gwyn and Evan had often used this alternative for night adventures, he knew. It was not easy for Tŵm to join in their games since he lived further away but Evan's farm was nearer. Sent to bed early, the two boys liked nothing better than to slip out and play in the dark. Under cover of night, they would play cops and robbers, spying through neighbours' windows and creeping around their gardens. Gwyn always escaped via the apple tree outside his window. A thick branch spread horizontally, directly underneath the sill. It was easy to open the window, swing his legs over the sill on to the branch, and then shin down the trunk to the ground. Tŵm was certain in his own mind that this was how Gwyn left the cottage that fateful night. There would have been no squeaking doors or creaking floorboards to worry about. However, he said nothing, lacking the courage to intervene in such solemn proceedings. In any case, he couldn't see that it mattered how Gwyn got out of his house that night. It only mattered what had happened afterwards.

"Mrs. Parry." The coroner paused. "Mrs. Parry, I am sorry to have to ask you these questions but it is essential that we establish the facts."

Ruth nodded.

"How was your son's state of mind in the days before his death?"

Tŵm held his breath. He had hoped that question would not have been raised. Even Ruth Parry couldn't cope with that scenario, he was sure.

"What do you mean?"

"Allow me to clarify. Was he depressed, disturbed? Was he behaving normally?"

Understanding dawned. As Tŵm watched Ruth set her jaw and looked directly into the coroner's eyes.

She was adamant. "My son was neither depressed nor disturbed. He was a perfectly normal young man."

"Mrs. Parry, you must excuse me asking you such things but some young men have been badly affected by their experiences in the war. There have been cases of young men taking their own lives."

Ruth forgot herself despite the formality of the proceedings. Tŵm had never before heard her raise her voice. "It is an insult to Gwyn's memory to even suggest such a thing. What you are suggesting is inconceivable. Gwyn knew how wrong that would be. It would be a sin against God and a crime against his country."

"I have to explore every avenue."

"I realise that but it is pointless to explore that one. Gwyn was proud of serving his country. He would never consider doing anything that would bring shame on his father, his regiment or his family."

"The question had to be asked, Mrs. Parry."

Tŵm, though he didn't possess Ruth's certainty, tended to agree with her. True, from the little he'd said, Gwyn had been badly affected by fighting at the Front, but he would have been all too well aware of the impact that his death would have on his mother. That alone would have prevented him from carrying out the deed, even if he had the inclination to do so.

After such complex analysis, the coroner's summing up was brief and to the point. Some facts were clear. The victim was identified, the cause of death established and the recovery of the body recounted. However, the exact circumstances preceding the death, the reason why Gwyn Parry entered the water, the nature of the head wound and the cause of the bruising all remained unknown. His state of mind at the time of the incident also remained a mystery.

There could be no other verdict – an open one.

Corn Month

The inquest inhabited Tŵm's mind, permeating every recess with an intensity that defied resistance. He dissected it, treating each part like a specimen to be examined. He had no idea why Gwyn would go out after dark and then end up drowned in Pwll Berw. Where was he going? What was he doing? Was he meeting someone? A girl? Then there was the head wound. Had Gwyn hit his head before or after he entered the water? Or had someone hit it for him? If someone else had hit him that would explain Gwyn, a non-swimmer, being in the water. An assailant could have struck a blow and then Gwyn might have fallen in. Or he could have been pushed. The questions span, spiralled, surged forward, sank back. Did he fall or was he pushed? Or did he throw himself in? And then hit his head? If he did then it must have taken tremendous courage.

Then there were the bruises. Immediately Tŵm began to feel uncomfortable. Uneasy at living with deceit, he did not want to go there. He circled the spot before forcing himself to look it full in the face. As he had left the court, Cadoc was waiting outside. Tŵm had done his best to avoid him, staying close to Dr. Owen. But Richard Owen's main concern was supporting Ruth who had walked out of the inquest, upright, head held high but with her face as white as Easter lilies. She ignored the hacks clamouring for a comment. Cadoc had found it easy to isolate Tŵm for the few seconds it took to say, "Glad ya 'eeded me warnin'. Thought ya'd wanna save yar own skin."

"Don't think I did what I did just because you told me to, Cadoc Morgan."

"No? Wot uvver reason would yar 'ave?"

Tŵm had watched Cadoc's muscular frame stride away. To his annoyance, Cadoc had raised his thumb over his right shoulder in a gesture which implied allegiance. The gesture sickened him. To think that Cadoc Morgan thought that he could be in league with him! But what else could he do? He had to protect Ruth Parry. That was more important than anything Cadoc Morgan thought or didn't think. Cadoc Morgan was just a thug. It really didn't matter what he believed.

What did matter though was that he, Tŵm Tudor, had withheld information from the police. Not only that but Tŵm knew that the police would most likely think it was vital evidence, even though Tŵm himself believed that it wasn't actually vital, just misleading. The coroner had spent a long time on the significance of that bruising. Tŵm remembered the words. "So, the bruising and the head wound may not be connected." Guilt seeped through the seams he had carefully sewn over his memory.

For he knew the pathologist was right. The bruises had been inflicted some time before. The Thursday evening before Easter Saturday to be precise. Maundy Thursday. He was sure though that they were not connected with Gwyn's death. The only way that they could be linked was if the same person inflicted the head wound and the bruises. Tŵm was willing to bet that was not the case. He thought it through.

Cadoc Morgan was a sadistic bully but he was no murderer. Tŵm was sure of that. Even if he had fought with Gwyn and Gwyn had fallen into the pool, Cadoc would have pulled him out. He would've stopped short of killing. Not for the right reasons to be sure. Morality wouldn't come into it. But Cadoc was not stupid. He had native cunning. It wasn't in Cadoc's nature to risk his own life and freedom just for the satisfaction of ending Gwyn's. Tŵm knew him too well. Cadoc liked to hurt people but he didn't like to hurt himself. He would always protect his own interests. And his interests would not be served by a life in prison or worse. Cadoc never lost control. It was one of the features that Tŵm found most distasteful about him. If Cadoc lashed out in temper that would be at least understandable. But he didn't. With Cadoc the hurt was planned, designed even. That was what made it so terrifying. Cadoc preferred live agony to death's release. Tŵm recalled one incident that had sickened him then and still sickened him now. It was one of those memories that he really wished he could erase but the acrid stench of it was seared indelibly on his mind.

Cadoc must have been about ten years old. The younger Tŵm was tagging along behind Evan and Gwyn as usual one Saturday afternoon. They encountered Gethin and Cadoc near the stream where they had clearly been making a dam. Bored of this activity they had moved on to something new. Crouched, heads together, poring over something which lay in their hands, they chose to ignore Evan and his pals who were racing twigs upstream of the dam.

Gethin was the first to speak. "Wanna see wot we're doin'?"

Evan, flanked by Gwyn and Tŵm, moved across towards Cadoc, who was now kneeling alongside something that was lying on the grass alongside the stream. At first Tŵm thought the Morgan brothers had found a dead rabbit, freshly killed by a fox or weasel. But then its leg twitched slightly.

"Have you found a rabbit that's been hurt?" asked Evan in all innocence. "Perhaps we should put it out of its misery." The three of them edged forward to see what was happening.

As he watched, understanding crept up on Tŵm. Far from putting the poor creature out of its misery, intensifying suffering was the whole point of the activity.

Gethin was holding the rabbit's back legs firmly with his right hand. His left hand pressed down on the shoulders so that the forelegs splayed across the earth. Unable to move, the rabbit was helpless. A slight heaving was the only sign of life.

Cadoc Morgan was experimenting. Between his thumb and forefinger, he had a long thorn which he was sharpening to an even finer point with a penknife. "Keep 'im still Gethin." With medical precision he moved the thorn towards the rabbit. Tŵm heard a pop. He forced himself to look. Blood and liquid were trickling down the rabbit's face from the left eye socket. Cadoc raised the thorn again.

"No," Tŵm and Gwyn shouted in unison. Evan took a different approach. He launched himself forward grabbing at Cadoc's bony wrist, trying to wrench the thorn from his hand. But it was just too late. The other eye had already exploded into liquid. Gethin, taken by surprise, loosened his grip. The blinded rabbit shot forward, bashed straight into a sapling, then crawled off into the long grass.

"Wot ya do that for?" Cadoc was indignant.

"The poor creature," said Tŵm, appalled by what he had seen. "Why would you do that?"

Cadoc was sulky. "I jus' wanted t' see what'd 'appen."

"But think of the suffering you've caused. And he can't live now. He won't be able to find his way back to his burrow. He'll take days to die and he'll be frightened."

"It 'asn't got a burrow."

"What do you mean?" asked Evan.

"I got it from an 'utch. It's Luned's rabbit."

Luned was in school with them. A tubby, red cheeked girl, her dark plaits bounced as she had made her way up to Mr. Pugh the previous day.

"Yes, Luned, what is it?"

"Cadoc Morgan. He stole my pencil and jabbed it into my hand." She displayed the back of her hand which was bleeding slightly and starting to bruise.

"He did, did he? Cadoc Morgan, come here."

Cadoc had received three stout blows for that escapade. He was not going to let it lie.

"She deserved it. She shouldn't 'ave shopped me in."

"You shouldn't have hurt the rabbit. He hadn't done anything to you. He doesn't deserve to suffer. Were you going to kill him?" Tŵm asked.

"No, course not. I were going to put it back in the 'utch so she could see wot 'ad 'appened to it. Now ya've spoilt that."

"You bastard." Evan spat out the word in disgust. Tŵm could not voice such a term but Evan had no such compunction.

Cadoc shrugged his shoulders. "I dunna care wot ya think. I'll tell Luned ya lost 'er rabbit." He swaggered off, back towards the village, Gethin alongside.

"We'll have to find him, "Tŵm said to the others. "We can't leave him in that state. He must be put out of his misery."

Tŵm became more and more desperate as the night closed in. He moved forward gingerly on his hands and knees parting the long stalks of grass with his hands, looking under gorse bushes and delving deep underneath reeds and ferns.

Evan consoled him. "We've done everything we can."

"But it's not enough. We must find him." Tŵm was adamant. He couldn't bear to think of the rabbit suffering in the darkness of his day.

"He must've crawled somewhere safe to die," said Gwyn.

"You're probably right," Tŵm answered, "but he must be terrified. We have to find him."

It was pitch dark by the time they were forced to give up.

For the next few nights Tŵm found it difficult to sleep, plagued by images of sharp blades tearing through soft, vulnerable tissue. After a tortuous week, by the Saturday, he was at least able to tell himself that the rabbit must be dead and no longer suffering. It was cold comfort though. He would never forgive himself for not finding the poor creature.

Evan took his own revenge. One of the Morgan's field gates mysteriously was left open one night creating an escape route for sheep eager to explore. Cadoc and Gethin suffered a leathering. Griff Morgan, convinced one of his sons must've left it open, blamed them for "carelessness or laziness or both." It took them three days to retrieve their scattered flock from neighbouring farms.

The Thursday after the inquest Caron travelled to Carreg-y-Bedd in the trap with Emyr. He had several errands to run. He told Caron to pick up Siôn's boots that had been taken to the cobbler for soling while he went to see Weyland Philpin, who had been sharpening some tools for him. As they passed the 'Lamb and Lion', Caron turned her eyes towards the common next to it, hoping to spot Abram about his chores.

She couldn't help herself. Involuntarily, the words escaped her lips. "Tad, the Gypsies have gone." The shock was like a physical blow; the result, a leaden lump in her stomach.

Emyr was only vaguely interested. "They're Romanies. They've moved on. Likely they'll want to find better grass for the horses now the common's been grazed. They won't have gone far though at this time of year. There's still plenty of work about."

Caron didn't know how she got through the morning. Panic gripped her. She might never see Abram again. She couldn't go looking for him. It was unthinkable. She had never gone any distance without Mam and Tad. The furthest she had ever been was the seaside in Rhyl on a day trip with the chapel. She clutched on to Tad's comment, "They won't have gone far." If that was indeed the case then she could at least ride out on Jac and perhaps discover the new camp.

She had to wait until Saturday morning to fulfil her plan as Jac was needed on the farm the next day. Up early, keen to avoid any awkward questions from Mali, she followed the rutted track that led to the clearing where she had first met Abram. The day was already warm. Sitting down, she trailed her hand through the pool, tears of water sparkling in the early morning sunlight as they fell through her fingers. Remembering their first meeting, the memory of Abram's presence was almost tangible. She could feel her neck tingling in anticipation of him drawing near, placing his hands on her shoulders, turning her to face him. Unable to prevent herself, she turned round, half expecting to see him approach. But the clearing was empty; the only sound a summer breeze breathing gently through the leaves. Caron sat, solitary, lost in thought. She fingered the tiny bag that hung hidden underneath her blouse. In it lay the rush ring Abram had given her. Though not good at needlework, she had found a scrap of silky material in Nain's workbox, sewn a pouch and hung it round her neck with a discarded shoe lace. It sufficed. Abram's gift lay next to her skin. Leaving the ring on her finger was unthinkable.

Time passed. He was not coming. He had gone. And she had no idea where. Sighing, she untethered Jac and climbed slowly aboard, leaving him a long rein to walk slowly back to Cwyn-y-Gwynt. Choosing a different track, she wound her way through the lower reaches of the forest. There was nothing to hurry for; she had lost all sense of purpose. The oaks and beeches thinned as she neared the lane that led back towards home. A pungent smell struck her nostrils. Smoke! But she couldn't see anything. The lane was within sight when she spotted a newly made track to her left. Undergrowth had been cleared recently, branches snapped off to allow wider access, brambles clipped back. Curious she turned Jac down the track. It could be a tramp of course but she was not nervous. Not on Jac. She could easily gallop away if need be. She rounded a corner, taking care to hold Jac's head high as he stepped over tree roots obstructing the way. The smell of smoke grew stronger. Only a little way ahead she saw where it was coming from – a camp fire. The scent of burning wood hung heavy in the still air of a warm morning. A tongue of joy licked a soothing balm deep inside Caron. She looked round. There were the two Gypsy caravans. She recognised them instantly. One red and cream, painted with elaborate curlicues, interspersed with russet apples and deep purple plums, its central panel displaying a jet black horse, proudly feathered; the other caravan, leaf green with brightly coloured birds featured on the side – woodpeckers, a chaffinch, blue tits, robins and swallows. Surrounding them were raised motifs of cerise daisies and mustard roses. Three horses grazed alongside. A dark bay, a portly piebald and a skewbald. Caron recognised Brân at once, his chestnut mane distinctive against his white neck. Unthinkingly she rode straight into the camp.

"Good mornin' young gel." Moses' head had appeared in the top opening of the stable door of the red caravan. He opened the bottom half and walked towards her.

"Been out ridin' 'ave yer? Ye're a way from Cwyn-y-Gwynt aren't yer?"

Caron nodded.

"Would yer like t' join us for breakfast?"

She nodded again and slipped down from Jac's back. Moses brought a tether and left Jac to graze with the others. He nickered at Brân before tearing hungrily at the lush grass.

Moses' understanding of horses was evident. "Seems t'ey 'ave met before," he said, chewing on tobacco.

Caron flushed, her pale skin deepening as Abram appeared from the same van. He smiled at her. "Hello Caron."

"Yer two know each ot'er?" asked Moses.

"We met once out ridin' in t' forest," explained Abram.

Moses shot a glance at his son. "Well, I've just asked yer friend t' sup wi' us." He turned to Caron. "Come an' be seated." He indicated some logs that had been dragged round the fire. "T'is is me woman, Grizell."

The woman who came out of the caravan did not welcome Caron. Her jet black hair was tied back under a sky blue scarf. Dark, deep set eyes narrowed suspiciously as she assessed the stranger. Without putting herself out to greet Caron, she placed a plate of eggs on a rough-hewn plank of wood by the fire.

"Keep 'em duck eggs warm while I get t' bread," she instructed Abram. She soon returned with crusty bread already torn into chunks, shooing in front of her two younger children who Abram introduced as his sister, Esmeralda and his cousin, Matthew. Esmeralda stared at Caron, twisting a strand of unexpectedly fair hair round a grubby finger. Matthew showed little interest in the new arrival, preferring to weigh up which was the biggest egg.

The upper half of the green caravan door opened to reveal a young girl, perhaps three or four years younger than Caron, rubbing sleep out of her eyes. "I smell food," she said to no-one in particular.

Moses laughed. "T'ought thet would get yer up Silvaina. Where's yer Ma and Da?"

"Said t'ey was goin' out early. Da's been offered some chickens."

To Caron, Moses said, "Silvaina's a real layabout in t' mornin'."

An older woman with skin like polished beechnut, followed Silvaina out of the van. She sported several wide gold bracelets fitted tightly round both her arms. Spotting Caron, she stopped, folded her arms, looked at Moses and asked, "'Who's t'is t'en?"

Moses explained. "Caron Tudor. She were ridin' in t' forest an' came across us. I know 'er Tad. Work fer 'im a' times."

The woman walked towards Caron. "Pleased t'meet yer." Her smile revealed spaces where teeth should be and a single gold tooth isolated in her left upper jaw. "I'm Seraphina. Come t' 'ave yer fortune read 'ave yer?" Walking awkwardly towards them, she put her hands on her ample hips and looked Caron up and down. She had a natural air of authority. "Ye're way too pretty fer yer own good." She laughed. "T'ose eyes'll break a few 'earts." Turning her attention to the food, she began helping Grizell to dish out eggs and bread on to platters. Grizell handed one to Caron, furrowing her brow as she did so. Following their example, Caron broke the yolk with the crust and then used the bread to scoop up the egg itself. She was unexpectedly hungry. The last couple of days she had been merely picking at her food. As she broke her hunk of bread a piece of it fell on her knee. She picked it up and raised it to her mouth.

"No! Don't do thet! I'll get you some more." Abram reached for the loaf.

"Don't do what?"

"T' bread. It's touched yer skirt."

"It's fine Abram. It's still clean."

"No, it's not. T'row it to one of t' dogs."

Caron looked at the two whippets lying on the caravan steps.

Abram continued. "It's not clean. It's *mochadi*."

"What's that?"

"It means somethin' dirty. Yer can't eat food if it's touched yer clothes. It's t' same if someone's sick. Yer can't use t'eir t'ings."

Caron, confused and realising she had a lot to learn about Romany ways, did as she was told, tore the rejected bread in half and threw the pieces to the dogs. They gulped them ravenously.

Despite Grizell's hostility, Caron felt unaccountably at home. At Cwyn-y-Gwynt, meals were austere affairs. Mali presided over a formal table, where 'manners maketh the man' and topics of conversation were severely restricted. Village and chapel affairs were favoured; the latest escapades of the suffragettes were not. Accepting that she was mature and wise enough to warrant a vote, Mali did not approve of the suffragettes campaigning for women under thirty to be given the same privilege. "Young flibbertigibbets. Think they know everything and they know nothing. No experience of life!"

Breakfast with the Gypsies was very different. Relaxed, slow, no-one was hurrying. Taking time to enjoy the food, they chatted about whether they needed a new horse, "Sal's gettin' on a bit now," about work in the harvest fields and about skinning the rabbits for that night's meal. Caron let the conversation drift over her, not confident enough to join in unless asked a direct question. Feeling that she couldn't use first names for adults and too embarrassed to speak to Abram, she was restricted in any case to addressing the children.

Esmeralda was sitting next to her. "Do you like eggs?" Caron asked her. Esmeralda smiled shyly and nodded.

"Yer won't get much out of 'er," Seraphina broke in. "Shy as a young fox cub, she is." She turned her attention to Caron. "D' yer ride out often?"

"As much as I can but Jac's needed on the farm so it's mostly Saturday and Sunday. I love riding and I love being in the forest."

Seraphina nodded her understanding. "Used t' 'elp me Da break in young 'orses when I were a young kid. Sat me first 'orse when I were two." She laughed. "No 'orse'd want t' carry me now wi' me weight."

Caron didn't know whether it would be more polite to agree or to disagree. In turmoil she said nothing.

Talk turned to the Denbigh show. "Should be good weather fer it t'is yeer," Abram chipped in.

Caron, feeling on safer ground, replied, "My Tad usually competes in the sheepdog trials as well as showing the sheep. I like watching the horse jumping."

"Ay, 'tis a good day," said Moses.

They were interrupted by the arrival of another couple who emerged unexpectedly from behind them.

"Smelt t' food 'ave yer?" Moses chuckled.

The man was wrestling with a wooden crate. Cackles and squawks filled the air. "Got four 'ens 'ere," the man said proudly. "Good layers too, I've been told. A real bargin 'cos auld Albert owed me a favour. 'elped 'im dig over 'is potato patch las' week."

Seraphina bent down to inspect the new arrivals. She held out her hand. Solomon pulled a wad of cash out of his pocket and gave it to her. "Keep us goin' fer a while. Made a fair penny I did, pickin' currants in Carreg. Real glut this yeer. All t' wimmin makin' jam. Got some o' thet too."

The hens continued to kick up a racket until they were released into a pen of wooden rails, shored up with thick branches and tied together with string. It had clearly been purpose built. Immediately peace descended as the hens started scratching at the earth and pecking at the grass. Low clucking indicated their contentment.

"Won' be short of eggs fer a bit," announced the man.

"Solomon," said Moses to Caron by way of explanation. "'is woman is sister to Grizell."

While Caron was still working out the family relationships, Solomon bowed extravagantly towards Caron. "Comp'ny," he commented. "Who is t'is luv'ly lady?"

Caron reddened. "Emyr Tudor's girl," Moses replied.

"Don' tek after yer Tad d'yer?" Solomon boomed at her. He spoke like the auctioneer at the market, as if convinced that if he didn't bellow someone would miss what he was saying. "Nor yer Mam either, fer thet matter. Face that'd put t' fear of God up Howell Griffith's bull." He laughed.

"Now Solomon," remonstrated Moses, "don't yer go rippin' 'er Mam apart in front of 'er."

"Sorry," Solomon said. "Didn't mean no 'arm." As he smiled at Caron, his eyes danced with vigour. The rest of his face was all hair. Eyebrows, moustache, beard, sideburns, all vied for superiority but had to admit defeat to the mass of jet black curls springing from beneath a battered felt hat. A cigarette hung from the left side of his lower lip, wagging to and fro in time with his words.

The woman with him, joined Moses in condemnation. "Shut yer mouth, Solomon, yer daft 'aporth. Can't yer see ye're upsettin' t' girl. She's not used t' yer nonsense." She offered Caron her hand. "I'm Valentina. Pleased t' meet yer. Don't tek any notice of Solomon. Where t'ere's no sense, t'ere's no feelin'!" She aimed a blow at Solomon. Well used to Valentina's ways, he swerved sideways to avoid the flat of her hand making contact with his ear.

Caron, unused to public displays of violence between grown-ups, was unsure how to react. She was rescued by Abram. Quiet until now, he could see that she was overwhelmed. "P'raps yer'd better be gettin' back. T'ey'll be wond'rin' where yer are. T'ey might be worried about yer."

Caron smiled at him gratefully. "Yes, I'd better ride back. It must be late."

"Sun's right up now," Moses agreed. "Come an' see us again, why don't yer? Abram can bring yer in t' evenin' fer some food an' some music. Isn't thet so, Abram?" Not waiting for Abram's reply, Moses continued. "Tek t' girl back to t' lane," he ordered.

"It's fine. I know the way," Caron responded.

"Now, we don't wan' yer gettin' lost do we? Yer Tad'd never forgive me. Abram, get 'er 'orse."

Abram untied Jac, brought him over to her and gave her a leg up on to his back. Leading Jac back down the way she had come in to the camp, he said to her, "A bit much fer yer meetin' us all at once. Do yer remember all our names?"

"I do," she answered. "You have a kind family. But who's Seraphina? Is she your Nain?"

"Yeah. She's my Ma's Ma. She's t' phuri dai, t' old woman. She's in charge."

"Not Moses then?" Caron asked, surprised.

"No, of course not. 'e doesn't 'ave 'er wisdom."

"Your Mam's a bit scary," Caron ventured.

"Ma don't like strangers thet's all. Takes 'er time gettin' t' know yer." He grinned at her, then laughed out loud. "Fancy yer turnin' up just like thet. An' I'd been wondrin' 'ow I were goin' t' manage t' see yer again."

"Really?" For the first time that morning, Caron looked directly into Abram's eyes. "I didn't know you were camped in the forest. I just knew you'd left Carreg. I thought I wasn't ever going to see you again."

"Now why would yer t'ink thet? After our last meetin' too." Caron, embarrassed at this reference to their previous liaison, averted her gaze. Tightening the rein, Abram drew Jac to a halt. Drawing Caron down from Jac into his arms, he repeated the kisses of their previous encounter and then sent her home with the taste of him lingering on her lips.

"Kept 'er quiet didn't yer?" was Moses' only comment on Abram's return to the camp.

Tŵm was on his way to see Howell and Olwen Griffiths. Emyr had said, "They'll be pleased to see you Tŵm and while you're there ask Howell if I can borrow some Luddington's Lambing Oil. I'm running low." Guilty that he hadn't been for a while and guilty too that he didn't want to go at all, he cycled at a snail's pace in the gentle warmth of a Welsh summer day. He would much have preferred to be moving the young sheep onto the hay fields now that the grass was coming through rather than talking about his dead friend. Speaking about Evan only served to remind him how much he missed him. Was it really over three years since Evan had gone? He hoped that sometime he would obtain some comfort from happy memories of times they'd shared. But not yet. Not yet. As he pedalled on, he told himself that, on balance, he would feel worse if he didn't go than if he did.

Olwen's expression of delight only increased Tŵm's sense of self-loathing. He should have visited before now. How long was it since he had seen her?

Olwen answered for him. "Tŵm, how lovely to see you. I haven't spoken to you since Gwyn's funeral."

"Good morning Mrs. Griffiths. Is it that long?" He made an uneasy excuse. "I've been very busy helping Tad on the farm but with the reasonable weather in May and June we're well ahead now."

"I quite understand Tŵm. We farmers have to work with the weather, don't we? I'll make you a cup of tea and I've just made some griddle scones. Would you like one?"

Tŵm sat at the well-scrubbed kitchen table, munching away. Now that he was there, he felt able to relax. The thought of visiting was much worse than the actuality. Evan's mother took such pleasure in his visit that she made it easy for him, when in fact he should be trying to make it easier for her. With an understanding beyond his years, Tŵm guessed that it must be difficult for Olwen Griffiths to see him living when her son's life had so cruelly been wrenched away from him. Deliberately choosing non-sensitive topics, he updated Olwen on the number of lambs born that year, the sweetness of this year's hay and the forthcoming corn harvest. Their conversation took on an easy cadence. Being a farmer's wife herself, Olwen was interested in progress at Cwyn-y-Gwynt.

"We're not doing as well as you," she said. "But then we're short of help. Catrin's so far away and Ebrill has her hands full with three youngsters."

"How are they all?" asked Tŵm.

"Catrin and Charles are doing really well. Business is good and she's expecting her first baby early December. We don't see much of them though."

Tŵm was not surprised to hear this. He had never warmed to Catrin. Evan used to say of her, "My sister's like a blinkered horse. She sees her own way ahead but never looks to the side to see what anyone else wants or needs." Desperate to escape the farm, she had gone into service in Liverpool, met Charles at a dance and married as soon as decently possible. Charles was the youngest of three brothers, both of whom had been killed, one in Arras and one, tragically very near the end of the war, at Havrincourt. Charles had taken over the running of his parent's hotel which he was set to inherit. Catrin had managed to line her nest not with duck feathers but with goose down.

"And Ebrill?"

"She's as well as can be expected given her circumstances. She's moved in with us now. Bringing up three youngsters alone on a war widow's pension is not easy Tŵm. She needs help and it's nice for us to have the grandchildren with us. Little Evan is nine now you know."

Tŵm did know. On occasion he had seen Ebrill taking the children to school, the older girls fussing over their little brother. Ebrill had been particularly close to Evan and had named her youngest child after him well before any threat of war loomed. Her husband, Harri, had been killed at Mametz Wood. As a result, she had done everything possible to persuade Evan not to enlist. "Don't leave me," she had pleaded. "I simply couldn't bear it if you were taken from me as well." Evan, with characteristic optimism, fully believing in his own invincibility, had replied, "The Huns'll have to watch out once I'm there. Don't worry Ebrill, I can take care of myself."

Evan's picture in its carved frame of blue forget-me-nots, stood centrally on the mantelpiece, taking pride of place. Thankfully it was not the still life of a staged photograph taken in a studio. That would not have been the real Evan. Tŵm had been with him when the photo was taken. They had been at the Denbigh Show and a photographer had captured the young Evan to perfection, his dark eyes dancing with enjoyment, his slightly crooked smile, his floppy hair. To Tŵm the picture, despite its small size, dominated the room.

Olwen Griffiths noticed the direction of his gaze. "We have another one that the army sent us, you know. Have I ever shown it you?"

Tŵm shook his head.

"I'll get it."

Tŵm looked round the room. On one side of the huge fireplace that embraced the cooking range were oval, sepia portraits of long-gone family ancestors. On the other side was a proud plaque reading:

1914 The Great War 1918

Lest we forget

Killed	908,986
Wounded	2,000,000
Missing	191,000
Total	3,099,986

The Path of Duty was the way to glory.

And one of those 908,986 was Evan, Tŵm thought. Behind every number was a mother, father, son or brother who had a family like the Griffiths', a family who had loved him. Every soldier had a life to live that ended too soon in mud and filth, blood and misery.

Olwen wasn't gone long. The photograph looked very like all the others Tŵm had seen of soldiers in uniform. It was curious how official photos drained the soldiers of their personality and made them all look the same. Stiff, formal and posed, the picture gave little indication of individuality. It was a soldier rather than Evan. Tŵm would not have instantly recognised Evan if he hadn't known it was him. Evan stared unsmiling into the distance, his face an expressionless mask. The only sign of Evan's irrepressible nature was the cap worn at a slightly jaunty angle.

"I prefer the other one," Tŵm told Olwen.

"So do I, but I'm proud of this one. It shows how loyal he was to King and Country and how brave."

Tŵm would have been more comfortable to continue discussing the farm but Olwen wanted to talk about Evan. Tŵm had heard the stories many times before but if it helped Olwen to repeat them then he was content to listen.

"I remember parting from him at the station. Full of the joys of spring he was, though it was actually early summer. As you know, he turned eighteen just two weeks before Gwyn's birthday on June 1st. They had both received their call up papers at about the same time along with a railway warrant asking them to present themselves at Kinmel Camp. Midsummer's Day it was when we took them both to Denbigh to catch the train. Ruth Parry came with us of course. Being Ruth, she didn't shed a tear when they got on that train, even though it must've been so hard for her with Thomas already gone. 'Whatever happens is God's will,' she said to me. I just wish I had half her fortitude. Evan had to unwind Ebrill's arms from his neck, she hugged him so close. Howell told him to look after himself and write regularly. Gwyn didn't say much but then he never did, did he? Always kept himself to himself. Was bound to be like that really with being brought up by Ruth. The Parrys never did go in for displays of emotion. Gwyn was chalk white though, I do remember that. Evan, of course, was talking non-stop. I recall he said to Ruth, 'I'll look after Gwyn, don't you worry.' He was bouncing with excitement at the prospect of the training, seeing a new country, being part of what he called, a great adventure. 'I can't wait to be off,' he said as he hugged me. 'What a lark!' I can see his face now. He looked so *happy*. Then he slung an arm round Gwyn's shoulders and they both got on the train, threw their bags in a compartment and then Evan pressed his nose against the window just as he used to do as a child at the sweet shop in town."

Olwen smiled at the memory.

"I half expected him to say, 'Mam, buy me liquorice allsorts.' Loved those he did. The window was part way pulled down and filthy with soot. Playing the fool made his nose all dirty. He couldn't hear me telling him with the noise from the engine so I pointed at my nose, then his, then rubbed mine. I didn't want him arriving for training with a dirty face. Wouldn't make a good impression that, would it? Then he stepped back, rubbed his nose with his sleeve, gave us all a wave, grabbed Gwyn's arm and pulled him down onto the seats as the train pulled out." She paused. "That was the last time I saw him."

Twm allowed Olwen to ramble on. He allowed her words to drift over him, all too familiar with what she was saying. Olwen had moved on to Evan's letters. "So good about writing he was. I was surprised because he was never much of a writer before. Liked being outside he did. But I think he realised we were all worried about him and the one thing you could always say about Evan was that he loved his family. Always looked after me he did, young as he was. Such a good boy, the best son anyone could have had. Never caused me a moment's trouble. After the girls left home, he'd come and help me cook the supper or churn the butter. 'Don't want your arm to ache do we Mam?' he'd say to me. Yet often he'd been outside helping Howell spread muck or feed pigs. Boundless energy he had. Never stopped."

Twm, used to Olwen's rapid changes of subject, only had to nod, smile and mutter an occasional, "Yes, he did," to keep Olwen in full flow. This suited him. It wasn't that he minded hearing Olwen's memories of her son; it was just that they weren't his memories. His recollection of Evan differed somewhat from Olwen's. Understandable, Twm thought, to place her lost son firmly on an unassailable pedestal. It wasn't that Olwen's memories were inaccurate; more that they were embellished, coloured in by love and loss. It was certainly true that Evan cared deeply for his family and did his best to look after them. But he was no angel. It certainly wasn't quite true to say that he had, 'Never caused a moment's trouble.' Evan was often in trouble. Nothing serious to be sure. Evan was as honest as the day was long. Straight as a die, as Emyr would say. But he was full of mischief. Twm well remembered one day at Tan-y-Graig. Emyr had come over to help Howell with some fencing and the boys, left to their own devices, wandered over to the house. Evan decided to plague his Nain, who was visiting and had decided to help by baking bread in the kitchen. She had brought the flour and yeast from the pantry and placed it on the table. While she was occupied fetching some warm water from the range, Evan sneaked in, picked up the flour and took it back to the pantry. When his Nain walked back to the table with the jug of water, they watched as she searched everywhere for the flour. "Going mad I am," they heard her say. "I could've sworn I brought it out already." Later on, when she was sitting down with a cup of tea waiting for the bread to bake, Evan came in and tied the strings of her pinny to the cross bar on the back of the kitchen chair. When she stood up, the chair stood up with her. "Evan," she scolded, "untie me at once. What a scamp you are."

Evan's practical jokes didn't stop there. Twm well remembered the time Catrin had got all dressed up for a birthday party. He and Twm were in the stackyard by the water butt. Evan was scooping up water in his hands and throwing it at Twm who was laughing and dodging. Catrin unwisely walked across the yard saying, "Look at me Evan. What do you think of the dress Mam made for me?" Evan, pretending he hadn't heard her, scooped up another handful of water, pretended to aim at Twm but successfully drenched Catrin.

"Oh sorry, Catrin, my hand slipped. Are you OK?" He smiled crookedly at her, minus his two front teeth, his eyes sparkling with fun. Catrin stood there, water dripping from her newly washed dark, glossy hair down on to her sprigged cotton frock. Olwen, wiping her clean, told her, "It was just an accident Catrin. Don't make a fuss. You know Evan wouldn't do it on purpose." Catrin stuck out her tongue at a laughing Evan and got soundly told off for being so rude.

Twm remembered another time too when Evan played what he termed 'a trick' on his sister. Always neat as a new pin, she hated any kind of mess or dirt. This irritated Evan who was never happier than when he was plastered in mud or covered in hay seeds. One afternoon he had the extraordinary good fortune to find a half-rotted crow in the hay loft. It must have flown in but couldn't find its way out again. Never one to waste an opportunity, Evan wrapped it in newspaper and tucked it beneath Catrin's clothes in her chest of drawers. The next morning, Olwen sniffed and said, "Catrin, does your jersey need a wash? It doesn't smell too good to me."

"It is clean Mam. It was washed last Monday."

Catrin walked to school as usual but as the heat from her body permeated the wool the rank smell became overpowering.

"Stinky Griffiths, stinky Griffiths," Catrin's peers had taunted. She didn't lose the nickname until years later when she left for Liverpool.

Before Catrin could realise what had happened, Evan had removed the culprit and thrown it in the midden. Olwen washed all Catrin's jerseys several times but never quite managed to rid them of the smell. "I can't understand it," she said to Catrin. "You need to be more careful about where you sit in future. You must have leant against something very unpleasant."

Evan regaled Twm and Gwyn with his triumph. "She deserved it," he maintained when Twm objected. "She's always getting me into trouble. Runs and tells Mam when I don't wipe my boots and bring clods of earth into the kitchen. 'He's done it again Mam,' she'll cry. 'Shall I tell him off for you?' Ebrill doesn't behave like that. She sweeps it up before Mam can see it."

Twm, lost in memories, realised he wasn't listening closely as Olwen passed him a letter. He had seen the letters before but he would have to show an interest and read them again. The first one was all about the training camp.

Dear Mam, Tad and all the family

You mustn't worry about me. I'm having a fine time here at Kinmel. Our training is good preparation for being in France or wherever I'm going. It's teaching me to take care of myself. The camp extends about four miles over towards the coast near Rhyl. Bodelwyddan Castle is our HQ. The village too is part of the camp. I was walking down Artillery Row yesterday evening and I could see the sea. Beautiful it was, with the sun shining on the water. It was like when you and Tad took us children to the seaside in the summer and you told us that the setting sun was pulling the water up to its chin like we did with the sheets when you tucked us up in bed. One day we went down into Llandudno and did drill on the beach. Right by the pier it was. That was hard work as the wet sand sucked at our boots and made it heavy going. My muscles ached for days afterwards.

I can't believe how big the camp is. It stretches into the distance. It's just topping! There must be thousands of us here and I've made some grand chums. Gwyn and I are lucky as we're sleeping in barrack cabins which are basically wooden huts. The name 'cabin' makes them sound small but they each hold 180 men. Others are sleeping in bell tents. Our cabin is next to one of the cook houses so we can smell our dinner cooking. They feed us well with plenty of meat and potatoes to get our strength up to fight the enemy. There's a parade ground of course so we can practise our marching. But I didn't expect there to be a post office, where I will post this letter, and shops. I can buy a Daily Mail, my favourite Wills cigarettes and my liquorice allsorts. We call this part of the camp, Tintown. There's even a brewery here and a club where we can all go to get a pint. Don't worry, I'm not drinking much beer at all but it's nice to rest after a hard day. Don't suppose we'll get much of a rest at the Front! The buildings are real posh, not like the cabins, and timbered in black and white. One of the biggest buildings is the hospital but I haven't been in that.

We've been kitted out now so I have a cap, strong boots, a uniform and a greatcoat. I wish you could see me all dressed up in it. I look so smart. You would be really proud of me.

You know me Mam, I like to be kept busy and we're certainly busy here with all the drills and marching. Physical fitness is very important before we go off to fight the Hun so there's lots of exercising in PT classes. Of course, I was fit already with working on the farm but you should see some of the townies huffing and puffing!

I've learnt so much, so many new things. We've been taught to use weapons too as part of attack practice. Some of the lads have been chosen to train in the use of machine guns or rifles. Others are becoming experts in signalling or wiring. The ones who will be stretcher bearers are learning first aid. I haven't been put in a special group and neither has Gwyn so probably we'll be in the infantry. Gwyn isn't enjoying it as much as me but don't tell his Mam that. No need to upset her. Poor Gwyn is more of an artist than a fighter. He thinks marching and exercising are really boring. All thumbs he was, learning to use a rifle. Got into terrible trouble, he did. I can't tell you the words one of the Corporals yelled at him the other day when he only fired twice in a minute. You have to take the safety catch off, slide the bolt and load the chamber. Then you take aim and fire, sliding the bolt after every time you pull the trigger. I can already fire eleven shots a minute and I'm getting faster all the time. When I'm a real expert, I'll be able to fire the 'Mad Minute'. That's fifteen, but to do that I have to re-load and it takes a lot of practice. Apparently sixteen is the record here.

Gwyn told me he didn't want to kill another man, German or not. I told him, 'You'll change your mind real fast Gwyn if it's Fritz or you.' Shooting is second nature for me. Remember how Tad took me out to shoot rabbits when I was just a small lad. I brought you back a brace for the pot so many times. Last week the sergeant praised my target shooting with my trusty Lee Enfield. He said to me, 'You'll make a great sniper, you will lad. Pick off the Hun as though they're ducks on a fairground stall!'

We've been practising our shooting in real trenches just like the ones in France and Belgium. That'll make a big difference to us when we get over there as we'll know what to do. I can't wait to go now. The Hun'd better watch out when I get there. I'll show 'em what's what.

I'll write again when I get to wherever I'm going. You won't know me when I get home, I've built up so many new muscles! I'm sure I'll be bigger and stronger than Tad!

Love Evan

"Such a long letter Twm especially when you consider he couldn't have had much time for writing. Always had a lot to say for himself did Evan. Told me everything he did. When he came home from school, I got every little detail of his day. Better than the girls he was for that," Olwen reminisced.

Twm smiled. The letter, full of news, was so like Evan. He had always packed so much into every day, bouncing with enthusiasm, embracing every new experience, meeting everything life threw at him, head on. However, despite Olwen thinking that he told her everything, Twm knew for certain that Evan hadn't mentioned quite all his new experiences in the letters to his family. Gwyn had told him, not long after his return from the war, in an unexpected moment of confidence that Evan had disappeared from the training camp on more than one occasion.

"I was really worried. Evan and I always made our way back to the cabin together after a meal in the canteen and a visit to the club. Evan said to me, 'You go along to the club Gwyn and I'll see you later.' I asked him where he was going and he replied, 'Ask no questions Gwyn and you'll get no lies'."

Even Tŵm was surprised at this. Evan's reply was more than unusual. Open as the day is long, he had no secrets.

Gwyn continued. "I lay in my bunk in the pitch dark, worried sick. Evan would be in serious trouble if any officer found out he wasn't there. It even crossed my mind that he'd deserted. Then I dismissed that as nonsense. Evan was enjoying himself far too much to run away. He was actually looking forward to going to fight whereas I was in a sick funk. He did eventually come back sometime in the middle of the night. I heard him slip in and after that I was able to go to sleep."

"So, where'd he been?" Tŵm had asked.

Gwyn had turned bright red and dropped his voice. "Tŵm, there were lots of girls hanging around the entrance to the camp. Grand entrance it was too. Massive pillars with stone lions on top, guarding the gates and surveying everyone entering the camp. Made me feel very important when I went through for the first time."

Tŵm, baffled by Gwyn's sudden change of direction, asked, "So what? What have girls by the gates got to do with Evan's disappearance?"

Gwyn paused. "Tŵm, you know. They were *those* kind of girls."

"No, I don't know Gwyn. What do you mean?" Tŵm grew hot at remembering his own naïvety. Gwyn and Evan had left him so far behind, not only geographically, but physically and emotionally too. Gwyn had been incapable of using the word. Tŵm had not made it easy for him. "They were... they were..." His words came out in a rush. "Ladies of the night."

"Ladies of the night...?" Realisation dawned. "Oh, I see."

Tŵm felt as awkward as Gwyn. It was not something they had ever discussed. "You mean Evan went with one of these women?"

Gwyn nodded. "Evan wanted to try everything. Everything he couldn't do in Carreg-y-Bedd, smoking fags, coming back intoxicated..."

Tŵm was pragmatic. "Oh well, I suppose he thought that as he might get killed, he'd better find out what it was like."

This comment prompted Gwyn to find his voice. "Evan never thought he was going to be killed. He thought he was going to live forever. Said he'd be dashed if any Hun was going to get near him."

Tŵm, curious, couldn't resist the next question. "And did you...?"

"Of course not." Gwyn was horrified. "Evan vanished a few times before we left for the port but I never went with him. I couldn't let my Mam and Tad down like that. They would've been ashamed of me if they'd known."

"But they wouldn't have known," Tŵm argued, logical as always.

"But I would've known," Gwyn had replied. "I couldn't have lived with myself."

Tŵm steered the conversation into safer waters. "How did he get back into the camp?"

"Well, a lot of the camp was fenced in with posts and wire but not all of it. It was too big. So Evan just found an unfenced section and then dodged back in. That part was easy. I don't know how he found his way round the camp. I was always getting lost but he seemed to have a map in his head. He never got caught, though one time it was a close-run thing."

"Why, what happened?" Tŵm asked.

"Evan came back later than usual that time. Told me later he'd been having a specially good time and winked at me. It was almost dawn when he got back and the camp was stirring. The sergeant had already been in to make sure we were getting up. Evan's bed was empty and made up. The sergeant was asking where Evan was when Evan came in behind him. The sergeant barked out, 'Griffiths, where've you been?' Evan was as cool as a cucumber. 'Caught short I'm afraid, Sarge.' But the sergeant was suspicious. 'You seem to have found time to get kitted out.' Evan was so quick. 'Can't go wanderin' about with no clothes on, can I Sarge?' The sergeant didn't give up easily. 'Your bunk is made up.' And do you know what Evan said? He said, 'Just efficient, aren't I?' He was brilliant. I couldn't have carried it off. I really couldn't. It was bare faced cheek, that's what it was. And do you know he got clean away with it."

Tŵm smiled again at recalling their conversation. He could just imagine it. Evan had the cheek of the devil. Maybe that was why Gwyn had told him about it, because he wanted Tŵm to share in the memory of Evan's sense of mischief, to remember how special he was. Though he was happy to talk about the training camp, Gwyn was reluctant to share his experiences at the Front. Tŵm, curious to find out what it was really like on the battlefields, had initially interrogated Gwyn but mostly to no avail.

"Oh, come on Gwyn. Tell me what it was really like there. Did you shoot any Germans? Did you see anybody killed?"

Gwyn had been patient but firm. "Tŵm, trust me. You don't want to know. You don't know how lucky you are not to know what it was like."

Now, at nearly twenty, Tŵm squirmed at the naïve insensitivity of the questions from his younger self. During the years since Armistice Day, more and more news had emerged in the papers of the conditions suffered by the soldiers. He himself, had seen a cripple, an ex-soldier with one artificial leg begging on the streets of Wrexham and another wearing a tin mask, covering up what remained of a face. Gwyn had been right. Some things it was better not to know.

Twm dragged his attention back to Olwen. She had moved on. He caught the name, Bethan.

"Our Bethan?" he asked.

"Yes, of course."

Twm flushed, hoping that Olwen hadn't realised that he hadn't been paying attention. He struggled to catch up.

"Always coming over here she was. All sorts of excuses she made. Out for a walk, bringing extra cakes from the baking, chapel news, messages from her mother and so it went on. Then once she got here, it would only be a couple of minutes before she asked, 'Is Evan here?' You probably didn't realise Twm. No reason why you should. Real sweet on him she was."

Twm was astonished. "Bethan? Our Bethan? Bethan liked Evan? Are you sure? Evan never mentioned it to me."

"Well, he wouldn't would he? You and Gwyn would've teased him unmercifully. I think he was embarrassed about it. Tried to disappear when she turned up. I had to remind him about his manners. If I'm honest, I don't think he was that keen on her. Bethan took life a bit too seriously for Evan."

Twm silently agreed. Bethan viewed mirth as needless frivolity. A match with Evan would not have been made in heaven. He remembered that Evan had once called her 'boring'.

On his way home Twm had plenty of time to think about what Olwen had said. He still found it almost impossible to believe. Bethan had never shown the slightest interest in the opposite sex as far as he was aware. Not that he had ever thought about his sister's feelings much. They didn't have a lot in common. Bethan had low horizons, fully content with her world of home, farm, village and chapel, whereas he wanted so much more. Twm had never imagined her leaving home, even to get married. Now that he was thinking about it, he supposed that he envisaged her as a future maiden aunt even though she was only just twenty-two. The others were different. Now that he had stopped for a moment to consider the future of his siblings and discounting Siôn as too young, it seemed to him likely that Brad would marry a suitable farmer's wife and have a brood of children. He couldn't see Caron spending her life alone either. She was his favourite, there was no question. Lively and intelligent, she shared his zest for exploring life's opportunities. Too young to have been badly affected by world events, she bubbled with optimism. Life to her was an exciting adventure story unfolding page by page. If Evan had lived, she not Bethan, would have been the perfect match for him. Tŵm worried about Caron. He knew, because they had spoken about it, that Carreg-y-Bedd stifled her, that she found the chapel dull and more than slightly menacing. The strict régime of Cwyn-y-Gwynt meant that she "couldn't be me" she had once told him. He hoped that they would both have the chance to fly the nest at some point. Not that he wanted to abandon his family. Far from it. But their dreams were not his dreams.

Still, it was no use worrying about the future at the moment. There were too many problems in the present. First and foremost, was he going to tell anyone about the fight or was he going to keep it a guilty secret? The burden of undivulged knowledge continued to weigh him down, growing heavier by the day. It would be such a relief to tell what he knew, whether to the police or to Richard Owen or both. But lightening his own load by telling someone else may just make matters worse. Worse for Ruth Parry and certainly worse for him.

The nagging intruder that was always there at the back of his mind engulfed him; the dread that he may be arrested as a criminal, his family's wrath, the fear of public notoriety, the destruction of his dreams. In such a circumstance, Dr. Owen could not vouch for his protégé's honesty and recommend him for medical school.

He forced himself to work through his dilemma. His conclusion was soundly deduced. If he had been going to broadcast the news of Gwyn's fight with the Morgans on the evening of Maundy Thursday then he should have done it first, not last, when Gwyn's body had been found. To explain now would cause endless trouble and would, in all likelihood, prove futile.

He mulled over each point in turn. Knowing that Gwyn had been fighting with the Morgan brothers would hardly improve the situation for Ruth Parry, especially when she found out the reason. He owed it to Gwyn not to cause more suffering for Ruth. She was so proud of both Thomas and Gwyn. Better that he took the strain than pass it on to Ruth. She simply couldn't be put through any more, not a police investigation, not a reliving of the Easter events, not a revisiting of the idea that Gwyn might have taken an ultimately final decision and most of all not something that shook her unswerving pride in her son.

The continual threats from Cadoc were empty ones he was sure, designed purely to protect Cadoc himself. Cadoc didn't trust him that was certain. He clearly didn't grasp the reason why Tŵm was so unlikely to inform on him, probably because compassion for others did not figure highly in his approach to life.

He reasoned too that if Gethin or Cadoc hadn't pushed Gwyn into the pool as a follow up to the Thursday fight, then the previous tussle was irrelevant, a red herring that could focus attention in the wrong direction. He forced himself to face the worst scenario: that the Morgans did push Gwyn into the pool and had not been arrested. But try as he might Tŵm could not believe that of them. Ruffians they certainly were, but killers? Surely not.

He tried to stand back and examine why he couldn't believe that of them. Was he fooling himself? Trying to give himself an excuse not to act because it could destroy his own life? He couldn't rid himself of this thought. It ate away at him like fly strike in lambs. Whatever he decided to do or not do, the indisputable fact was that nothing he did would bring Gwyn back. Gwyn would stay dead. He had to focus now on the living.

The Carreg-y-Bedd show took place in the last week of August just before the harvest. It came as a welcome relief to Tŵm, a limbo of a day when he could pretend life was normal. It proved to be a good day for the Tudors. Bethan won the floral art competition as well as the craft prize for her knitted shawl, Mali won best raspberry jam and Emyr came runner up in the sheepdog trials. He was not best pleased. "Jono should've won. He ran out well but then he had some bad luck. The sheep went off the line of the fetch and were in danger of missing the gate. He realigned them just in time and put them through the fetch gate, but the run suffered for that," he grumbled.

Relaxing in the produce tent, Tŵm enjoyed a strong cup of tea and a light scone laced with fruit.

"Afternoon Tŵm." It was Howell Griffiths, Tan-y-Graig.

"Oh, hello Mr. Griffiths. Enjoying the afternoon?"

"Certainly am. Little Evan's just won the eleven and under show jumping on that bright bay pony I bought him. Moses found it for me. If anyone knows a good horse when he sees one, it's him. Said to me, 'Best to buy a black or bay. Stay away from greys and chestnuts, especially for children.' He was right as well. Little Evan's having a high old time. He's going to hunt the pony this winter. Called him Madoc he has."

Tŵm was pleased. "Just like his Uncle then. Competitive."

"Yes Tŵm. Fearless he is. Just like Evan. Ebrill did well to name him after her brother. You should've seen him in the jump off. Came round the last corner so fast, the pony had to take off on one leg. Shaved three seconds off the previous winning time. I wish Evan could've seen it. He'd have been so proud."

"I'm sure he would've, Mr. Griffiths. Little Evan must be a great comfort to you."

"He is Tŵm, he is. I don't know what we'd do without him. Of course, we love the girls too. And though poor Ebrill couldn't afford to keep her home, it's been a blessing in disguise, her coming back to us. Better for her 'cos she's not by herself and better for us as we can enjoy the grandchildren. Nothing will ever make up for Evan's loss of course but it does help to have them all there."

Tŵm nodded. "Evan wouldn't have wanted everyone to be miserable. He made the most of every moment. He would want you to do the same."

"I know, I know. But losing a son is a terrible thing Tŵm. I hope you never find out what it's like. Children shouldn't go before their parents. It's not the natural order of things. You don't get over it you know. You learn to live with it because you have to but it doesn't get any easier. But God was good enough to give us our grandchildren. The person I feel sorry for is Ruth Parry. She has no-one."

"And to make it worse Mr. Griffiths, we don't know the truth of what happened. I can't stop thinking about that."

"Neither can I Tŵm; neither can I."

The Tudors began the harvest early, starting it in late August since, "The beard is almost dropping off and the fields are already white," Brad told Emyr when he was sent to check it. Unlike the hay gathering which involved most of the local farmers, Emyr called upon help from local cottagers to harvest the barley. He allowed several families to plant potatoes in one of his fields, preparing the ground for them, weeding and hoeing the crop, supplying manure and then delivering the potatoes to them when they were ready to eat. All the cottagers had to do was supply the seed potatoes themselves. In return they worked with Emyr to pick his own potato crop and helped with the barley. In the past, though only three fields at Cwyn-y-Gwynt were laid to barley, scything had been a long, slow job. Even an experienced scyther could only cut an acre in a day. This had caused Emyr to invest in a reaping machine. Drawn by Samson and Delilah, it saved many days of work. After being cut the barley lay on the ground for nine days before binding. Two years after the end of the war, the reaping machine had been joined by a string-tying binder which had greatly reduced the work involved, though the sheaves still had to be built into stooks and left to dry. Some farmers liked to build field ricks, the tâs sopyn, and leave them in the fields until Christmas but Emyr preferred to wait for a dry day, carry the crop to the stack yard and build up the stacks there, thatching them with straw to keep them waterproof and then roping them. This was where Moses and Abram came into their own, Moses teaching his son the old craft. Having the stacks in the stackyard meant that threshing throughout the winter and removing the beards with a jumper was an easier task as the barley did not have to be carried so far. Anything that saved time and effort in the cold months was worth doing. "Better to have more work now and less later," Emyr always said to his sons. "Keep us ahead of ourselves."

"If we get any more ahead, we'll meet ourselves coming back!" laughed Tŵm.

Tŵm, pleased to have a distraction from Gwyn inhabiting his mind, threw himself into the harvest with enthusiasm. Emyr, watching him, thought to himself that maybe he would make a farmer of Tŵm yet. Though he had sympathy with his son's plans, there was no doubting that Mali had a point. Tŵm was the eldest son, he was a good lad, honest and hard-working. Cwyn-y-Gwynt would rightly be his one day.

For once the two brothers worked together as one. It was good to see it. Emyr sent up a silent prayer of thanks to the God who had allowed him to keep his sons while so many had lost theirs. Just an accident of birth he thought, that meant his sons were too young to go to war. He reflected on Ruth Parry, Howell and Olwen Griffiths, Gwilym Bowen and so many others whose lives had been all but destroyed by forces beyond their control. His family had escaped unscathed. Over the years, as far back as he could remember, the Tudors had been spared any such tragedies. A cloud suddenly passed over the sun, blocking out the sunshine for a moment and Emyr shivered. Perhaps I'm tempting fate he thought. No-one knows what the future holds. It's in the hands of God.

Hedgehog Month

By the time Moses and Abram were roofing the stacks it was well into September. Caron watched them from her bedroom window. Moses' patience and Abram's willingness to learn were evident in the proficient dexterity of their fingers through the long hours of the day. To Mali's surprise Caron was more helpful than usual, offering to take out food and drinks. The first time she went out she was disconcerted by a wink from Moses and a look from Abram that held her gaze. Try as she might, she couldn't stay away. When she knew refreshments were due, she turned up in the kitchen with uncharacteristic reliability. Fortunately, Mali, all too well aware of the necessity for helpers, did not pay much attention. On the final day Caron watched as the two Gypsies finished the last stack, anchoring the ropes with heavy stones that secured the thatch against the strongest of winds.

Emyr went over to talk to them, paid them and came back into the house as they detached the horses from their picket hobbles in the field next to the stackyard and rode through the farm gate. Caron determined to go downstairs so that she could coincidentally meet her father in the kitchen. He would likely know the Gypsies' intentions.

"Good job done there," Emyr was announcing to Mali as she entered the room. "Moses is a true craftsman."

"How much did you have to pay him?" Mali was more concerned with the cost than admiration of his expertise.

"Little enough." Emyr was non-committal. "I'm going to miss his help."

Caron couldn't prevent herself. "What do you mean?"

"They're on their way tomorrow. That's the way of the Romanies. They've stayed here longer than usual. Itching to move on I would think. Anyway, as Moses says, he has to follow the work. He's in demand during the harvest with those special skills of his."

Caron felt a lurch of fear. "Where are they going?"

"I don't know. I didn't ask."

It was too late in the day for Caron to even contemplate finding an excuse to go out. The next day she rose early, caught up Jac and was out before anyone else was up. This time she rode directly to the camp, picking her way purposefully down the track as the early morning light shafted through the beech trees, no longer caring what excuse she was going to give when she got there.

She was too late.

All that was left was the circle of grey ash that had been a living fire. Other than that, the only sign of habitation was flattened grass, some broken branches and a faint smell of what Caron recognised as chicken mess. She dismounted to touch the ash. It was lukewarm. She trickled the powder through her fingers watching as the slight breeze made it drift through the air, coughing as the dust tickled her throat. The Gypsies must have left while it was still dark. Angry with herself for not getting up even earlier, she remounted and made her way back down the path. Now that she was looking, she could see clearly where the wheels had sunk into slightly softer ground but once she was back on the lane, she had no idea which way the families had gone. Turning back into the forest, without consciously choosing a direction, she found herself on the path leading up to Moel Coch where she and Abram had raced just three months before. Reliving the experience, she let Jac go and he flew up towards the rock they had used as their finishing line. He stopped by himself, his sides heaving with the effort. Caron slipped off him to give him a rest. Sitting by the rock, she held the reins in her hand. Brushing her hair back from her face she realised her cheeks were wet with tears. As Jac quietly cropped the grass she buried her face into his mane and sobbed for what she had lost.

Caron meandered back to Cwyn-y-Gwynt, deep in her own thoughts. Her late arrival drew down a tirade from Mali. "You're always going off. I wish I had time to ride round the countryside like her ladyship with never a thought in the world for all the jobs that need doing. You don't pull your weight Caron. I'm going to make you a list of jobs for today. Bethan can have some time off. She does twice the work you do. You can start by taking out all the rugs, hanging them over the line and giving them a good beating. I need to get jobs like that done before the weather turns and the nights draw in."

"Can I help? That sounds like fun." Siôn stood in front of Caron, his face upturned to hers.

She laughed despite herself. "It isn't, but yes you can." Taking Siôn's hand, she said, "Come on, we'll get the bedside rag rugs first."

Later Twm found them in the garden, covered in dust. "The rugs are clean but we're filthy," Caron told him. "I'm going to have to get out the bath later, heat some water and wash my hair as well." She ran her hand through her thick curls. "My hair feels stiff with dust."

"You look exhausted Caron." Tŵm's concern was evident in his voice.

"Well, I had an early start, a long ride and now this. Mam's got a long list for me yet."

"You make sure you get a drink and a sit down before you start on the next job. You're really pale."

He looked more closely at his sister. Underneath the coating of dust her skin was as white as parchment.

"Honestly Tŵm, please don't worry, I'm fine."

"Well, you look after yourself. I'm going away for a few days."

Caron was startled. A member of the family leaving Cwyn-y-Gwynt was a more than unusual occurrence. "Really! Where are you going?"

"To Anglesey. Now the corn harvest's finished there's a bit of a breathing space. Tad and Brad can manage carting the straw and I'll be back before we start to bring in the potatoes and later on harvest the oats."

Unaccountably Caron felt a tremor of panic. She didn't want Tŵm to go away even for a short time, especially now that Abram was no longer there. She relied on his dependable presence, she realised, far more than she did on Mam and Tad. But she was being selfish, she told herself.

"I'm going to Dr. Owen's family in Newborough. He's arranged for me to stay with them again. Remember, I stayed with them once before when Gwyn came with me during the summer of '19 just after the 'flu epidemic had passed its peak. I'd been helping the doctor day and night so he said I deserved a holiday and arranged for me to go to his parents. He told me to take Gwyn for company. He said it would do Gwyn good too after his spell at the Front."

"Of course, I remember. I wouldn't forget that you went to Llanddwyn Island would I?"

Tŵm smiled. "Ever the romantic, Caron!" He knew how badly his sister wanted to visit Llanddwyn.

"I wish I could take you with me and then you could see it for yourself but I can't ask to bring another visitor. It would be impolite. I really enjoyed staying with the Owen family and I know you'd like them too. They were so good to me. With Dr. Owen's father being a doctor too he was happy to talk to me about new developments in medicine. He's still practising but doesn't do as much as he used to now that his youngest son, Huw, is living with them. It's so sad. Huw lost an eye and suffered shrapnel injuries in the war and takes some looking after, I believe. Dr. Owen told me that his brother has severe pain in his back as the surgeons couldn't remove all the shrapnel."

"Why are you going this time?" Caron asked.

"Oh, Caron, I haven't given up on wanting a career as a doctor despite Mam being against it. You'd think she'd be pleased but when I raise it, then all I get is that I'm the oldest son and as such will inherit Cwyn-y-Gwynt. But there's plenty of farmers who pass on the farm to a younger son. Some first-born sons move to another farm when they get married and then a younger son farms with his parents until they become too old to work. Then he takes over. But even if I were the younger son, I still don't think she'd approve of me doing anything except farming. To Mam, the farm matters far more than Brad and I. All she wants is more land and then of course it takes more people to farm it. But Mam won't listen. You know what she's like. More land; more status." Twm paused, then laughed. "The funny thing is that if I got married and brought a new wife here to Cwyn-y-Gwynt, I don't think Mam would like it one bit. She's wouldn't take kindly to another woman in her kitchen. She'd still have to rule the roost!"

"You're right there!" Caron agreed. She felt guilty. She was aware of the ongoing arguments but had been too wrapped up in her own problems to pay much attention. "You're not thinking of getting married are you Twm?"

He laughed again. "No, of course not. I'm far too young and anyway I haven't got a girlfriend. I don't want to get married for a fair, few years yet."

"I'll bet Mam's not best pleased at you going to Anglesey. She'll think Dr. Owen's family will encourage you to be a doctor even more."

"You're right there Caron. She wasn't best pleased. But I told her that it would be rude to turn down the invitation when they were being so kind to me because I'd lost my friend."

Caron changed the subject. "Why can't a daughter take over the farm Twm? Why does it have to be a son?"

"It can Caron, and it sometimes is, especially if there's only daughters in the family. Think of Cwyn-y-Gwynt. Nain told me it came down to her and then, when she passes on, it will be Mam's and then, from what Mam says, mine. But in my experience, it's usually sons as they can do the hard, physical work outside. That's not fit work for women. Daughters either marry and their husbands move in to look after the farm or they go to live with their husband on his farm. Those who don't marry, stay to look after their Mam and Tad in their old age. That's the way of the world."

"I think girls are just as good at working as boys, Twm. Look how Howell Griffiths had a Land Army girl to help in 1917 when Evan left for the Front. Martha, I think her name was. He told Tad she was as strong as any man. It didn't matter what he asked her to do, picking stones, cutting hay, she was always willing to try her best. He only paid her a pound a week plus her keep."

"Yes, you're right, he did say that," Twm replied. "But despite what you say there's some work that's too heavy for women. Most of them are just not as strong as men. But they can still do important jobs. In the war some women made shells in the munition factories. Tough and dangerous work it was; others joined the fire brigade or drove ambulances. Women doing men's work and what's more doing it well, means that now the war's over, things are changing. Nothing's ever going to be the same. We've got women jurors, women studying for degrees at Oxford and our first woman M.P. And women can vote now. That's a huge change."

"Not unless they're over thirty and quite rich!"

"True, but the suffragettes are fighting to change that. It won't be long until all women will be able to vote, mark my words!"

"That would be quite something, Twm. I'd love to be able to vote. I'd vote for Lloyd George. At least he's Welsh."

"He's a fine Welshman Caron. We owe him a lot. Played a big part in winning the war if you ask Tad, though not everyone agrees. Dr. Owen wouldn't for instance. He's a Conservative through and through."

"How do you know Twm? Did he tell you?"

"No, he didn't but he said once that Lloyd George was responsible for reducing spending on defence and that meant we were short of armaments when the war started. He said that Lloyd George helped the sick and the poor but he left Britain vulnerable. Dr. Owen was quite angry and said that the cuts undoubtedly caused more casualties at the beginning of the conflict.

Tad has a different view of Lloyd George. In 1915 we ran out of artillery shells. The papers said it was a national scandal and that many of our brave soldiers lost their lives because of it. Tad says that Lloyd George put everything right because once he was made Minister of Munitions, he set up new factories and employed more people so that production of shells increased massively. He was so successful that he became Prime Minister the next year."

"Well in my view, it's simple," Caron replied. "We won the war and he was our leader."

"We certainly did. And let's hope we never face another one in our lifetimes."

Caron, realising that Twm must be thinking of Evan, changed the subject.

"So how will visiting Dr. Owen's family help you to become a doctor Twm?"

"Dr. Owen Senior has got an extensive library of medical books and he's been kind enough to say that he'll lend me some. I want to keep up with my studies as much as I can so that when I do go away to train, I won't be behind all the others."

"It doesn't sound much fun to me Tŵm. Whenever I've looked at your books, they seem very boring. Give me a good story any day."

Tŵm smiled. "I find them more exciting than one of your yarns. The pace of development in medical knowledge nowadays is nothing short of astounding. Dr. Owen was telling me he's read about research into diabetes in Canada. Two doctors have discovered a substance called insulin that can bring a patient out of a coma. I can't wait to go to Anglesey again. Dr. Owen is taking me to Rhyl in his new car to catch the train. He said I can try driving it on the way. I'm very excited about that! The Owen family have said they'll collect me from Llangefni station."

Mali's shrill voice intruded. "Caron, Caron, where are you? Haven't you finished that job yet? I need you to peel potatoes and carrots. Now!"

Caron sighed with resignation. "You have a good time Tŵm."

"I hope to. But it won't be the same without Gwyn. It will bring back so many memories."

Two days later, Tŵm was sitting on a rocky outcrop at Llanddwyn Island. He had left the substantial stone house near Newborough early, made his way down the lane that led to the sea, through Newborough Warren and then on to the beach. After a lengthy walk along the shoreline, he finally reached his destination: Llanddwyn Island.

Just as Gwyn and he had done years earlier, Tŵm climbed the steep path edged with white stones up to the lighthouse, Tŵr Mawr, and gazed out towards Ireland. Vague recollections of a school lesson resurfaced. Something about ancient druids transporting white stones to sacred sites so that reflected moonlight would illuminate their rituals. To the south west, the protective arm of the Llŷn Peninsula curved round the slate grey sea while, to the south east, Snowdonia could be glimpsed at times through the morning mist. Tŵm was pleased he'd started out so early. With only the cormorants and sandpipers for company, he at last found the isolation he craved.

Was it really only three years ago that he had visited this place with Gwyn? That had been such a different day. The last time he had seated himself on these rocks, the sun beat down on his back, perspiration trickled down his brow and he was relieved to remove his knitted socks and bathe his sweaty feet in the cool waves. They had walked along the beach in the warmth of an early September sun, high in the sky. The island had not looked to be far. "Let's walk to the lighthouse," Gwyn had suggested. It had been deceptive, much further than they thought. It was hard work walking on the sand in the heat, carrying fishing gear.

By the time they got there, Twm was glad to throw off his clothes and swim out from a sandy cove. A strong swimmer, he revelled in the silkiness of the water cleansing his skin, soothing his tired muscles. Gwyn sat on the beach watching him, then paddled idly in the edges of the sea lapping gently against the shore. Later they drank from a spring and fell on the ham sandwiches, raspberries and oat cakes provided by Mrs. Owen. Surprised to find not only the lighthouse but also cottages, which had been homes to the pilots who guided slate carrying ships through the sandbanks of the Menai Straits, they explored further. Near the ruins of an ancient church, they discovered two incongruously modern crosses. One of them, the Celtic cross, commemorated the death of St. Dwynwen in 465 AD. Twm knew the legend well. Nain had recounted it one winter evening as they sat by a smouldering log fire in the oak beamed parlour. Caron couldn't have been much more than six years old. Twm couldn't remember why they were there. It wasn't usual to light a fire in the parlour. Normally they would all gather around the kitchen range. Neither could he remember why the rest of the family were not there. In the sing-song voice, she reserved for stories, Nain settled herself between her two grandchildren and began.

"It was deep in the mists of time when Welsh princes ruled ancient kingdoms. Dwynwen, daughter of King Brychan Brycheiniog of Brecon fell in love with a prince who, hearing tales of magical Welsh mountains, had sailed over from Ireland to see them for himself. Maelon Dafodrill he was named. As a matter of courtesy, he visited the court of King Brycheiniog to bring greetings from Ireland. The king greeted him with feasting and dancing. He had many beautiful daughters but Dwynwen was the most beautiful of all. She had skin as white as a dove and hair as gold as ripe corn in the summer sun. Tall and graceful, her emerald eyes looked deep into Maelon's. She fell in love at first sight."

"Emerald, Nain? Were they the same colour as mine?" Caron was already deeply involved in the story. Twm smiled at the memory. He had always preferred to listen quietly but Caron could never wait patiently to find out what happened next.

"They were child, they were. Just the same as yours. That's because you are a true child of Wales. I wouldn't be surprised if you were not descended from King Brycheiniog himself."

Nain continued. "So Dwynwen fell in love with Maelon but the king had made other plans for her. He had promised her to a suitor, another Welsh prince who was rich and had a strong army to help Brycheiniog protect his kingdom from the attacks of English invaders. Dwynwen knew of her father's wishes but she did not love this prince. Secretly she decided to become a nun rather than marry him. For Dwynwen was not only beautiful, she was good and kind. Her heart was pure as the driven snow and she could not bear to marry a man whom she did not love.

Foolishly she revealed her love for Maelon to her father. The king was furious. He forbad her to marry Maelon and ordered her to marry a prince of his choice. One dark night Dwynwen met Maelon secretly beneath the castle walls, declared her love for him and told him what her father had said. She hoped beyond hope that Maelon would ask her to escape with him far over the sea to Ireland. But her hopes were dashed. Maelon rejected her, saying that their union was not possible. He told Dwynwen that her father, the King, would follow them with his knights, that they would both be killed and that it would cause a war between Wales and Ireland. No matter how much Dwynwen wept and pleaded, Maelon would not give in."

"What a cruel man, Nain."

"Well, maybe cariad, it may seem so but wait to hear what happens next. In tears, Dwynwen fled deep into the forest surrounding the castle. Finding a hidden glade, she knelt and prayed to God to help her overcome her despair and erase Maelon from her memory. Then she laid down her head on a mossy bank and cried herself to sleep. She dreamt that an angel came to her in the depths of the night and gave her a potion for Maelon to drink. When she woke the next morning, the rays of the early morning sun glanced off a glass phial, the colour of violets. Thinking it was a love potion, Dwynwen made her way back to the castle and at the next meal she poured a glass of wine for Maelon and mixed in the love draught. Tragically, instead of Maelon falling desperately in love with her, he turned into a block of freezing ice."

"Served him right," Caron broke in, speaking with certainty.

Nain continued. "Heartbroken, Dwynwen fled on her beautiful white steed to Ynys Llanddwyn. Leaving her horse to graze, she walked down to the sea. A path led her to a magical cove where she drank deeply from a spring emerging from a cleft in the rocks that edged the tiny bay. The fresh water, bubbling up from the time-worn stones which formed a pool in a natural rock basin, was like fine wine and clear as crystal. Dwynwen looked down into the water as though it were a mirror. In its depth she could see a single golden fish. By the light of the silver moon, she lay down by the life-giving spring. Again, she prayed to God and then was lulled to sleep by the sound of the waves breaking gently against the shore. That night she dreamt that God would grant her three wishes. When, at sunrise, the screaming of the gulls woke her, she remembered her vivid dream.

She knelt down on the soft sand and committed her wishes to the gentle breeze. Her first wish was for Maelon to return to the warmth of life. The second wish was for her memories of him to vanish into the sea mist so that her suffering would be soothed."

Caron could not contain herself, Twm remembered. "And the third?"

"That all lovers who visit Llanddwyn will discover if they will live happily ever after."

"What happened to Dwynwen, Nain?"

"She lived contentedly on Llanddwyn Island for the rest of her life. All three wishes were granted. Maelon returned to life and to Ireland and married an Irish lass. Her other suitor married one of her sisters so Dwynwen's father, the king, got the wealth and the protection he craved. He allowed Dwynwen to stay on Llanddwyn. She became a nun and built a church and a convent there. When she was dying, she asked to be taken to where she could see, through a cleft in the rock, the sun setting over the sea towards Ireland."

At this point, Caron had begun to weep. Twm recalled that she said, "But that's so sad. I wanted the story to have a happy ending."

"God doesn't always give us what we want cariad and sometimes that is for the best. We don't always know God's plans for us. The story does have a happy ending even if it isn't a romantic one for her. Dwynwen became St. Dwynwen, the patron saint of lovers. Since her death, pilgrim lovers have visited the island through the centuries hoping to find out if they will live happily ever after, Dwynwen's third wish. So, though she did not marry Maelon, she wanted other lovers to find the happiness that eluded her."

"How do the lovers find out if they're going to be happy in the future, Nain?"

"Well, any sweethearts who visit Llanddwyn must search for Dwynwen's sacred spring, for the golden fish predicts the fortunes of each couple. Each man is tested to see if he will stay true to his lady love. Remember Maelon did not stay true to Dwynwen so she did not want other women to suffer the same fate."

"How are they tested, Nain?"

"The lady throws a handful of breadcrumbs into the water, then lays a silk handkerchief on the surface. If the golden fish swims to the surface and makes the water bubble then fortune will be fair and good luck will follow. If the water stays still, then the woman must beware as her loved one is likely to be unfaithful to her in the future."

"What would she do Nain, if she found that out?"

"Well, she would have to make a decision, wouldn't she? She could stay with him and hope that he doesn't break her heart or she could choose to leave him and avoid despair in the future."

"What would you do Nain?"

"I would trust St. Dwynwen, rather than any man."

"Then I would do the same."

"Even if the magic fish makes the water ripple, there is one more thing that the lovers must do to secure a happy future."

"What?" asked Caron

"Both the lovers must search the beaches for a white pebble shimmering with light. They must each take a pebble with them and keep it safe."

"Why?"

"Because the pebbles are love tokens from the isle of St. Dwynwen. They cast a spell to make sure that love will last."

"Do you know why the pebbles sparkle Caron?"

She shook her head.

"It's because aeons ago, at the birth of the world, moonlight was trapped deep inside them."

Twm remembered every detail of Nain's story. He had heard it many times as Caron asked to listen to it again and again. She never tired of it. Nain was careful not to repeat it when Mali was there. Once Mali had come into the kitchen unexpectedly to find Nain assuring Caron again that, with her emerald eyes, she was sure to be descended from a Welsh princess, probably one of Dwynwen's sisters.

Mali had exploded with temper. "Filling the child's head with such rubbish. Giving her ideas above her station. I won't have it." Twm had noticed that after that Nain had been careful to tell Caron her tales when Mali was safely out of the way.

Twm looked out towards the western isle. Older and wiser now, he was aware that Nain had embellished the original story for Caron's benefit, making it her own in the way that only she could. Nain really did have a talent for storytelling, thought Twm, picturing Caron's rapt expression.

Gwyn had asked, "Who's Dwynwen?" when he saw the inscription on the cross. Tŵm had treated him to a potted version of Nain's tale rather expecting Gwyn to scoff at it. To his surprise Gwyn's reaction had been entirely different.

"It's easy to believe a love story in a setting such as this," he had said, sweeping his arm across the landscape. In the afternoon, after they had caught several fine mackerel and a couple of bass to take back for the evening meal, Gwyn had settled down to sketch. The picture he produced was striking. The forefront was dominated by the huge cross. In the background was the lighthouse, framed by a stormy sea. Despite the clear, sunny day and the tourists enjoying the beaches, Gwyn had drawn a threatening sky, empty beaches, desolate rocks. "I wanted to sketch Dwynwen's anguish," he explained.

"It looks more like Calgary than Wales," Tŵm had commented.

"There are many ways to suffer, Tŵm," Gwyn had answered as he rolled up his picture. Later, when they had admired his handiwork, he had given it to the Owen family as a thank you present. Framed, it had pride of place on their parlour wall.

It was certainly too chilly to swim today. Tŵm watched a young sandpiper wading in the shallows. It wouldn't be long before it left for warmer climes, he knew. He rather envied it. Welsh winters were more to be endured than enjoyed. Against the background sound of the breaking waves, he could hear the strident calls of the oystercatchers as they searched for cockles. On the ridges of the rocks the guillemots sat huddled against the wind, hunched up like old soldiers. Tŵm picked up a handful of wave-washed pebbles and allowed them to trail through his fingers. Amidst the kaleidoscope of colours, a few sparkled bright white. What was it Nain had said about white stones? He searched his memory. It came back to him. Lovers, intent on a happy future, should take one home as a talisman. He remembered that Nain had once told Caron that the pebbles glistened with frozen moonlight from long, long ago, trapped deep within the stones.

Well, there was no point in him taking home a stone. He did not have a lover or even the prospect of one. Not that he was interested in finding a lover in any case. Tŵm had a different focus. His vocation gnawed inside him. He knew that hunger could only be relieved by fulfilling his dream. Picking out a hunk of white quartz, he stood up and hurled it as far out to sea as he could, watching it arc through the air before disappearing under the surface of the water. Having second thoughts, he searched for another, this time carefully selecting it from the myriad of pebbles, strewn amongst the lines of seaweed washed up onto the sand. The one he chose, though not quite a Snowdon Diamond, was smooth, egg shaped, glittering like crystal in the gloom of the overcast morning. He would take it back as a present for Caron. She would love it. She had questioned him eagerly after his return from Ynys Llanddwyn that last time when he had visited with Gwyn. "Did you see Dwynwen's spring? The golden fish? And the cleft in the rock where she gazed on the sunset as she faded away?"

He hadn't. He and Gwyn had been more intent on hunting mackerel than chasing myths. This time he wouldn't disappoint her. He would take her back a symbol of eternal love, blessed by St. Dwynwen herself. Feeling obligated, he started searching for the well. After a long time scrambling on rocks made slippy by wet lichen, he discovered a likely site on the north side of the island, below a cleft rock. The small pool was edged by craggy rocks, shading the surface. Water cascaded from the pool down into the sea below. On one side, marram grass, triumphing over the rock face, grew down to the rim itself. Tŵm smiled to himself. There was no sign of a golden fish or indeed of any fish at all. To retain some stability, Tŵm grabbed a hunk of grass and reached down with his other hand into the pool itself. The water was icy cold. At least he could tell Caron that he had visited the shrine of St. Dwynwen. Last time, with Gwyn, they hadn't even tried to search for it. By the time Gwyn had finished his sketch and they had caught their fish, they had been obliged to make their way back so that Mrs. Owen had time to fillet and cook their spoils for the evening meal.

Feeling that he had fulfilled his duty, Tŵm wandered back to the cove he had visited earlier. Now he had space to reflect, he tried to piece together the past, hoping to make sense out of the present.

Gwyn had wanted to sketch Dwynwen's emotion, explaining that he wanted to capture Dwynwen's heartbreak at her lover's rejection. He had certainly succeeded. The picture ached with despair. Tŵm had objected.

"But Gwyn, Dwynwen found happiness here. Maelon vanished from her memory, she devoted herself to God and to the joy of other lovers."

"Eventually yes. But she had to go through the heartbreak first and that was what she felt when she first arrived in Llanddwyn. It's my first visit here too so I feel in tune with her."

Tŵm was shocked. "Why on earth would you feel in tune with her? You haven't had your heart broken."

"You make all these assumptions Tŵm. You don't know everything about my life." His anger made him more open than usual. "I know what it is to be in love."

Twm stared at Gwyn in absolute amazement. A lifetime lay within the three years that separated the two friends. In that chasm lay the battlefields of Northern France and, it seemed, an affair of the heart.

"Did you fall in love in France, Gwyn?"

Gwyn laughed despite his previous irritation. Twm was still just a boy.

"Oh, Twm you have no idea... no, of course I didn't. My whole focus was survival. It took all my energy just to get through each day."

"Then... ?"

Twm's question hung in the air between them. And that's where it stayed. Gwyn had no intention of answering it. Shrugging it off as, "Not important," he changed tack. "Bet I can make one of these stones do more bounces than you!"

"Bet you can't," Twm retorted searching round for suitable flat missiles. After several disputes, fifteen minutes later they declared a draw. The foam atop the rippling waves had made it impossible to agree accurate counts.

The moment of confidence had vanished. Gwyn had retreated behind his personal dry stone wall. For him to remove a stone and allow his friend a glimpse into his mind was a rare occurrence. Even with Twm, he often preferred to erect a barrier.

They had walked back at a leisurely pace, conversation rendered unnecessary by the scrunch of the sand under their feet, the lapping of the waves and the screaming of the gulls. Only a few people were left on the beach; some walking dogs, others gathering belongings. Comfortable in Twm's company, Gwyn had never felt the need to fill in the silences. Drilled in good manners, he could however be sociable when required and that evening it was required. Conversation over dinner centred on places worth visiting in Anglesey such as Beaumaris Castle.

"I'll take you there in the horse and trap," offered William Owen stroking his moustache. "The cycle car will only take two. I must buy a proper car soon. Something more solid. It would suit us much better."

Twm smiled. The doctor loved his engines and had been one of the first to buy a cycle car, maintaining that he needed it to reach his patients more quickly. Twm had seen him tinkering with the gearbox, absorbed in the task. It was as much a toy as a necessity, Twm thought.

The doctor began planning the next day. "Beaumaris is the last of Edward I's castles. He never actually finished building it. We Welsh were rebelling against unjust English rule and Edward decided that a new castle crammed full of soldiers would be a good way of keeping us under control. Newborough has a special link with the castle because the population here is descended from the notorious residents of Llanfaes."

"Why notorious? And where's Llanfaes?" asked Gwyn showing a polite interest.

"Because Llanfaes put up the most resistance of all and it was situated right next to where Beaumaris is now. It was a flourishing royal township by all accounts. When Edward finally overcame the opposition, he refused to allow the settlement to exist. He forced all the people to move to a completely new settlement which was named Newborough. I like to think that my family have inherited the courage and tenacity of their mediaeval ancestors. We have been here for generations. Their blood courses through our veins."

William Owen struck the table with a clenched fist. He would not have sounded out of place in the chapel pulpit, thought Tŵm.

"Why didn't Edward complete the castle?" asked Tŵm.

"Because he had trouble with the Scots and they took his attention away from Wales. The English were always trying to impose their rule on the Celts but even if they sometimes triumphed by brute force, they were never able to conquer our spirit. Still can't. I expect you saw plenty of the Welsh spirit Gwyn when you were off fighting the Hun. In the Royal Welch, weren't you?"

Gwyn nodded. Tŵm saw the panic in Gwyn's eyes. Tŵm knew he would not want to be questioned about his battlefield experiences.

Launching in to rescue his friend he rapidly changed the subject. "The history of Anglesey is fascinating Dr. Owen. Are there any other ancient sites?"

Dr. Owen, pleased the boys were showing an interest in local history, regaled them with stories about ancient burial chambers. "There's one just up the road at Llandaniel. It's called Bryn Celli Ddu. I've heard a rumour that it's going to be excavated sometime in the next few years. I'll take you there if you like."

Tŵm and Gwyn had enjoyed not only a visit to Beaumaris with a stop at Llanddaniel on the way but also had been taken over the Menai Bridge to Caernarfon Castle, another of Edward I's strongholds.

The screech of a seagull jolted Tŵm out of his reverie. He could feel a fine drizzle brushing his cheeks. He must get back. After all he was supposed to be scouring Dr. Owen's library for books that would extend his knowledge. Looking up he saw threatening dark clouds approaching over the sea like men of arms appearing over the horizon.

Thrusting Caron's moon stone deep into his pocket Tŵm turned his face towards Newborough. It would take a while to walk back.

When Twm returned to Cwyn-y-Gwynt he was pleased he had made the effort to find Caron's stone. She was more than delighted; she was overwhelmed.

"Oh, Twm, it's the nicest present I've ever had. Thank you, thank you, thank you. I'm going to show it to Nain as soon as Mam's out. I'll keep it forever." As an afterthought she added, "Did you have a good time Twm?"

Twm smiled at her pretended interest. "Not in your terms Caron but certainly in mine. I read a number of books, discussed medical matters with Dr. Owen Senior and he's lent me some books to bring home. Our Dr. Owen will return them when I've finished with them."

Caron glanced at several hefty tomes and added, "I'm glad it's not me reading them."

"Well, I won't get much reading done until after the potato and fruit harvests. You'll have to help too."

Caron wrinkled her nose. "I don't mind picking the apples, pears and damsons and I love collecting blackberries in the hedgerows but how I hate potatoes. The soil makes my hands so dirty, rough and sore. Your skin is much tougher than mine with all your work outside."

"I thought you told me girls were just as good as men at all the farming jobs," Twm teased her.

Caron, realising she'd been caught out, tossed her mane of auburn curls, decided not to retaliate and escaped with, "I think Mam's calling me."

One unseasonably warm day, Siôn and Caron were sent to gather the last of the plums. "We have a glut and we can't waste them," Mali had said. The tree was so weighted down that the lower branches brushed the ground and the fruit looked as though the flesh would burst through the skin. Caron and Siôn, seduced by the golden, honeyed scent and the humming of the bees, picked in silence, every so often stopping to devour a rosy globe that burst in their mouths as syrupy, sticky, glorious nectar.

Suddenly Siôn screamed. He had bit into a plum and had disturbed a drunken wasp which had been harmlessly lying back inside a tempting hollow. Siôn, not renowned for his bravery, sobbed as a portion of his bottom lip grotesquely ballooned up to disguise most of the upper. With casual cruelty, Brad mocked his younger brother. "Siôn, you could join the circus as a freak."

"Brad, leave him alone. He's in pain." Caron, putting her arm round Siôn, took him in to the kitchen where she soaked some muslin in vinegar and told Siôn to hold it on the swelling. He hadn't received much sympathy from Mali either, "Serves you right Siôn. It's retribution that's what it is. You shouldn't have been eating the plums, you should've been collecting them."

Siôn curled up into a ball in Nain's armchair in the kitchen. It was the only chair that bore a semblance of comfort with its paper thin, tapestry cushion, Mali not seeing the necessity of being seated on anything other than hard, bare wood.

Harvest Festival proved unsettled and the Tudors thought it prudent to take umbrellas to chapel.

Before they left home, Nain said, "I love the harvest service. I'm going to miss going today but it's threatening to rain and I don't want to get caught in a heavy shower. Always been a wonderful show of produce in Carreg-y-Bedd, there has. Those who are grateful for God's bounty receive a better crop the next year. That's how it works."

"Nain, that just can't be true," replied a sceptical Twm. "You can't mean to say that next year's harvest is dependent on a few prayers in Ebenezer! It's more likely to be affected by the weather!"

Mali intervened. "Twm, hold your tongue. Who do you think sends our weather? Don't you dare contradict your Nain. She's quite right. Think of the Bible. We reap what we sow; Galatians, if I'm not mistaken."

"But Mam that's a metaphor I'm sure." Twm wasn't going to give up.

"Twm, I said that's enough." Mali's tone was threatening. Twm thought better of continuing.

As always Ebenezer's altar was surrounded with plump marrows, slim, elegant runner beans, upright leeks standing proudly to attention, bulging peas, bouquets of cabbages, spotless carrots and scrubbed potatoes, all jostling for position with fine pears tinged with pink, baskets of cooking and eating apples, velvety, purple damsons and Nature's plenty in the form of late, wild bilberries and early blackberries. Vases of brightly coloured dahlias bloomed on window ledges.

Blessing the produce, Daniel Ellis informed the congregation that it would be shared out after the service, "To our old people, those wounded in the war, bereaved families and those stricken by poverty."

Caron, despite her longing for Abram, was enjoying,
'We plough the fields and scatter,
The good seed on the land.'

And as she had always done as a child, she sang lustily.

To Tŵm, it was as though Ebenezer was retaliating as the hymn bore testament to the truth of Nain and Mali's earlier words.

'But it is fed and water'd
By God's Almighty Hand;
He sends the snow in Winter,
The warmth to swell the grain,
The breezes and the sunshine
And soft refreshing rain.'

The congregation, as they left the chapel, found themselves subject to God's refreshment.

"It's a good thing we brought the umbrellas," Emyr commented as people pulled coats over their heads and rushed away to find shelter at home.

"And a good thing my Mam stayed at home," added Mali.

Caron knew it was more than unlikely that Moses and his family would return at this time of year but she couldn't resist glancing across at the empty space that now lay between the chapel and the 'Lamb and Lion'. It was as if the Gypsies had never been there.

No sooner had the plums been dealt with, than the potato harvest started. An early frost meant conditions were perfect. Most of the cottagers had three to five rows of potatoes but first they had to help Emyr with his crop as payment for their soil rent. Caron heaved a sigh as she surveyed the field. Even with the cottager's help the job would take days. But the potatoes were important. Part of the Tudors' staple diet, they also fed the pigs and hens. At least Caron thought, she didn't have to dig. They worked in pairs, one digging, one picking. While Tŵm forked the moist earth, Caron picked out the potatoes and collected them in a basket. As each basket filled up, she carried it to the flat cart by the field gate. Tŵm, noticing her struggling with the weight, offered to carry for her. To Tŵm's surprise, Caron, normally fiercely independent, accepted gratefully.

The work was back-breaking, dirty and tedious. The break seemed a long time coming. Tŵm fell on the hunks of bread, cheese and ham that Mali provided along with cooling draughts of water. "Aren't you hungry?" he asked Caron, noticing that she was only nibbling at the edge of a piece of cheese and hadn't taken any of the bread.

"You have my bread Tŵm. You're bigger than me so you need more. I think I'm too tired to eat much. Don't you just hate doing this?"

She did indeed look exhausted, Tŵm thought. Maybe potato harvesting was too much for her slight frame. "I'd rather be doing something else, yes, but it's got to be done. We have to eat." He glanced sideways at his sister. She was ashen.

"Just look at my hands. Torn to shreds on stones and grit. And my back. It hurts so much. She stood up, leant backwards to try to reverse the damage caused by bending over and used her hands to massage her muscles. "I don't ever remember it as bad as this." Her voice caught in her throat and Tom studied her more intently. Was he imagining it or were there tears in her eyes?

"You have a longer rest sis. You might feel better then."

"No, I can't. Everyone else has re-started. Mam'll be over to put a broom behind us, as she would say. You know what she's like."

Tŵm knew she was right. "Come on then, let's get on. The sooner we start, the sooner we'll finish."

Three hours later they were all still hard at it. Tŵm, concentrating on his shallow digging, tossed the fading tops on one side. He stood up to ease his own aching back, pressing his hands hard against his hip bones. Furrowing his brow against the sun, lower in the sky now, he turned to speak to Caron. "About ten minutes to finish this row, I reckon. Then you can go in and help Mam with the supper."

Caron didn't answer. Bent over, sorting the crop, she stood upright to look at him. Then, to Tŵm's dismay, she swayed and sank to the ground.

"Caron! What's the matter?" Tŵm was with her in two strides. Making use of his medical knowledge he tilted her head back, checked her breathing and felt for her pulse. Placing the basket of potatoes under her feet, he raised her legs to encourage the blood flow to the brain. Gently he stroked her hair back, "Caron, Caron, can you hear me?"

Caron stirred. "What happened?"

"You fainted that's all. You'll be fine but you've worked for too long and need to rest."

"What's happened Tŵm? Is she ill?" For once Bethan seemed genuinely concerned. He saw a number of others looking their way.

"She's fine Bethan. Just overdone it, I think. I'll take her inside."

Caron stood, shakily leaned on Twm's shoulder and together they made their way to the farm kitchen. "Don't tell Mam I fainted; she'll be cross with me again. She's always saying I don't work as hard as Bethan and Bethan's still out there."

"For the moment we'll tell her that you're tired and don't feel well. No need for her to know the detail yet." Twm, of all people, understood what Mali could be like. "But I'm sure Brad or Bethan will tell her what happened. Everybody saw you on the ground."

Mali, busy cooking the supper, lived down to their expectations. "I have no sympathy my girl. It's your own fault if you're tired. You get up at all hours to ride that horse, wasting time. Then you pick at your food. I cook you nourishing, substantial food and then you waste it. Waste, waste, waste. Goodness knows where you'll end up. You've been brought up to know the value of hard work. Everybody else is still out there getting in the harvest and you... you are in here having a *rest*." Her voice dripped with sarcasm.

"Let her alone Mam. She doesn't feel well. Just look at her face."

"Twm you get back out to the field. She's taken you away from your work too."

Twm hesitated, not wanting to leave Caron to Mali's mercy.

"You go Twm. I'll be fine." Caron's voice was firm.

"You heard your sister. Now go on." Mali's tone brooked no argument.

Reluctantly, Twm obeyed. Once he'd gone Mali looked more closely at her daughter. "You look washed out. I want no more nonsense with your meals. You'll eat whatever is put in front of you and you'll eat every scrap. Is that clear?"

"Yes, Mam." Caron just wanted the haranguing to end. She'd have promised anything to stop Mali's strident tones ringing in her ears. She knew Mali was right in one sense. She hadn't been eating. Abram filled her head. The thought of not seeing him again made her feel physically sick. Lovesick. But she knew she must eat. She had drawn attention to herself by fainting and the last thing she wanted was for anyone to suspect that her illness was due to missing Abram. Mali's venom was mild compared to what Caron would be subjected to if her mother knew about her friendship with a Gypsy boy.

Siôn wandered into the kitchen. He was filthy from head to toe, soil caked in his hair and over his boots. "Have you been picking potatoes or rolling in them?" Mali asked. "The best place for you is the pigsty."

Caron laughed. She was relieved at the distraction. "I'll get the bath out shall I Mam and scrub him?"

"Yes, it's about time you did something useful. And Siôn make sure you wash behind your ears or you'll be growing potatoes there as well!"

"Mam, what's fainting? I saw Caron lying down and Bethan said she'd fainted."

"Fainted! Did you faint Caron? Don't you dare not eat properly tonight! It's your own fault you're ill. I've never fainted in my life. Siôn, go outside and take those dirty clothes off. You're dripping soil all over the floor."

At supper, when everyone had cleaned up, Twm noticed Caron eating everything on her plate. Slowly, it was true, but she did eat it, though she had little choice since Mali was watching her like a hawk.

Later Caron put Siôn to bed. "Come on you, up the wooden hill. I can see your eyes closing."

Twm came up behind her. "You look better. I'm pleased you were sensible and ate all your food. You can't work hard on an empty stomach. It's the body's fuel you know. Why weren't you eating anyway?"

"I don't know Twm. I just felt poorly and was off my food. I feel much better now. A good night's sleep and I'll be as right as rain in the morning. I'll be off to bed as soon as I've read Siôn the next few pages of a Morgan Humphreys adventure story."

"I'm off soon myself. It's been a long day." In reality Twm wanted some thinking time. It had been a tiring day but Twm was both strong and young. His body could take the punishment of hard graft, even enjoy it in a strange kind of way. Physical exhaustion was pleasurable in that it delivered the satisfaction of a day well spent and dreamless slumber. It was certainly less draining than mental acrobatics where tortuous thoughts were not only dispiriting but resulted in him tossing and turning through the small hours.

Once in bed, he thought back to that conversation with Gwyn on Llanddwyn. It was bothering him. He had an insistent feeling that there was something significant about it; something he was missing. What was it Gwyn had said? First, he had admitted to being 'in tune' with Dwynwen. Then astonishingly he had confessed that he had been, or was, in love. He had spoken of suffering and heartbreak. Twm dug deep to find Gwyn's exact words. "I know what it is to be in love." Who on earth could Gwyn have been in love with? And if it wasn't during the war but afterwards, then Gwyn had to have fallen in love in Carreg-y- Bedd. He would surely have known if Gwyn had been courting a girl. There would have been no need to keep it secret. Twm undertook a quick mental survey of girls in the village of a similar age to Gwyn. It didn't take long. Harriet and Alice Craddock were way out of reach. Alice was affianced to a military man from Scarborough while Harriet spent most of her time with friends in London. He supposed it would have been possible for Gwyn to yearn for one of them from a distance but it wasn't likely. He would never have encountered them for long enough to develop a passion. Tŵm also discounted Bronwen Morgan. Gwyn loathed all the Morgans. In fact, he was frightened of them. Their aggression was an affront to his gentleness.

There were a few girls who had been in school with them but Gwyn had never so much as indicated even a flutter of interest. He positively disliked Luned who all those years ago had lost her rabbit to Cadoc's cruelty. Luned, who had a tendency to enjoy telling tales, had once incurred Gwyn's wrath for telling Mr. Pugh that "Evan Griffiths copied Tŵm Tudor's homework." Both Tŵm and Evan got thrashed for that, Evan for copying and Tŵm for allowing him to copy. Of the others, Ann had gone to work in Chester, Ceri had already married a solicitor from St. Asaph, Rachel had gone away to train as a teacher and Anwen was helping her Mam in the shop. Tŵm couldn't even recall Gwyn ever speaking to Anwen, who was one of the few young women left working in the village. In any case Anwen was, to be charitable, somewhat on the tubby side. She wasn't the sort of girl a man fell passionately in love with. Tŵm thought of Nia Bowen telling him that Bethan was 'sweet' on Evan but that Evan showed no interest in her. Maybe Gwyn too had been 'sweet' on a girl who did not reciprocate. But, if that were the case, then who it was he had no idea.

As September drew to a close, Tŵm felt as though he were in limbo. It was weeks since the inquest. Was that it? Was it all over? Gwyn was dead and still no-one knew how or why. Would it remain so for ever? What can I do, he wondered? He couldn't bear the thought of living out his life without any answers to any of his questions. To make matters worse everyone else seemed satisfied with the open verdict. Most put Gwyn's drowning down to a tragic accident. Why couldn't he be satisfied with that?

When Tŵm asked Emyr if he ever wondered what had happened to Gwyn, the answer he got was, "Let Gwyn rest in peace Tŵm. It's tragic you've lost your two friends but many have lost more than that..." He turned his head to check they were alone and that Mali wasn't within hearing distance. "Bloody war. Hugh Vaughan from Mwrog Street in Ruthin lost all three of his sons. Terrible losses in that street, there were."

Ruth Parry accepted the fact of her son's death and didn't seem to want to explore what she termed, 'Gwyn's accident,' while the Bowens were too occupied dwelling on their own loss to muse on Gwyn.

The only person who seemed to share his curiosity was Dr. Owen but it wasn't so much personal, more that the mystery was an affront to his scientific mind. "Such a strange business," he said to Tŵm one morning. "I keep questioning why Gwyn ended up in that pool. Unexplained deaths nag at my mind. I hope we discover the answer one day."

Partial illumination came from an unexpected quarter. The last day of September was a Saturday. After feeding the stock, Tŵm had a few hours free. Emyr had recently acquired a second-hand bicycle so Tŵm loaded the basket with damson and blackcurrant jam, apples and pears, freewheeled down the bank that led towards Carreg-y-Bedd and was soon knocking on Ruth Parry's door.

"So good of your Mam," Ruth commented as she stored the jars away in the kitchen. "It'll be a taste of summer on a cold winter's day."

As usual Tŵm undertook some chores, making a bonfire from hedge cuttings, chopping wood for the fires and digging up yet more potatoes. "I'm an expert at this Mrs. Parry," he laughed. "You don't know how many hours I've spent at home searching in the soil to find these."

"You are good to me Tŵm. In your free time too."

"I'm pleased to help," Tŵm replied. "I've spent many happy hours here with Gwyn and I know he would want me to give you a hand. He and Evan were my closest friends. I miss them both every single day."

Despite herself a shadow passed momentarily over Ruth's face. "I do too Tŵm. I comfort myself with knowing they are with God and that Thomas is looking after them but it is hard not to hear Gwyn's voice." Tŵm looked up. Such a confidence from Ruth was more than unusual. Taking an extraordinary risk, he patted her hand. Unused to physical contact, she flinched but did not move it away.

"I know I can't take Gwyn's place, Mrs. Parry but while I'm alive you'll always have a son of sorts."

Ruth smiled. "You're a good lad Tŵm but you have your own life to live. You can't always be bothering with me."

"You're no bother, Mrs. Parry."

Just as quickly as the blacksmith snatched his fingers away when he happened to brush against a red-hot horseshoe, Ruth changed the subject. The conversation had veered dangerously close to emotion. "Let me make you a drink Tŵm. You must be thirsty. That smoke from the bonfire catches the back of the throat." Though Ruth had ruptured the connection, Tŵm felt that at least there had been a moment when their spirits had touched.

Fortified with toast and tea, Tŵm left shortly afterwards. The bike had been a good idea. It was much quicker than walking even with the hills to climb. Thinking Dr. Owen may be home on a Saturday, he thought there was time to call there. He hadn't had chance to tell him much about the Anglesey visit with the daylight hours being filled with fruit and potatoes. But he was unlucky. Dr. Owen was out. Their conversation would have to wait a little longer. Riding back Tŵm chanced upon Cadoc Morgan emerging from Maldwyn Price's slaughter yard. He decided to cycle past and ignore him but Cadoc spoke up.

"Well, look who it is! If it's not Tŵm Tudor posin' on a bike. Feered to stop are ya?"

Tŵm slowed. He didn't want Cadoc Morgan to think that he had the upper hand. "Pnawn da, Cadoc. What are you up to today?"

"Up to, up to. That's typ'cal of ya. Why should ya think I'm up t' anythin'?"

"Because you always are Cadoc. That's why."

Cadoc's handsome face, reddened with rage. "Bin looking af'er that sister of your'n 'ave ya?"

Tŵm placed his foot on the ground and stopped completely, taking care to stay the opposite side of the lane from Cadoc. If Cadoc started anything, he wanted to be able to get away. It wasn't lack of courage so much as practicality. He knew he hadn't got a cat in hell's chance of beating Cadoc in a fist fight.

"I've told you before Cadoc. Stay away from Caron."

"Caron. Cadoc. Go nicely together don' they?" Cadoc marred his handsome face by creasing it into a sneer. Tŵm wondered whether Caron would indeed be taken in by Cadoc's Celtic good looks if he pursued her. It struck him again that, to a girl, Cadoc's black, curly hair and strong, masculine features would probably prove attractive. Cadoc certainly bore a striking resemblance to his sister, Bronwen. No-one could overlook the fact that they were siblings.

"Cadoc, if you so much as look at Caron I'll..."

"You'll wot? Don' think ya scare me Tŵm Tudor. I'd look forward t' givin' ya a thrashin'. A cat can look at a queen, canna it? No-one'd wanna look at yar other sister, would they? Looks like 'er Mam. Face like a constipated ferret."

Tŵm, not wanting to trade blows, ignored the insult to Bethan. Dropping his voice, he repeated, "Cadoc, I've warned you. Don't go near Caron."

Cadoc wasn't going to give up. It was too much fun goading Twm. "Pretty as a picture she is. Body like those gals on the tobacco cards. I'd love to tek 'er for a canter. Doesna tek after yar Mam and Tad. Makes ya wonder where she came from."

Knowing that Cadoc was merely taunting him, Twm kept himself under control. "I'm not rising to the bait Cadoc. You can say what you like."

"Know she's got a boyfriend d'ya? I were in the f'rest one mornin', rabbitin'. Saw them together I did. If ya ask me she's already bin spoilt. Nuthin' but a slut. Not that I wouldna mind a piece of the action anyways."

This took Twm unawares. Shocked, he forgot his resolution not to trade insults. "You're just making it up Cadoc. I know your game. You're trying to rile me. In any case if we're talking about sisters, yours is no better than she should be. Already got herself a reputation she has."

As soon as the words issued from his mouth, Twm was sorry he'd uttered them. It was a low blow and Twm felt he'd sunk to Cadoc's level. Blowsy and audacious, Bronwen Morgan, it was true, had often been the subject of gossip. She was certainly very attractive in an untamed sort of way. She swept back her thick mane of black curls with a red ribbon, better to show off her creamy complexion, her violet eyes which spoke of wantonness and the curve of sensuous lips. She had a predilection, unique in Carreg-y-Bedd, for low cut necklines and high-ranking men. It was rumoured that she'd even had a tryst with Humphrey Craddock himself. Certainly, Nerys Philpin had seen a girl with dark hair enjoying a ride in the new Model T Ford he'd had for his birthday. "I'm sure it was Bronwen Morgan. All swanky she was," she had been heard to say to Rhian Hughes. "No-one can mistake those curls." One Sunday after chapel Twm had heard Nerys Philpin tell Mali that Bronwen had "dallied" with several local farmers, "but only the ones with more than a hundred acres." Despite her provocative appearance it seemed that Bronwen was ruled by her head not her heaving bosom.

"Don' ya start on our Bron." Cadoc was livid now. "At least she's a proper woman not like that dried-out stick ya call an older sister." Cadoc, now in full flow, could not restrain himself. He flung out a last triumphant card. "Think yar too good for 'er I s'pose. Yar friend didna think the same way. Mad for 'er 'e were."

Shocked into silence Twm did not immediately respond. Eventually he managed,

"What do you mean?"

"That streak o' tap water ya called a friend. The dead one. 'e were crazy 'bout our Bron."

"How could you possibly know that?"

Cadoc, enjoying his superior knowledge was happy to oblige. "Caught 'im one day, didna I."

"Caught him what?"

"Drawin' 'er picture he were. 'bout six months ago. Couple o' weeks before 'e drown'd. I caught 'im sneakin' aroun' Lane End. Behind the blackcurrants 'e were. Watchin' 'er. She were plantin' beans in the cold frames. Creepy it were. Bron didna half laugh when I called 'er over and 'eld up 'er face. Spit of her, I 'ave to admit. 'Wot makes ya think I'd ever be int'rested in ya, Gwyn Parry. I've got bigger fish to fry,' she told ' im. So then I screwed up 'is picture an' sent 'im off with a flea in 'is ear, I did. Got into trouble with Bron 'cos it were a good picture an' she wan'ed to keep it."

Lane End was very much a no-go area in Carreg-y-Bedd. The Morgans lived in a cottage down a dead end. Hanging on the fence was a sign, that looked as though it had been painted by a five-year-old, pronouncing this dwelling to have been christened, Hendreforgan, so declaring to all and sundry that this was the home of the Morgans. Yet Tŵm could never recall anyone using that name; it was always referred to as Lane End. The road past it led to nowhere. It transformed itself into a green lane, ultimately barred by a rusty gate that had to be heaved upwards if anyone wanted to squeeze through. Not that there was much point in gaining access, as on the other side were just fields grazed by the Bowens' sheep. No-one would have any reason to venture down Lane End unless they were visiting the Morgans and very few did visit the Morgans. True the minister and the doctor made rare appearances but social small talk was not the Morgans' way. If the truth be known most of the god-fearing inhabitants of Carreg-y-Bedd were a little nervous of the Morgan family who, for the most part, lived outside the comfortable bubble of chapel activities, social gatherings and community events. Griff Morgan had spent some time at His Majesty's pleasure, only for petty theft and poaching, but nevertheless such dishonesty made him an outcast. His wife, Beti, unkempt and confrontational, kept herself to herself and was rarely seen in Carreg. Gethin and Cadoc were known to be hostile, their arrogance unpopular with folk who practised self-effacement. Worst of all they were known to partake in copious amounts of beer drinking at the 'Lamb and Lion'. As for Bronwen she was dismissed as a 'hussy'.

Tŵm, in reality at a loss, felt he had to say something. "I don't know why you think I'll believe anything you say Cadoc."

"Please yisself." Cadoc, with an air of triumph turned to go.

Seizing the opportunity, Tŵm cycled off, thoughts scrambling for priority. Once well out of sight, he turned off the lane down a well-worn track which he knew led to a birch coppice. Dismounting, he propped up his bike and sat down, leaning his back against a convenient trunk. He had to mull this over.

Tŵm wouldn't have entertained the concept of Gwyn suffering from unrequited love if it hadn't been for Gwyn's words to him on Llanddwyn Island. But Gwyn had admitted that he knew what it was to be in love. That was astonishing in itself. But typical of Gwyn he had volunteered no further information and Tŵm had too much respect for Gwyn to intrude into, what was clearly, private territory.

But Bronwen Morgan! And if Gwyn had fallen in love with her, he must have hidden his passion for quite some time. Tŵm had dismissed her as a candidate for Gwyn's affections. No-one could have been more unlikely. They were as different as chalk and cheese. Gwyn, reserved, honest, devout; Bronwen, devil-may-care, rebellious, easy with her favours. It didn't make sense. But Tŵm could not think of any other possible reason why Gwyn should make an appearance in Lane End. He would certainly not have been paying a visit to the Morgans. And the drawing. Tŵm could think of lots of words to describe Cadoc Morgan but imaginative was not one of them. There was no way on God's earth that Cadoc could have made up such a story. It was too far-fetched. Gwyn lurking in the Morgans' garden, surreptitiously creating a portrait of Bronwen... No-one could have dreamt that one up, especially not Cadoc.

So, what did it mean? Did it have any significance regarding Gwyn's death? To accept that Gwyn was infatuated with Bronwen was difficult enough, but to conceive of Gwyn hurling himself into the murky depths of Pwll Berw because Bronwen Morgan had humiliated him defied belief, especially two weeks after the event itself. In Tŵm's view, even if Gwyn was still suffering the pangs of unrequited affection, he wouldn't put Ruth through the double agony of a death which would result in an absence of salvation. Moreover, Gwyn had always been so sensible. He would surely have realised that such a fancy would pass.

Some considerable time elapsed before Tŵm climbed back onto his bike and pedalled back to Cwyn-y-Gwynt. He had to come to terms with his new knowledge before he returned home. Gwyn's secret love was just one small part of the whole picture, he said to himself, but the canvas was still rent with jagged holes. Until they were mended, he wouldn't discover what really happened to Gwyn on that fateful Easter Saturday.

Harvest Month

Cwyn-y-Gwynt was a hive of activity. Excitement was too close to emotion to be considered healthy in the Tudor household but certainly there was an air of expectancy. The Carreg-y-Bedd country fair was to be held on the Saturday at Tan-y-Graig with a friendly football game and competitions in hedging, ditching and shoeing but the highlight was to be the ploughing contest. Tŵm had decided to leave the Tudor challenge to Brad. He knew he would have little chance of winning. Though competent enough, Tŵm didn't care enough about the art of straight furrows to be fiercely competitive. In any case, if he entered, he knew he would lose to Brad and he didn't want to give Brad the chance to lord it over him. He was happy though to help his brother in his quest for local fame by walking alongside Delilah's head, keeping her straight on the turf, to make sure Samson walked in the newly turned furrow. Tŵm had seen Brad operate before and been full of admiration for his skilful turning of such huge beasts and his ability to keep them straight by controlling both the plough and the traces, leaning into the weight as he did so. Brad, endowed with Mali's proud nature, was intent on proving himself in the community. It wasn't the fifteen shillings first prize that attracted him; more the local renown. In Brad's class the ploughmen had to prepare a drill for turnips. Each furrow had to be five inches deep and nine inches broad. Whoever ploughed the straightest and nearest the gauge was the winner. Ifan Evans, resplendent in bowler, waistcoat complete with watch chain and a white buttonhole, was coming all the way from Llanrwst to judge the entrants.

The morning of the fair Caron and Tŵm helped Emyr wash, groom, plait and braid Samson and Delilah before decking them out with brasses. The previous evening all the family, even Siôn, had polished brasses and saddle soaped harness. "Use some elbow grease on those traces," Mali had said to her youngest son. "Don't just slide your cloth across the top."

"It's not elbow grease I'm worried about," Caron replied. "It's horse grease from their coats. Washing it off before soaping the leather is a mucky job. Samson and Delilah are going to be sparkling clean and I'm going to be filthy. Just look at my nails, ingrained with dirt. I like cleaning tack but I wish I didn't get so dirty."

Mali was clear. "That doesn't matter at all Caron. No-one's going to be looking at you. It's the horses that matter. Brad doesn't want to be seen with a grubby team."

"Pass me those coupling straps," Emyr said to Twm, "and I'll start putting everything back together. One day Siôn you'll have to learn how to do this."

"I can't Tad," replied Siôn looking at the massed tangle of leather. "It's impossible."

"There's only one way to learn," replied Emyr.

"What's that?" Siôn was plaintive.

Brad laughed. "The same way we've all learnt Siôn. All the pieces are piled up and then you stay there all day trying again and again until you manage to buckle it together correctly. You get no supper till it's done. You'll never forget how to do it after that. I learnt how to do it when I was ten."

Siôn, tearful, said, "I'll never be able to do it by then. I'm ten next month."

Caron leapt to Siôn's defence. "Stop teasing him Brad. Siôn, you won't have to do it until you're much older if you don't want to and Twm will teach you what to do first. It'll be fine, I promise."

Emyr consoled Siôn further. "If things carry on the way they are Siôn, you won't need to learn how to do it."

"What do you mean Tad?" Caron asked.

"Horses'll be replaced by tractors before too long. Shame really. There's nothing like the bond between man and horse. But progress is progress and we must move with the times. It'll save a lot of work that's for sure. I wouldn't be surprised if next year's competition has a tractor section."

Caron was shocked. "It won't be as much fun Tad, as with the horses."

Brad intervened excitedly. "No, it'll be much better. We'll get the ploughing done in a fraction of the time."

Mali tried to dampen his spirits. "A tractor! We couldn't afford one. Our name isn't Craddock."

Emyr supported his son. "That's where you're wrong Mali. There's a Ford tractor for sale in Llangollen at Sun's Motor Company. £190 it is. Then Edwards of Denbigh have got a Moline. Howell Griffiths was telling me the other day. Don't know how much it is though."

"£190! £190! Emyr Tudor, are you out of your mind? You'll be wanting a car next, like that doctor."

Emyr, unruffled, continued. "Just think Mali. A strong working horse is at least sixty guineas. That's one hundred and twenty for two horses. Then they have to be fed and shod. We spend a small fortune with Weyland Philpin.

And there's the vet to pay when necessary. You're always complaining about his sky-high charges. Look at the time we'd save too. Selling Samson and Delilah would nearly pay for a tractor."

Mali was undeterred. "But you wouldn't sell the horses surely. You'd still need them. What if the tractor broke down? Then there'd be the cost of repairs and fuel. I don't like the idea of them. Smelly, noisy things they are."

"Well, they're the future of farming Mali. As I said before, we've got to move with the times if we want to make a decent living. A tractor does the work of five horses, so they say, and it only eats when it's working! And it's not just for ploughing. We could do harrowing, harvesting, planting. There are all manner of attachments. Howell Griffiths is going to buy one, I believe."

There was a long pause from Mali before she ventured, "Oh, if Tan-y-Graig is going to buy one then perhaps you should look into it Emyr. We've got more acreage than they have."

The next day it wasn't only Brad who was involved in the forthcoming competition. The country fair committee, though not running a stock and horse show, had decided to hold a sheep class so Emyr entered his best Welsh Mountain ram, spending a satisfying couple of hours trimming and brushing his fleece. "It's the only livestock event of the day," Emyr told Mali. "Just a bit of local, friendly rivalry that's all. Must make an effort." The Carreg-y-Bedd women just as, if not more competitive than the men, enjoyed showing off their skills in baking and preserves. Mali had entered her cheese scones, oatcakes and a jar of chutney.

The morning of the fair dawned dry but overcast. Emyr tapped the barometer that graced the kitchen wall. "At least it's not raining. Pressure's falling though."

"It is threatening Tad," Brad answered. "May brighten up later. Hope it doesn't rain. Don't want the earth to be too heavy and sticky. Spoil it for everyone and after all that work we've put in on Samson and Delilah we want them to look their best, not be drenched in water."

Emyr, practical as always, answered, "Well, we'll just have to wait and see."

Caron, despite her misery, was looking forward to the fair. She had arranged to meet Dee Philpin, the blacksmith's daughter. She hadn't seen much of her since she left school as Dee suffered from ill health but they'd always been good friends, often getting into trouble in class for giggling and chattering.

The two girls met up as soon as they reached Tan-y-Graig, Dee's pale fragility providing a stark contrast to Caron's robust good health. Caron, shocked at her friend's wan face asked, "Are you sure you feel well enough to be here Dee?"

Dee, dismissing Caron's concerns, answered, "Of course. I'm just a bit tired."

Since the unfortunate episode in the potato field and fearful of Mali's wrath, Caron had learnt to shelve her heartache at meal times and even found herself hungry at times. Not that she had abandoned hope of finding Abram though. She clung on to something she had heard from Emyr. "Mark my words. Those Gypsies'll be back before the nights draw in. There's too much work around here for them to stay away for long."

Brad's class was due to start at eleven. Caron and Dee jostled for position amongst a crowd of spectators. Six teams were competing. Samson and Delilah looked superb, ready to use their power to strain into the collars, their bright bay coats gleaming like conkers. Along the line, blacks, browns and dapple greys awaited their turn. There was a cheer as the judge gave the signal to start.

"They're not in the lead," Dee remarked to Caron. She could see her father not far away from Ifan Evans, prepared to restore a shoe if one happened to be cast in the thick earth.

"It's not a race," Caron told her. "The judging is all about the furrows. Samson and Delilah are moving slow and steady." She paused, then added, "I love seeing the ground change from grassland to thick, rich soil. It looks just like soft, brown corduroy." Brad turned expertly at the end of the first furrow and made his way back, the rich loam churning satisfyingly behind him. As he made his way down the third, Caron heard Twm, who was ensuring Delilah kept in line, shout something to the crowd. It seemed there was a dispute of sorts by the edge of the first furrow.

Caron and Dee craned their necks. "What's going on?" asked Dee.

"Don't know but Gethin Morgan's in the midst of it. Let's move nearer."

As the two girls neared the throng surrounding Gethin, it became clear that an argument had broken out between Gethin and Emyr, who had been watching his son's skilful progress with great satisfaction.

"I didna do it on purpose," Gethin was assuring Emyr.

"Yes, you did. You were sly but I saw you. You trampled in Brad's furrow deliberately to break down the edge. Cheating, that's what it is."

"Ya canna prove that. Someone pushed me an' I fell forrard."

"A likely story. You get away from that edge this minute or I'll call the judge over."

Muttering and grumbling, Gethin, puffing smoke rings as a gesture of defiance, shambled slowly over towards the refreshment tent. Whatever was the truth of the matter, it didn't affect the outcome. Brad raised the trophy for the second year in succession.

"Chip off the old block," Emyr said to no-one in particular but grinning widely. "Won a fair number of them in my youth."

It was a successful day for the Tudors. Mali won the oatcakes competition but had to be content with second place for her scones, giving way with bad grace to Ruth Parry. She explained her defeat to Emyr. "They felt sorry for her, I'm sure."

"Oh, come Mali, Ruth Parry's always made a tasty scone."

"That's right Mam," said Twm, supporting his father. "She often gives me one to eat when I visit and they're very good." Seeing Mali's face, he hastily added, "But of course they're not quite like yours." He wasn't going to risk not being offered a freshly baked treat the next time Mali made them.

"My chutney didn't get a prize at all. I asked the judges why and they said it tasted bitter, probably due to too much vinegar."

Emyr, trying to redeem himself, consoled her. "Well, I think your chutney's perfect with cheese, Mali. I don't understand how it didn't win. Anyway, we can't complain. We've done well overall. I'm delighted with second place. Idris Jones' ram is a fine specimen, isn't he? I don't mind being runner up to him; he deserves it."

Twm, watching his younger brother cover himself in glory, was not in the least bit envious. Ploughing a straight furrow was not a priority in his life. He had other, far more important, concerns.

One of those concerns suddenly laid his hand on Twm's shoulder. "Twm Tudor. Gettin' yar Tad to fight yar battles now are ya?" Cadoc's sarcastic tone was unmistakeable.

Twm turned. "I've no idea what you are talking about Cadoc."

"Yes, ya do. Yar Tad. Accusin' Gethin like that. Someone pushed 'im. 'e didna do it deliberately."

Twm held Cadoc's confrontational stare. "Cadoc, I'm not going to quarrel with you about this. You're just trying to cause trouble. Brad won that Challenge Cup fair and square." He dropped his eyes. His gaze fell on Cadoc's shirt. His stomach flipped.

"Cadoc, your shirt's ripped. You've lost the second button down. Just above your waistcoat."

"So wot?"

"Well, it's odd that's all."

"Tŵm Tudor yar nuffin but a daft bastard. I lose buttons all the time. So must ya, workin' on the land. Wot's odd about it?"

Tŵm, jolted by the sudden knowledge that he may have been wrong about Cadoc's innocence, launched into an attack. "It's just a coincidence then that Gwyn Parry had a shirt button just like that in his pocket when they found him drowned? Might he have pulled it off in that fight he had with you?"

Cadoc paused. It was a long pause. He narrowed his eyes and stared at Tŵm.

"Ya did know abou' the scuffle we 'ad. I knew it. I knew 'e would've told ya."

"Yes, he did tell me Cadoc. He told me all about it."

"Did 'e tell ya 'e 'it me first?"

"I don't believe that Cadoc!"

"Ya can believe wot ya like. Gethin saw what 'appened. 'e saw it all."

"So, there were two of you beating up Gwyn were there? Two on one. That's really brave!"

"No, I won fair an' square all by meself. Didna need any 'elp from our Gethin. At least ya've 'ad the sense to keep it quiet." He smirked, "Scared of me an' Gethin ent ya?"

Tŵm couldn't let Cadoc get away with that. "Don't think for one moment Cadoc that I'm frightened of you two."

"Then why 'ave ya kept quiet then?" Cadoc sneered. "Runnin' to the police is jus' wot I'd expect from a Tudor."

"My silence is nothing whatsoever to do with you Cadoc. The only person I'm concerned about is Ruth Parry. If it gets out that you and Gwyn had a fight, the police'll want to know what was said. That'll give you the chance to repeat your lies over and over again and the whole neighbourhood will think Gwyn was a coward. I don't want Gwyn's memory tainted like that. Neither do I want his Mam to feel shame. It's her pride in Thomas and Gwyn that's keeping her going. If she lost that, I don't know how she'd manage. You called him 'windy'. He told me."

"Wot's wrong with that? 'e were windy. I were only tellin' the truth. Me mate, Rhodri, were in the 9th. Told me a few stories 'bout yar precious friend. Rhodri said, one mornin' not long before Evan Griffiths went west, our lines was gettin' a real batterin'. The shellin' were non-stop an' the lad next to yar friend got blown to buggery. The army would've told 'is family 'e were 'missin'. 'e were certainly that. An' then our lads saw thousands of Bosche in front of 'em. Comin' in waves they was. Some was already in our wire nearby, so Rhodri said. Ev'rybody fired rapidly at anythin' that moved.

Ev'rybody 'cept yar friend. 'e got 'imself in a funk 'ole. Would've bin court martialled an' shot 'e would, 'cept Evan Griffiths stood 'im up, shoved 'is rifle in 'is 'and told 'im to play 'is part. An' that's not the only story I 'ave an' all."

Tŵm paused. "You only heard the story second hand, Cadoc. You don't know that it's true and even if it were, anybody would be scared in that situation."

"Wouldna stop ya doin' yar duty tho', would it? I'll 'ave ya know that I fought with real 'eroes. Some was ex-miners. Jus' the men ya'd want to fight by ya. Ya don' want a shiverin' wreck alongside ya. Like yar friend. Las' thing ya need."

"The war's over now Cadoc. I'll tell you what. I'll carry on keeping quiet about the fight if you promise not to repeat that story to anyone else. You don't know that it's true and as I said before it'll upset Mrs. Parry. She's gone through enough. That might've been Gwyn's first battle. Perhaps after that he mustered his courage and fought like a lion."

"Yeah, yeah. Pigs might fly! Once yella, always yella if ya ask me. People need t' know who were brave an' who weren't. Only fair. An' anyways I know 'e were still windy. Fri'ttened 'im to death I did."

Tŵm decided to take the bull by the horns. Cadoc couldn't do much to him in the middle of the fair.

"Cadoc, did Gwyn pull the button off your shirt while you were beating him up that Thursday night or did that happen when you shoved him in the pool?"

"Ay, ay. Wot are ya accusin' me of Tŵm Tudor? I 'ad nothin' to do with 'is drownin' an' I dunna know 'ow it 'appened."

"So you say. But you admit to having a scrap with him just two days before."

"I may've given 'im a leatherin' but I didna kill 'im. Anyways 'e deserved 'is beatin'."

"How's that Cadoc? It sounds to me as though Gwyn had every right to be angry with you."

"But that weren't why I 'it 'im."

Tŵm leapt on the discrepancy. "Oh, so you did hit him first?"

"I might've done. I canna remember."

"You're just a liar Cadoc. Through and through. I don't believe a word you say."

Further conversation was prevented by the appearance of Emyr, "Tŵm can you come and help with the horses? We need to be getting home."

As Twm turned to follow his Tad, Cadoc put his index finger to his lips before he swaggered away.

It had been a good day Caron thought. At her ease with Dee, she had relaxed and just enjoyed the fair. With a start she realised she hadn't thought of Abram for a few hours and felt unaccountably guilty. Still anxious about her friend, she decided to walk back with her to the blacksmith's cottage. It was only a couple of miles but they hadn't even gone half way when Caron realised Dee was struggling. She turned to her friend and was shocked to see how pale she was.

Dee leaned on a stile by the side of the road. "Can we just sit on this for a minute and have a rest?"

"Of course. Are you alright?"

"I'm just a bit breathless. We've been standing all day."

Caron, used to constant chores with Mali's voice echoing in the background, "No slacking my girl, you've got young legs; you don't need to sit down," saw nothing unusual with being on her feet all day.

Her friend was gasping for breath, then started to cough. "I'll be fine in a minute. I get these turns sometimes. I just need to rest and then they go off."

"We shouldn't have walked. There were lots of people going back to the village in traps. One of them would've taken us. Have you been to see Dr. Owen?"

"Oh yes. He's told me to sleep with the bedroom windows wide open and keep the room cold even in winter. The very best thing he said is fresh air. That and lots of rest. I'll be better soon I'm sure."

Fortunately, as they were speaking, they heard the rattling chug of a car engine behind them. Dr. Owen came round a corner and into sight. Caron waved at him and he pulled up beside them, turning off the engine and climbing out of the driver's seat.

"Oh, Dr. Owen we're so pleased to see you. Dee isn't very well."

Richard Owen strode over to Dee. "Come on now, Dee let's get you into the car. Caron, you squeeze into the back first." Caron did as she was told, the pleasure of having her first ride in a car spoilt by the sight of Dee sinking gratefully on to the passenger seat, taking a deep breath and starting to cough again. "Just breathe normally," the doctor told her. "The spasm will stop in a minute." He waited until she was quiet and calm, cranked up the car and they set off for Carreg-y-Bedd. Dee admitted to Caron that she had a pain in her chest but was otherwise quiet on the drive which only took a few minutes. Caron watched as the hedges flashed by. She had never been so fast in her life before.

Nerys Philpin, hearing the uncommon sound of a car outside Yr Efail, came out of the cottage door.

"Is she alright doctor?"

"She's fine now. Overdid it a little bit." Turning to Dee, he said, "I told you to take it easy, didn't I?"

Dee nodded. "Sorry doctor. Tad took me in the trap this morning so I thought I'd be alright to walk home. It's been so much fun being with Caron."

"Yes, well I'm glad you had a good time. Mrs. Philpin, I'll come to see Dee tomorrow and examine her. We'll have a chat about what to do next to make her feel a bit better."

As Dee walked through the door with her mother, Dr. Owen turned to Caron. "Do you want me to take you home Caron?"

"Oh, no doctor but thank you. I don't want to put you to any trouble."

"It's no trouble. It will only take a few minutes and I'll enjoy the drive. Come on, get in. You can go in the front this time."

"Then thank you. It is getting dark." Once settled comfortably, she asked, "Will Dee get better soon?"

"I hope so Caron. But she needs looking after, rest and plenty of fresh air. I'm sure she would appreciate your company if you had time to visit."

"I will, doctor but I don't see her very often as Mam keeps me very busy. I hadn't seen her for some time and her cough seems much worse. What's wrong with her? Can you help her? And is it catching? Mam won't like it if I bring illness back home."

"As for what's wrong with her, I'm afraid I cannot tell you that Caron. As a doctor I'm not allowed to discuss my patients' illnesses with anybody outside their family. Neither can I discuss treatment but I promise you, I'm doing everything I can. And you don't need to worry about catching it. It's not the sort of cough that's highly contagious. It's possible to catch it but it's not that likely for a strong, healthy girl like you, unless you're living with her. Better to be safe than sorry though. Don't get too near if Dee has a coughing spasm. Perhaps you could go out for a short walk with her. That would do her good."

Caron's concern was immediate. "I'll try to see her more often, doctor."

"You do that Caron. You're a good girl."

As the doctor started the engine again, Caron reflected on his words. If only he knew. She knew she wasn't a good girl. She was wicked. Very wicked. She had met a boy alone in the forest and allowed him to kiss her. Nothing could be more sinful. She determined to make amends. Even if she had sinful thoughts, she could at least do some good deeds. She would start by visiting Dee and maybe she could visit Ruth Parry too. Ruth would be glad of some company. She had a reasonable chance of getting time off from her chores. Mali liked people to think that the Tudors were the sort of family who helped those who were not fortunate enough to have been born a Tudor.

Richard Owen, acutely aware of Caron's silence as he drove to Cwyn-y-Gwynt, put it down to shyness and anxiety about her friend. He tried to make her feel more at ease. "So what do you think of my car Caron?"

"It's grand doctor. Just grand. And so fast. It must save so much time."

"It does Caron. It helps me get to my patients much more quickly. It's not an exaggeration to say that I'm sure it will save lives in an emergency."

"And it will be dry and warm in winter. Better than a trap." Caron had vivid memories of being soaked to the skin on her way to chapel and sitting through the reading meeting, shivering in wet clothes.

The doctor laughed. "It will certainly keep me dry but I gather it's very cold and I'll need blankets in the winter."

Caron lapsed back into silence. Richard Owen tried again. "How have you been occupying yourself lately Caron? Been helping your Mam, have you?"

Caron was polite. "Yes, doctor. We've all been busy with the harvesting. It's been hard work." Not for the first time Richard Owen wondered how Twm and Caron had turned out to be such fine young people, given their mother's iron grip. He had no illusions about Mali Tudor. Not that Twm had ever been overly critical of his mother; he was too conscious of family loyalties for that. But Richard was more than capable of reading between the lines. He didn't care much either for Brad. Bethan, he thought of as sour, strait-laced and lacking in compassion. He remembered a time he had spoken to her after chapel, not long after Gwilym Bowen had returned a broken man. Nia had brought Gwilym to the chapel that day, hoping that seeing old friends would aid his recovery. During the sermon, Gwilym had stood up, stared at the altar, waved his arms in the air and shouted out unintelligible utterances punctuated with obscene words. It had caused quite a stir. Nia, suffused with shame, had helped him outside, while the congregation determinedly kept their eyes fixed on Daniel Ellis who, ignoring the rude interruption, gamely continued with his sermon based on Jesus casting out an unclean demon in Luke 4.

Richard had followed Nia out.

"I can't bring him again, can I doctor?"

"Of course you can Mrs. Bowen. He's ill. Jesus asked that the sick be brought to him for healing. Gwilym has every right to be in chapel."

"But his behaviour will be the talk of the village."

Richard had been reassuring. "I wouldn't worry about that."

"Well, I do doctor, I do. I'm going to take him back now before everyone comes out. Come on Gwil, let's go home." She had buttoned up his coat for him, taken his arm and started to hurry him down the path. Gwilym had stumbled.

"Careful, he's disoriented. Take it slowly."

The strains of 'Love Divine, All Loves Excelling', could be heard drifting from the chapel. "They're singing, the last hymn doctor. We must get away before everyone comes out." Nia had been adamant.

Richard had returned to the service, entering his pew on, 'Jesu, Thou art all compassion.'

Bit short on pity in Carreg-y-Bedd chapel he had thought to himself. His view had been confirmed when the congregation made its way outside. Bethan was first, directing her comments to him and to Ruth Parry. "Shocking doctor, don't you think? Blasphemy in the middle of the sermon. I didn't know such words existed." She pursed her mouth, drawing her thin lips into an even finer line.

Richard had kept his temper under control with difficulty. "He's sick, Bethan. He's been badly affected by his war experiences."

Bethan had retaliated. "He may be sick, but he's upsetting decent, god-fearing people. He shouldn't be let out. Others have been through the war too but they don't feel the need to bellow out obscenities in God's house."

Mali had followed this up with, "Gone funny in the head hasn't he doctor? You'd think Nia Bowen would have more control over him. Bethan's right, Nia shouldn't bring him out if that's the way he's going to behave. Needs hiding away where he can't do any harm. If you ask me, he's barmy and he'd be better off in Denbigh asylum. If my boys had gone to France, I would hope they'd fight bravely, not show themselves to be cowards."

Ruth Parry had joined in, "I can at least be grateful that both my men were heroes. But the doctor's right Mali, we don't know what horrors Mr. Bowen saw. We should feel sorry for him. True, his language was unseemly but I don't think he knew what he was saying. Let's hope that with God's mercy he'll get better."

Richard had smiled at her, relieved to find that there was pity in Ebenezer;

it just wasn't to be found in the souls of Mali and Bethan Tudor.

Mali, naturally, had to have the last word. "Perhaps so Ruth, but you can't tell me that Gwilym Bowen wouldn't be best locked away from respectable people until the time that God, in His goodness, delivers him from madness."

Richard had known he was fighting a losing battle. Prejudice was not going to be dismantled, especially while it had the wall of holy virtue protecting it.

Lost in thought, he realised Caron had spoken to him but he did not catch what she had said. "Sorry Caron. I couldn't hear over the noise of the engine. What did you say?"

Caron turned a frightened face to him. "Doctor, you've always been so kind to Twm. Could I come to talk to you? By myself. Not with Mam."

"What's the matter Caron? I can stop the car and you can tell me now if you like."

"No, there's no time. Mam will be expecting me back."

"Caron, if you're ill it would be usual for your Mam to be there as you're still a child under twenty-one. I can come to Cwyn-y-Gwynt if you want."

"No, doctor. Please don't do that. It doesn't matter. Forget I said anything."

"Caron, I can't do that now that you've mentioned it. Look if you're worried about something, of course you can come to my house and we'll talk about it."

"Thank you doctor but I haven't got any money to pay you. I don't feel ill anyway. I need to talk to someone and I can't think of anyone else."

"Then you must come to see me by yourself Caron. I don't like to think of you worrying about anything. And don't worry about paying. You just want to talk to me and you say you don't think you're ill so you wouldn't have to pay anything anyway. I'm sure I'll be able to put your mind at rest."

"It won't be easy for me to get away doctor and if anyone sees me going to your house, they'd ask Mam what was the matter."

"You just call when you can slip away and hopefully nobody will see you and I'll be in. If I'm not you can just try again. How about that?"

"Oh, thank you doctor. I'll do that. Not sure when it'll be though."

Caron was so relieved that she allowed Mali's wrath at her returning in the doctor's car, to drift over her. Mali had not been best pleased to see her emerge from Richard Owen's prize possession. "Honestly Caron, how could you put the doctor out like that? You've got feet, haven't you? You could have walked. Don't ever do that again you lazy girl."

It was more than two weeks before Caron finally managed to knock on the doctor's door. She had not forgotten her resolution to visit Dee and took advantage of a wet Saturday to ask if she could go to the Philpins. It had been raining on and off all day so she couldn't work outside and Mali was annoyed at her getting 'under my feet' in the kitchen. Mali approved of visiting the sick as long as it didn't disrupt her daily chores.

Mali addressed Nain. "Always been a weakling that Dee Philpin. Remember when she was born. Scrawny she was. And tiny. Wasn't expected to live. Born a couple of months before our Caron. Yet people always thought Caron was the older one. Real bouncing baby Caron was, glowing with health."

Nain nodded her agreement.

"Dee had a lot of time away from school," Caron concurred, "I always missed her."

Mali was scathing. "You do talk nonsense Caron. What on earth do you mean? Missed her! You had lots of other friends."

"I know Mam but Dee was my special friend. I could talk to her about anything and she would listen."

"You weren't in school to talk. You were there to work, Caron Tudor. Mr. Pugh always told me you were a daydreamer and a chatterer. 'Mrs. Tudor,' he said, 'Caron doesn't concentrate. Always sucking her pencil and staring out of the window.' Ashamed of you I was. Especially with Twm doing so well. Bethan always worked hard too but of course she wasn't as clever as Twm," pronounced Mali, ignoring the fact that her elder daughter was rolling out some pastry at the kitchen table.

Bethan, long immune to criticism, was unperturbed. "Twm's always been wrapped up in his books. Wouldn't suit me. I like to keep my hands busy."

"Go and see your friend if you must Caron but don't be too late back. It's getting dark early now. You can take Nerys Philpin some butter. Really fresh it is. It will do Dee good. Build her up a bit."

Caron waited for a break in the rain before wrapping herself up in an old coat of Twm's to walk down the lanes to the village. The weather had turned chilly and the freshening wind whipped up the scarlet in her cheeks. She made her way round to the back door, passing the open-ended square arch which formed the smithy itself. Many a time she had watched as Samson and Delilah were led in over the cobbles to be tied up on the back wall. To the left was the dark cavern of the smithy, with its huge fire, a blessing in winter, a curse on hot summer days. It was so familiar, the swish of the bellows, worked by Old Bill, Weyland's assistant, to keep the heat in the flames, the stench of burnt hoof, the hiss of glowing horseshoes as they were plunged into icy water before being nailed to the foot. But today it was empty and cold.

Nerys Philpin answered the door at her first knock. "Goodness, Caron. Come in and get dry. Fancy coming out in this weather."

"I've come to see Dee. I was worried about her. She looked so ill after the ploughing competition. I thought if there was a break in the rain, we could have a short walk round the village." Caron looked round the small kitchen. There was no sign of Dee. Two bentwood chairs were pulled up before the range. A meaty smell wafted from a blackened saucepan bubbling away on the fire.

"Having stew we are today. Got a nice piece of shin from Maldwyn Price. Mind, you have to be careful buying from him. I wouldn't buy a pheasant without its head for fear it'd turn out to be a chicken."

Caron laughed. The butcher had a dubious reputation. "The stew smells good. Where's Dee? Has she gone out?"

"Of course, you've not heard. Dee's not here. Dr. Owen thought it best that she went to the sanatorium for a while. Gone to Llangwyfan she has."

"Llangwyfan?" Caron was puzzled.

"Near Denbigh it is. Dr. Owen says it has all the latest treatments to make Dee better. Lucky we are. Just over two years ago it was opened by no less than King George and Queen Mary! They sailed on the Britannia to Holyhead, took the train to Denbigh, then drove by road to Llandyrnog. The doctor told me."

Caron took a deep breath. "What's the matter with Dee Mrs. Philpin?"

Nerys Philpin's eyes filled with tears. Caron, unused to any display of emotion from adults, shifted uneasily in her chair.

"Tuberculosis, it is." Nia said it slowly, rolling it round her tongue, making sure each syllable was correct. "Don't know how she managed to pick it up. Of course, she's always been a bit on the sickly side. No resistance, see. Could've happened anywhere. Children drop in and out of school. Take those from Tŷ Celyn. What was their name?"

"Boyle?" offered Caron.

"Oh, yes. That's it. The Boyles. Could've been them. Always looked unkempt to me. Then there's the Gypsies. I told her not to go near them but I caught her taking them windfalls on more than one occasion. So kind-hearted she is. Well, wondering's not going to do any good is it? She's got it and we've got to live with it."

"When did she go, Mrs. Philpin?"

"It's a few days ago now. Yes, that's right, last Thursday. The doctor said that a spare bed had become available unexpectedly and that we were lucky because normally there's quite a wait. Though he said there's not much risk of it spreading in the village, he seemed worried about Weyland and me catching it and said the sooner Dee was in hospital, the better it would be for everyone. Then he was kind enough to come with me and Dee. Weyland couldn't come. He had to shoe the Craddock's hunters. Went in the doctor's new car we did."

"What sort of place is it Mrs. Philpin?"

"Oh, real grand it is. Brand new. Some patients pay to be there, the doctor said, but they have a section for those who can't. Not that it wasn't hard leaving her behind. Sobbed her heart out she did. And they wouldn't let her keep the knick-knacks she'd taken with her. Just a photo, an ornament from Llandudno and some books. Said they didn't encourage personal possessions. There's a library there so she'll be happy if she can get her hands on some nice stories. Always got her head in a book, she has."

"What will she do all day?"

"Well, during the day the beds are wheeled outside so she's got plenty to look at."

"Sounds cold at this time of year, Mrs. Philpin."

"That's the point Caron. It's part of the treatment. Lots of cold, fresh Welsh air and good food. I'll take this butter for her when I next go. So good of your Mam. Please thank her for me."

"I will. Could I have Dee's address too and then I can write to her."

"Yes, I'll get it for you now. That'd be lovely. It'll cheer her up no end to get a letter from you."

Caron had expected to spend a couple of hours with Dee and, mindful of the doctor's advice about not being too close, perhaps go for a walk. As she left the Philpin's cottage, it occurred to her that since she was not expected back for a few hours, this might be a good opportunity to speak to Dr. Owen, especially since it was now raining so heavily there was no-one about to see her making her way to his stone double-fronted house, Tŷ Faenor. She wondered quite how she was going to broach the subject. Maybe he wouldn't be in. The thought immediately brought relief. If he wasn't in, she wouldn't need to tell him and she could put it off. But then, if she couldn't speak to him, she was going to have to come back and she would still have to worry. Whether he was in or out, it wasn't going to be an easy afternoon.

Richard Owen was in. He was dozing in his favourite armchair in front of the fire. His hands rested on the cracked, brown leather of the arms. This was a rare occurrence as he did not indulge in day-time rests but he had been up most of the previous night with a severe case of pneumonia. He had been grateful for his car on the way home.

He heard the doorbell and sighed. "No peace for the wicked," he muttered to himself as he pressed against the arms to pull himself out of his chair. He fully expected to see Ieuwan Benyon, Moelfre, whose wife he had been monitoring closely. She was getting on in years to have another baby and the birth was imminent.

He pulled the bolt and opened the front door. Startled to see Caron rather than Ieuwan's tawny beard, he gathered his wits as she told him, "I went to see Dee but she's gone to a special hospital. Oh, you'll know that of course."

The doctor ushered her in. "Don't worry about your friend Caron. She's in the best place for all the latest treatments. Come in to my study. I've lit a fire and it's warm in there." He seated himself opposite her and seeing her obvious nervousness got straight to the point. Better that she got whatever it was off her chest. "Caron, my dear, how can I help you?"

Caron took his cue. "I've been a naughty girl Doctor."

"I can't believe that Caron. I don't know any better young people than you and Tŵm. I know Tŵm is very good to Ruth Parry and you said you have just been to visit the Philpins."

"That's different doctor. I've been more than naughty; I've been wicked."

Caron started to cry; great, racking sobs that shook her whole body. Richard Owen brought her a glass of water and waited for her to calm down.

"Whenever you're ready, Caron, I'm here to listen."

"I'm so ashamed doctor. But I couldn't help myself. I loved him so much you see."

The doctor tried to hide his surprise but he was astonished. Surely Caron Tudor hadn't got a boyfriend. He hadn't heard any gossip of that nature and his housekeeper, Glenda, would have certainly have delighted in telling him. Though he tried to discourage her, she always said, "You need to know the truth about the lives of your patients, doctor. They'll only try to pull the wool over your eyes and it's my duty to see that your eyes are wide open." Relieved that Glenda had gone to see her sister in Ruthin that afternoon so would not know of Caron's visit, he continued with, "Take it slowly Caron, start at the beginning and explain to me what happened."

Caron's narrative took some time to unwind, peppered as it was with the twists and turns of Nain's stories and of feeling sinful in the chapel. It culminated with, "I allowed him to kiss me doctor and even worse, I enjoyed it."

Richard Owen suppressed a smile and a simultaneous desire to say, 'Is that all?' Caron was so upset; he had to take her seriously. Besides Mali Tudor would be incandescent with rage if she knew that Caron had met a young lad alone.

Almost as though she'd read his thoughts, Caron added, "I haven't told my Mam, doctor."

He decided to understate the case. "That was probably a wise decision Caron. She would be very cross with you. Not that I'm encouraging you to be deceitful but from what you say this young man hasn't been seen around these parts for a while so you may well never see him again. There's no point in drawing down your Mam's wrath. There's no harm done. You've just had a hard lesson in life, that's all."

Caron began to sob again. "You don't understand doctor. I love him. I know I shouldn't but I do. And I can't bear it if I never see him again."

Richard Owen felt for her. Young love. So painful. "I do understand Caron. Please trust me." Immediately he uttered the tacit admission, he wished he hadn't. However, he needn't have worried. Caron didn't even seem to register that she'd heard. She moved on to another topic.

"There's something else doctor."

"Yes?"

Caron's face was suffused with embarrassment. "I haven't been unclean for a long time."

"Unclean?" It took Richard a few moments to realise. "Oh, I see. Is that what your Mam calls it?"

"Yes, doctor."

"How long Caron?"

"Since June. Four months."

"Caron, you're young. Not every girl menstruates regularly every month. Have you felt ill at all or had any pains?"

"No, but I have fainted when I was picking potatoes and I haven't been eating properly because I feel sick sometimes. I just thought that was because I was so unhappy."

"Caron, did Abram, do anything else to you other than kiss you?"

"No, doctor, he only kissed me. He kissed me with his lips on my lips. Then he kissed me with his body."

"Kissed you with his body Caron?"

"That's what he said. He said there were two ways of kissing, one with the lips and one with the body."

Illumination struck Richard Owen. "Caron, has your Mam ever explained the facts of life to you?"

"Oh, yes doctor." Caron could not see the relevance of this question.

"What did she say?"

Mali's words were engraved on Caron's mind, she had heard them so many times.

"She said, 'It's a fact of life that we're born to die. So, you must lead a good life not an evil one. Then you'll go to heaven and not to hell'."

The doctor muttered an imprecation. "Did she ever explain where babies came from?" Caron was astonished. "No."

"What did she say when you started your flow?" The word was commonly used by the Carreg-y-Bedd young girls so Richard suspected Caron would know it.

She did. "Mam said it was a curse that all women had to bear and that I mustn't make a fuss over it." Caron thought back to her discomfiture at being given torn up rags to "soak it all up" and her lecture on washing them out in cold water in an old bucket kept outside hidden under the viburnum. "And don't hang them out on the line," Mali had said. "You don't want the men to see them. Hang them inside that thick hawthorn hedge at the end of the garden."

"Is that all?"

"Yes. She's never mentioned it again."

Richard Owen was aware of a familiar anger. In Carreg-y-Bedd the pious trussed up bodily pleasures in a straitjacket of religious rulings, moral statutes and taboos. To an educated man nurtured in a liberal household, the narrow prejudices were not only absurd but were the source of much unhappiness.

"I think I had better examine you Caron."

"I don't have five shillings, doctor."

As he had done so many times before when his patients had no money, Richard Owen freely offered his expertise. As he so often said to his father, "What can I do? I can't not treat a sick child or dress the wound of an old farmer who has scythed his leg just because they have no money. Anyway, the rich pay handsomely so their fees cover the poor."

Richard Owen, sensitive to Caron's inexperience of matters medical – with Caron's rude health, he didn't think she'd ever received a doctor's visit – explained to her what he was going to do before he attempted to palpate her abdomen.

Then he settled Caron back into a chair before beginning. "Caron. You haven't had a flow during July, August or September and I have examined you. Then you told me that you fainted in the potato field and that you weren't eating because you were feeling sick."

Caron couldn't help interrupting. "Am I ill doctor? What's wrong with me?"

Richard was gentle. "Caron, I believe you may be going to have a baby."

He expected horror or fear but in fact Caron simply looked astonished.

"A baby? But how can I have a baby? I'm not married."

"Abram," he replied. "The body kiss. That's what married people do."

Caron looked even more confused. "So I shouldn't have allowed the body kiss. Is that it doctor? But it was so nice. I felt so close to him."

If he had been a lesser person, Richard Owen could have allowed himself amusement at her naïvety. In contrast, he was furious at the conscious withholding of information. The school's contribution to sexuality was limited to the purity of the Virgin Mary in the nativity story while the chapel's interpretation was largely based on the 'detestable abominations' of Sodom and Gomorrah and the 'lustful desires of the flesh'. As a consequence, carnal knowledge for the devout in Carreg-y-Bedd made an abrupt arrival along with the woollen blankets, the 'carthenni', on the wedding night. The Biblical words shrouded rather than revealed the real meanings. The doctor doubted whether Caron was even half aware of the definition of 'lust', let alone whether she understood the nature of homosexuality in Sodom and Gomorrah. The village lads had a better understanding. Their comprehension began with furtive, playground jokes, progressed to knowledge gleaned through the activities of rams and bulls and culminated in bawdy talk in the 'Lamb and Lion'.

Though he was disappointed with the gipsy lad, the doctor's pragmatic view was that lads will be lads. The full extent of his wrath was reserved for Mali Tudor. For Mali and others like her, the animalistic side of life was shrouded in dark nights and the prison of the marital bedroom. What sort of mother was she to allow her daughter to remain in such ignorance? Did she really believe that silence provided a protective moat that would ensure virginal purity?

"Doctor, what am I going to do? Mam'll kill me." Caron looked pleadingly at him as if expecting him to provide an instant solution.

Richard Owen was firm.

"You will have to tell her Caron."

"But not yet doctor, do I?"

Explaining the gestation period, the doctor explained that she would 'show' soon. In his opinion she was fifteen to sixteen weeks. Soon it would be impossible to hide the fact of her pregnancy. Caron's loose, baggy hand knitted jerseys and bulky flannel skirts worn with boots could hide a swelling abdomen for some time yet but not for ever. She could delay the evil day probably beyond Christmas but come February, Mali would have to be told.

"When the time comes, would you like me to tell her Caron?"

"Oh, would you doctor?"

"If it will make it easier for you, then I will." Whether it would be easier the doctor questioned. Nothing with Mali Tudor was easy. She would be outraged. But his prime priority was to alleviate Caron's anxiety.

"Caron, you are a healthy, strong young woman. You will be fine. As to the practicalities of the birth and looking after the baby, well we'll face those problems when they arrive. It won't do you or the baby any good to worry. I'll let you get used to what's happened and then we'll speak again. It would be best if you could come to see me every four weeks or so, then I can just check you're keeping well."

"If I can get away doctor I will but it may be difficult."

"Just come if you can Caron. Now shall I take you back?"

"No but thank you. Mam and Tad would wonder why I was with you. I'll walk."

"And don't go riding that horse of yours Caron. A fall from him could cause both you and the baby some damage."

Caron gave her agreement but privately knew that Jac may prove her only way to see Abram alone, if he came back. Giving up riding would result in awkward questions. She was always getting into trouble for leaving her chores to ride Jac. To avoid suspicion she knew she needed to carry on as normal. In any case she had been riding all through the summer with no ill effects.

The walk home was not a happy one. The rods of rain reflected Caron's mood. Droplets clung to her red-gold hair and trickled down her nose and chin. She huddled deep into the protection of Twm's coat, wishing he were there with her. She thought back. It was only seconds. Surely it took much longer than that to create a human being. She didn't feel pregnant. She didn't feel anything. Perhaps Dr. Owen had made a mistake. Unconsciously her hands moved to encircle her belly. True it was fatter than it had been but it was still firm and hard. Caron, lean and lithe, was unused to carrying any weight. She had noticed the waistbands of her skirt had become a little tight and that she had to leave the button undone on the brown serge. But she hadn't thought anything of it. It couldn't be true. She would wake up tomorrow morning and the whole problem would have gone away.

The luxury of deliberation disappeared the next day with the onset of the fruit harvest. Siôn, Caron and Bethan collected the hazel nuts from the ground underneath the two nut trees that flourished beyond the rhubarb, where the garden bordered the stack yard. They spread out the nuts on newspaper in the attics so they would be ready for Christmas. Caron loved the plump nuts, swollen with nourishment, hiding shyly in their frilly autumn clothing that looked for all the world like elfin hats. She always liked to leave a few behind, covering them with leaves so that the squirrels could replenish their winter stores.

They started on the apples early on the 24th. It was Twm's twentieth birthday but in the Tudor household, birthdays did not disrupt work planned for that day. The only concessions were that Nain was baking a marble cake for them to enjoy that evening and that Twm had been presented with a new penknife to help him with daily tasks on the farm. He wondered idly if there would be a celebration for his coming of age in 1923. Emyr's voice penetrated his thoughts. His Tad usually worked in silence so this passionate outburst was more than unusual.

Emyr was regaling Mali. "I just can't believe it. Resigned! Resigned! And he won the war for us too. They're replacing him with Bonar Law. A nonentity! The country's gone crazy. We'll be losing the Empire next."

Twm was well aware of the reason for the outburst. His Tad was incensed by the resignation of Lloyd George, the Welsh Wizard as he called him. Since he'd heard the news he'd spoken of little else.

Emyr carried on. "Sheer talent got him where he was. Didn't have the advantages the other politicians had. Wasn't born with a silver spoon in his mouth. But cleverer than all of them put together. We were losing the war till he came along and sorted it all out. Practically out of ammunition we were. And now this happens. The country ought to be bloody grateful to him."

"Emyr! Emyr! I know you feel strongly about this but that's no reason to use foul language in front of the children."

Emyr carried on muttering under his breath.

Twm smiled. It was going to take some time...

The fragrant scent of apple lay heavy in the air. Wooden ladders were used to reach the highest branches. Mali issued commands. "Make sure you twist each one to separate the stem. If you pull at the branch, other apples will fall and get bruised. They won't keep then. And place them carefully in the baskets. Don't just throw them in. That will damage them too. Don't mix up the varieties."

Once a fair number had been picked, Bethan and Caron were responsible for carrying the baskets from the orchard into the kitchen and sorting the apples. Each one had to be checked, then wiped with a dry cloth. Windfalls stayed in the kitchen ready for immediate eating and for pies. Crisp, new born apples were packed off in their baskets to the two attic rooms, where they were placed in serried ranks on newspaper laid down on the boarded floors.

Mali issued more commands. "Don't let them touch mind. And make sure you put them in the right place." For the eating apples, she had covered one room with the 'Denbighshire Free Press'. The rosy stripes of Cox Cymraeg led the way, flanked by the sunset glow of the russet Croen Mochyn. The cookers inhabited the other room with the blushing Trwyn Mochyn and the pale Pig y Glomen occupying the free territory of the 'North Wales Times' and the polished, mottled Snowdon Queen pears marching down the centre on 'Y Gymraes'.

The larder was similarly under Mali's control. She and Nain spent long days bottling ruby coloured Denbigh plums and powdery coated damsons. These joined the neatly labelled raspberry, bilberry and blackcurrant jams and the bramble jelly stirred up when blackberries burst forth from among the thorns.

Picking the bilberries meant a long climb up to the moorland for the Tudor women. Despite the abundance on the bushes, the bowls took hours to fill with the tiny bilberries. Even more tedious was the task, allocated to the two sisters, of topping and tailing blackcurrants with tiny scissors kept for the purpose. To Caron, Bethan and Siôn, summer weeks were stained black or red, depending on the fruit in season. Most of their time was spent either gathering fruit or breathing in the heady scent of sugared sweetness colliding with tart juice, while jam bubbled away in brass preserving pans. Preparing enough food for the family was the main priority as October pointed its golden finger towards the long, freezing winter.

On the night of All Hallows, Nos Calan Gaeaf, Caron found herself alone in the room she shared with Bethan.

It wasn't so much that she hadn't been dwelling on her new situation, more that it didn't seem real. It was nearly a fortnight since the doctor's diagnosis and though she knew Dr. Owen wouldn't lie to her she still didn't feel any different. Now that the sick feeling had passed, she felt like the old Caron. Bundled up in her warm clothes, she didn't look any different either. But the main reason for her lack of anxiety was that she had a solution. She just needed to find Abram. She knew for certain that he would tell her what to do. He would probably marry her at once and carry her off to live with the Gypsies. From the little she had seen, it wouldn't be a bad life. They had caravans, plenty of food and horses. They also seemed to have fun. Fiddle playing, dancing, talking; all very different from Mali's constant haranguing. Gaiety was in short supply at Cwyn-y-Gwynt. There would be things that she would miss. Twm and Siôn definitely, but she could come to visit and they could come to visit her. Jac certainly, but maybe he could go with her. She had read somewhere that young brides often came with dowries. Jac could be her dowry.

In the bedroom she shared with Bethan, she sat in front of the mahogany dressing table with triple mirrors, adorned with china wash jug and bowl. She didn't really need to do it, she told herself, because she knew anyway what the answer would be but she would just do it for absolute proof. She idly traced the sky blue, rippled spout of the jug with her finger. A crack that began in the waist of the jug and made its journey outwards into the swelling hand painted body of the piece, separated a painted doe from her fawn, which was listening intently with pricked ears to some unknown sound emerging from the undergrowth.

Moving the pitcher and bowl to one side, Caron cast her mind back to Nain's words. "Start at the top and peel it round and round in one long piece." This would be easier said than done. To begin with, as she had thought, she had not found it easy to retrieve apples from the attic. A few days before All Hallows, Mali had visited the village to do some shopping. Seizing the opportunity, Caron had secreted a small kitchen knife under her clothing, removed the twig that secured the catch of the attic door and made her way up the stairs, wincing at every creak of the old oak boards. Thinking that eaters would generate better magic than sour cookers she had surveyed the rows of coxes and russets with dismay. It would be difficult enough to steal one apple, let alone two to use and one extra as insurance against the peel breaking. She decided that three of one type would leave a gaping hole that couldn't be disguised, so taking one eater of each variety and then picking up another russet that was fortuitously falling off the edge of the paper, she moved the others around to fill in the gaps, making sure to keep the carefully placed rows intact.

As she did so, a floorboard moved as she trod on it. It creaked ominously and Caron held her breath in case anyone had heard. Surely Nain couldn't hear as far away as the kitchen. She was just being silly. She relaxed and moved her toes. The board tilted slightly and she leant down to push it firmly back in place. In the dark cavity underneath, she caught a glimpse of something blue. Tipping the board further, she reached underneath and brought out a bundle of newspaper with some blue wool peeping out from one side. She opened up the paper to find a pair of knitted baby bootees with a buttoned ankle strap and three white flowers embroidered on the front. Dumbfounded, she wrapped them up again, replaced them and made sure the board was stable. Curious as she was, she realised she couldn't ask about them as doing so would raise awkward questions about why she had been in the attic.

Caron hid the apples and the knife in between her knitted jerseys in a drawer. The scent of them unnerved her. Not only did her garments emanate a cider-like odour but the aroma was evident in the bedroom itself. Fortunately, Bethan didn't seem to notice anything unusual or if she did, she certainly didn't say anything.

It was fortunate for Caron that Nos Calan Gaeaf fell on a Tuesday. Aware that she had no chance of undertaking supernatural activities at midnight, which seemed to her to be the ideal time, she settled for early evening when Bethan was with the minister. Though the Eisteddfod rehearsals had long since finished, Bethan was now helping with the sewing of costumes for the nativity play. She had invited Caron along, "You'll enjoy it. There's six women from Carreg and one of them is Ruth Parry."

"No, I won't enjoy it Bethan. I hate sewing. It's boring. Don't you remember when it took me weeks longer than anyone else to make a pinny in school and then it fell apart the first time I wore it?"

Bethan had sniffed. "You ought to make more of an effort Caron. It's important for every wife that she's able to make do and mend."

Caron turned her thoughts back to the pressing matter in hand. Retrieving the apples from their hiding place, she placed them in a row on top of the dressing table. The two Croen Mochyn and then the Cox Cymraeg. Where should she start? She picked up a russet first since she had two. Carefully inserting the tip of the knife by the stalk, she started to turn the apple against the blade. With the tip of her tongue held gently between her teeth, concentrating intensely, Caron slowly wound her way around the fruit. She was nearly there when the knife slipped, breaking in two the pink flushed curl. Cross with herself for being clumsy, she picked up the Cox. Practice makes perfect, she said to herself as she circled the fruit. This time she made it to the end, placed the peel carefully on the lace mat and then began to destroy the evidence by eating both the apples, including the cores.

Quartering the remaining russet and then slicing each piece into two, Caron inserted the knife through each section so they lay along the blade like beads on a string. Did Nain say the left shoulder or the right shoulder, she wondered. Holding the knife over the right, Caron looked deep into the mirror, the glow of the gas light creating a dark silhouette. She conjured up Abram's face in her mind, the contour of his jaw, the glint of his eye, the fall of his hair.

It was no use; Abram's image was there in her head but not in the mirror. Sighing, she thrust the knife, with its garland of apple segments, over her left shoulder. Giving the spell some time, she waited a few minutes. But it was just the same. Abram's presence simply did not inhabit the mirror. It might have been frightening if he had made an appearance, she told herself. Better that she try the second route.

Focusing hard on creating the mirage once more, she took a deep breath and threw the peel purposefully over her left shoulder. It landed beneath the window. It was going to form an 'A'. Realising that if she picked it up, it would lose its shape, she crouched down on the floor next to it. At first the peel simply looked exactly what it was, a curl of peel. But then she fancied that she could detect a 'G' or maybe a 'J'. It couldn't possibly be a 'Q'. She couldn't think of any male names that began with a 'Q'. She stared at it again, willing it to form an 'A'. Perhaps it was an 'S'. Disappointment struck her. Whether it was an 'S', a 'G' or a 'J', not even Caron's imagination could transform it into an 'A'. Perhaps she had not followed the ritual exactly. Well, it was no use, she couldn't try again as she had no more apples.

"Caron, Caron, what are you doing up there?" Mali's voice intruded into her thoughts.

"Coming Mam." Hastily she ate the last apple and stuffed the peel into her pocket to be disposed of outside.

Nos Calan Gaeaf had failed her. She must stop dwelling on a possible 'S' and concentrate instead on finding out if Abram and his family had already returned to the Llŷn to escape the worst of the Welsh winter's excesses. She had hopes that they hadn't. October had been dry and sunny, though a little on the chilly side. Often the month produced deluge after deluge. Caron could remember many an October where the cows had been up to their knees in mud with the ground squelching underfoot as she walked. This time it had been different with cold, crisp days easing the transition to winter. It was likely that Moses was earning some cash to last him through the winter by helping with the sheep, dipping them to protect against scab. In past years, he had been one of the potato pickers at Cwyn-y-Gwynt but this year, though Emyr would have been glad of the extra pair of hands, he had moved on to pastures new. The Gypsies are a law unto themselves, thought Caron, never sticking to a set routine, just going where their fancy or the work led them.

There was little chance, she knew, of tracking the movements of Abram's family. The Gypsies were not deliberately secretive; they just did not see the necessity of explaining their movements to non-Romanies. They probably wouldn't be that far away but ten miles was just as impossible for Caron as fifty or sixty. Mali would question a few hours absence and Caron's only mode of transport was Jac, who wasn't always available, and could only manage limited distances. An icy winter in Cwyn-y-Gwynt lay like a desolate mountain range between the two valleys of parting from Abram and being reunited with him.

Return of the Salmon

It was Tŵm who brought the news. He had been to the Bowens' farm, Ffynnon Ddu, to help out with some fencing. Sheep had been escaping from holes in the hedges. "He's not having a good day," Nia Bowen told Tŵm when he arrived. "Been crying he has. He's not done that before. First time." Nia, shocked, had found the crying more upsetting than the shouting.

"Perhaps that's a good thing," Tŵm reassured her, remembering the doctor's words about trauma being locked in. "I'm no doctor yet, though I hope to be one day, but maybe it's a sign he's getting better."

"I hadn't thought of it like that Tŵm. I thought he was getting worse." Nia smiled at him wearily.

"How is he now Mrs. Bowen? I can't fence without him. It needs two of us."

"Oh, he'll be helping you Tŵm. I just wanted to warn you that he might not be himself."

Tŵm was one of the few people who could cope with Gwilym Bowen's 'turns'. He just had the knack. Not frightened of Gwilym's appearance or of his odd mannerisms, he treated him just as he would Emyr. Gwilym worked in silence, every so often staring blankly at Tŵm as though he had never seen him before. Tŵm issued instructions which Gwilym followed to the letter. Whether it was his imagination, Tŵm wasn't sure, but it did seem to him that Gwilym was calmer. Certainly, there was no sign of a twitch. When they finally left the lower pasture, adjacent to the farm house, it was stockproof. Tŵm accompanied Gwilym back to the kitchen. Gwilym pressed down the latch and gave the door a heave, as it always stuck at the bottom. They found Nia seated at the table, her head in her hands. From the state of her reddened eyes, she had clearly been crying. Gwilym stopped and looked at her. Nia looked up at them. She had clearly been surprised by their unexpected entrance.

She won't want Gwilym to see her upset, Tŵm thought. There was a long, awkward pause. Tŵm tried to think of something to say; anything to fill the silence. Then Gwilym walked forward and put his arm round her shoulders. She leaned her head against him and he surrounded her with his other arm.

Nia started to sob but this time with joy. "He's never done that, Tŵm, never. Not since he came back from Ypres. You're right. I think he's turned a corner."

Tŵm left. They needed time alone.

He began to walk back, glad that though the wind was getting up, it wasn't raining. It wouldn't take too long to reach Cwyn-y-Gwynt. Deciding to return down a bridle path which skirted the forest, rather than go through the village, he smelt the smoke before he saw it.

"Nos da Tŵm."

"Nos da, Moses. What are you doing back? Thought you'd have made your way to the coast by now."

"Ay, we're late this yeer. No doubt abou' thet. Be goin' soon t'ough. Idris Jones, Tan-y-Waun, decided t' try winter wheat t'is yeer. Bit high up if yer ask me. Anyway 'e wanted some 'elp wi' t' sowin' so thet's where we've been."

"So why have you come back this way Moses?"

"Cadog Roberts, Banc-y-Defaid, 'as a mare fer sale. Sal's gettin' on a bit now so I wan' t' go an' see if I can do a deal. Real nice 'orse she is. Strong 'indquarters, short back, clean limbs, gud eye. Liver chestnut but yer can't 'ave everythin'. At least she not be 'n unlucky grey. An' she's got two white socks. Wouldn't call Cadog a friend 'zactly but it's better t'an t'ree or four."

Tŵm was bemused about the socks. "What do you mean Moses? About the socks and the friend?"

"Eh, lad, don' yer know t' old rhyme?

'Ave a 'orse wi' four white socks, keep it not a day,
'Ave a 'orse wi' three white socks, send it far away,
'Ave a 'orse wi' two white socks, sell it t' a friend,
'Ave a 'orse wi' one white sock, keep it till its end.

Lot o' truth in them lines. White socks mean white 'ooves an' t'ey're not as strong as t' black 'ooves."

"Oh, I see," said Tŵm, unravelling in his head Moses' comments about Cadog Roberts's mare. He smiled to himself. He would like to watch the duel between Cadog, known to be as tight as a rusty lock, and Moses, the grandmaster at horse dealing. He would back Moses any day.

This view was supported by Moses' next comment. "Should be able t' knock down t' price anyway. No 'orse looks good at blackb'rry pickin'. Winter coat comin' t'rough."

The wind was screaming round the gable end when Tŵm reached Cwyn-y-Gwynt. Struggling with the kitchen door, which threatened to tear itself from his hands, he was more than happy to reach the warmth of the range. Rubbing his hands together he turned to face Nain.

"Hard day Tŵm?" she asked.

"Not too bad. We did a good job."

"And how's Gwilym Bowen?"

"A little better, I think. He worked well."

"Such a pity. Bright as a button as a child. I feel very sorry for Nia Bowen. She has her work cut out there."

At that moment Mali came through the door. "Well, at least she's got a husband. Save your pity for Ruth Parry if you want to feel sorry for someone. I'm glad you're here Tŵm. Your Tad needs some help outside. Brad's not back from Yr Efail. Tad sent him to fetch the plough blade that was in for repair. Weyland Philpin must make a good living. He's always busy and his prices seem to go up every month."

Tŵm reluctantly removed himself from the proximity of the range to go back out into the cold night air. As he did so, Emyr appeared. Seeing his son was on his way out, he observed, "Tŵm, you can stay inside. I've finished. It didn't take me as long as I thought."

"Supper won't be long," Mali told him. "Where's Caron? I need her to help. Bethan's at a society meeting at the chapel. Caron's always sneaking off to her bedroom. I just don't know what's the matter with her. If she's got her head in a book again, I'll give her what for."

Shouting for her younger daughter resulted in Caron appearing almost immediately. As the Tudors sat down for chicken broth and freshly baked bread, the conversation turned to equine matters.

"I think I'll send Cariad to the next horse sale. She's never going to be any good. Has a mind of her own and won't work well with another horse. She has to be in charge." Emyr looked relieved at the prospect. He had spent many a futile hour trying to train Cariad to work with Samson.

"Bit like my Mali then!" Nain laughed.

Emyr allowed himself a smile. He would never have got away with such a comment but Nain always went where a spouse feared to tread.

Fortunately, Mali took it as a compliment. "Someone has to take charge of family affairs and I'm best placed to do that. You're too busy with the farm Emyr. Though I say it myself, I'm first-rate at organisation."

Emyr took the sensible route. Expert at placating Mali, he responded with, "You certainly are. I don't know where we'd all be without you."

Caron diverted the conversation back to Cariad. "Oh no, Tad. Please don't sell Cariad. She just needs some more time. And Delilah's getting older. She needs less work." Caron always became attached to the animals, especially the horses and hated to see any of them depart the farm.

"No, I've made up my mind. Samson still has years left in him. Delilah should keep going for a bit yet. But you're right Caron, she needs to do less work. I must buy in a youngster. Part trained. That would mean we could use the new horse sooner rather than later. I'd like to get a mare; then we can breed from her too. I think I'll go to the next horse sale. It's at the end of the month."

"Funny you should say you're in the market for a horse Tad. I was speaking to Moses earlier and he's looking to buy a mare from Cadog Roberts of all people."

Emyr laughed. "I don't envy Moses trying to do a deal with that old skinflint. I didn't realise Cadog had a mare for sale but it must be a good one or Moses wouldn't be interested."

"I didn't know the Gypsies were back," Caron's voice interrupted. "It's late for them to still be here."

"I think it's short-lived," Twm replied. "Only until Moses acquires his horse."

"Moses'll run rings round Cadog." Emyr laughed. "Deserves it as well. Mean old devil."

Mali jumped in. "Language, Emyr, language!"

Emyr ignored her. Accomplished at shutting her out, it was as though he hadn't even heard her.

"Where was Moses, Twm?" Caron, sensing this may be her last chance, was insistent.

"I was just getting to the end of the green lane that winds round in between Ffynnon Ddu and the forest. The caravans were on that wide verge where the lane joins the road. Nice, sheltered spot for them. It's surrounded by holly trees."

"That'll please Moses!" Nain exclaimed.

Puzzled, Twm asked, "Why?"

"Romanies feel secure near what they call the trees of God. Serves a dual purpose. Physical and spiritual protection."

"I didn't know that. Why the holly tree?"

Nain replied, "I think the prickly leaves are the crown of thorns and the red berries the blood of Christ."

"Would seem to make sense," Twm said.

Mali sniffed. "Load of pagan nonsense."

"You don't want to dismiss Gypsy beliefs so easily," Nain interjected. "Your Hen Taid told me a story about a Gypsy child. She caught the measles; nasty disease. Can be fatal. She had it real bad. Her Hen Nain cured her with powdered holly leaves. She made them into a tea and got the child to drink it. Girl was at death's door but within a day she was sitting up in bed. Cures whooping cough too."

Twm, shocked, said, "Sounds downright dangerous to me. I'd rather have a proper doctor."

"Quite," agreed Mali. "If I was ever ill, not that I am, I'd trust modern medicine not some witch's brew. It's 1922 for goodness' sake not 1622."

"There's not much can be done for measles." Twm couldn't resist using his knowledge. "Dark room, rest, lots to drink."

Caron, uninterested in talk of diseases, had found out what she needed to know. It was probably her last chance to see Abram. And see him she must. She knew the bridle path well, having ridden Jac along it many times.

"Is Jac being used tomorrow?" She had spoken out loud without really thinking.

It was Emyr who answered. "No, he isn't. Why? Do you want to ride him? He could do with some exercise. You haven't taken him out much lately."

Caron, grateful for this encouragement, answered. "Yes, I think I will."

Mali's response was immediate. "Then you've got another think coming, Caron Tudor. You needn't think you're going off riding, leaving Bethan and I to do all the work."

"Oh, please Mam. Just this once. The weather'll be getting bad soon and I won't be able to go. Tad said that Jac needed the exercise. I promise I'll do all the jobs when I get back."

Emyr supported her. "Let her go, Mali. She's right, Jac needs the exercise. And it won't do Caron any harm either. She's looking a bit peaky. Needs some fresh air."

Mali grudgingly agreed but with a toss of her head to indicate her displeasure. "It's bedroom cleaning day tomorrow and don't think Bethan will do your work for you. It'll be left for you so don't be away too long."

The next morning Caron, remembering the last time, when Moses and his family had left the camp in the forest before she got there, rose when it was still dark. Trying not to disturb Bethan, she hastily dragged on her clothes and crept out to find a surprised Jac still lying down. Deftly she tacked him up complete with saddle. Dr. Owen's advice had hit home. Soon she was riding in the direction of Ffynnon Ddu. It didn't matter that it was still dark; she knew every track intimately. Jac, though well accustomed to rough ground stumbled over a clod of earth at one point, throwing Caron on to his broad neck. She manoeuvred herself back into the saddle, remembering again Dr. Owen's caution about falling off. Well, it couldn't be helped. The risk was worth taking. She had to see Abram.

This time she knew where she was headed and before long she could see the dark shapes of the caravans silhouetted against the lightening sky. Nothing stirred. She was too early. She would look ridiculous if she turned up in the camp now. She could have no possible excuse for being there.

Jac nickered to Brân and Sal who neighed back. Panicking, Caron turned Jac and despite the grey half-light cantered him away, heading into the forest rather than risking early risers at Ffynnon Ddu catching sight of her. After about half a mile she reined in Jac and dismounted, allowing him to regain his breath. She hadn't thought it through. In desperation she had simply ridden towards Abram but Abram was with his family. If she waited for a while until the Gypsies woke, she could ride to the camp but she needed to see Abram alone and there would be no chance of that as she wouldn't need escorting out of the forest like last time since the caravans were right next to the lane. Additionally, she was worried about how suspicious it would look to turn up at the camp so early. She couldn't plead it was an accident since Moses would know that Twm was likely to have told her where they were. She thrust her arm through Jac's reins as he nibbled at the short grass and sat down on a hummock beneath an old elm. What was she to do?

Caron didn't know how long she had been sitting there when she heard the sound of hooves. Looking up she saw Brân approaching. Abram slipped to the ground, loosed Brân as usual, and seated himself beside her.

"How'd you know I was here?"

"'eard Brân whinnyin'. Knew t'ere mus' be 'nother 'orse around. T'would be unlikely thet anyone else 'cept yer would be out t'is early. Saw Jac's 'oofmarks an' followed 'em."

"I wanted to see you."

"Well, I'm 'appy t' see yer too." Immediately Caron felt Abram's lips on her mouth, arms round her body, reaching for her breasts, and pushing up her skirt. He began to breathe heavily. "Come back fer more kissin' 'ave yer?"

"No, no." She thrust him away.

"What's t' matter? Yer seemed t' like t' body kisses las' time."

"I didn't realise... I didn't know that it could cause..."

"Cause what?"

He sat back down, leaving a rift between their bodies. Caron, needing the comfort of closeness, edged towards him. She shivered. The air had an icy edge. Abram put his arm round her shoulders.

"Come 'ere. Yer cold."

"Abram, I have to speak to you."

"Well, I'm 'ere an' I'm list'ning."

Now that she had the chance, Caron was speechless. What could she say? How could she possibly explain without using forbidden words?

"Abram, I'm not well."

"Not well? What's t' matter wi' you? Yer look t' picture of 'ealth t' me."

"Yes, well, it's not that I'm sick..."

"If yer not sick, t'en 'ow can yer be not well?" Abram teased her. Despite the pressing nature of her confession, Caron had to fight off the desire to kiss him. Searching for courage, she took his hand in hers.

The words fell over each other. "Abram, I'm going to have a child."

Abram was silent for a long time, a very long time. Whatever Caron had expected it wasn't this. She didn't say anything else. There was nothing else to say. So she waited. What she hoped was that Abram would provide her with a solution. Tell her what to do, what to say, help her extricate herself from the predicament she found herself in.

Eventually Abram turned to her. "So, whose child is it? Who's t' father?"

It took a while for the significance of his words to sink in.

Caron flushed red with embarrassment. "What can you mean? You are, of course."

"T'ere's no of course abou' 't. We didn't... we didn't do what pe'ple need t' do t' mek a baby. 'ave yer lain wi' someone else?" Abram's anger was evident in his raised tone.

Caron stared at him in utter disbelief. "Someone else? Dwi'n dy garu di. I love you. Only you." Realising she had voiced her feelings, she stopped in confusion.

"I don' believe yer. Yer must've been wi' someone else."

"Abram, I haven't been with anyone else. You must believe me. I love you and I thought you loved me."

"Love, love. It's a bit soon fer thet ain't it? Yer t' first girl I touched. I don' want a woman an' a baby yet. If yer 'aven't been wi' another man, t' doctor must've made a mistake."

Caron, suffused with relief, answered, "Do you think so? Do you really think so? Dr. Owen is a good doctor."

"All doctors can mek mistakes. Now put 't out of yer 'ead an' stop worryin'. 'ave you got a kiss fer me? T'en I mus' get back. I'll be missed."

"I won't see you again for a long time, will I?"

"Not 'ill Easter. No' thet long."

Trying to keep calm, Caron asked, "Where will you go?"

"T' Llŷn. Prob'ly near Llanbedrog. Good, sheltered spot t'ere. Less lik'ly to 'ave snow."

Strangely Caron was no longer so upset about not seeing Abram. She had got used to it. For the last few weeks, the dread of having to impart such shocking news to Mali had displaced the fear of separation.

Riding back to Cwyn-y-Gwynt on a loose rein, Caron's mood was lightened. Abram had reassured her. It was all a misunderstanding. She must have misled Dr. Owen. Unintentionally of course but perhaps she didn't tell him the right things. She determined to put it all out of her mind.

Emyr was in the yard when she returned. He was nursing a bill hook. "You must've been out early. Jac had already gone when I went to feed the stock." Not expecting a reply, he continued, "Brad and I are going to start laying that hawthorn hedge today between the five acre and the potato field. Be a long job, but a job well done."

"Is Twm helping?"

"No, I've told him to move the ewes in with the ram. Shouldn't be too bad a job with Jono. That'll mean the lambs'll be born when the weather improves. Don't want them arriving too early."

Caron took Emyr by surprise by asking if she could help.

"Don't know what help you're going to be but you can if you want. You'd better check that your Mam doesn't want you first."

As it turned out Mali wouldn't allow Caron outside until the bedrooms were cleaned. It was a Thursday and that meant, barring a sudden death, the dust had to be removed from Cwyn-y-Gwynt's second storey. Mali's dictum was, 'Cleanliness is next to godliness'.

When Caron eventually managed to walk over to Twm, he had nearly finished. "When will they lamb Twm?"

Twm, busy sending Jono after a ewe that had broken from the flock, didn't look up. "Gestation period is about five months, so April."

"Is that the same as people?"

Twm laughed. "No, women are nine months."

"And how does the ram... well you know?"

Twm, used to biological matters, explained in a matter of fact way, choosing his words carefully.

"I didn't know that. About rutting."

"Well, what did you think happened? It's the same with the cows and horses."

"I hadn't thought about it much. Tŵm, is it the same with people?"

"Yes." Tŵm, shocked at his sister's question, flushed bright red. "But I don't think it's a suitable topic for me to speak to a girl about. 'Specially my sister. Anyway, you don't need to worry about that. You're not getting married." He whistled to Jono to walk up.

Caron, mulling over her new information, was further relieved. She hadn't done anything like Tŵm described.

"Caron, watch where you're walking. Keep away from that ram. They get aggressive during the rut." Tŵm's voice was urgent.

Caron made for the gate, giving the ram a wide berth. It was going to be alright. She could forget about it.

November 11th happened to fall on a Saturday.

"We're going to have a war memorial soon in Ruthin. The council decided last spring," announced Emyr. He watched the clock carefully that morning. "Remember that at the eleventh hour," he announced at breakfast, "we'll all respect the Great Silence and think of those who were lost in the war. Whatever you're doing at that time, you stop and reflect. I won't have anyone in this family muttering a single word during that two minutes." Emyr's tone resonated with his strong feeling. "We owe them a huge debt of gratitude. We still live in a free country and it's all due to soldiers like Evan."

Later when Nain's long case clock struck the hour, Caron leant her floured hands, sticky from making suet pastry, on the window sill and watched as Emyr paused in his walk across the yard and stood with his head bowed. She turned her thoughts to Evan. As a friend of Tŵm's, he had often visited Cwyn-y-Gwynt to either help with some jobs when extra hands were needed or to go rabbiting, fishing or exploring the forest. She had liked him. A lot. You couldn't not like Evan, she thought. He filled a room with his presence. Irreverent and funny, he had often been at the receiving end of Mali's sharp tongue. "Evan Griffiths, you'll get yourself into trouble one day, mark my words." Full of life and vigour, it was easy to imagine that the door would open and he would walk in. "Look you, Caron. Have you made that pie 'specially for me? You must've known I was calling." His deep, musical lilt was so clear in her head that she looked round half-expecting to see his face and find that news of his death had all been a terrible mistake. She found it impossible to visualise a dead Evan, stretched out on the battlefield, his voice silenced.

Out in the barn Twm stood stock still next to the pitchfork he had been using to toss hay down into the hay racks in the stalls. His mind too was filled with Evan. How could Evan have got himself killed? He had always seemed invincible. How had a mere German got the better of him? Evan had enjoyed not only muscular strength but native cunning. With a confidence that in anyone else might be termed arrogance, Evan simply had no fear of anyone or anything. Even Cadoc Morgan was wary of him. He remembered one day after school when Cadoc was scrapping with young Hywel Morris over a broken pencil.

Cadoc had been vociferous. "Ya snapped me pencil in 'alf."

"I never did," snivelled Hywel.

"Yes, ya did. Ya saw it'd dropped on the floor so ya picked it up an' broke it in 'alf. Now I'm gonna break you in 'alf."

Hywel shuffled backwards against a wall and Cadoc saw his chance. He grabbed both Hywel's wrists and pinned him against the bricks.

Suddenly there was a hand on Cadoc's shoulder. "Pick on someone your own size Cadoc Morgan." It was Evan.

"An' who's gonna stop me?"

"I am."

Cadoc, still keeping a tight hold on Hywel, twisted his head round and looked directly into Evan's eyes. He saw steely determination.

"A'right. I'll let it go jus' this once. But," he turned to Hywel, "if it 'appens again I won' be so forgivin'. I'll 'ave summat special in store for ya." He left the threat hanging in the air and swaggered off with, "'ey Gethin, wait for me."

"Yella," commented Gwyn. "He was scared of you Evan."

"And so he should be," retorted Evan. "I would've hammered him into the ground."

"Rather you than me," Twm commented. "He's tough is Cadoc."

"Not as tough as me though," answered Evan. "And I had right on my side. I would've beaten him to a pulp and he knew it."

Twm was dragged back to the present by Emyr's, "Twm have you finished feeding the hay?" The two minutes was over and duty called. Remembering more about Evan would have to wait for tomorrow's memorial service.

Ebenenezer was packed. Everyone was there to remember Armistice Day, most wearing poppies. Emyr had driven the trap into Ruthin the day before to buy them for his family. "I'm sure wearing a poppy is going to become a tradition," he said to Mali. "And it's such a good way of raising money for those who've lost limbs."

"Nonsense Emyr, it's an American fad. It won't last."

Despite the chill in the air Nain had come with them. "When I think of the sacrifices those men made, I feel I must be prepared to suffer some discomfort myself," she had told Mali. Twm allowed himself to drift along on the waves of haunting music that filled the chapel. Daniel Ellis had chosen a new hymn, sent to him by a friend in London, and the words '*I Vow To Thee My Country*' held special resonance when he thought once again of Evan. '*That lays upon the altar the dearest and the best.*' Evan certainly was the dearest and the best. Dear to his family, his friends and astonishingly to Bethan. Gwyn had told him that he "couldn't have coped" in France without Evan. What was it he'd said? Oh yes...

"He looked after me Twm. He kept me safe. Most of all he got me through when I was sick with fear. I don't know what would've happened if he hadn't done that. I'd probably have been shot for desertion. He was more than a true friend. The word 'friend' doesn't do him justice. He was my saviour."

Twm thought back to one early afternoon when he had at last gained some insight into Gwyn's war. He and his friend had taken a break from checking the sheep for foot rot. Summer flies had increased the number suffering from the condition. Twm remembered that they had leant their backs against a handy buckthorn and munched pork pies that Bethan had baked the day before. It had been a sunny day and they had sat for too long enjoying the warmth. Their conversation had turned, as it so often did, to Evan.

"I just wish Evan was here to enjoy sunshine and pies," Twm said. "Simple pleasures, I know, but it's so sad he can't share in our day."

Gwyn had smiled. "If he'd lived Twm, I doubt very much that he'd be sat here with us. He'd have been off doing something exciting. He told me that after the war was over, he wanted to fly a plane like Alcock and Brown and become a movie star like Douglas Fairbanks! I remember teasing him and saying, 'Both at the same time?' 'Why not?' he answered. 'Life's for living. And I intend to live every second to the full'."

"And I bet he would've as well," Twm answered. "He certainly had the looks of a movie star and he could act as well. I'll never forget him mimicking Mr. Pugh or as he called him, Mr. Poo. My sides ached from laughing." Twm paused. A shadow passed over his face. "Sometimes I feel guilty for enjoying life when Evan can't. It's as though everything is spoilt with him not here."

Gwyn suddenly became very serious. "If you feel that Tŵm, then think how bad it is for me. I'm here and Evan isn't. And he deserves to be sitting here with you and I don't."

"Of course, you deserve to be here Gwyn. You fought for King and Country as well."

"But not bravely Tŵm. Not like Evan. He was a real soldier. I wasn't."

"Gwyn, we're not all natural soldiers. I wouldn't have made a good soldier either. I don't think I could've killed anyone, even a German. We each have our talents. You're a fine artist. Evan couldn't draw a straight line."

Gwyn allowed himself a wry smile. "Yes, but at the Front, being able to fight was a lot more useful than being able to draw. And you would've been able to kill the Hun, Tŵm. If it were you or him, you would've done it, I'm sure of that. But I wouldn't be here if it wasn't for Evan. He literally saved my life more than once. Tŵm, I was a coward. I have to face it."

"I'm sure every soldier was frightened Gwyn, just like you."

"It's true a lot were. But I was worse than most. One time, we'd spent a couple of weeks in the support trenches but then we were moved to the front line. We were told the enemy would attack the next day. I was so scared, I got diarrhoea. I told Evan I was going to report sick with dysentery to the commanding officer. 'No, you're not Gwyn. You're going to stay here with me. I'll see you alright. You wouldn't be the first to try that one and if you tell him that you're ill the captain will watch you like a hawk. There's a big difference between dysentery and being shit scared and they know the difference. They'll get you for malingering. Before you turn round, they'll make a spectacle of you and handcuff you to a post for hours. Then again, if they count it as cowardice before the enemy you'll end up before a court martial and I wouldn't give much for your chances if that happened'."

"Did they really shoot our own men Gwyn? I've heard rumours but did it really happen?"

"Yes Tŵm. Evan saved me from both death and dishonour at least twice."

"Twice? What was the other time?"

"I was on sentinel duty. It was a cardinal sin to go to sleep on duty because that would put everyone in grave danger. But I was exhausted. We all were. I dozed off and woke to Evan shaking me. 'Gwyn, Gwyn. For God's sake Gwyn, wake up.' I dragged myself back to consciousness to find Evan's face looking anxiously in to mine. 'I knew you were tired Gwyn and thought you might drift off. The captain is on his way to check everyone. It's curtains if he finds you asleep'."

Twm, aware that, unusually, Gwyn was talking about the battlefield, seized the opportunity. He knew it may not arise again. "Gwyn, why was Evan awarded the Military Medal? I know he rescued another soldier. His Mam told me but none of us know the detail. Were you there?"

Gwyn paused before replying. "I certainly was Twm. Perhaps I should've told you before but it's hard to talk about what happened... out there. If I talk about Evan, I have to talk about me as well. And that's tough. Very tough. And I don't want you to suffer my fate." Twm was startled. "What do you mean?"

"I don't want you to share the pictures that haunt my head. Once they're there, they're there forever. It's like trying to dig solid rock out of the earth. You cannot shift them no matter how hard you try. But I think I've been wrong not to tell you about Evan. He was your friend too and you should know just how brave he was. I haven't even told my Mam because I didn't want her to know what my Tad and I went through; I wanted to spare her that."

Then pride suffused his voice. "You've never seen anything so plucky. Such a shame he didn't live to receive his gallantry award but he was killed only a few days later." He paused again, clearly struggling to voice those images breathing in his head. Unaccountably he began in what sounded like the middle of the story.

"The thing was Twm, none of us could see. Thick mist, made worse by smoke, shrouded everything. If I think about it, then even now I can taste the acrid smell in the back of my throat. I was choking and coughing. To make it worse my eyes were stinging from the gas that hung in the air. I kept rubbing them. Bad as it was, we'd been lucky as most of the shells had landed further down the line. We were on the edge of it. The noise was deafening with the constant bombardment. I just didn't know where I was or what to do next so I stayed on the fire step and kept my head down."

"Where was Evan?"

"I thought he was next to me. I had my eyes shut against the onslaught of the deafening noise; planes roaring overhead, shells thudding, artillery firing. I was praying for it all to be over. My throat was closing up so the last thing I wanted to do was talk. Then I heard Evan shouting at me, 'Gwyn, Gwyn, help us down.' His voice seemed to come from above me. I just thought it was my confusion. But it wasn't. I looked upwards and there was Evan on the parapet with a body draped across his shoulders. Evan ducked his head, slid the torso forward into my outstretched arms and then skidded down a scaling ladder. As you know, Evan was built like a Shorthorn bull but I staggered backwards under the weight. All I could do was stutter out, 'What? How?'

'It's the chap who was on the barbed wire in front of us. I couldn't leave him there,' Evan told me. He'd only gone and rescued a lad from off the wire in the middle of No Man's Land. I couldn't believe he'd pulled such a stunt but he had," Gwyn went on.

"Did many soldiers get trapped on wire?"

"Oh, Tŵm, you have no idea. Way too many ended up like that. This fellow had been groaning for hours. To my shame, I just wanted him to stop. The sound was getting on all our nerves. Sid, one of the gunners, voiced what we were all thinking. 'Wish he'd hurry up and die. I can't stand it any longer.' The only one who did anything about it was Evan. I didn't see exactly what he did. I was too busy keeping my head down. It was the others who told me. They said Evan waited for a break in the shelling and then made for the nearest shell hole as fast as he could, given mud up to his knees. Apparently, he dived for cover just in time as the machine guns strafed the ground around him. Then he started to crawl to the wire. He wouldn't have made it I'm sure but the Boche must've realised what he was doing because they stopped firing."

"Why?" Tŵm asked.

"I honestly don't know. Maybe they saw that Evan was not firing at them but just saving a fellow soldier or perhaps the groaning was getting to them too. After all they're human as well. Terrible tales were told about the enemy you know. Some said they cut off children's hands and ears; others that they used the fat from Allied corpses to make soap. I didn't believe much of it. Most of the Huns I saw were young boys and just like us they were terrified for the most part. I'll never forget one day, not long after Evan was killed, when I saw a group of our lads herding German prisoners along a sunken road. It was hard to tell who was in the worst state; us or them. There was a young British officer in charge but he was on the point of collapse with exhaustion and thirst. His knees started to buckle and you'll never guess what happened Tŵm?"

"What?"

"This German handed him his water bottle. Just like that. His water bottle! Can you believe it? I'll never forget his face. Had round spectacles and a trimmed moustache. I remember wondering how he'd managed to keep it tidy on the battlefield. Mind you, I had seen some soldiers using the water in shell holes to give themselves a shave."

Tŵm tried to divert Gwyn back to his story. "And Evan?"

"Oh, where was I?"

"The wire. The soldier was stuck on the wire."

"Stuck is the right word, Tŵm. Like a stuck pig he was. Hung over the fence like a flag over a coffin. From a distance he looked almost graceful, swaying there in the breeze. Been there for hours. Must've been well-nigh impossible to lift him off but Evan managed it. I could see from his shoulder titles, he was a young lad from the Cheshires. Fighting alongside us they were. The wire had torn him to shreds. The worst was his face. Half ripped away it was. I suppose dragging him off the embedded wire had slashed his skin even more. Blood was seeping through his uniform. Evan was covered in it."

"Did the soldier survive?" Tŵm enquired.

"I don't know. He was in a bad way. The stretcher bearers took him off to the field hospital. Never saw him again. Thing was we saw so many wounded. We never knew who lived and who died."

"Evan richly deserved his medal then. He showed extraordinary courage."

"Courageous Tŵm, yes, but foolhardy as well. By rights, Evan shouldn't have survived. If they'd started with the machine guns again, he'd have been shot to pieces. But that was Evan all over. Act first and think later. You know what he was like."

Tŵm did know what Evan was like. He knew only too well. He had vivid memories of an escapade where they were more than lucky to elude detection. It had all been Evan's idea. It always was.

"Let's go to Bryn-y-Castell."

Tŵm and Gwyn looked at each other. "What do you mean?" Gwyn asked.

Tŵm was puzzled. "Do you mean the woods, the park or the lake? We'll have to ask permission if we're going to do that. And what for? We're not allowed to fish or shoot on estate land or on any of the farms. Do you mean just to explore?"

"Well, exploring's a good idea but I don't mean that. I mean the house."

Puzzlement changed to incredulity. "The house? You've got to be kidding!"

But Evan wasn't kidding. "Aren't you just a little curious? Don't you want to see what it's like, see how the Craddocks live?"

"But we can't Evan." Tŵm was sarcastic. "What are we going to do? March up to the front entrance and ask to look around?"

"Well no. That mightn't work," conceded Evan. "But Llinos Rowlands has started cleaning there now she's left school. I'm sure she'd let us in through the side door if I asked her nicely. I know her really well."

Yes, I'll bet you do, thought Tŵm. Llinos, younger than them, was slim, pert and pretty. Evan was popular with the female population of Carreg-y-Bedd. They were drawn to his easy charm like moths to a flame.

Gwyn was immediately concerned. "She'll lose her job Evan, if she gets caught."

Evan was not to be deterred. "But it's up to us not to get caught."

Tŵm decided to use sarcasm. It was always a handy weapon with Evan. "And when exactly do you think this guided tour of the mansion can take place? I suppose you're going to arrange for the Craddocks themselves to go out or are we going to somehow dodge round them without them noticing us?"

This time Tŵm's plan failed. Evan was undeterred. "Tŵm you're reading my mind! I happen to know that none of the Craddocks are at home today. They've gone off to a funeral. Lady Craddock's godmother has died. Llinos told me." Evan's crooked grin was at its most mischievous.

"You want to go now?" Gwyn was struggling to take in this novel venture. "But we're supposed to be fishing. If we go back without any trout, your Mam is going to want to know why, Tŵm. She's depending on fish for supper."

"We can always say we had an unlucky day." Evan had an answer for everything. "If we go now, Llinos'll be there. She's only there in the mornings."

"How do you know Llinos'll open the door? There's lots of servants working there."

Evan shifted uncomfortably on the river bank. "I've been there a couple of times before. Not in the house. Just to meet Llinos. She scrubs out the back hall mid-morning so if she hears a knock, she knows it's me. We grab a quick five minutes for a 'chat'. He winked at Gwyn conspiratorially. Her Mam doesn't like her seeing me you see. Says she's too young."

"Evan, you're a dark horse." Tŵm was startled. It hadn't crossed his mind that Evan had been seeing girls.

Half an hour later found them outside a side entrance to Bryn-y-Castell. They hadn't risked the main drive but had crossed the estate grounds, narrowly missing a couple of grooms exercising two horses, by hiding behind the Shooting Lodge. It was a toss-up whether Gwyn or Tŵm was the more uncomfortable but Evan had been persuasive.

"What harm can it do? It's not as though we're going to steal anything. We just want to look that's all."

Despite his reservations, Tŵm too wanted to see inside. Evan was right; it would be interesting to see where the Craddocks lived.

Gwyn voiced his trepidation, "We're going to get into terrible trouble."

"Only if we get caught. And we won't." Evan's confidence was contagious. Even Twm, naturally cautious, was infected. The door opened instantly after Evan's gentle rapping.

Llinos must've been waiting, thought Twm. Her face lit up at the sight of Evan but then quickly fell as she noticed his two companions. "I didn't say you could bring friends Evan."

"Only thought of it this morning. Seemed a good idea. Oh, come on Llinos. Live a little dangerously! Let's have some fun!" He put his arm round her shoulders and gave her a quick squeeze.

She blushed. "Oh, alright but you'll have to be quick. The other housemaids are busy in the bedrooms, the cook and her helpers are in the kitchen and the butler's gone off on an errand." She ushered them in. "Take your boots off. They'll make too much noise. Then follow me. We need to be very quick."

Doing as they were told, they crept silently behind her in stocking feet. Evan had a large hole in one of his socks, Twm noticed. His big toe was poking through. Llinos led them through to an oak panelled hall, dominated by the family coat of arms, from which led a carved staircase. Glossy tables displayed vases of pink roses and cream gladioli jostling for position with fine china ornaments. They sped silently across the Persian rugs into a vast drawing room dominated by a stone fireplace and furnished with deep settees, comfortable arm chairs, a huge cabinet inlaid with ivory and several, fine occasional tables displaying photographs of the Craddocks and their dogs. Craddock ancestors surveyed proceedings from lofty oil paintings. The eyes made Twm feel as though he were being watched. His skin prickled.

"Hurry up," Llinos urged them as they tried to take it all in. She moved them back into the hall and then opened another door. It proved to be the dining room with a mahogany table stretching into the distance surrounded by twelve upright chairs upholstered in crimson velvet. A massive sideboard with a marble top dominated the far wall. Heavy, cherry-coloured drapes hung at the sash windows.

Suddenly a bell rang. Llinos panicked. "There's someone at the door. The footman'll see you. Hide under the table in case he comes in here."

Squashed in between chair legs, along with Gwyn and Evan, Twm had a few moments to reflect on his precarious position. How could he have allowed Evan to persuade him? It was more than stupid. It was downright dangerous. It could lead, at best, to Sir Edward Craddock speaking to Emyr and at worst to a thrashing at home and arrest by the police. 'Wanting to have a look round' sounded a lame excuse even to Twm. No-one would believe them. They'd think they were there to steal things. He looked at Gwyn. He was shaking with fear.

They could hear voices in the hall. "Sir Edward and Lady Craddock are away today I'm afraid. Can I take a message?"

Tŵm recognised Daniel Ellis' reed thin voice. He couldn't quite make out the reply. He heard footsteps and then the door shutting. Then, to his horror, the dining room door opened. It was the footman.

"I thought I heard someone in here," he said to Llinos, who'd taken a cloth out of her pocket and was attempting to rub at the sideboard.

"Just giving it a quick polish," she answered.

"I thought it was always done on a Friday."

Llinos was quick to reply. "It is but the windows have been open and it's got a bit dusty." To her relief the footman accepted her explanation and disappeared. "Come on, you must go immediately," she hissed at them.

They padded back the way they'd come and were out of the side door within seconds, pulling on their boots, not stopping to do up the laces.

"Never do that to me again Evan," Tŵm told him. "We had a narrow escape."

Evan, refusing to be chastened, simply replied, "I told you we wouldn't get caught. And we saw the rooms. Live in the lap of luxury, don't they? Bet none of our pals have seen in there."

"Not that we can tell anyone we've seen it," interrupted Gwyn, "or they'll ask us how we know what it's like."

Tŵm, deep in his reverie, was dragged back to the present by Binyon's words:

> 'They shall grow not old, as we that are left grow old:
> Age shall not weary them, nor the years condemn.
> At the going down of the sun and in the morning,
> We will remember them.'

The images of Gwyn and Evan had loomed large, more real than the worshippers around him. There were times that Tŵm could scarcely believe that his two friends were not still with him and this was one of them. But he at least knew the reason for Evan's death. He was slaughtered by the Hun as so many others were. But Gwyn. Who knew what had happened to him? And why? Tŵm resolved once more to get to the truth of the matter.

Bethan had been providing Daniel Ellis with the pleasure of her company now for several months. She was looking forward to the opportunities that the Christmas services offered. After Eisteddfod practices were over, she volunteered for teaching the children's group at Sunday School, playing the organ and leading Bible classes.

"Always at the chapel," Emyr grumbled. "I can never find her when I want her."

Mali defended Bethan. "Don't criticise her for serving God, Emyr. There's a few others round here who would do well to follow Bethan's example. Never see them in chapel from one month's end to the next. Don't help with anything. She's a good girl. You should be proud of her."

"She's never here." Emyr was not going to give up. "She's at the chapel most evenings, barely here at all on a Sunday and now she tells me she's going to write some letters for the minister. Organising visiting preachers, that sort of thing."

"Well, I don't see how any of this affects you Emyr."

"It means Caron has to do more in the house and can't help as much outside. She's good with the animals. It helps if she feeds the chickens, grooms the horses and takes the slop to the pigs. Leaves Brad and Twm more time for the heavy work. Bethan would do well to remember that charity begins at home, in my view."

Mali sniffed. "I'm glad Caron's useful for something. She takes hours longer than Bethan to clean and cook. And she seems to have slowed up even more of late. Lives in her head, that's her problem. I don't know how she's going to end up."

"Oh, she'll be fine, Mali. Don't worry about her. She's a good lass. A bit giddy I grant you but her heart's in the right place."

"I'm more concerned about her hands than her heart Emyr. Ten thumbs she has."

It was true that Caron's fumblings were no match for Bethan's deft fingers, equally good at shaping butter, darning socks, knitting jerseys or dicing vegetables for cawl. Bethan's household skills were a match for Brad's dexterity with dry stone walls or a difficult calving.

Caron was only too aware of her grievous lack of proficiency. She had often wondered why she hadn't inherited the Tudor practicality. It would have made her life so much easier if she could produce well risen scones or a neatly hemmed sheet. The problem was that she didn't know what she wanted to be. Her parents and siblings knew their place. Emyr and Brad were born to be farmers; Mali's and Bethan's vocation lay in hearth and home; Twm's dreams lay with medicine. Only Siôn's young path had yet to unfold.

Thinking of the future reminded Caron of Dee and how her friend couldn't plan what she wanted to do until she was better. It couldn't be very pleasant lying in bed all the time. Dee must be bored. Caron determined to write the promised letter and as soon as possible. Accordingly, that night she sat at the kitchen table after supper with pen, ink and paper.

"You're a caring girl Caron," Nain said. "Dee will be glad to get your letter. It will cheer her up. What are you going to say?"

Caron had no idea. She couldn't risk telling Dee about Abram. Mali may well decide to read the letter before Caron had chance to hide it in an envelope. Then again, Dee's Mam and Tad may read it after Dee had received it. Anyway, she wasn't sure how Dee would react. She would certainly be surprised and she might even be disgusted. Dee was a good girl, obedient and well mannered, the last thing in the world she would want would be to bring shame on her parents, as Caron had, by meeting a boy alone. Caron couldn't decide if Dee would understand or if she would condemn her friend's behaviour as stupid or wrong.

In the end she restricted her news to the farm activities, the chapel gatherings and the fact that, despite her objections, Emyr was going to sell Cariad and buy a new horse. Dipping her nib for the final time into the black ink, she finished the letter by sending everyone's good wishes for a speedy recovery and signed it, 'Love Caron'.

Mali put out her hand. "I just want to check the spelling. You don't want to send it with any mistakes in it."

Caron handed it over. She had been right. Mali was going to read it. Thankfully even Mali couldn't object to the simple catalogue of events. However, she couldn't resist a final dig. "Love Caron," she uttered contemptuously. "She's not your sister. You need to change that and write 'sincerely'."

"But I'll have to write it all again Mam."

"Yes, you will."

"Then please can I have another piece of writing paper."

"Paper's expensive Caron. I haven't got it to waste. Alright, just this once, you can leave it but don't write 'Love' again."

"No, Mam." With relief Caron licked the envelope to seal it. She would take the letter to the post office the next day.

Late November saw Bethan on a mission. In June she had passed into her twenty third year. Time was moving on. Her project had not been going well. True she spent every moment possible with Daniel Ellis but she did not seem to be making progress. She couldn't understand it. After all she had devoted herself to the service of both Daniel and the chapel. What more could he possibly want? She had moulded herself into the ideal minister's wife. No-one in Carreg-y-Bedd was more moral, more obedient to God's Word, more devout or more dedicated to community service.

Not only that but she was unparalleled in the household skills of neatness, cleanliness, and thriftiness, able to produce economical yet tasty meals, grow fine produce and repair a torn clerical collar. She was more than useful to him, she knew that. So why hadn't Daniel asked her? She had provided the opportunity for him more than once, ensuring that they were alone in either his house or God's house. But it was of no use. Daniel had remained formal, business-like, distant, confining himself to conversations concerning event dates and times, the arrangement of refreshments and the selection of appropriate psalms.

It wasn't as though she had any competition. Daniel certainly had shown no indication of interest in any other woman in the congregation. She was certain of that. She had been checking. She scrutinised every sidelong glance, each moment of eye contact during the sermon. Daniel's gaze did not seem to linger on Sarah Bevan, Manon Price, Lowri Pritchard or indeed any of the more than adequate supply of single females caused by the shortage of husbands after the war. In fact, as the words from Galatians rang from the pulpit, *'This I say then, walk in the Spirit, and you shall not fulfil the lust of the flesh,'* his holy contemplation seemed not to discriminate between the safely espoused and the dangerously independent.

Bethan found Daniel a difficult man to age but she guessed at approaching maturity since she knew that Ebenezer was not his first chapel. Blandly expressionless, his features lacked both laughter and worry lines. He believed life was a serious business and needed to be approached with impassivity. Surely, she thought at his stage of life he should understand that it was simply inconceivable that a minister should not have a wife. She had drawn his attention to the advantages of a spouse by displaying her culinary skills, taking him samples of her drop scones and a jam sponge. Then one afternoon, noticing a pile of mending, she had performed more intimate tasks, repairing a rent in some trousers and sewing on buttons. Giving the situation considerable thought she realised with a start that she was already fulfilling most of the duties of a minister's wife. All except one of course. She shuddered. That didn't bear thinking about. Especially with Daniel Ellis. But it was unavoidable. That she knew. The unpleasant wifely duty, of which she knew little beyond the fact that it must be endured, along with the pangs of child birth, was part of the married purity of the one flesh.

The solution came to her relatively quickly. She needed to withdraw all her help. With no-one to play the organ, oversee rehearsals, teach Sunday School, help the children to memorise and recite verses, lead Bible classes and help with letters, Daniel would soon see that she was invaluable. She began her plan immediately by developing an unfortunate sore throat and cough that prevented her from discussing matters theological.

If she had expected a triumphant climax to her machinations, she was to be disappointed. Her efforts were in vain. Rather than cancelling the Bible class, Daniel enlisted the willing help of Lowri Pritchard. Then to add to Bethan's mortification, Mali stepped in to recount parables to the Sunday School and Gareth Bevan took over playing the organ. It seemed she wasn't indispensable. She would have to offer what Mali and Gareth could not before Lowri Pritchard seized her chance of occupying the vacant pew.

Making a speedy recovery by the next Tuesday, Bethan determined to stay behind after debating the Second Book of Corinthians Chapter 4 with the Bible class.

"Mr. Ellis, I wondered if you would care to help me choose the texts for next week? The group feel we should focus on comfort in times of grief. I want to make sure I echo what you say in the pulpit."

"Very wise Miss Tudor. After all we don't want any ambiguity confusing the congregation. I would suggest Ecclesiastes 3 Verses 1-4. I think it puts tragedy in perspective.

'For everything there is a season, and a time for every matter under heaven: a time to be born, and a time to die; a time to plant, and a time to pluck up what is planted; a time to kill, and a time to heal; a time to break down, and a time to build up; a time to weep, and a time to laugh; a time to mourn, and a time to dance'."

Bethan responded with, "So many families have lost sons in the war. The holy texts provide comfort for them as they struggle to come to terms with their loss. Of course, I'm still unmarried so haven't yet experienced the joy of children. I do hope to have children in the future though. I expect you do too, don't you Mr. Ellis?"

Daniel Ellis, ignoring the question, proceeded with, "Then I would follow on with John 3, verses 16-17, reminding them that God too lost his own Son:

'For God so loved the world, that he gave his only Son, that whoever believes

in him should not perish but have eternal life.'

And finally, of course the resurrection, to remind people that they will meet their loved ones again in heaven.

1 Thessalonians Chapter 4, verses 13-18 is ideal.

'But we do not want you to be uninformed, brothers, about those who are asleep, that you may not grieve as others do who have no hope. For since we believe that Jesus died and rose again, even so, through Jesus, God will bring with him those who have fallen asleep.'

I believe that if you direct the discussion around those three texts, God will Himself comfort the grieving."

"Thank you very much Mr. Ellis. That is of great help to me. I find I rely more and more on your spiritual guidance. I don't know how I would manage without you." Bethan allowed her hand to unintentionally brush his hand as she said the words.

Daniel Ellis drew his fingers away sharply, to clutch at the Bible that lay on the table. He held it before him as though for protection.

"If that's all, then I think you'd better be getting back to the farm. It will be a cold, dark walk though you have the goodness of the Lord to protect you."

Bethan tried again. "It's cold but it's not wet. I can stay to talk about the readings further."

"No, you have given enough of your time. I insist that you go home."

Bethan sighed. She had given him the pleasure of her extended company as well as the chance to talk about children and marriage. It had been to no avail. She didn't expect him to fall in love with her. Her time for that had long since disappeared. But she did expect him to see the practical advantages of becoming her life's companion.

"Mr. Ellis." She took a risk. "Daniel."

Daniel Ellis' face became suffused with crimson.

"That is just too familiar, Miss Tudor. We are alone. I must protest."

Bethan decided to forge ahead, to seize the initiative. "We have a lot in common, you and I: a strong belief in God, a desire to help the community, a life of service to others. Could I dare to hope that we may share a future together?"

The implication took a while to register. When it did, Daniel Ellis' discomfiture manifested itself in anger. "How could you suggest...? So improper! So unseemly! I must ask you to leave at once and never raise the subject again."

To her chagrin, Bethan found herself hustled outside. On the long walk home, she had time to muse on her humiliation. Alright, it had been a step too far, too soon. But she would have felt worse if she hadn't raised the possibility of lifelong commitment. After all she couldn't wait much longer.

She put the conversation behind her and switched her thoughts to Trefor.

Emyr was as true as his word. One morning, his enthusiasm not dampened by Welsh drizzle, he rose at four in order to walk Cariad the few miles to Ruthin station. "I'll put her in a wagon on the train. It's a much bigger horse auction at Abergele than it is in Ruthin," he said to Tŵm. "With a bit of luck, I'll get a good price there." He and Tŵm had spent a couple of hours the previous day making sure Cariad looked her best. Her dark bay coat was shining, her hooves oiled and glistening, her two white socks and narrow blaze pristine white. "We'll plait her up," he told Tŵm, "but won't bother with flights and loops, rolls and rings. It's not as if she's going in a showing competition. I want her to look her best but I don't want to spend hours and hours decorating her. That won't push up her price. They'll buy her on conformation and strength, not prettiness."

Caron too got up early to say goodbye to Cariad. She was in tears as she threw her arms round Cariad's huge neck and laid her face against her. "I don't know how you can part with her Tad. She's part of the family."

"Now, now Caron. Don't go upsetting yourself. Cariad's a work horse, not a pet. Every animal on this farm must earn its keep. The cats have to hunt the rats, Jono has to round up the sheep and as for the horses, well we couldn't farm without them. Cariad doesn't pull her weight. She'll go to a good home, don't you fear."

"How can you be sure Tad? If she's not a good work horse then why would somebody buy her?"

"She is a good work horse Caron but not in a team. She's too much of an individual for that. Likes all the attention and wants her own way. Just won't listen to the other horse. She'll make a good horse for a farmer who wants a single horse to pull a small plough or a roller. She'll be ideal for that."

Prising Caron from Cariad, Emyr clipped the lead rein on to the head collar. "Now stop worrying and go and get my dinner. I think your Mam's put up some bread and a bit of mutton along with two apples wrapped in pastry." He looked up at the sky. "I'm glad the rain's going off. Cariad'll look better dry."

He called to Tŵm, "I'll be gone all day," and followed this with, "You and

Brad can manage ploughing the stubble I'm sure."

Twm nodded his assent as Cariad clattered out of the yard for the last time.

By the time Emyr returned it was already dark. He was not alone. Caron, hearing hooves striking the cobbles, left the stew she was stirring and raced out of the kitchen. "She didn't sell then Tad! Oh, I'm so glad you've brought her back." She followed Emyr into the stable.

"Since you're here Caron you can fill the racks with hay. Just go into the loft will you and throw it down." He lit the lantern and held it up. Caron stopped in her tracks. The young Shire horse in front of her was not Cariad.

"Cariad's gone to a good home Caron; you don't need to worry. Young farmer from the other side of Corwen. Just starting out by himself. He was very pleased to find a young, strong mare. I told him she played up in a team and he said it didn't matter as he'd only have the one horse. Wanted her to haul logs, clear the land, pull a plough. Cariad has fallen on her feet, well hooves anyway. He laughed. The lad knew horses and she took to him straight away. I got a good price for her too. Now what do you think of this young lady?"

Caron stood back. "She's a nice horse Tad." The horse in front of her was jet black with four white stockings and a white star on her forehead.

"She certainly is, isn't she? A real beauty. Clean limbed as well. Had to pay more than I was expecting but she's worth every penny. Rising four she is, so she's not fully trained yet." Emyr was teetering on the edge of excitement. Like his daughter, he loved his horses. "She'll be at her best by the time Delilah retires."

"She's not the same colour as Samson. They won't look as good together when you use the wagon for a Sunday School outing or take the choir to an eisteddfod. Nor will the team be likely to win at shows."

"That's true Caron but she was by far the best horse there. And the most important thing is how she works. It's just a bonus to win at the shows. I can always show her in hand by herself. And as for social events, I'm not one of those farmers who like to show off as you well know."

Twm came in to the stable. "I wondered what was going on, you were so long," he said to Caron. Then he gave a slow whistle of appreciation. "What a splendid horse. You made a good choice there, Tad."

"I did, didn't I? I'm very pleased with her. She's a true black. Has a black muzzle. You can help me train her Twm. I was just telling Caron that she wasn't cheap but you get what you pay for. At least I got three guineas back as luck money. Thought I might have a foal out of her as well. Caron would you like to name her? She hasn't got a name as yet."

"Then we'll call her Black Beauty. Because she is."

Emyr had vivid memories of an inconsolable Caron when Ginger died in the book of the same name. Her tears were only surpassed by the ones shed when she read the story of the hound, Gelert, mistakenly slain by Prince Llywelyn, after a wolf attacked his baby son. Gelert had protected the baby, who was alive, well and hidden under the cradle, by killing the wolf. His blood-stained jaws had led Llywelyn to think that the dog had savaged the baby so he stabbed Gelert in a fit of rage. When he discovered the truth, Llywelyn never smiled again. The story haunted Caron still and she only had to think of it, for tears to spring to her eyes. Emyr, knowing his daughter's sensitive nature, asked, "Are you sure?"

"Yes Tad, I am."

"Then that's settled then. Black Beauty she is."

Caron's distress over the loss of Cariad paled into insignificance a few days later when another inhabitant of Cwyn-y-Gwynt met her destined end.

On the day Caron had been dreading she asked if she could go out riding on Jac. Mali had been firm in her answer. It was out of the question. She was needed for the work that was to follow.

So Caron found herself in the hayloft trying to block out the squealing. But no matter what she did or how tightly she pressed her index fingers into her ears, it was no use. The piercing shrieks continued unabated. She wanted it to stop. But then she hated herself for that. It made her a part of it all. If there was silence it meant that Susie was gone. At least she wasn't down there with the rest of the family; not yet anyway. It didn't matter in any case that she wasn't there. She could picture it all too clearly. Susie rolled on to her back, Twm and her father grasping her back legs and holding them together, Brad and Mali clutching her front legs just as firmly and Maldwyn Price, the butcher, standing astride her head with his knife raised; the bowl ready and waiting for the torrent of blood that would pour out. Caron had been a part of it too many times. At eight, she had been forced to hold the bowl. When she objected her Mam, puffing with exertion, had simply said, "You want to eat don't you?" and that was the end of that.

Caron dropped her hands, realising that an unnatural silence had descended on the farmyard. It was over. Gertie and Millie, she knew, would be huddled together at the back of the sty. Normally at this time, they would be snuffling in the corners of their yard, searching for scraps, real or imagined, left over from feed time. But they knew. She knew they knew. Nurturers turned killers. They sensed too that their turn would come. One mid-January; one toward the end of February. She wondered which one would be first. Knowing full well what awaited her, she made her way slowly down the loft ladder, through the barn and out onto the cobbled yard.

'No longer Susie' was already hanging head down, blood dripping slowly now into a bucket from a gaping gash. She had mis-timed it. She was too early. Maldwyn Price drew his knife and with the precision that stemmed from years of practice, slit the carcase from stem to stern. She caught the whisper of swishing stomach and guts spilling out into a steaming heap on to the floor of the pen. Emyr preferred to pay for the butcher's expertise rather than do it himself. "It's much quicker and cleaner if Maldwyn does it," he always said. Caron suspected that he didn't want to do it himself but didn't want to admit that to Mali. She would have seen it as a sign of weakness.

"Caron, come here." Her Mam had spotted her. She had no option. Mali handed her the wooden spoon to stir the blood that would become black puddings. She knew there was no shortening the allotted time. Mali would not allow the puddings to be spoilt by lack of stirring at this stage.

The execution may have been swift but the wake was long and lingering. Susie's corpse would be on display for days. The sweet, tangy scent of blood clung to Caron's nostrils. Combined with the acrid mix of tallow, singed bristles and hot skin, the scent of dead pig would hang in the air, permeating clothes and hair. There was no escape, even in the bedroom that she shared with Bethan. Worse still, she must encounter slabs of Susie for weeks on end. She would be sent to the cellar to find a chunk of meat, saltpetre packed round the bone, suitable for a Sabbath repast. Sides of bacon and plump, rounded hams would hang from kitchen hooks; the staple diet of the winter months. Once Susie was cooked, strangely Caron found the eating of her easier to bear than the constant guilty confrontation with grisly body parts.

Cooked Susie was a long way removed from the live Susie who grunted a morning greeting when Caron poured the slops into the trough. Sausages, chops, boiled trotters, belly crackling, bread and dripping were comfort foods on freezing winter days. The one exception was the seemingly endless brawn. She always pushed it around her plate with distaste, trying hard not to think of Susie's piggy eyes following her every movement round the sty. It had to be eaten though. "Waste not; want not," was one of her mother's favourite maxims. Caron was always scolded for smothering her brawn in brown sauce to try to camouflage its origins. Sauce too cost money.

All in all, it hadn't been a good month for Caron and she reached December with a growing sense of loss and despair. Abram had gone and though losing Cariad and Susie could not be compared, their absence increased her feelings of instability and insecurity. Then there was the harsh reality of Dee suffering in a hospital, miles away from home, and the haunting memories of Evan, brought forcibly back by the memorial service. No, there was no doubt about it; November had changed her world.

God's Month

A few days after Bethan's failure to capture Daniel Ellis' heart, a letter arrived for her at Cwyn-y-Gwynt. Mali, opened and read it before passing it to her daughter.

"Have you done anything to upset the minister Bethan?"

Though inwardly apprehensive, outwardly Bethan remained calm. "No, of course not. Why?"

"Because you have a letter here from him, thanking you for all your help but stating that other people are taking over most of your duties. It does seem a little strange. I don't recall anything like this happening in the chapel before."

Bethan scanned the missive.

Dear Miss Tudor

As minister, I am highly appreciative of the service you have given to the community, to the chapel and of course to God. As you are fully aware, the major posts of responsibility in the Chapel, such as conducting prayer meetings, are only open to the male members of the congregation but you have been so kind as to offer your services in many of the minor roles.

However, I am concerned about over-burdening you. To take on such a work load is admirable but it must be taking time away from your family commitments. I would not want chapel obligations to cause any kind of rift between you and your loved ones.

In addition, you must be aware that other members of the chapel community welcome the chance to be of service to others. I have several people who would like to partake in certain activities, only to find that you are, shall I say, the current incumbent. It is only right that they too have the opportunity to enjoy the gratitude of the congregation.

Since I have had positive replies from your letters to guest preachers, I find I no longer have a need for any help with paperwork as I have fewer sermons to write. Of course, the deacons will continue to manage chapel funds and the letting of pews and will organise accommodation for visiting preachers. With reference to the Bible Reading group, I have decided that every week a new personage will chair the discussions. This will increase the involvement of every member of the group and bring them closer to their God.

I am particularly anxious about the strain imposed by your Sunday School duties. Not only do you select the hymns, the passages of catechism, the prayers and writing exercises but you have also undertaken to write the teachers' minutes, balance the account books, check the attendance registers and organise the annual outing. That is a heavy load for one person, however willing. My intention is to have three Sunday School teachers from now on as I have a number of participants eager to take on the roles. This will give you a well-earned rest as more volunteers mean that there is no longer a need for your services.

I am sure you will understand and share in my concerns and support me in my resolutions. I do not want to deprive you completely of serving the community so you may still play the organ on alternate Sundays; Gareth Bevan will play on the other occasions. You will, I am sure, want to continue on the rota of ladies who clean God's house and provide refreshments on special days.

Thank you again for all your invaluable help in the past.

With gratitude
Daniel Ellis

Bethan's first reaction was relief. It would have proven very embarrassing to be alone with the minister. The only tasks left to her were public ones. He had been very clever in ridding the two of them of even the remotest possibility of conversing with each other. Paradoxically, at the same time, she felt the humiliation of rejection. She had worked very hard and knew she had fulfilled her duties more than satisfactorily. And for it to end like this!

Mali was not going to let the issue go. "I don't know, Bethan. He seems grateful for all you've done but to dismiss you like that from nearly everything... all you're left with is occasional organ playing and a skivvy's position. People will talk."

"Oh, Mam, what he says is quite right. Chapel was making it difficult for me to help you when you needed me. Tad was complaining about that. If you look at it that way, it was quite thoughtful of him to consider my welfare. Not everyone would've done that. Then he does have a point about other people being given a chance. Everyone wants a place in the chapel family. Perhaps I was a bit selfish in doing as much as I did. Time for someone else to take over now."

"Well, I suppose so Bethan but if I find out that you've upset him then you'll be in real trouble." An idea struck her. "You've just reminded me about your Tad. He did complain, that's true. What was it the minister said?" She soon found the sentence she was searching for. "'It must be taking your time away from your family commitments and from daily chores.' I hope your Tad hasn't had a quiet word with Mr. Ellis about the time you've been spending there! Woe betide him if he has! He'll have me to deal with if he's caused people to gossip."

"Surely not Mam." Bethan had the grace to feel somewhat guilty.

"Well, I hope not. I'll go to ask him now." Mali could soon be heard shouting in the stackyard. "Emyr, Emyr. Where are you? I want a word with you. Now!"

She found Emyr in the shippon and showed him the minister's letter. He immediately denied any interference. Knowing her husband as well as she did, Mali could see that Emyr was as surprised and bewildered as she was. She calmed down.

Bethan, for once, was unworried about Mali's threats. The only two people who knew the truth about what had taken place were Daniel Ellis and Bethan herself. She certainly was not going to divulge that information and she was sure the minister would not. She was safe.

Mali was right on one count though. People did talk. Nerys Philpin was the first to raise the matter with Ruth Parry. "Strange business that. Bethan Tudor was so involved in chapel business and now she's out on her ear. Wonder what's happened."

But they were left to wonder. Bethan was right. Daniel Ellis had no intention of discussing the issue.

Caron shivered as she dressed in bed underneath the blankets. She was used to taking her clothes downstairs and getting dressed in front of the fire but with her swelling tummy that was out of the question.

There were few visitors to Cwyn-y-Gwynt in December. The short days meant that essential tasks had to be crammed into fewer hours leaving little time for the luxury of social chit-chat.

That made it all the more surprising when a stocky roan pony clattered into the yard through the damp drizzle. Mali, hearing the hooves, stopped kneading dough and made her way to the window.

"Good heavens, it's Weyland Philpin," she informed Nain. "He hardly ever leaves his forge. What's he doing here? Perhaps Emyr needs something heavy repairing but he hasn't said anything to me." She watched as Weyland awkwardly removed his bulk from the pony's back, handed him over to Brad and made his way to the back door.

"Caron, carry on with the bread." She went to greet their visitor. "Weyland, what an unexpected pleasure. Please do come in."

Caron looked up as her friend's father made his way into the house. His heavy features were as leaden as the anvil with which he worked. As a child she had been frightened by his rough appearance but she had come to realise that his rather threatening face hid a kind heart. Bushy dark sideburns framed his face while a bulbous nose, reddened through constant close contact with hot embers, sat above full lips adorned with a heavy moustache.

Taking the seat Mali offered him, he unusually got straight to the point, omitting the obligatory pleasantries. Gruffly he started with, "Nerys sent me. I come with bad news."

Then he sat, bent his head and said nothing. Nain made a drink from the freshly boiled kettle and passed it to him. He wrapped his huge, calloused hands around the cup. "It's Dee. She's passed on."

"Passed on? Passed on? Do you mean she's been moved from Llangwyfan to a different hospital?" Mali enquired.

Again, there was a long silence.

"No, I don't mean that. I mean she's gone. Gone forever."

Realisation dawned. "You don't mean she's died?" Nain asked.

"Ay, I do. I do mean that. She's not here anymore."

Caron stopped kneading the bread and stared at Weyland.

"Dee? Dee? She can't be dead. She went into hospital for them to make her better. What's happened?"

Weyland Philpin broke down and sobbed. Caron had never before seen a man cry. Weyland was a strong man in every sense of the word. Muscular, with huge sinewed arms and legs resembling the trunks of ancient yew trees, it seemed impossible, thought Caron, that he could weep like a woman. "My only child. How can I carry on?"

Mali, unused to, what she considered to be, unedifying displays of emotion, decided brisk practicality would be the best approach. "Caron go and fetch your Tad. Weyland, pull yourself together. You have Nerys to think of and a business to run. Life carries on. Whatever life throws at us, we must bear it with God's help."

"God, God! Don't mention God to me. Where was He when Dee needed him? That's what I'd like to know."

"It's not for us to question God's will Weyland. You will be reunited with

Dee when you too reach God's arms."

"I wish I had your faith Mrs. Tudor. But I don't. When you're dead, you're dead. Extinction, that's all we've got to look forward to."

During the exchange, Emyr, alerted by Caron, had emerged from the barn and entered the kitchen, closely followed by Tŵm. Emyr laid a clumsy hand on Weyland's shoulder and applied pressure to relay sympathy. "Tell us what happened."

It took a good half hour to extract the facts from Weyland who kept digressing into tales of Dee's childhood. "She never was one for mischief," he kept saying. "All she wanted to do was help her mother. Loved nothing better than baking cakes. Made a tasty, spiced plum cake, she did."

It seemed that Dee's lung disease had advanced too far to be cured. "She just wasted away so quickly," her father told them. "Went to skin and bone. Then the coughing took a lot out of her as well. By the end she was exhausted. She couldn't carry on. I think she'd had enough and ran out of the energy to fight it. Llangwyfan did its best. Complete bed rest, no exertion at all. She couldn't walk across the room without being breathless."

"Did they give her any treatment?" asked Nain.

"Well, they made sure she had good food. Beef, eggs, cheese. That sort of stuff. Built her up I suppose. Didn't work did it?"

"Did you go to see her there?" Mali contributed.

"We went to see her whenever we could. It took some arranging. It's a long way. Train to Denbigh. Then my cousin, Wyn, took us in his pony and trap. He lives near the station. The room she was in was freezing cold. Had the windows wide open even though it was winter. Said she must have fresh air. Didn't do her any good if you ask me. It stands to reason you need to keep a child warm to get her better."

Tŵm couldn't resist. "No, Mr. Philpin. Cold, fresh air is part of the treatment."

He stopped as Emyr held up his hand to him. "That's enough Tŵm. Let Mr. Philpin have his say."

It didn't seem that Weyland Philpin had registered Tŵm's comment. He continued as though there hadn't been an interjection. "Dr. Owen called to tell us that Dee was worse and we should go in to see her but we didn't realise it would be for the last time. We were sitting with her and Nerys was holding her hand when she had a coughing spasm. Suddenly blood streamed out from her nose and mouth so I grabbed the bowl by her bedside and held it in front of her."

A graphic picture of Susie's passing flashed into Caron's mind. Nain, glancing across at her and noticing her stricken face, tried to remonstrate with Weyland, "I don't think..." But it was no use. Weyland was intent on finishing his story.

"The bowl was full in seconds but the blood was still gushing out. And that was it. Her head dropped back and she'd gone. An haemorrhage they said it was."

Nain tried to deliver what comfort she could. "It was quick then. She couldn't have known anything about it. That's something to be grateful for."

"Yes, that at least was a blessing." Weyland turned to Caron. "Caron, I have a letter here for you. Dee was very pleased to receive your letter and hear all the news. She showed it to us and said how kind it was of you to take the time to write it. It meant a lot to her. I found it under her pillow after she'd... well afterwards."

Despite her grief, Caron shuddered with relief that she hadn't mentioned Abram in her letter to Dee.

Weyland handed an envelope to Caron, who wiped sticky hands on her pinny before taking it. "We haven't opened it. It was addressed to you."

"Do you mind if I read it later Mr. Philpin? Your news is such a shock and I feel shaky." Thinking of Mali, she chose her words carefully. "I was so very fond of Dee."

Mali was quick to respond. "You'll do no such thing Caron. Mr. Philpin will want to know what it says. He's her Tad and he has a right to know."

"Nay, nay. Leave the girl alone Mrs. Tudor. She's right. It's a shock for all of us. Let her have some time to take it all in."

Mali sniffed. "Well, if you say so Weyland. I'm sure I'm very sorry for your loss. Please give my condolences to Nerys."

"I will indeed." Weyland rose to go. "The funeral will be Tuesday week. I hope you will find the time to come."

"We most certainly will," Emyr responded. "We will all be there to pay our respects."

"Diolch. That means a lot to Nerys and me. We've spent some time deciding on hymns. We thought we'd have, 'Loved ones gone before'."

"Very suitable," Nain agreed. "I love that hymn. We sang it at my dear husband's funeral. God rest his soul. If I remember the words rightly, they go:

'Loved ones have gone before
Whose pilgrim days are done
I soon shall greet them on that shore

Where partings are unknown.'

Or something like that anyway. You couldn't have chosen anything better. It reminds us that we will meet our loved ones again in the world after this. Death isn't an end. You must comfort yourself with that. It's a beginning."

Weyland smiled fleetingly. "I wish I believed that Mrs. Reece. The separation is so hard to bear."

When the blacksmith had left, Mali turned to Caron. "Well, come on, open the letter."

Emyr intervened. "No, Mali. As Weyland said, give her some time. You go upstairs Caron and read your friend's words. You can tell your Mam afterwards what it says."

Caron flashed him a grateful look.

Safe upstairs, she lay on her bed and tried to decipher Dee's rather spidery handwriting. She smiled as she recalled Mr. Pugh's acid comment as he disdainfully threw Dee's homework across the desk. "Dee Philpin, do you seriously expect me to read that? It looks as though someone has flicked paint across the page."

But Dee's writing had never improved. Its skeletal lines, a sad echo of its owner's physical state, crawled painfully from left to right.

Dear Caron

I was so thankful to receive your letter. It brightened up a dull day. Nothing ever happens other than a lucky patient gets to go home or an unlucky one gets sicker or worse.

Llangwyfan is a new building, clean, modern and surrounded by pine trees. Their lovely scent fills the air, helping to disguise the stink of disinfectant but sadly they can't take away the most powerful smells - of sickness, fear and distress.

There's only women and children here. I' m glad about that. I wouldn't want any boys seeing me in my bedclothes.

So you can get some idea of what my life is like, I've written you a diary of my typical day.

5.30am Temperature taken.

7am Wake up.

7.30am Bedpan. Bedwash (I used to be able to wash at the basin in my room but I'm not allowed out of bed now.)

8.30am Breakfast. Porridge, bacon, egg and fried bread. (They won't even let me feed myself now.)

8.30am – 11.30 am Bedrest. One pillow as I have to lie flat. Windows wide open so very cold. Room cleaned by nurses. Lino washed. At least something to watch.

11.30am Doctor visits. Examines me. Sputum test.

12.30pm Dinner. Stew, potatoes, rice pudding. (We have a lot of food especially meat. I thought I'd get fat as they won't let me exercise yet but I'm getting thinner.)

1.30 – 5.30pm Bedrest. Read books. Mam and Tad visit when they can. It's hard for them to get here and they're not allowed to hug me. Sometimes I see children crying outside. They can't come in to see their Mam or sister and just have to wave to them through the window.

5.30pm Supper. Cold meat and potatoes.

6.30 – 8.00pm Bedrest.

8.00pm Weighing.

9.30pm Sleep.

As you can see Caron, the days are very boring. I'm not allowed to do anything except lie here. They used to take my bed outside some days but I haven't been well enough for that lately.

When I get better, I will be able to get up to the toilet and to have a wash. Then if I improve, I will be able to go out for a short walk. That would be really nice.

The doctors are talking about collapsing one of my lungs. They want to give my lung a rest. I'm very scared about that. I'd rather die. I'm not scared of dying. After all it's only like sleeping but without waking up. But I'm frightened of pain. I get a bad pain in my chest sometimes and I can't take a deep breath without it hurting but I think an operation would give me worse pain and I don't want that.

I don't know how or why I got this terrible disease. I wish I did.

Pam fi Dyw? Why me God?

Sorry, Caron but I do feel miserable at times. Life is made a bit more bearable by a kind nurse here, called Clara. She tells me about her boyfriend, Sam, and about their plans for getting married. She puts her arm round me when I'm coughing and tells me not to be frightened because she'll always stay with me till I feel better. It's hard to be brave but she makes it a bit easier. One day she was coughing and I asked her if she was worried about catching my

*illness from me. She said she was but that she needed the money as Sam had
lost his job.*

*Some of the nurses frighten me. They are so strict about keeping to the
rules. I got caught out of bed one day. I was so bored that I went to look out of
the window. From my bed I can only see a branch of a tree. Well, I was told off
severely, I can tell you. I was told I was, 'A disgrace, an ungrateful, disobedient
girl who was undoing all the good that they had done me so far'. I'm not going
to risk being shouted at again. I suppose the nurse was only doing her job but
she made me cry. I'm not used to being shouted at. The only person who's ever
shouted at me before was Mr. Pugh and he shouted at everybody so I didn't
feel singled out.*

*The worst is being homesick. I miss my Mam and Tad, I miss you and I
miss Tiger. Mam said she would make sure Tiger had lots of cuddles while I
was away but he has only ever wanted me to stroke him ever since he was a
kitten.*

*I know it's difficult to get to see me but it would be nice if you could write
again.*

Love Dee

Caron allowed herself the luxury of quiet weeping. She couldn't believe Dee
was dead and she couldn't bear the thought of Dee being so unhappy before
she died. Added to this was a strong sense of guilt. Ever since she had met
Abram, she had badly neglected Dee. A mind full of romance left little room
for anything or anyone else. What sort of friend had she proven to be? And
now it was too late.

The guilt was intensified by the striking difference, made plain in Dee's
letter, of her life compared to that of her friend's. Poor Dee had been confined
to a small room and all she'd had to look forward to was being able to go to
the toilet by herself. It must have been like being in prison. She, Caron, had
all the space of Cwyn-y-Gwynt, lots of people to talk to and she was strong
and healthy.

She might be in a bit of a pickle at the moment and if the doctor was
right then she had Mali's wrath to face but she must keep it in perspective.
Nothing that was going to happen to her could possibly be as bad as what
had happened to Dee.

'An unlucky one gets sicker or worse'. Caron tried to imagine what it must
have been like for Dee to talk to someone one morning and then the next day
find that person was no longer there. It was no use. She had no idea. Cwyn-y-

Gwynt, cradled away from the struggles on the battlefields, had sheltered the childhood Caron from harsh reality. The closest death she had encountered was Gwyn Parry's and even then, she'd had no direct involvement. She had just seen the effect it had left on the living; Ruth Parry particularly of course but also Tŵm. Since Gwyn died, Tŵm had been withdrawn, brooding even. She hadn't paid enough attention to him. Her own worries had taken precedence. But now she thought about it, she realised Tŵm had lost his old, easy-going manner, his tendency to chat amicably with his favourite sister. With a pang, it struck her that both she and Tŵm had lost their best friends. She wished she had comforted her brother more.

She was not only a failure as a friend; she was also a failure as a sister. She couldn't do anything about Dee now. Dee was gone. But she could do something about Tŵm. Laying her head on the bolster for a moment, she resolved to change, to stop thinking solely about her own troubles.

Caron's reverie was rudely interrupted by footsteps on the stairs. Mali was not to be deterred for long. "Have you read the letter Caron? What does it say?"

Caron handed it over. There was no point in doing anything else.

"Well, I don't know," Mali commented. "What a silly girl, going against doctors' orders; they must know best especially in a special hospital like that. Not that getting out of bed would've made any difference, it doesn't look like. From what Mr. Philpin said she was too ill to recover anyway. And I don't see any reason why she had to give you all that unnecessary medical detail. Such things shouldn't be talked about. Toilets indeed! And other words that would never pass my lips! Then the fuss she makes about being homesick! She should've been grateful she was in the best place. At least it gave her a chance."

"Mam, Mam. Dee's dead. Dead! She was only eighteen. She won't be able to get married, have children or find any kind of happiness. It's so unfair. And all you can do is criticise her!"

"I shall ignore that last remark Caron, since you're upset. And what makes you think that life is fair?"

With Christmas approaching Tŵm decided to go into Carreg-y-Bedd. His well-worn boots had a hole in the sole and needed mending before the winter really set in. However, he had another reason for wanting to go out. The 'Lamb and Lion' was playing host to a rare troupe of clog dancers and he wanted to watch them. They were on tour and had a fine reputation for both dancing and for lively tunes. Knowing that Mali would condemn the double sin of crossing the threshold of a drinking establishment, let alone indulging in the dubious pleasures of music and dance, he decided discretion was the better part of valour.

"I'll probably call in on the Griffiths' or the Bowens," he told Mali. "so don't keep supper for me. I'm sure they'll give me a bite."

Walking on new leather, he reached the 'Lamb and Lion' as it opened its doors. The Long Room was being used for the occasion. Presiding over the event was the landlord, Bryn Powell. He was clearly enjoying himself, his creased countenance much in evidence as he did his best to organise his customers.

"'ey Bryn, 'ave ya bin waterin' down the ale? It's criminal it is, sixpence a pint for gnat's piss."

Tŵm turned his head. Cadoc. That meant Gethin wouldn't be far away. It had been a while since Tŵm had seen the Morgans. Not that it worried him. An absence of Morgans was only to be welcomed. He decided to stay well away from them. It was easy to merge with the crowd as most people were pressing forward to get into the front row. Tŵm wedged himself behind the bulk of Ieuwan Benyon. He glanced across at Cadoc who was puffing away on a Craven A. He didn't seem to share his brother's preference for Woodbines. Unexpectedly, rather than Gethin, Bronwen was standing next to Cadoc. Tŵm, not fully able to escape the chapel philosophy, felt the shock of surprise. A woman in the 'Lamb and Lion'! But then the Morgans lived according to their own rules.

It wasn't long before the fiddlers made their entrance, followed by the four clog dancers. Tŵm found himself tapping his foot in time with the rhythm of the steps. The audience showed their enthusiastic appreciation by clapping and stamping, the noise reaching a crescendo with the high leaps of the 'toby stepping'. Then there was a pause as Bryn Powell emerged with a candle in a brass holder. He placed it carefully on the floor in the centre of the dancers. The fiddles started up again; the men tapped their way round the candle. There was a roar of applause as a burly, bewhiskered dancer deftly snuffed out the candle with a quick movement of his clogs.

It was over. Tŵm edged his way towards the door. He couldn't be too late or Mali would start asking questions.

Cadoc spotted him. "Not man enuff for beer," he sneered. "Surprised ya Mam allowed ya to come." Tŵm hadn't dared to drink, knowing the smell would taint his breath. Thinking it best to ignore Cadoc, he carried on through the door, emerging into the chilly night air.

A voice behind him said, "Hello Tŵm. It's some time since I saw ya."

Tŵm turned. "Good evening Bronwen. Going home are you?"

"Yes. Thought I'd get out o' there while Cadoc can still stand up. I don' want the bother of gettin' 'im 'ome."

Tŵm thought this plan seemed eminently sensible. He wouldn't want to deal with a drunken Cadoc either. He glanced at Bronwen. Tŵm was not totally immune to the charms of the fair sex. It was just that he had other priorities. There was no doubt about it, Bronwen, with her upright carriage and fine bone structure, was a beauty. There was no-one to rival her, he was sure, not only in Carreg-y-Bedd but in the whole of North Wales. Shame she was a Morgan.

"I'll walk with you through the village, Bronwen. It's dark. Not pleasant to be out by yourself."

Bronwen tossed her head. "I can look after meself Tŵm Tudor. But I'll walk with ya to the beginnin' of Lane End since ya goin' back 'ome that way."

"I've not seen you for a while Bronwen. What have you been up to?"

Bronwen bridled. "Oh, this an' that. I don't like yar tone Tŵm Tudor. What do ya mean, up to?"

"I didn't mean anything by it, Bronwen. Just a figure of speech. Wondered whether you were thinking of getting yourself a position somewhere."

"No, Mam an' Tad need me at 'ome. Bein' the only girl, I 'ave to 'elp in the 'ouse and with growin' the food. Tad, Gethin an' Cadoc take a lot of feedin'."

Tŵm took a risk. "They'll have to manage without you when you get married."

"An' wot makes ya think I'm goin' to do that?" Bronwen was immediately on the attack.

"Nothing. It's just that lots of people decide to do just that."

"Well, not me Tŵm. I got more bloody sense. I'm not breedin' a pile of kids an' slavin' for some poverty-stricken chap." Used to male attention, she suddenly became coquettish. "Tŵm Tudor. Fancy ya raisin' the subject of marriage. Are ya askin' me to go out with ya?"

Tŵm was at a loss. Startled by hearing a woman swear, he was even more shocked by Bronwen's effrontery. The last thing in the world he wanted to do was to step out with Bronwen Morgan. Even if he wanted to, which he didn't, it would automatically lead to a leathering from Cadoc and Gethin. But to answer, 'No,' sounded blunt and discourteous.

He prevaricated. "Oh, Bronwen, I know you wouldn't be interested in courting me."

Bronwen stopped and turned to him. Looking directly into his eyes, she increased his discomfiture. "Don't know why you say that Tŵm." She traced around the outline of his jaw with her finger. "Ya'r not a bad lookin' lad. Strong body, 'onest face, kind blue eyes. An' in time, the owner of Cwyn-y-Gwynt. Ya'r not a bad catch for any girl."

Still holding his gaze, she raised her lips to his and kissed him long and hard. Tŵm, despite himself, succumbed to the delightful sin of his first kiss. Bronwen pulled back suddenly and Tŵm felt a stinging slap on his cheek.

"Tŵm Tudor. How dare ya kiss me without me permission! Wot kind of girl do ya think I am? Wait till I tell Cadoc wot you've done. 'e'll give ya wot for."

Tŵm, taken aback, handled the situation clumsily. "But I didn't. You kissed me."

"Y'ar nothin' but a liar Tŵm Tudor. Takin' advantage of a girl in the dark like that. Jus' like ya frend y'ar."

Tŵm, despite his confusion and sensing an opportunity, recovered himself. "Bronwen, stop playing games. You know perfectly well I didn't do anything wrong. What do you mean about my friend?"

"Ya'll 'ave a 'ard time provin' ya didna force me. Nobody to see ya, were there? And as for yar friend. Weird 'e were. Lurkin' behind trees tryin' to draw me picture. I were real mad with Cadoc though. Ruined me portrait 'e did. It were a good likeness. I could've kept it. Cadoc said 'e didna wan' that creep droolin' over me picture. That's why 'e wrecked it. Threw it back at 'im 'e did. Told 'im 'e were lucky 'e didna ram it down 'is throat. Real funny it were seein' that Gwyn Parry scrabblin' about on the ground to pick it up before 'e ran away with 'is tail between 'is legs. Cadoc said 'e were just the same during the war. Enemy'd always see the back of 'im, not the front. Real yella."

This was too much for Tŵm. "And how would Cadoc know that?"

Tŵm got the same story that he'd had from Cadoc. "Cos 'is friend were in the 9th. Same as Gwyn an' Evan. Cadoc's friend told 'im that Gwyn Parry were a disgrace. Not like 'is pal Evan Griffiths. Fought like a lion 'e did. Got a medal didna 'e? Blood of Owain Glyndŵr without a doubt. Shame 'e didna come back. I would've stepped out with 'im. So 'andsome 'e were. Them deep, dark eyes! 'nuff to make a girl's stomach flip over."

Tŵm paused for a moment. He hoped Cadoc hadn't denounced Gwyn to anyone else other than Gethin and Bronwen.

"I hope you're not going to be spreading this in the village, Bronwen. You don't want Ruth Parry to hear lies about her son."

Bronwen sniffed. "I believe wot Cadoc told me. 'e 'as no reason to lie. If

Gwyn Parry 'ad bin so brave, 'e would've come 'ome with a medal as well wouldn't 'e? An' as for Ruth Parry. Always goin' on abou' God an' 'eaven. Me, I'd rather enjoy the 'ere an' now, not the if an' when."

Appealing to Bronwen's better nature was not, Tŵm knew, a good move. But he had no option. "Please Bronwen, don't make it any worse for Ruth Parry than it already is. She's suffered so much tragedy and she's all alone."

"I wunna promise Tŵm. The truth is the truth. People need to know wot Gwyn Parry were really like. Maybe it's God's justice that 'e ended up in Pwll Berw."

"That's a terrible thing to say Bronwen." Tŵm's shock was evident in his voice. "No-one deserves a fate like that. And Gwyn was a good man."

Bronwen shrugged her shoulders. "Doesna matter if ya'r good or bad when ya'r fightin' does it? Bullets don't choose only the bad. An' 'e were good at dodgin' bullets by all accounts."

Tŵm tried again. "Bronwen don't go upsetting Ruth Parry. Please."

Bronwen shrugged. "I'm not the only one who says so. If she doesna 'ear it from me, she'll 'ear it from summ'on else. Anyways what'll ya give me if I do wot ya want Tŵm? Another kiss? Ya kiss better than yar friend, I'll say that."

Tŵm was silent as her words sunk in. "Bronwen! You kissed Gwyn? So, you must've known he liked you before he drew that picture. You led him on, didn't you? And you didn't tell Cadoc that. Put all the blame on Gwyn you did. Accused him of creeping up on you. I wouldn't be surprised if you encouraged him to draw your portrait and then pretended you didn't know he was doing it."

"So, wot if I did? 'e might've been lily livered but 'e were good at drawin'. Wanted a picture of meself dinna I? Nothin' wrong in that. 'e must've known I weren't interested in 'im. Not me type. Couldna get rid of 'im after I said I'd swop 'im a kiss for a picture. Were always trailin' around after me. Clingin' 'e were. Like duckweed."

Tŵm, not trusting himself to voice his anger, contented himself with retorting, "Well, you don't have to worry about Gwyn hanging around you any more do you Bronwen?"

"No, I don't but now I've got ya botherin' me."

"Well, I'll not bother you any longer Bronwen. I wish you Nos Da."

Tŵm, thankful to draw an unpleasant conversation to a close, saw Bronwen flounce off down Lane End.

Daniel Ellis had endured an arduous month. The previous year Gwyn Parry had been a huge help to him, always ready to lead a Bible reading group or a society meeting, his devotion to God reflected in every word he spoke. How he missed Gwyn's reverence and dedication. If he'd lived, he might well have become a minister himself or at the very least, a deacon. It had been so fulfilling to take him under his wing and encourage him to hear and heed God's calling.

Daniel was also, in part, regretting his hasty action in ridding himself of the attentions of Bethan Tudor. She had certainly been very useful in lightening his load. But no, it had been a deed well done. How could she have thought...? Women were indeed a dangerous species. It all harked back to Eve of course. Enticing men into snares. Such lewdness as that shown by Bethan Tudor could not be tolerated.

The Christmas season was always filled with choir practices, the uplifting harmony of the hymn festival, Cymanfa Ganu, prayer meetings, Bible classes and nativity play rehearsals. Then there were the competitions for singing solos, short stories, poems and handicrafts. Though he had plenty of willing helpers, Daniel felt obliged to be present on most of these occasions as the inhabitants of Carreg-y-Bedd did like to have their efforts applauded. Anwen, the daughter of Rhian Hughes from the shop, had been only too willing to step into the breach, left by Bethan, as the Sunday School teacher for the younger children's group. He had considered her unsuitable for the adult group which surely needed more gravitas than Anwen's simplistic, naïve approach to matters Biblical could provide.

Anwen hounded him continually with, "Oh, Mr. Ellis please can I have a word? Do you think the story of the Good Samaritan is suitable for five-year-olds or will the robbers frighten them?" Or "Just a word, Mr. Ellis. Could I have your view on Cain and Abel? So appropriate for Carreg-y-Bedd with Cain being a tiller of the ground and Abel being a keeper of sheep. But do you think the slaying will encourage wildness among the boys especially since God allows Cain to get away with it in my view?"

"I wouldn't say Cain gets away with it exactly," Daniel had retorted, taking the criticism of God personally. "If I recall correctly God places a curse on Cain tilling the ground and condemns him to wander the earth as a fugitive."

"That may be so Mr. Ellis but He protects Cain from being slain by placing His mark on him. What happened to 'an eye for an eye, a tooth for a tooth', that's what I'd like to know?"

"I prefer to believe that doctrine was superseded by Matthew advising us to turn the other cheek. I'm surprised at you Miss Hughes. I didn't see you as an advocate of violence."

Anwen Hughes pushed back a stray lock that had escaped from her tightly pinned hair. "And what would have happened Mr. Ellis if we had turned the other cheek to the Kaiser? I ask you that. We'd have been overrun with the Boche, that's for sure."

For once Daniel Ellis was confounded. "There's an element of truth in that Miss Hughes, I have to agree. But remember what it says in Romans, *'Do not be overcome by evil but overcome evil with good'*. That's not quite the same as revenge is it? The outcome of the war was a foregone conclusion; we had right on our side. I thank God though that I did not have to raise a weapon myself. During the war, my calling, thrust upon me by God, lay in providing comfort to those more indirectly involved, who had loved ones in the thick of the fighting. I am not a violent man Miss Hughes; I am a man of peace, rather like Jesus himself. Perhaps we could find something a little more acceptable than Cain and Abel. What about the parable of the Good Shepherd, if you want to use a story the children will understand?"

"Perhaps that would be better," Anwen conceded. "Thank you for your help, Mr Ellis." She looked directly into his eyes as she flattered his choice. "You always know the right thing to do. I depend on your judgement so much. You do realise that don't you? Perhaps we could meet every week for a conversation about the Holy Scriptures. I'd be quite willing to come to your home so we would not have to endure annoying interruptions." She smiled as winningly as she could, given the prominence of her front teeth.

Daniel Ellis, horrified, kept his composure. How many more brazen hussies was he going to have to withstand? Was no man safe from their predatory claws?

He responded with calm firmness. "I really don't think that will be necessary Miss Hughes. I trust in your ability to make sensible choices."

Anwen Hughes sighed. Without the blessing of a pretty face, it seemed she was condemned to never having a comfortable home of her own.

The afternoon of Christmas Eve found Caron sitting on her bed. Disappointingly it was raining. She had hoped for snow but the whole month had been warmer than usual and there was little chance of a magical white Christmas. She was heavily tired. Mali had wrung the neck of a fat Rhode Island Red the previous day, had plucked and drawn it and it was now hanging naked ready for stuffing. Since Christmas Eve happened to be on a Sunday, much of the preparation for God's special day had taken place the day before, on the Saturday. The morning had been spent making stock from the giblets, peeling root vegetables and baking. Five weeks earlier the plum pudding had been made, tied up in muslin and placed in the churning room. Emyr and Brad brought in a small tree from the forest; Caron hung it with small packages of nuts and sweets, fir cones and biscuits. Nain decorated the pictures and the mantle pieces with branches of scarlet-berried holly.

Caron cupped her stomach in her hands. She could no longer forget about her condition. Rather, it was now on her mind the whole time. Her swollen belly was beginning to remind her of the shape of the ewes come March or April. She had not returned to see Richard Owen but she was now beginning to realise that he had been right. She could no longer deny that there was new life growing inside her. Still able to hide her shame under layers of winter clothing, it would not be long before she would have to admit the truth to Mali. She wondered how long she could wait before she was forced to speak. Frankly she was terrified, knowing for certain that however violent she imagined Mali's reaction to be, it would, in all probability, be worse than that. Mali was proud of the fact that, "There has never been any illegitimacy in my family. All fine, upstanding, god-fearing people they were." Bastards happened to other families, not to anyone who was a Maddock, a Reece or a Tudor.

Normally Caron loved Christmas; the scent of pine, the carol singing, the food, and the modest gifts they exchanged. Christmas week she sang, with her usual gusto, in Ebenezer. 'The First Nowell' was her favourite carol. She loved the story, cupped in a lilting melody, of the shepherds looking after their sheep on a cold winter's night and then following the star wherever it went. Every Christmas Eve, creating her own ritual, she ventured into the frosty night air, watched the sheep huddling together for warmth in the fields near the farmhouse and gazed up at the sky. At such a miraculous time, it was easy to imagine the Christmas story happening near Carreg-y-Bedd itself.

But this year it was different. She was just going through the motions. Dee's funeral had been heart breaking. Ebenezer had sobbed with collective, tangible grief. The whole population of Carreg-y-Bedd and its surrounding farms came to mourn the loss of such a young life. Too many knew what it was to lose a child.

"So very sad that Dee was an only child," Olwen Griffiths said to Mali Tudor. "Just like Gwyn Parry. I don't know how Weyland and Nerys will find the strength to go on. At least I've got Ebrill and Catrin and their families. I have a lot to be grateful for."

"That's why it's a safeguard to have several children," replied Mali. "You never know what's going to happen."

Caron tried her best to enjoy Christmas. She made 'taffi,' the buttery toffee that was always a part of their Christmas celebrations, baked cakes and biscuits and watched the nativity play in chapel. Particularly taken with the perfume she had created from rose petals gathered in the summer months, she begged Tŵm to ask Dr. Owen for small glass medicine bottles and he had obliged. Nain, Mam and Bethan would be pleased she was sure. She bought sweets for Siôn and made small plum cakes for Tad, Tŵm and Brad. It would be the last Christmas for the old Caron, she knew. Next year; well, she couldn't think what next year would be like. Mali was not going to accept a bastard in the house. She determined to see Dr. Owen again. He would tell her what to do.

Christmas Day proved to be better than Caron expected. Starting in darkness at six o'clock, the candlelit plygain, celebrating the dawn of Christmas morning, had taken place while she was still slumbering. Later, during the preaching meeting, the singers sang carols from the Bardd a Byrddau before finishing with the haunting music of 'Caniad San Silin' and emerging into the light. She made sure to sing enthusiastically to conceal both the sinful bulge underneath her coat and her sorrow at Dee's absence. Mali would be seriously displeased at any public display of distress. No-one was to notice there was anything different about her. But it was no use pretending. She may not *seem* any different but she *was* very different. In 1923 she would become a Mam. She would no longer be that slip of a girl from Cwyn-y-Gwynt. It was impossible to look beyond April. A wet Welsh mist hung over the rest of the year.

Caron looked up to see that the deacons had chosen John Hughes, Rhian's husband, the cobbler, to read the gospel. She resolved to respond to the magic of the Christmas story. This year it was Matthew's words, '*When his mother Mary had been betrothed to Joseph before they came together, she was found to be with child of the Holy Spirit.*'

Before they 'came together'. Is that what she and Abram had done? But what was it Abram had said to her? "We didn't do what people need to do to make a baby," or something like that. She allowed herself to indulge in a flight of fancy. Perhaps a similar thing had happened to her. She listened closely to the rest of the passage. Joseph had found the fact that Mary was with child, shameful and wanted to divorce her quietly. Mali, like Joseph, was certainly going to find her daughter's situation shameful and never want to see her again. But if the doctor was right then Caron doubted if separation from her family would be 'quiet'. Mali would have plenty to say on the matter before her daughter disappeared from her sight.

The narrative progressed. John Hughes' droning voice described how Mary was rescued from her disgrace by an angel appearing to explain to Joseph that it was God's plan that *a virgin shall conceive and bear a son* who shall be called Jesus. Caron took a deep breath. Even her vivid imagination stopped short of a holy apparition dropping in to extricate her from her predicament. Suffused with guilt, she realised she had been comparing her quandary to that of the Virgin Mary. That was more than sinful. It was blasphemous. Would she never become a good person like Mam or Bethan? Her salvation came in the form of *'Away in a Manger'*. Putting disturbing thoughts on one side she joined in thankfully. Twm, glancing across at her, was pleased to see her enjoying the singing.

He had found the chapel meeting a pleasurable torment. Like Caron he enjoyed the reassuring rhythm of the familiar carols, the traditional stories of the journey to Bethlehem, the shepherds guarding their flocks and wise men bearing gifts. But the Christmas season only served to remind him of how swiftly time was passing. Was it really only five years since Evan and Gwyn were worshipping here with him? 1917 seemed a lifetime away. So much had changed; so many families ravaged, dreams wrecked, futures ripped away. It struck him that many of those he knew so well lived with grief gnawing away as a rat chews a hole in the base of a barn door. For some it would not be possible to be whole again: the Bowens, the Griffiths', Ruth Parry and so many others.

As he sat there, listening to the words that Daniel Ellis had carefully selected for the special birthday, Gwyn and Evan breathing along with him, he recognised how affected he was by the absence of his friends. He missed them; he missed them badly. At one time he had kindred spirits with whom to share his thoughts; now all he did was ponder and deliberate alone.

Taking stock, he became aware that he had been treading water for months. Grief had changed him. Spared the searing agony served up to his friends' families, he was nonetheless enduring his own drawn-out misery. It had sapped his energy, his drive, his spirit. He had allowed the days to pass because it was easier not to make a decision, easier not to fight Mali, easier just to drift on the ebb and flow of daily activity. Isolated from Tudor thinking by virtue of intellect and open mindedness, he had lacked the courage to choose his own way. Berating himself for his inactivity, he resolved that things must change. He couldn't carry on with the corrosive sensation of doing something other than what he should be doing. 1923 was a new year and for Tŵm it had to be a new beginning. He owed it to his friends. They had been denied the chance to live out their chosen futures; he would be letting them down if he failed to live his.

Bethan was forced to spend the chapel celebrations observing her lost love. Now that he was no longer a prospective spouse, she was able to judge him more dispassionately. Daniel Ellis could certainly not be termed handsome. But then he couldn't be termed ugly either. If she were honest, he was just ordinary, nondescript even. He had no features of any significance; no Roman nose, no bushy eyebrows, no receding chin. He was the sort of man who blended into the background, who no-one would pay any attention to, if he were not the minister. It was his role that made him a man of consequence in Carreg-y-Bedd not his physical presence. Accustomed to God's house rather than labouring outside in all weathers, his complexion was pallid; his hands smooth. His sermons, though illustrating appropriate moral lessons, were underpinned by intellect rather than passion. It was unfortunate, she thought, that his God had failed to provide him with the twin engines necessary for God's Word to be driven home to the congregation; a powerful voice and strong emotion.

It was a shame her scheme had ended in disappointment. But in only a week's time it would be a new year; time for a new plan. She would be turning the same age as the century itself. She must ask her Mam when they were next going to visit their cousins. After all, Llanrwst was a very attractive place and it had an excellent bakery.

Later that same day, Caron, determined to revel in her last innocent Christmas, enjoyed the plum pudding that had been wrapped in an old piece of sheet and boiled in the copper. She was genuinely pleased to receive lavender soap from Tŵm, a newly knitted scarf from Nain, a woollen jersey from the ever-practical Mali, fruit gums from Siôn and caramels from Bethan. Especially pleased with the oversized fawn jersey, after Christmas Day was over, she wore it almost constantly, causing Mali to comment, "I'm glad you like your Christmas present Caron but it has got to be washed at some time."

Remembering her promise to herself to talk to Tŵm about Gwyn, she managed, by dint of subterfuge, to share in a conversation with him on the night of Christmas Day. When he braved the cold night air to feed the cattle and horses, she went out with him, offering to mix the horse feeds while he saw to the hay and water.

As they worked in harmony, filling and carrying buckets, Caron, rather awkwardly said, "Tŵm, a New Year makes you think doesn't it?"

"It certainly makes you look back and look forward." Tŵm agreed.

Caron laughed. "Just like Nain's Cadi!" Then determined not to miss her chance she became serious. "Do you miss Gwyn a lot? I miss Dee all the time."

"I do Caron, I do. Life will never be the same. Everything's changed and I feel very lonely at times. I used to talk to Evan and Gwyn all the time."

Caron, feeling a pang of guilt again, answered, "You've always got me to talk to."

Tŵm smiled at her. "I know, Caron. But it's not the same. I talk about different things with you than I did with them."

Seeing her face fall, he hastily added. "Boy talk I mean. You're my special sister and no-one's more important to me than you. But I don't want to lumber you with my... torment." He chose the word carefully. Torment was exactly it. He thought back to Cadoc tormenting Luned's rabbit. Just as Cadoc prodded the rabbit with the thorn so his mind was constantly needled by speculation. "To be honest with you Caron, it's worse not knowing what happened to Gwyn than it is missing him. Not solving the mystery makes me feel as though I'm letting him down."

Caron, seeing Tŵm's distress, put her arms round him. "Oh, Tŵm I hadn't realised you were thinking that. We've both lost our closest friend but at least I know why Dee died. There's a logic to it. It must be unbearable not to know. I can see that now. Let's hope 1923 brings you some answers."

"I hope so too," replied Tŵm, "but it's difficult to know how to find out those answers." He searched his sister's face. "Never mind about me. Are you alright Caron? You don't seem to have been yourself lately."

Caron very nearly blurted out that she was going to become a mother but stopped herself just in time. After what he'd just told her, the last thing she wanted to do was add to Tŵm's worries.

"I'm fine Tŵm. Really. It'll take me some time yet to adjust to Dee not being there. That's all."

Tŵm accepted her explanation. After all he was in the same position himself.

Once the Lord's birthday was over, the final few days of December proved to be uneventful. St. Stephen's Day was noteworthy only for the overcast sky promising storms which arrived in full force within twenty-four hours and lasted for three days. The Tudors, in common with their neighbours, battened down the hatches, venturing out only to feed the stock and milk the cows. "We can afford to wait until the storms blow over before preparing for next year's cycle," Emyr told his sons, looking up at the threatening sky with a critical eye.

Confined to the house and forced to spend far more time with each other than usual, Mali arranged for them to occupy themselves with useful pastimes. After Caron and Bethan had polished all the brass, she collected together heaps of mending and darning, allocating a pile each to Bethan, Nain and Caron. "It's a fine opportunity to get all the jobs done," she told them. Still on her first sock, Caron eyed Bethan's growing heap of neat darning with dismay. It was going to take her hours longer than her sister. Finishing it at last, she laid it on one side with a sigh of relief.

Mali, in the middle of turning a sheet, reached for Caron's effort. "It just won't do Caron. Look at the difference between yours and Bethan's. There's going to be a hole again in this in no time." Taking a small pair of scissors, she began to snip away at Caron's irregular stitches. "Start again and this time do it properly!" Turning to Nain, she went on, "Mam, just help me with this sheet, will you? If you could help me spread it across the table, I'll be able to cut it and then turn the ends into the middle. It'll last another year at least."

Caron looked over to the scullery where her brothers were cleaning and repairing horse tack. Emyr, who had been making a new rake handle, was not going to allow them to waste their time either. Caron could see him instructing Brad in the use of a curved needle. "There's a weakness in that cheek strap. The stitching's rotted. Could cause an accident. Best to check it all over now before we come to use it again. Brad, like Bethan, was proving to be adept with his fingers. "Tidy job that," Emyr observed on checking it.

Caron, though not envying Brad his repairs, would much have preferred to be washing and soaping leather. She loved breathing in the heady scent of horse and saddle soap. It reminded her of the liberating joy of rides in the forest on Jac. Thinking of galloping Jac brought Abram to the forefront of her mind. While she was sitting sewing, where, she wondered, was he? What was he doing? What was he thinking? Was he thinking of her? They hadn't parted on good terms. He hadn't said he would miss her and he'd more or less accused her of seeing another lover. But he had kissed her. She clung on to that. He'd kissed her long and hard. Perhaps he was simply being brave and manly about their parting. And her news must have come as a shock to him so it was no wonder, he'd reacted as he did.

At that moment she felt a fluttering in her belly and instinctively clasped her hands across the movement, jabbing her finger with her needle in the process. What on earth was that she asked herself? Her hands encasing her swollen body could feel just how large she had become. She forced herself to face the truth. There was no denying it. New life was growing inside her.

Month of the Snow

New Year's Day proved to be yet another trial for Caron. Siôn wanted to take part in Calennig but was considered too young to walk round the village by himself. Mali, in her wisdom, decided that Caron should accompany him on the journey to meet up with his friends.

"You'll have to go early mind. Straight after breakfast. You can't miss chapel just because it's Calennig. We'll meet you there at the usual time."

Siôn, excited, had spent most of the previous afternoon studding several Pig y Glomen apples with cloves, hazel nuts and a few of Mali's precious raisins. He decorated each one with a sprig of holly. Twm helped him make tripods out of twigs to form a nesting place for each apple. He stood back to admire his handiwork.

"We can wish everyone good luck with these, after we've finished singing," Siôn said with satisfaction. "They'll look grand on windowsills or mantlepieces. Mam, have you got a bag for my presents? I hope most people have got some sweets left over from Christmas."

"Siôn Tudor! You might not get any presents. Not everyone can afford to give you things. If people *are* good enough to give you something, then just remember your manners and thank them." As she spoke, Mali handed over butter muslin, fashioned into a triangular bag by means of three knots.

"I will Mam."

They set off as ordered just after breakfast. "Don't be late. You need to finish in time for the preaching meeting," Nain called after them. "Remember it's bad luck anyway to carry on with Calennig after noon."

Caron set out holding Siôn's hand. She was dreading someone spotting her increased weight and decided she would stand behind the group as they sang. Not wanting to burden herself with long walks in between the farms, she suggested to Gareth Bevan, who seemed to have taken charge of the youngsters, that they tour the village houses. To her relief he agreed.

In Siôn's terms, the morning was already a success, the muslin bag groaning with nuts, sweets and pennies as they knocked on what Caron told Siôn would be the last door. "Remember we have to meet Mam and Tad in plenty of time for the service."

"Oh, Caron, please let's carry on. Just one more house after this one."

"No, Siôn. We're going to Ebenezer now. Your bag's already full." Chapel had never seemed so attractive. At least she could sit down. Her legs and back were aching; an unaccustomed feeling.

They stood outside the final house and sang Happy New Year greetings to Ruth Parry.

Klennigi, Klennigi,
Blwyddyn Newydd dda i chi,
Ac I bawb sydd yn y tŷ,
Dyma fy nymuniad i,
Blwyddyn Newydd dda i chi,
Klennigi, Klennigi.

Caron felt uneasy. It didn't seem right somehow. After all, the last thing Ruth Parry was going to have was a Happy New Year. But that thought did not seem to have crossed the mind of Gareth Bevan. "We don't want to miss anybody out," he said.

Ruth opened the door and dropped some jelly babies into the bags. To Caron's surprise she had her left arm in plaster.

Caron made her way round to the front of the group. "Mrs. Parry, you've hurt yourself. What happened?"

Ruth dismissed the accident. "Oh, hello Caron. Nice to see you. Oh, just a fall. Nothing to worry about. It'll be better soon. I'm not in pain. It's just a nuisance." Changing the subject and looking closely at Caron she commented, "You're looking really well Caron. Must be your Mam's good food and lots of fresh air. Have you put on weight?"

Caron flushed. If Ruth Parry had noticed a difference in her appearance, there was a chance that others would as well. "I don't think so Mrs. Parry. I've just got lots of clothes on to keep myself warm."

The arduous duties of Christmas had taken their toll on Daniel Ellis; rehearsals for the nativity play, extra services, competitions, sermons, the choral festival. He was exhausted. And he paid the price. January was warm, windy and wet with more winter sun than anyone could remember seeing since 1910. Despite the clement conditions, the minister developed a nasty cough. After battling with it for three days he took to his bed and called the doctor. Richard Owen was less busy than usual which he put down to the winter sunlight creating an unseasonal optimism in his patients.

"It will take about two weeks," he told Daniel.

"Two weeks! What about the chapel sermons?"

Richard Owen was placatory. "If you give me the details, I'll contact another minister for you. I know you all help each other out when one of you is ill." He went on, "You need bed rest, plenty of drinks and to keep warm. Light a fire in the bedroom."

"A fire, doctor? In the bedroom? That'll increase my coal bill."

"Well, it's either that or sleeping downstairs and keeping a fire lit all the time in the sitting room. You must keep warm. We don't want you ending up with pneumonia. Before you go to bed a stiff brandy wouldn't go amiss either."

Daniel Ellis, shocked to the core, failed to cover the contempt in his reply. "Doctor, you cannot be serious. Alcohol has not, and will not, ever pass my lips. The demon drink is Satan's own lifeblood. It causes men to fall victim to other, perhaps worse, temptations."

The doctor, accustomed to his 'fashionable' views branding him a member of the devil's party rather than God's holy band, did not rise to the bait. "Well, do what you wish about the brandy but make sure you rest near a warm fire."

Deciding it would be beneficial to be placatory, he continued with, "You have a reputation you know for ignoring your own well-being to work tirelessly for your flock. But you cannot help them if you lack the strength to do so. As you are well aware, we are but frail mortals. The power of the spirit can at times be overcome by the weakness of the body."

Richard's use of God's language smoothed Daniel's ruffled feathers. "I know you're right doctor but it's hard not to answer the cries of my congregation."

"For a dedicated minister such as you, it must be well-nigh impossible." Richard smiled as he placed his hand comfortingly on the minister's shoulder. As he did so, he felt Daniel stiffen. Presumably physical contact may taint a minister's soul, Richard thought.

Daniel Ellis cleared his throat. "Since you're here doctor, I wonder if I could take further advantage of your medical knowledge."

"I would be happy to help." Richard, sensing the minister's nervousness, became briskly professional.

"I'm afraid the matter is really, well, delicate. I take it that anything I say is completely confidential."

"Of course. I am bound by my Hippocratic oath."

"By the nature of my profession people come to me for advice. They confide in me, doctor. These confidences, one doesn't always want to hear, especially if they involve sins that shouldn't speak their name, but I am duty bound to help." Beads of perspiration appeared on the minister's brow.

He's feverish, thought Richard. He decided to be reassuring. "I have many medical conversations which are difficult to say the least. It is my duty too, to speak about sensitive issues."

"This is why I am speaking to you now, doctor. I knew you would understand the dilemma I have been forced to deal with. You too must have to discuss..." He paused. "Bodily functions."

Richard tried to relieve the burden. "If a villager has asked you about a medical matter, Mr Ellis, then I suggest you ask them to visit me."

Daniel sighed. "If only it were that simple, doctor. This situation does not concern bodily illness; it is more a matter of a sick mind."

Richard's thoughts turned to Gwilym Bowen. Had the minister had cause to visit the Bowens? His last conversation with Nia Bowen had led him to think that it would be a long time before she and her husband darkened the door of the chapel again. Daniel Ellis was silent. It was clear he did not know what to say next. "Please go on," Richard said to him.

"Are there mental sicknesses that cause physical abnormalities doctor?"

"There may be," Richard answered, "but I need more information to be able to help you."

The perspiration began to drip again from the minister's brow. "The matter we are discussing concerns unnatural aberrations. One of my flock, a man, is fighting a battle with the devil. He has asked for my advice."

"And what is this man's problem?"

"He is attracted towards someone he shouldn't be."

Richard relaxed. So, all this subterfuge was a simple matter of advising some miscreant who was coveting someone else's wife. That the minister thought of this as 'abnormal' did not surprise him in the slightest.

"Surely Mr. Ellis you have dealt with such matters before. The man needs to be advised of the consequences of breaking up a family. He must find a woman who is free to love him."

Daniel squirmed uncomfortably. "No, doctor. You don't understand. His proclivities do not lie that way."

Realisation dawned. The doctor decided to put Daniel out of his misery. He was clearly not going to be able to voice it. "Am I correct in thinking that this person may be drawn towards a member of the same sex?"

"Yes. I apologise for having to speak about such perversion doctor but I have to respond in some way to this sinner's request for help."

Richard tried to clarify the situation. "I have to ask you, has the man given in to his impulses? Is there a second man in the community who is sharing in this behaviour?"

"I don't think so doctor. From talking to him, he hasn't given in to evil practices. He realises that such acts would be unspeakably gross, is disgusted with himself and wishes to be cured. But as you know from Biblical teachings, evil thoughts are as bad as evil deeds."

"I'm not sure I agree with you there Mr. Ellis. However, I bow to your greater knowledge. You know more about the Word of God than I do. What I can say is that, from a medical point of view, aberrations of this nature may well be pathological."

"Does that mean this man can be cured, that the poison in his mind can be neutralised?"

"From what I have read, a cure is not easily achieved," replied Richard.

"So, what help can I offer him? I am sure he is going to raise this matter with me again and my main concern is to prevent him from falling into the abyss."

"In this situation, there is little medicine can do. My advice would be based on common sense rather than scientific research. I would advise him to lead a busy life which does not allow him time to dwell on sexual matters." Richard saw Daniel shudder at the voicing of such a word but he pressed on. "Then he must control his impulses. He needs to place himself in a situation where there is no possibility that he can translate thought into action. Marry a good woman, have some children and put, what may hopefully be a passing phase, behind him."

"Rather like Christ in the wilderness. 'Get thee behind me, Satan'."

"Quite. It seems sensible to put temptation well out of harm's way and lead a normal life. Is that of help to you?"

"It is doctor and thank you. I repeat that this conversation will go no further will it?"

"Absolutely not. The pact between doctor and patient is just the same as that between the priest and the confessional."

The doctor's comparison of the chapel with the 'one true church' drew a grimace from Daniel but he thought it best to ignore what he perceived to be an insult to his God.

Tŵm disliked January. As far as he was concerned it had no redeeming features. Long, dark days; wet, muddy fields. He wasn't fond of farming any month of the year but there were enjoyable days to be had in the sunshine of June and July. As a result, he was the first to offer his services when Emyr said he needed someone to go to Yr Efail. He needed Weyland Philpin to sharpen the axe. Daily chopping of winter wood for the fires had blunted its edge. For Tŵm, after spending a cold, damp morning moving the sheep to graze the turnip field, any distraction was welcome.

"You just never know what the weather's going to do," Emyr said to him. "We've been lucky this winter but that's not to say it will continue. We're due some cold weather in my view and I don't want to spend longer than needed chopping sticks on the block."

A trip to Carreg-y-Bedd, Tŵm thought, was better than slicing turnips for fodder or, even worse, the back breaking work of early muck spreading to increase the summer yield. He set off, with the axe over his shoulder, whistling '*Pack up your Troubles*' as he strode out toward Carreg-y-Bedd. Soon he was presenting the blunt axe to Weyland Philpin, who inspected it carefully. "Had a fair bit of use, this," he pronounced.

"Yes, well, it is winter," replied Tŵm.

"It'll take some sharpening, this will."

"I'll leave it with you, Mr. Philpin. I've got some letters to post and Mam wants paraffin and lamp-wicks from the shop." Tŵm wanted to get away. Shocked by Weyland's appearance he was at a loss to know what to say to him. The blacksmith seemed to have aged twenty years since December. His cheekbones protruded like the hip bones of an ancient cow; skin hung slackly beneath his jaw.

After exchanging pleasantries with Rhian Hughes, Tŵm returned to find the axe ready and waiting, propped up against the wall of the smithy. He noticed flakes of whitewash scattered across the brick floor next to pared hoof cuttings. How unlike the blacksmith thought Tŵm. Normally the smithy was scrupulously neat and clean, every tool secured in its place by a hook on the wall, the floor swept and scrubbed, cleaner than those inside the cottages. No, there was no doubt about it. Weyland was letting things go.

As he paid for the sharpening, disconcertingly Weyland seemed to read his thoughts. "I can see you looking round Tŵm. It's not as tidy as it used to be is it?"

Tŵm, embarrassed, stuttered, "No, it's fine Mr Philpin. I wasn't, I didn't mean to..."

Weyland took pity on him. "It's OK Tŵm. I know it's a mess." He choked on his words, echoing what he'd said to Mali when he brought the news of Dee's death. "You see, nothing matters anymore."

Tŵm, silenced, pressed Weyland's hand, picked up the axe and left. What was there to say?

He had plenty to think about on the way home. So many people in Carreg-y-Bedd were missing loved ones, many because of the war but some had faced peacetime tragedies. He was fully aware that the Tudor family had escaped lightly over the years. He was the one who had suffered the most, losing his two closest friends. And now Caron had lost her friend too. He wondered, not for the first time, about the randomness of death and wished that he had Ruth Parry's strong belief that she would see Thomas and Gwyn again in a better place. Plagued with doubt, he was denied the security of faith. He attended chapel as a good Christian should, largely because it was expected but also because the chapel family provided a warm protective blanket in times of need. To Tŵm the benefits of benevolent humanitarianism were worth the public acceptance of theological doctrine.

As Tŵm wound his way through the network of lanes that led to Cwyn-y-Gwynt, he heard someone walking towards him, concealed behind the next corner. Slowing slightly, he came face to face with Cadoc Morgan. Though it wouldn't even cross his mind to use it, he gripped the handle of the axe for security. It might make Cadoc think twice before he started anything.

"Cadoc, what are you doing out this way?"

"Bin checkin' traps 'aven't I?"

"And likely on someone else's land," retorted Tŵm.

Tŵm could see the head of a ferret emerging from Cadoc's left pocket. Cadoc, feeling the movement, pushed it back down out of sight. "Don' know why ya say that. Ya know Gethin an' me are labourin' on the farms so we're allowed to trap. None of yar bus'ness any'ow. Anyways I'm glad I run into ya. Wanta put ya right on a few things. Las' time we was speakin' we didna get chance to finish our conversation. First though, I 'ear you an' our Bron 'ad a chat."

"So?"

"Bron told me ya didna' be'ave very well either. Made a pass at 'er by all accounts. No way t' treat a lady."

"Then she told you wrong Cadoc. And Bronwen's no lady."

"I'll ignore that Tŵm Tudor. It's the only thing we 'ave in common i'nt it? Pretty sisters."

"Now don't you start on about Caron. I've told you to leave her alone."

"Told ya! Told ya! Since when've I done wot Tŵm Tudor told me!"

Tŵm decided they weren't getting anywhere. "What is it you want to put me right on, Cadoc?"

"Yar friend. 'tisn't wot ya think. Wot did 'e tell ya about our little squabble?"

"It was more than a 'little squabble' from what I hear Cadoc. Gwyn said you called him 'windy'. He said he was on his way back from working at Cwyn-y-Gwynt, he bumped into you and you taunted him and that led to a fight."

"Did 'e indeed? 'e didna tell ya the whole story then."

"Cadoc, I'd rather believe Gwyn than you. Are you going to tell me you didn't call him windy?"

"Oh, I called 'im windy a'right but that were because 'e wouldna put up 'is fists an' fight like a man. An' I didna bump into 'im. I went lookin' for 'im. Knew 'e'd be walkin' back 'ome."

Tŵm stared at Cadoc. "Why on earth would you do that? What did Gwyn ever do to you?"

"It weren't wot 'e did to me. It were wot 'e did to our Bron."

"Cadoc, you already told me Gwyn drew a picture of Bronwen and she told me her version as well. It didn't warrant beating up Gwyn."

"It weren't jus' that. 'e didna give up."

Tŵm was startled. "What do you mean, he didn't give up?"

"Pest'rin' our Bron. 'e just wouldna leave 'er alone. I 'ad to stop 'im some'ow."

"By pushing him into Pwll Berw," I suppose.

"Now don't start. I niver did that."

Despite not trusting Cadoc, Tŵm was conscious of wanting to know what he had to say. After all it might throw light on what happened to Gwyn. "Well go on then. I'm listening."

"That Gwyn Parry. 'e kept followin' our Bron around."

"Oh, come on Cadoc! Gwyn spent all day working at Cwyn-y-Gwynt. He couldn't have. He didn't have the time."

"It weren't in the day. It were in the ev'nin'. When our Bron went out at night 'e were like 'er shadow. Terrifyin' for 'er it were."

"I wouldn't have thought your Bron was easily frightened Cadoc, especially of Gwyn. He wouldn't have hurt a fly."

"That's not the point is it? The thing is 'e were followin' 'er. She 'ad no privacy."

"Cadoc, what was Bronwen doing out at night anyway?"

"Our Bron 'as friends don' she? She can go where she likes."

Probably meeting the latest man friend, thought Tŵm but thought better of saying so. There was no point in antagonising Cadoc further. It might stop him talking.

Cadoc continued. "Anyways it all came to an 'ead didna it."

"Why? What happened?" asked Tŵm, interested, despite himself.

"The Wed'sday of Easter week it were. Bron came back 'ome in an 'ell of a state. She'd been down to the 'Lamb an' Lion' to meet a few friends, she 'ad. On the way back, she 'eard steps behind 'er. Night were drawin' in. She were real fri'ttened, she were. So, she stopped, turned roun' an' shouted out, 'Gwyn Parry. Is that you? Are ya followin' me again?'"

"And are you telling me it *was* Gwyn?"

"Damn right I am. When she turned roun' 'e slunk be'ind that big 'orse chestnut tree near the chapel. But 'e weren't quick enough for Bron. She'd already spotted 'im. So she marched over there an' confronted 'im."

Tŵm was sarcastic. "She wasn't very scared, then was she?"

"She were still by the 'ouses weren't she? She could've knocked on a door for 'elp."

Tŵm laughed. "I think the last thing she needed was help."

"It's not funny Tŵm Tudor. Fri'ttenin' a girl like that. Creepy it were."

Tŵm moved him on. "So what did Gwyn say? I'm sure he wouldn't have meant to frighten her."

"Accordin' to Bron, 'e said 'zactly that. Then 'e followed it up with summat int'restin'." Cadoc paused for dramatic effect before continuing. "You'll niver guess wot 'e said then."

"Oh, just get on with it Cadoc." Tŵm was getting impatient.

Cadoc puffed out his cheeks, savouring the moment. "'e only went an' told our Bron that 'e loved 'er, didna 'e."

Tŵm, not knowing how to respond, opted for silence.

Cadoc, triumphant, continued. "That's got ya, 'asn't it Tŵm Tudor? Don't know wot t' say now, d' ya?"

Tŵm regained his composure. "What did Bronwen do?"

"Wot d' ya think she did? She laughed, didna she. She told me she stood there with 'er 'ands on 'er 'ips an' laughed an' laughed."

"Then that was cruel Cadoc. She could at least have taken him seriously."

"Seriously? Seriously? Are ya kiddin'? Our Bron an' Gwyn Parry? She'd 'ave to be desp'rate. An' she certainly i'nt that."

"So what happened next?"

"She sent 'im 'ome with 'is tail between 'is legs of course. Told 'im she wouldn't step out with 'im if 'e were the last lad left in Carreg-y-Bedd. Told 'im when she married it would be someone with standin', not a yella farm labourer without a penny to 'is name."

Tŵm retaliated. "So basically, Gwyn's crime, in your eyes, was to tell Bronwen that he loved her. She humiliated him. Then you followed that by beating him up."

"It weren't my fault. I 'ad prov'cation didna I?"

"How's that Cadoc?"

"Well, I knew 'e'd be comin' 'ome from yar place didna I? So I went to meet 'im. To tell 'im to stay away from our Bron an' to stop followin' 'er around. An' that's 'zactly wot I did. But 'e woudna listen. Told me Bron might change 'er mind in time. Pigs might fly! So I told 'im 'e'd better do as I said or it'd be the worse for 'im."

"So you threatened him."

"I wouldna put it like that."

"Well, I would. So why did you hit him?"

"'cos 'e jus' wouldna promise not to follow Bron. Said 'e were savin' 'er from 'erself an' she'd realise soon enuff that 'e were 'er best option. Crazy if ya ask me."

Tŵm considered what he'd just heard. He didn't trust Cadoc an inch. But what he said was plausible. It fitted with Bronwen's tale about the sketch. What possible reason could Gwyn have had for drawing Bronwen other than that he was attracted to her? True she was striking but Gwyn had usually drawn pictures that told a story, that had some kind of meaning, not simply portraits. And Gwyn wouldn't have wanted to tell Tŵm about Bronwen. He would've been too embarrassed. So it did make sense that he explained his bruises to Tŵm by telling him a half truth about Cadoc's taunts. He certainly wouldn't have wanted his Mam to know either. Ruth would have been disgusted at the very whiff of an illicit liaison.

"Say I give you the benefit of the doubt, Cadoc. Why didn't you tell the police what happened? At least that would've explained the bruises. If what you say is true, then it would've helped their investigation. They could've discounted the bruising as not associated with his death."

"Oh, yeah, yeah, I don' think so. I've got a bit of a reputation 'aven't I? An' my Tad's been in the nick. The coppers aren't goin' to believe a Morgan, are they? I'm not stupid."

Tŵm saw the sense of this. "I do see..."

"So ya believe me now, do ya?"

"I don't know." Grudgingly he added, "It does make sense. Why didn't you tell me before?"

"Niver got chance, did I? I were more concerned that ya kept ya mouth shut. Puts a different slant on things doesna it?"

"What do you mean Cadoc?"

"Gwyn Parry were rejected by our Bron weren't 'e? If ya ask me he chucked 'imself in the pond. All this talk of someone doin' 'im in. Load of nonsense."

"We can't know Cadoc, can we? I knew Gwyn very well. I honestly can't see him doing anything like that. He wouldn't do that to his Mam. And he'd see it as sinful. He came back from France closer to God than when he went."

"God knows why!" Cadoc laughed at his own joke. "Godless place. If ya'd saw wot I'd seen, the last thing ya'd believe in is God."

From what he'd heard of the battlefield, Tŵm tended to agree. "I must be getting on now Cadoc. As you said, you've put me right. But don't think you come out of this well because you don't. Lying in wait for Gwyn and then punching him just for falling in love with Bronwen. One day you'll get your comeuppance from someone."

"It won't be from ya will it Tŵm Tudor? Yella like ya friend."

Tŵm ignored him, settled the axe firmly on his shoulder and strode back to Cwyn-y-Gwynt deep in thought.

In mid-January a second letter arrived at Cwyn-y-Gwynt addressed to Bethan. This time Mali was out shopping for foodstuffs so Bethan enjoyed the novel luxury of opening her own communication.

Dear Miss Tudor

I believe I may have been a little hasty in the letter I wrote to you in December.

The chapel has missed your valuable services and so have I.

I would be grateful if you could come to see me, at your convenience, so that we could discuss you resuming some of the duties that you so kindly relinquished in order that others could bathe in the light of God's grace.

Yours truly

Daniel Ellis

Bethan, not wishing to appear too eager, made her way to Tŷ Capel the very next morning and by noon she was fully reinstated as a servant of God.

It was the third week in January by the time Caron managed to make it as far as Richard Owen's house. It had proven difficult to get away. Excuses for travelling into the village were in short supply on dark winter days. Salvation came in the unlikely form of Ruth Parry. "Do you think you could spare Caron for a few hours?" she had asked Mali.

Ruth did not like to ask for help but this time she had managed to swallow her pride due to her broken arm. "Such a stupid accident," she said to Mali. "I tripped on the hem of my skirt and fell down the stairs. Dr. Owen set it for me but I'm finding the household tasks difficult, especially since it's my left arm and I'm left-handed."

Mail sniffed by way of reply. "Must be difficult anyway, doing everything back to front, Ruth. Goodness knows why you're asking for Caron and not Bethan. Bethan would do your chores in half the time it would take Caron."

"Well, I know you rely on Bethan so much, Mali. I don't like to take her away from you."

"That's true Ruth. The speed Bethan works means that it's like having two pairs of extra hands. In any case it'll do Caron good to have a busy day. She's way too fond of sitting around reading a book or riding that horse."

Mali sent an anxious Caron over to Carreg-y-Bedd early. Ruth Parry had already noticed a difference in her appearance. Caron just hoped the bulky jersey Mali had given her for Christmas would shroud her plumpness. Despite the long walk, it was only nine o'clock when she knocked on Ruth's door.

Ruth was waiting for her, cleaning equipment ready to hand. "It's the extra jobs Caron rather than the daily ones. I'm so slow I haven't been able to get round to them. Though I know I'm lucky. At least my arm will be better in a few weeks. How those poor soldiers manage for a lifetime, I just don't know. And some of them have lost both arms and even another limb as well. I heard they get sixteen shillings a week for a lost arm and less than that if it's part of an arm. Money never makes up for that kind of loss. I saw one poor man begging in Denbigh just before Christmas. All dressed up he was in a suit and hat. He'd lost an arm and his left leg was just a stump. I put sixpence in his cap. Could ill afford it but still, there's always someone worse off. We must do what we can to help others. That's what Jesus did. I'm going to visit Nerys Philpin later. She's not too good by all accounts."

Caron's eyes filled with tears.

Ruth noticing, put out her hand to touch Caron's. "Oh, my dear, I'm so sorry. She was your friend, wasn't she?"

"She was Mrs. Parry. My best friend and I miss her. But you mustn't worry about upsetting me. After all it's much worse for Mr. and Mrs. Philpin than for me. Your visit will help them I'm sure."

"I hope so. We're in the same situation you see. She'll know that I understand."

Caron did see. They had both experienced the cruel loss of only children. Propping each other up, sharing the pain, may well provide some small comfort. Caron, with her child safe in her ever-expanding belly, was suffused with remorse. So many times, she had wished her child did not exist, that he or she would simply vanish, that her life would return to normal. She berated herself for her selfishness. Overwhelmed by her dilemma she hadn't given much thought to soothing the pain of others. Ruth Parry, in contrast, had lost her whole family but spent her time helping others who were suffering. She really was a true Christian; her kindness a lesson to others. Once again Caron resolved to be a better person. She would start today. At least she could help Ruth with the chores.

Finding new energy, by eleven o'clock Caron had poured carbolic down the drains, scrubbed out the clothes boiler and the bathtub with turpentine, cleaned the copper kettle with buttermilk and polished the brass with a mixture of emery powder and paraffin. With the brass door knobs, Ruth had cut a circular hole in a piece of cardboard and placed it over the knob itself to avoid the powder soiling the wooden doors. "If a job's worth doing, it's worth doing properly," Ruth told her.

When they at last sat down mid-morning for a welcome cup of tea Ruth said, "You're doing well. Thank you, Caron. But you do look hot. Why don't you take off that thick jersey?"

Caron, pink faced and sweating, panicked at the thought of exposing her body. "Oh, no I'm fine," she replied quickly. "I feel the cold and it's raw outside today."

"Well, I'm sure you'd be better without it but it's up to you."

Caron changed the subject. "What else needs doing?"

"The windows need cleaning, if you wouldn't mind. You can polish the glass with vinegar and newspaper. Then if you've got time you can move on to the furniture and floors. You can scrub the linoleum by mixing a drop of paraffin with the water. I don't know how I'd manage without paraffin. Gets rid of the grease and buffs it up to a lovely shine it does. It's lethal to woodworm as well. I use an old knitting needle, dip it in the paraffin then push it down the holes. Works a treat. You don't need to do that today though. I just want you to polish the table and dresser. I love the smell of beeswax, don't you?"

"I do Mrs. Parry but Mam mixes ours with turps and soap. It doesn't smell half as nice but she says it brings up a better shine."

"She's right but she's got a lot more furniture to clean than I have. Doesn't seem worth going to all that trouble for just a couple of items."

By the time they stopped for a very late dinner of boiled bacon and apple tart, Ruth Parry's small home was transformed. Always spick and span, it was now gleaming, the cold winter light glancing off the dark oak, brass and copper.

"I'm sorry I can't pay you Caron, but you know how I'm fixed. The price of everything nowadays! Goes up all the time. Butter's a shilling a pound now and tea, one and tuppence. And I can't work at the moment. Lady Craddock said she would carry on paying me, but I wouldn't hear of it. I couldn't take pay for work I haven't done!"

"I wouldn't dream of taking anything, even if you could afford it Mrs. Parry. I'm pleased to help."

"You and Twm are such kind young people. Your Mam's done a fine job of bringing you up." Ruth looked more closely at Caron. "I've asked you to do too much, Caron. You look peaky."

Caron was indeed weary but not wanting to admit this she answered, "I'm fine Mrs. Parry, really. The tasty food has given me all my energy back."

"Yes, it's a great relief to cook boiled bacon whenever I want. I'll never forget the rationing. And we were the lucky ones living in the countryside. We were already growing our own fruit and vegetables and we could always shoot a rabbit for the pot. Your Mam and Tad were so kind sending me butter and ham. The worst was the sugar. Three quarters of a pound a week! I don't know how your Mam managed with all the mouths she has to feed."

Caron smiled inwardly but said nothing. Mali had seen what was coming and had stockpiled bags of sugar, justifying her store by saying, "We're more than doing our bit for the war effort with growing food to feed the nation. I'm not having my men go hungry when they're working so hard."

Ruth continued with, "Well, I expect your Mam won't give you anything else to do after working so hard today."

Caron did not reply. She thought it most unlikely that Mali would take pity on her but was loath to criticise her Mam in front of Mrs. Parry.

It took but ten minutes for Caron to walk the short distance to Richard Owen's house. There was no reply to her tentative knock on the front door so she walked back down the path to the front gate. Her hand was on the latch when, as luck would have it, Richard Owen returned from his daily constitutional.

"Hello Caron. How nice to see you. Please come in. I'll ask Glenda to fetch us some tea and cake. I'll tell her I encountered you on my walk and invited you to take tea with me before your cold journey back to Cwyn-y-Gwynt. Then she won't wonder why you called."

Caron turned and followed him into the house. As always there were glowing coals in the grate to keep the study warm.

The doctor turned to her. "I expected you to visit before this. It's important that I examine you."

"I couldn't get away doctor without anybody knowing."

Richard nodded his understanding. As Glenda brought in a sponge cake and a pot of tea, Richard sympathised with Caron about Dee's death and Caron explained that she had been helping Ruth Parry with some chores. Good, thought Richard, Glenda would have nothing to gossip about. He waited until Glenda came to remove the crockery, then immediately said, "Right, let's see how you are progressing."

The examination did not take long. "You're perfectly healthy Caron and so is your baby. I can hear the heartbeat with my stethoscope."

Despite her anxiety, Caron felt a flutter of excitement. "Really doctor?"

"Yes, he or she is alive and kicking. Have you been able to feel the baby moving?"

"I don't know doctor. What should it feel like?"

"Women describe it to me as like having butterflies in their stomach but stronger. You'll be able to see your stomach moving as a hand or foot pushes against you."

"I have had odd feelings in my stomach doctor. I wondered what they were. What will happen next?"

"The quickening will increase Caron as the time of your confinement draws near. You may find that you have backache and want to pass water a lot. I estimate that your baby will be due towards the end of March. I must ask you whether you have told your Mam and Tad?"

"No, doctor. I have told no-one. Not even Tŵm, though I nearly told him."

"Your Mam may have been angry Caron if you'd told Tŵm before her."

"You're right there doctor but she wouldn't have known. Neither Tŵm or I would've told her."

"I don't believe you can hide your pregnancy much longer Caron. You will have to tell your family."

"I can't doctor. I just can't. I'm too scared." Richard Owen could see that this was an understatement. Caron looked terrified.

"Caron, think. If you don't tell them, then one day you will go into labour if you manage to conceal your condition for that long, which I don't believe you can. The birth will come as a terrible shock to them and you may not receive the medical help you need early enough in your labour."

Caron was looking confused. "Doctor, what's labour?"

Richard Owen sighed. "Weren't you at home when your Mam had Siôn?" he asked.

"No, doctor. Mam had a bit of a backache in the morning so I was sent to the Philpins for the day. When I got back in the evening, Siôn had arrived."

Gently Richard explained to Caron the fate that awaited her. He was careful not to frighten her but wanted her to know the reality of what lay in store. Ignorance already had much to answer for. Surprisingly she seemed unperturbed at the prospect of pain. This calmness was soon explained.

"However bad it is doctor, it can't be worse than having to tell Mam what I've done."

Richard Owen, sensing her despair, felt driven to help. "Caron I'll tell her for you but you will have to be there. And speaking of what you've done, I need to ask you a few questions. Last time you told me about the body kiss. I'm sorry to intrude but I need to ask you a little more about it."

Caron flushed beetroot.

"I know you don't want to talk about it, Caron but I have to ask. I need to know what happened. You can trust me. You know that don't you? And please try not to feel embarrassed. I know it's new to you but I'm a doctor and I'm used to speaking about these matters."

Caron nodded.

"Right. This body kiss. Did Abram remove your undergarments?"

Caron shook her head.

"Did he push up your skirt?"

She nodded.

"Did he remove his trousers?"

Again, she shook her head.

Richard Owen was puzzled. Either Carreg-y-Bedd had been chosen by God for the second immaculate conception or Caron was lying. Even though she did not want to speak about what happened, he couldn't believe that she was untruthful.

He tried again. Perhaps she had misunderstood. "So, he didn't take his trousers off Caron but did he move his trousers at all?"

"He might've Doctor. I think I felt him fiddle with his buttons. I just don't know. He pressed himself against me again and again."

"Then what happened Caron?"

"He gave a groan and stopped pushing against me."

"Caron, I'm sorry I have to ask you this. Did he make you damp?"

"Yes, doctor. I was quite wet. I did wonder why that was but just thought it was the dew on the grass."

Richard sighed inwardly. The poor girl was still a virgin. He had had a glimpse of her undergarments in the examination. Wide, loose drawers. The Gypsy lad had clearly been able to push the flimsy material to one side, rub himself against her body and ejaculate. An unlikely scenario for conception but by no means impossible.

And now her life was ruined. By a million to one chance. Richard Owen knew Carreg-y-Bedd too well. The community would be merciless, particularly given the paternity of the child. Richard Owen was not one of those who held Mali Tudor in high esteem. She was quite capable of doing that for herself he thought wryly. Despite his view that she had lorded it over Carreg-y-Bedd for way too long with her holier than thou attitude, he felt a pang of sympathy for her. She would be totally humiliated and there were many who would enjoy Mali Tudor's public downfall. Then there was Twm to think of. Such a fine, young man. This would damage his reputation too.

He turned to Caron. "Caron, if you would accept one piece of advice, it is not to tell anyone who is the father of this child. I know the pressure put on you to name the boy will be great but I believe it will make your situation worse."

Caron agreed. She knew immediately that he was right. To bear a bastard was bad enough but Mali's response to her grandchild being the result of her daughter's fornication with a Gypsy lad was beyond even Caron's imagining.

"How long can we leave telling my Mam, doctor?"

Richard did a quick calculation. "The baby's arrival is likely to be the end of March or the beginning of April but babies sometimes arrive early. I think we could leave it three weeks if you can manage to hide your stomach under loose clothes. You're lucky it's winter-time. That means I could come to tell your Mam and Tad in early February." Consulting his calendar, he continued, "Saturday 10th. I'll drive over in the afternoon and we'll tell them then."

Caron did not reply. February 10th would be the worst day of her life. That she knew. What she didn't know was what would happen after that.

She couldn't even guess since the circumstances were completely outside her control.

Richard Owen, seeing her obvious distress, was at a loss to know how to console her. Her plight was inescapable. He was reminded of the helplessness he'd felt when confronted with the ruination of Ruth Parry's life. At least Ruth could cling on to her pride in Thomas' sacrifice and in Gwyn's military service but Caron was going to have to live with shame. Thinking about divulging Caron's secret, he realised with a start that even he was anxious about it. Mali Tudor was a formidable woman.

St. Dwynwen's Day was marked by a crisp frost and a few flakes of snow. January had been wetter and warmer than usual and Emyr was pleased to see more typical winter weather. "Good, this'll break up the soil after ploughing. Just what we need," he said watching Nain holding the toasting fork over the fire, tipping it to one side to check if the bread was ready. "Put plenty of butter on that please Eira. It's a cold morning." After consuming his toast, he whistled as he went out to do the feeds.

"I'm glad somebody's happy," remarked Nain. "I'm feeling the cold. There was ice on the inside of my bedroom window panes this morning. My chilblains are playing up too. Tomorrow I'll have to save some of the contents of my chamber pot to soak them in."

Bethan shuddered and asked, "Are you wearing those bed socks I knitted for you at Christmas?"

"I am and I put my feet on the hot water bottle last night but of course it was cold by this morning."

Mali spoke firmly. "You're better off not putting your feet directly on to the stone Mam. That only makes the chilblains worse."

"So you say Mali, so you say but it's so nice to feel the warmth through the socks."

Their exchange was interrupted by a knock on the door. "Mrs. Tudor, parcel for you."

"Goodness, Jones the post, is early this morning," remarked Nain recognising the voice.

Mali opened the door to be handed a small parcel, addressed unexpectedly to Bethan. "It's for you," Mali told her.

Bethan was startled, "I never get parcels."

Finding the scissors first, she beat Mali to it, neatly cut off the string and sealing wax and then folded the paper before opening the box that was inside.

"Oh, Bethan, hurry up," Caron urged her. "Just tear the paper off."

Bethan set her mouth in a firm line. "Nonsense, Caron. It can be used again. 'Waste not; want not'."

"Bethan's quite right Caron," echoed Mali. "Don't be so impatient."

Bethan lifted the lid from the box to find a carved, wooden spoon with a glowing, satin finish. The design was simple. The bowl of the spoon was at the base, a heart at the top and the two were connected by intertwined arms forming a figure of eight.

"It's a love spoon," exclaimed Nain. "Of course, I'd forgotten what day it is. The 25th January. Dydd Santes Dwynwen. Who on earth has sent you that Bethan?"

Bethan turned towards her. "I have no idea."

"It's very plain," commented Caron. "I like the ones with lucky horseshoes and fearsome dragons."

"Nonsense Caron, the decorative ones are in bad taste. This one is simple and dignified. It must've been sent by someone respectable," Mali pronounced.

Bethan pulled out a card from the box and read the inscription. 'To Miss Tudor. To express my highest regard.'

"Not very romantic," Nain contributed.

"But an appropriate sentiment for an admirer," Mali retorted.

Nain was not easily going to give ground. "Mali, whoever he is doesn't even call her, Bethan."

"That would be forward, I think. A lasting bond is based on mutual respect not emotion. You can see from his words that this man respects Bethan."

"I would agree with you there Mali. But there has to be space for affection as well."

"Fondness is built up over time."

Bethan had said nothing throughout this exchange. Astonished at receiving an anonymous gift for the first time in her life, she could only hope that she had guessed correctly about the giver. He must have changed his mind, thought better of what he had written in his letter. The indignity of her rejection was not an easy memory but it did look as though she had been more than forgiven. Her spirits rose as she removed dried flowers from a nail protruding from the beam above the fireplace and substituted her little spoon.

Watching her sister, Caron felt for the rush ring she always wore round her neck and next to her skin. She could feel it even through her thick woollen jersey. That was a proper love token she thought. Love spoons were displayed on the wall; a public affirmation of a promise to a loved one. Her gift was private; a secret between the two of them. It meant a lot more.

'High regard!' She couldn't imagine Abram using that phrase to her. He'd told her that her hair was beautiful, the colour of autumn leaves. She hugged his words to her. She'd be willing to bet that no man had said anything of that nature to Bethan. Bethan's hair was more comparable to wire wool than autumn leaves. Thinking of this Caron giggled. It brought Mali's wrath down upon her head.

"What are you smiling about Caron Tudor? What's funny?"

"Nothing Mam. I'm just happy for Bethan."

Mali, unconvinced, finished with a flourish. "We'll have to wait and see if you manage to find a husband as worthy and respectable as Bethan's is likely to be."

Little Black Month

Daniel Ellis arrived at Cwyn-y-Gwynt along with a damp drizzle that seeped into every crevice of his long coat. He had followed the doctor's advice and had been rewarded with a reasonably rapid recovery. His cough had nearly gone. He hoped that he didn't catch a chill from the wet conditions but Daniel was the type of man who once he had decided on a course of action, wanted to carry it out as expeditiously as possible. He had chosen a Saturday for his errand, guessing that Emyr may well be able to take a break from the daily grind.

Mali, alone in the kitchen, greeted him. "What an unexpected pleasure Mr. Ellis. Please come in and join us for some refreshment."

Thanking her, Daniel divested himself of his wet garment. Mali hung it on the back of a chair and placed it in front of the range where it steamed gently. She was thankful that she had polished the warming pan only that morning. The minister could not fail to notice that her home was spanking clean.

Nain greeted him with, "Mr. Ellis, how nice to see you. I'm sorry I haven't been to chapel for a few weeks. I want to come but my legs won't let me. The arthritis gets to me when it's cold and damp. I can't stand and I can't kneel."

"I quite understand," Daniel Ellis replied. "I'll look forward to seeing you in the spring when the weather improves."

Following a brief exchange about the most recent sermon and as Mali made some tea and offered him two sparsely buttered Welsh cakes, Daniel asked, "Is Mr. Tudor available?"

"He's outside." Mali was puzzled. Emyr had little to do with chapel matters beyond attending every Sunday. He was too busy on the farm.

"I would be grateful if you could ask him to step inside."

Mali, direct as always, asked, "Is this anything to do with Bethan? Has she upset you again in any way? I will speak to her most severely if she has."

"It is to do with Miss Tudor but she hasn't upset me in any way. Quite the contrary. However, I would prefer to speak to Mr. Tudor if you would be so kind."

Mali, inwardly seething at being shut out of what was clearly a matter of significance, had little option but to do as she was asked. She called for Caron who, despite the cold, was staying out of the way upstairs on the pretext of tidying her bedroom drawers. "Go and fetch your Tad. The minister would like to have a word with him."

It was only a few moments before Emyr arrived with Caron.

"I hope I haven't disturbed you, Mr. Tudor."

Emyr reassured him. "No, no. I was only in the barn. What can I do for you?"

Looking around at Mali, Nain and Caron, Daniel was firm. "I would prefer not to have a female audience Mr. Tudor. Perhaps we could converse in the parlour?"

Mali, affronted by being subsumed into a group that included Nain and Caron, sniffed loudly. Grudgingly she said, "Emyr will have to open the curtains for you. It will be cold too. I haven't lit a fire in there. We don't use the room much in the winter."

Emyr, slightly embarrassed, turned to the minister. "It's no problem. Please follow me." He ushered Daniel into the Tudor's best room, firmly closing the door behind them, then seated him in an armchair in between a sideboard, where formal family portraits jostled for position with cups won in eisteddfods past and a small table on which a clasped Bible was proudly displayed. Two Staffordshire spaniels with carrot-coloured ears stared down upon them from the mantelpiece. Emyr closed the lid of the walnut piano. "Bethan's been practising hymns," he said by way of explanation.

"Miss Tudor's an excellent musician. Her skill shows us that every home should have a pianoforte. This looks to be a fine instrument," Daniel Ellis contributed politely. "Who tunes it for you?"

"Robotham and Piercy of Chester. All I have to do is go to the Castle Hotel in Ruthin to book a visit." Emyr fingered the candle stubs. "I must remember to ask Bethan to put new candles in the holders. They burn down so quickly at this time of year."

Back in the kitchen, Mali was mystified. "Well," Mali said to Nain, "I wonder what that's all about."

Nain was pragmatic. "I'm sure we'll find out soon enough." Seating herself in her chair, she resumed her darning.

Mali vented her spleen on Caron. "What are you hanging around for? Whatever they're talking about, it's none of your business. Go and do something useful."

Caron, pleased at the dismissal, retreated to her bedroom, this time to escape into 'Wuthering Heights,' lent to her secretively a few months ago by Dee. She could comfort herself with the unbreakable bond between Catherine and the 'Gypsy', Heathcliff. Now Dee had gone the book was hers to keep, a memento of her friend, who had written her name in the front.

It was about fifteen minutes later when Emyr and Daniel Ellis emerged from the parlour. "You were right Mali, it was chilly in there," said Emyr smiling and rubbing his hands. "Make us some more tea."

Mali, itching to know what had taken place, replied with, "Was your conversation satisfactory?"

Emyr gave nothing away. "Yes, very pleasing. I will explain later."

Disappointed, Mali had to sit through what she considered to be a boring exchange about the chapel accounts. When Daniel Ellis at last said, "I think the rain is easing now. It's very wet for February. I'd better be getting back," she seized his drying coat and then immediately opened the back door. He left highly satisfied with having engineered his own salvation.

As soon as the minister had disappeared from sight, Mali turned to Emyr. "Well?"

"Well, what?"

"Emyr, you are annoying in the extreme. You know what. What did the minister want?"

Emyr paused. This was a moment to savour. It wasn't often he had the upper hand. "Mali, you know you always say the Tudors are the envy of the neighbourhood. Well, it seems you're right. Daniel Ellis can't wait to join us."

"What do you mean? Join us?"

Nain interrupted. "Oh, Mali, haven't you realised. Surely, it's obvious. I did wonder if it were that, when he wanted to speak to Emyr, especially so soon after that gift arriving for Bethan."

Mali became aggressive. "Emyr Tudor, tell me immediately. I want to know. I'm not putting up with secrets in my own house."

Emyr put her out of her misery. "The minister has asked for Bethan's hand in marriage."

Mali sat down heavily. "And I thought she'd upset him. What a privilege! Bethan's a very lucky young woman that his eye has fallen upon her. Goodness, I' m going to have to write to Cousin Enid. Poor Trefor. Well, he's just too late. If he'd wanted her, he should've spoken up earlier. There's always Caron of course. Won't make him as good a wife as Bethan but he's not to know that. What exactly did the minister say Emyr?"

"Not much really. Just spoke about God's guidance in selecting a helpmeet for his journey through life."

"Did he say why he had chosen Bethan?"

"To an extent. He spoke about her virtues, her dependability, her high principles and above all her work ethic. He sang your praises too. Said she had turned out well because of her upbringing in a devout Christian family."

Mali preened. "And he's right of course. I've brought them all up to be decent, respectable human beings."

"I may have played a part too, Mali."

Mali was dismissive. "Oh, yes, Emyr. To an extent. But it's the mother who raises the children. The father has to concentrate on providing a living. Did he say anything else?"

"Just that he thought Bethan would make an ideal minister's wife as she had all the qualities he was looking for."

"Doesn't sound very romantic to me. Makes her sound like a prize cow," Nain interjected. "Did he say he loved her?"

Emyr turned to her. "Well, no he didn't but that goes without saying doesn't it?"

"I don't think it does Emyr. I think it needs to be voiced." Nain was firm.

Mali was disparaging. "Oh, Mam don't be ridiculous. You can't expect a minister to speak of such matters. It would be highly inappropriate."

"Eira, I expect he will speak of love to Bethan herself, not to us," said Emyr trying to be placatory.

"You've got more confidence than I have then," Nain retorted. "Has he actually asked Bethan to marry him or has he spoken to you first? It's unusual to ask the father before the daughter."

Emyr relaxed. "Now that I do know. He hasn't spoken to Bethan as yet. He said he wanted to ask my permission first. He said he believed that was the proper way to go about matters. As a man of the cloth, he's bound to behave differently from the local lads."

"So how does he know she will accept?" Nain asked.

Mali was quick off the mark. "Of course, she will accept. How could she not?"

Nain continued to argue. "But we don't know if she loves him. He wouldn't attract me if I were a young woman."

"Mam, Mam. If marriage were based on attraction, few people would ever tie the knot. Sensible women accept a good man from a respectable family with enough money to live on."

"Is that what you did Mali?" Emyr asked quizzically.

Never missing her chance Mali responded, "In part. You came from a good family; you're an honest man and you work hard. But, as you know,

I was the one with the property. Without me your son wouldn't have an inheritance."

Nain bridled. "To be more precise Mali, I am the one with the property. Cwyn-y-Gwynt doesn't become yours until I'm pushing up the daisies."

Mali dismissed Nain with, "Oh yes, in legal terms Mam. But to all intents and purposes it's already mine. Emyr and I run the place. He knew what side his bread was buttered on when he married me, didn't you Emyr?" Without waiting for a reply, she went on, "Bethan's a Maddock through and through. As such she's a sensible woman. Anyway, she'll do as she's told."

"Remember she has Reece and Tudor blood as well." Nain responded.

"Technically yes, but the common sense and business acumen came down the Maddock line. We can trace our ancestry back through generations of land owners as you well know Mam."

"Where is Bethan anyway?" asked Nain, changing the subject, all too aware of Emyr's discomfiture.

"I sent her to the shop in the village. I needed a few things," Mali replied.

"It wasn't a good day to send her out. She'll be wet through," Nain objected.

"Nonsense. A bit of rain never hurt anyone. It's a good thing I did send her. Better that she wasn't here. It might've been embarrassing for the minister," Mali replied.

Nain looked at Emyr. "Are we to tell her what has taken place or is the minister going to ask for her hand himself?"

"He said we were to tell her of his proposal. He said he thought it unnecessary to speak to Bethan directly."

"Seems an odd way of doing things," Nain responded. "In my experience a man asks the girl first so that he can make sure she will accept before asking her father. Otherwise, it could prove to be embarrassing for all concerned."

"He did say that he was sure she would accept. I don't suppose he would've asked my permission if he wasn't sure."

At this, an unpleasant thought occurred to Mali. "I do hope Bethan hasn't been throwing herself at him."

Nain, for once feeling a little sorry for Bethan, came in with, "Oh no Mali, I'm certain that's not the case. Bethan never behaves in an improper manner. And remember she did receive a love spoon. It must've been from him."

"That's true Mam. Well, she'll be back soon. I can speak to her then."

"The love spoon was from Mr. Ellis," Emyr confirmed. "He said he wanted to give Bethan an indication of his intentions. Then if she didn't want him to make an offer, she had the chance to tell him. He took her silence on the matter as acceptance."

"To me it seems an unreliable method of determining a girl's feelings," added Nain, "especially since he didn't write his name on the card."

"Bethan must've had an inkling of who'd sent it," Emyr replied, "though she didn't let on. I wondered why she was spending so much time at the chapel. It's all clear to me now. There was a liaison going on under our noses and we didn't realise." He laughed. "Of all my children, I would've thought Bethan the least likely to have a secret love affair."

"I'm sure she and Mr. Ellis conducted themselves properly," Mali interrupted.

"Now, there I agree with you," Nain added. "We don't need to worry on that score. 'High regard' indeed! Only Daniel Ellis could've reduced an emotional gesture to a business transaction. I only hope Bethan knows what she's doing."

Bethan arrived back late, having waited in the shop for the rain to lessen before making her way back with the groceries. She had no idea of the joy that awaited her return. Mali had decided that it was much the best thing for her to enlighten Bethan as to her future. "After all, I am her mother," she said to Emyr when he pointed out that he was the one who had actually heard what the minister had to say. Emyr gave in and left the women to deal with women's matters.

Even Mali was surprised by Bethan's reaction. She had expected her to be pleased at the prospect of a settled life but was unprepared for Bethan's sheer delight. Nain was relieved. The girl must love Daniel Ellis after all, she thought. Though he was an unlikely man to sweep a girl off her feet, he must have hidden depths.

Bethan's joy was largely a result of her intense surprise at the speed with which her mission had finally been accomplished. She smiled to herself. It was all most satisfactory, especially since she'd had to endure the disappointment of early December. She was still unsure what had caused such a disruption in her carefully planned strategy, just as she was ignorant of what had caused Daniel to change his mind. Daniel. Daniel. She would be able to call him that now. She had thought of him as Daniel for many months but, with the exception of that one undignified incident, had respected the formality of their relationship and so had been unable to utter his name.

Bethan sighed with relief. At long last married bliss awaited her.

Tŵm did not have an easy February. Firstly, he discovered that Daniel Ellis was to be his brother-in-law. The minister was a man he had never warmed towards. He couldn't see them having a close friendship. They had nothing in common. Daniel's vocation was very different from Tŵm's. Tŵm was a regular chapel goer but attended more from expectation than from a driving need for spiritual guidance. His God was Medicine. He wanted to care for the body, not the soul, though 'care' was not a word that sprang easily to the lips when one thought of Daniel Ellis. In Tŵm's view, Daniel, though ostensibly a holy man, lacked the empathy necessary for real humanity. What was more, the new addition to the Tudor family was going to become a member sooner rather than later. The wedding was to take place in the spring. "Why wait longer for God to bless our union?" Daniel had said to Mali. Tŵm was relieved to find that Bethan would be going to live in Tŷ Capel, the minister's house, rather than Daniel Ellis moving into Cwyn-y-Gwynt. He was not going to miss his sister. Apart from exchanging civilities they had little to say to each other on any matter. Her absence might make Caron's life a little easier he thought. It may lessen Mali's tendency to hold Bethan up as a shining example.

Dwelling incessantly on Cadoc 'putting him right' did not make for a tranquil time either. Cadoc's words, 'If ya ask me he chucked 'imself in the pond,' span round and round, disturbing Tŵm's sleep and preoccupying his waking hours. Could Gwyn really have put an end to himself? Could he have immersed himself in Pwll Berw, felt the chilly waters close over his head, denied himself the instinctive push to the surface to gasp some air? And purely for the sake of Bronwen Morgan. Surely not. Tŵm was aware that there were people who allowed emotion to overcome good sense, propriety and consideration for others. But Gwyn? Gwyn had always looked after his mother especially after Thomas' death. Even if he were overwhelmed with feelings for Bronwen, surely he couldn't, wouldn't, knowingly cause such distress to Ruth. But then Bronwen had not shown any sensitivity. Instead, she had rejected him, humiliated him, laughed at his pain. Perhaps it was a moment of madness.

Tŵm knew that unless he could solve the puzzle, it would be difficult to move on with his life but now Cadoc had told him what had really happened on the Thursday evening, what else was there left to discover? The crux of the matter was that there were no witnesses as to whether Gwyn jumped or was pushed.

Tŵm's pondering was brought to an abrupt end by February 10th making its appearance.

Caron had been willing the short, dark days to pass slowly. They didn't.

Hiding her bulge was becoming more and more difficult. She couldn't fasten her skirt band and had resorted to using a length of string wound round the button on one side and knotted through the buttonhole on the other. The string she was using was becoming longer by the week. Over her vest and shirt, she wore her loose jersey. Despite the winter cold, she spent as much time away from the kitchen as she could, volunteering for jobs outside or errands. Meals were not such a problem. Her belly was hidden if she was seated at the long board table in the kitchen and if she sat in another chair, she was careful to keep her arms folded over her middle. For the past three weeks Mali had loomed large in Caron's mind. She felt as though she was going to have to face the fiery breath of the red dragon of Dinas Emrys itself.

Opening the curtains on the day she had been dreading, Caron could see it was raining heavily as it had done for much of the month. She knew there was much that could go wrong with the doctor's visit. Mali may go out. After all it was a Saturday. At this thought, Caron was conscious of a spurt of hope. But it was momentary. It was unlikely that Mali would venture out to the village in such conditions. Her thoughts turned to the doctor. The weather wouldn't put him off now that he had a car. However perhaps the car wouldn't start in such wet weather and the doctor wouldn't want to come in the pony and trap and risk a drenching. Hope reasserted itself.

Not wishing to risk extra wrath, Caron became unexpectedly helpful and was assigned cooking duties. Mali had skinned two rabbits, shot by Brad, and ordered Caron to make them into a pie. Caron retrieved them from the bucket of water in which they were soaking and queasily jointed them, removing the fat and silver skin. It was a job she hated but she felt she couldn't make her normal complaints. Putting down her knife, she placed the joints in a pot and added bacon, onions and carrots.

"I'll have to go to the attics to fetch apples," she said to Nain. "Tad won't want rabbit pie without apples."

"Don't you leave that knife by the fire," Nain replied. "It'll annoy the fairies."

Caron obediently moved the offending knife on to the table before embarking on her trip to the attic to fetch the Trwyn Mochyns that Emyr loved in his rabbit pie. She checked whether the blue bootees were still there and pondered again on who had hidden them and why. Maybe she would ask Nain now that she had a justifiable reason for being in the attic. Back in the kitchen with the rabbits bubbling away on the range, she made the pastry. Despite the time of year, the fire made the kitchen hot and Caron felt dizzy as she wielded the rolling pin. She must not faint again as she had in the potato field. It seemed so long ago now. If only she could sit down, she was sure she'd be alright.

A few minutes later, she was brought back to full consciousness by Nain. "Caron, Caron, drink this water."

Caron realised she was sitting on the chair that she had pushed back to roll out the pastry.

"You're lucky my girl. You fell back into the chair. You might've banged your head if it hadn't been there."

Caron became aware of a gamey cooking smell. "Oh, the rabbits. They'll be burnt."

Nain reassured her. "I've stirred them and added more water. They're fine. It's just a good thing they weren't already baking in the oven. Otherwise, we might've had burnt pastry. Now you sit there and sip that water. I'll finish off the pie." Using a ladle, she transferred the contents of the pot to a dish then expertly rolled the pastry round the pin and unfurled it over the rim. "There, all done. I'll just slip it in the oven and then I'll help you peel some potatoes."

Caron smiled at her gratefully. "Thank you, Nain."

"Before we do that Caron, I think we need to have a little talk don't you?"

Caron nodded her agreement as Nain pulled up a chair.

"Caron, you don't seem right to me. Are you ill?"

"Nain, I didn't sleep well last night."

"And why's that?"

Caron hesitated. "I was worrying."

"And what have you got to worry your pretty little head about? You have all your life in front of you, a comfortable home and a family to look after you. I know Carreg-y-Bedd isn't the most exciting place in the world for a young person but believe me when you read the newspapers there are many worse places to grow up."

"Oh, it's not that Nain. I love Carreg-y-Bedd. I wouldn't want to live in the city."

"Well, what is it then? Whatever you say, I can see you're not well and if that daughter of mine had taken the trouble to look closely at her own daughter she would've seen it too. You're always tired. There was that time you passed out while you were picking potatoes. I don't think you've been right since then. You don't seem to have lost weight though. Your face is puffy if anything. If I didn't know better..."

Nain was interrupted by Caron changing the subject. "Oh, Nain, while I remember, when I was fetching the apples for the pie, one of the floorboards came loose in the attic and you'll never guess what was underneath it!"

Nain paled. "I think I might Caron. Was it a pair of blue bootees?"

"Oh, you know," Caron replied, somewhat deflated. She had hoped to surprise Nain.

"Yes. I knew they were there but I wish you hadn't found them. I must hide them in a safer place." Nain looked anxious.

"Did you put them there?" asked Caron

"I did."

"Why?"

"Because shoes keep away the evil spirits, the ghosts, witches and demons. They bring good luck to a home too. But please don't tell your Mam that they're there Caron. You know she doesn't approve of what she calls 'superstitious nonsense'. She'd move them and that would bring bad luck."

"No, I won't tell her Nain. I promise. I don't want you to get into trouble. But whose bootees are they? Were they Twm's?"

"No, Caron. I can't lie to you. They weren't Twm's. Now don't ask me any more questions. Try to forget you've seen them."

Mali noisily entered the room dragging a sack. "If I've told Emyr once, I've told him a hundred times to fetch in a new bag of potatoes. Had to do it myself in the end." She looked at Caron sitting in the chair. "Haven't you got something better to do? I wish I had time to sit down and have a drink."

Nain leapt in. "Now, now Mali. Everything is fine. Caron's finished the rabbit pie and it's in the oven. We were just looking for more potatoes, weren't we Caron? Now, you've brought them, Caron and I will get them peeled and in the pan."

Mali was quietened. "Oh, well if the pie's in..."

"It's nearly ready. Only waiting for the pastry to brown. We just need to get a move on with the vegetables." Nain rolled up her sleeves and reached for her pinny as Caron stood up to help.

In minutes the potatoes were on the hot plate and coming to the boil. Caron laid the table and it wasn't long before Emyr, Brad and Twm could be seen washing their hands under the pump in the yard.

"Remember to put a plate out for Bethan," Mali reminded them. "She'll be soaked when she comes back from helping the minister. She's helping him reorganise his books."

Devouring the rabbit pie and mounds of mashed potatoes, Emyr commented, "Very good pie. Always much better with apple. We needed hot food; it's not easy working when you're drenched to the skin."

Mali sniffed. "Mam, you've done enough potatoes for two meals. You always peel too many. We could manage with less. They need to last till the next crop."

"You worry too much Mali. We've got plenty. Let the lads fill up their stomachs. They've been working hard and Brad and Siôn are growing boys."

They'd no sooner finished than a trap could be heard rolling into the yard.

Mali went to the window and rubbed the condensation off a pane. "Who can that be? I can't believe anyone would venture out in this weather without good reason. Even Bethan thought twice about going out this morning." She paused. "Goodness, it's Doctor Owen. What on earth can he want? And why's he in the trap and not that noisy car of his? You can't tell me he hasn't got a private income. He couldn't buy that car otherwise. And petrol's three and six a gallon so I'm told. His family must have money. Maybe he needs some help today from you Twm. Brad, go out and help him with the pony and trap. Put them under cover in the big barn. I'm sure he'll only be here a few minutes just to pick up Twm. Caron, get the table cleared and the pots washed."

Brad, pulled a sack over his head, tied it round his middle with string and went back out into rain that by this time was driving horizontally across the yard.

About ten minutes later, Mali thrust her head round the back door, wondering why Richard Owen had not come in. To her surprise she saw that Brad had unharnessed the pony and was in the process of leading him into a stable.

"Thank you Brad. Just rub him down will you and give him a wad of hay," she heard the doctor saying.

Puzzled by the prospect of Richard Owen coming in for what promised to be a lengthier visit than she had envisaged, she called to him, "To what do we owe this pleasure Doctor? What makes you come out to see us in conditions like these and where's your car?"

The doctor strode across the cobbles, smiled at Mali and said, "The car's broken down. It's in the garage with an oil leak. Such a good job I hadn't sold Dandy yet. I'll be glad to come into the warmth after being out in all this rain. Makes me appreciate that car."

Mali was quick to respond, glad that she had been proven right. "I told you those new-fangled motor cars can't be trusted, didn't I? Give me a good, reliable horse any day."

Divesting himself of his outer coat, Richard Owen hung it on the back of a chair by the fire. Steam began to rise slowly from the thick woollen material and the smell of wet dog pervaded the room. Nain offered him a cup of hot tea which he cupped gratefully in both hands.

"I didn't think you'd come," Caron blurted out, then realised her mistake and flushed crimson.

Mali pounced. "What nonsense are you talking Caron? You couldn't possibly have known that the doctor was going to call."

Richard, sensing an opening, replied, "Oh but she did."

Mali's look of astonishment said it all. For the second time in a month, she felt disadvantaged. It was not an experience she enjoyed.

Richard Owen took charge. "Mr. and Mrs. Tudor I need to speak with you about a serious and private matter. I see Bethan's not here thankfully but it would be best if you gave Twm and Brad a job to do outside and asked Siôn to help them."

Twm, open mouthed and wondering how the doctor could possibly have anything to do with Caron, gave Siôn a push towards the door. "Come on, you can help Brad and I finish replacing those two broken spokes on the big cart. He's already out there and we can do that inside the barn."

"And what about me?" Nain asked.

"I believe it would be better if you stayed. Your daughter and granddaughter may need you."

Mali reasserted herself in her own kitchen. "No. Mam, we don't know what the doctor's going to say. You go and have your afternoon nap."

Nain, courage bolstered by the presence of an outsider of some stature, stayed seated. "No, Mali," she said firmly. "This is clearly important. I'm staying."

Caron found her voice. "Mam, I want Nain to stay too."

Mali, distracted from the matter of her mother turned to Caron. "Do you know what this is about? What have you been up to?"

Richard Owen took charge once more. "Please would you all listen. I think it better if we draw up our chairs round the table. Then everyone can hear."

Emyr, perplexed, had been silent in the face of this unusual occurrence in his daily routine but now found his manners. "Come on, come on, do what the doctor asks."

He politely offered Richard his own arm chair at the head of the table. Richard took it. Caron sat next to him in order to position herself as far away as possible from Mali. Sandwiched between the doctor and Nain she felt slightly safer. It was not to last. She could see her Mam and Tad sitting opposite. Mali was glowering at her. For her daughter to have knowledge of a matter about which she knew nothing, was galling in the extreme. Caron looked down. Everyone else looked expectantly at the doctor.

Richard Owen knew that telling the Tudors was not going to be an easy task. He had rehearsed what he was going to say and how he was going to say it. But now that he was here, with their eyes fixed on his face, he couldn't remember one word of what he had so carefully prepared. He cleared his throat and began, "I'm afraid I have to tell you that Caron is not well." He hesitated. What had made him say that? It wasn't even true. Caron was in rude health. He was prevaricating. He opened his mouth to restart but before he could, Mali jumped in.

"What do you mean she's not well? And how would you know? Has she been to see you behind my back?"

Richard, realising that delaying tactics were not going to be helpful, took the plunge. It took him seven words to change life forever for the Tudor family. Later when he looked back on it, the whole incident seemed to have taken place in slow motion. No shell landing in a British trench could have wreaked more havoc. At first there was silence, followed closely by disbelief, then seemingly endless questions. Mali became hysterical; Emyr, his usual stolid self, though shaken, asked practical questions: "When is the child likely to be born?" and "Where will she have it?" Nain simply felt for Caron's hand under the table.

Mali was quite simply beside herself. In the space of a few moments, she had progressed from stunned disbelief to incandescent wrath. Her eyes bored into Caron's, her questions tempered only marginally by the doctor's presence. "Who's the father? How could you do this to me? What have I done to deserve this? Aren't you ashamed of yourself? When have you been alone with a lad?" And again, "Who's the father?"

Richard Owen did what he could. "Mrs. Tudor, please calm yourself. I appreciate it's a shock but Caron will need help from you." His words proved inflammatory.

"Help! Help! I'll give her help! What she needs is horse whipping. She's not been brought up to act like a common whore."

Caron bowed her head as though the verbal abuse was a physical burden. Richard, aware that Mali was likely to be restraining herself in front of him, knew that once he'd left, Caron would have to face Mali's unbridled fury. But he couldn't stay forever. He could only hope that Nain and Emyr would not allow Mali to go too far. In his view the poor girl was guilty of nothing but ignorance and naïvety.

This was not Mali's view. Once the doctor finally drove the trap out of the yard, she gave full vent to her anger. "You filthy, filthy, slut! You disgusting trollop! Now you tell me this minute who the lad is."

Caron, browbeaten by the tirade, summoned her strength to answer. "No, Mam I'm not telling you." Mali drew her hand back. The blow across Caron's cheekbone knocked her sideways.

Emyr intervened. "Enough is enough Mali. I know she's let us down but violence is not the answer. We have to work out what to do."

Mali, crying with frustration, retorted, "She deserves everything I've given her and more. I'll find out who she's been leading on if I have to beat it out of her." Again, she turned to Caron. "You can stop that snivelling. Get yourself up to your room. I don't want to see your brazen face."

Caron, grateful for any respite, did as she was told. "I hate her," she said to herself. "I hate her." Immediately she felt guilty. She's my Mam, she thought and it's sinful to hate her. The Bible says I must honour her. But I don't. I just don't. She closed her eyes only to see the eyes of the deacons condemning her sin. Curled up on the bed, she could hear every word of the furious argument that was still going on downstairs.

"She'll have to go. She can't stay here. I'd never be able to hold my head up again. And the chapel. I won't be able to show my face there. Just think what people will say. I'll be a laughing stock. I can hear Nerys Philpin now. 'Have you heard about Mali Tudor? Daughter's having a child and she's not married you know. From what I hear she doesn't even know who the father is. What does that tell you?' And Caron. I can barely speak her name. Never thinks about anyone but herself. She hasn't thought of Brad or Twm. What girl's going to marry into a family with that kind of skeleton in the cupboard?"

Emyr did his best. "Now Mali, calm down. We'll sort it out. I don't understand how it could've happened. She's never gone out to dances or indeed anywhere by herself. I would never have thought that my little Caron would do something like this. But I'm sure she'll tell us what's happened once you stop screaming at her."

Mali was not to be quietened. "Stop screaming! Stop screaming! I'll do more than scream when I get hold of her again."

Nain had said little. Even though she had begun to suspect that all was not right with Caron, she had dismissed her suspicions as nonsense. Just like Emyr, she was of the view that Caron had not had the opportunity, let alone the inclination. She also knew that trying to calm Mali would be counterproductive. Mali's nature was such that she felt morally obliged to be furious. Nain ventured, "I think we should sleep on it," she said, "and talk about it tomorrow. Let it sink in and then we can decide what to do."

Emyr assented. "Good idea. Pull yourself together Mali. We can't let Siôn know what's wrong." Mali set her mouth in one thin line but she nodded.

The door opened. Bethan was back, droplets of rain dripping from her hair. "What's going on? I could hear Mam shouting from outside. And why are the boys in the barn keeping out of the rain? They told me they weren't allowed in."

Mali couldn't resist. "It's your sister. You'll never guess what she's done. She's breeding a bastard." At first Bethan was perplexed. Then, seeing their faces, it sunk in.

"No, she can't be..." She turned to her father for reassurance.

"I'm afraid it's true Bethan," he affirmed. "The doctor came to tell us."

Bethan was puzzled. "The doctor? How would he know?"

"That's what I want to know," Mali replied grimly.

A thought struck Bethan. "But what about me? Daniel's a minister. If he finds out about this he isn't going to want to be associated with our family. He'll cancel the wedding!" She burst into tears.

Emyr had endured more than enough. Telling them he had to groom the horses, he went outside. Mali could cope with it.

Mali switched her attention to Bethan. "Nobody's going to find out about this Bethan. Nobody at all. I'm going to see to that."

The next morning when Caron came downstairs for breakfast, Emyr and her brothers were already outside. Stony faced silence from Mali and Bethan greeted her. Nain sat awkwardly in her chair, not wanting to say anything in front of Mali. Caron didn't know what to say so she said nothing, knowing that anything she said would bring further wrath down upon her head. Eating cold bacon and bread, she felt like a pariah. The silence was worse than the vitriol. Feeling like the accused waiting for the jury to pronounce in court, she had lain awake until the early hours, not even able to sob because of Bethan in the bed alongside hers. Before Bethan went to sleep, she had vented her spleen. Her invective differed from Mali in that it included the words 'stupid,' 'selfish' and 'thoughtless'. The outpouring concluded with, "You have ruined my life."

Mali couldn't resist for long. The silence was broken with, "You needn't think you can lie in bed in the morning just because you're *ill*." Her voice dripped with sarcasm.

Caron hung her head. "I'm not... I didn't... I was only a little late. I didn't go to sleep for ages last night."

"Well, it's no wonder is it? Heaping all this trouble onto the head of a decent family who don't deserve it."

"What's going to happen to me?"

"There are decisions to be made and I'm the one who'll make them. You will do exactly as you're told. If I had my way, you'd be thrown out of the house today and never darken our door again. You have your Tad to thank that you're still here this morning. That and the fact that your disgusting behaviour has to be kept a secret. It's humiliating enough that the doctor knows."

Nain ventured a comment. "You don't have to worry Mali. He can't tell anyone. Doctors swear an oath you know."

Mali ignored her.

"And the first thing, my girl, is giving me the name of the lad. He needs to be dealt with. Not that I blame him as much as you. You shouldn't have led him on and then given in to him."

Nain interrupted. "I don't see how you can deal with him, Mali. If you tell his family then everyone is going to know. You won't be able to keep it a secret."

This drew a response. "For once Mam, you're right. Best that he and his family don't know. But I need to know who it was."

Caron summoned up some courage. "Why Mam? Why do you need to know?"

"Don't you dare answer me back." Caron ducked as Mali raised her hand.

"It would be better for you if you tell me. I have to know who you've been sinning with. Then I can make sure you never see him again."

Caron did not answer. Silent revolution was less likely to result in retaliation than vocal rebelliousness. It was easier to stay silent. If Mali knew her secret, she would be even more savage if that were possible.

"You will tell me Caron or from this day on you are no longer my daughter."

"Mali, no!" Nain's horrified exclamation at last attracted Mali's attention.

"Mam, she's drawn this down upon her own head. She's not only let her family down but she insists on not telling us what we have a right to know."

"Mali, she isn't the first that this has happened to and she won't be the last."

"She's the first in the Maddock family. If you go back down the generations, there's no illegitimacy at all. And it's the same with the Reeces and the Tudors. God-fearing, respectable families, all of them. And that... that... hussy," Mali spat out the word, "has destroyed our reputation."

"Calm down, calm down Mali. It may not be as bad as you think."

Mali was incensed. "How can it possibly not be as bad as I think? It will probably be much worse. I've always been able to hold my head high in Carreg-y-Bedd. Respectability and reputation are everything. People will talk. If anyone finds out then Bethan's future is destroyed. How can a minister associate himself with this sort of scandal? Then there's Brad and Twm. Both held in high regard by all the neighbours. They can't help but be affected by this. Such a selfish girl. Never a thought for how her actions will affect her brothers and sister."

"Now be fair Mali. I don't suppose for one second that she deliberately set out to hurt them."

"Perhaps not. But thoughtlessness is next to godlessness in my view."

Caron moved out of arm's reach and tried again. "I wish you'd stop talking about me as though I'm not here."

"The way you've behaved, you don't deserve to be spoken to."

Nain diverted Mali. "I agree with you on one thing Mali. We do need to think about Bethan, Twm and Brad. It is best to hide what has happened. Easier for Caron too."

"I don't care about that. She doesn't deserve to have her life made easier."

"Mali, we need to give the situation some thought. I have an idea that might just work."

Mali regarded her mother. "Caron, get out of my sight. Make yourself useful and go and let out the hens and collect the eggs. Then you can feed the horses and clean them out."

Nain objected. "Mali, she shouldn't be doing any heavy work."

"If she loses the child it doesn't matter does it? Better that it doesn't arrive at all than live with such a stigma."

Caron did as she was told and left them to decide her fate.

Twm found out the shocking truth the same morning. He couldn't fail to notice that something terrible had happened. The atmosphere in Cwyn-y-Gwynt was thick with tension. Mali was either silent, her mouth set in a grim line, or screaming at Caron from behind closed doors. Bethan, with red swollen eyes, couldn't bring herself to speak to her sister, Nain was uncharacteristically silent and Emyr simply stayed outside despite the winter weather, not even venturing into the kitchen to thaw his cold hands.

It was Emyr who told him about Caron while they were feeding the stock before going to chapel. "You're old enough to know what's going on Twm but keep it to yourself and don't tell Brad. I can't trust him to keep it quiet. The fewer people who know, the better."

Twm was dumbfounded. Absorbed in agonising about Gwyn, he had not had an inkling of his sister's dilemma. He remembered the conversation about the sheep. What was it Caron had asked him? Oh, yes, about the rutting. It had been embarrassing. She had appeared to know nothing about the facts of life. Surely, she couldn't have been trying to fool him into believing in her innocence. Thinking back, he couldn't believe that of her. She had been genuinely ignorant and obviously bashful. So how... Just like Mali and Emyr, he couldn't understand how Caron had been able to meet a boy alone. In Cwyn-y-Gwynt, Mali controlled the chess board of family movements. Later that morning as Mali, Emyr and Nain were chatting to the Griffiths' after chapel, Twm saw his chance. Caron was standing alone, waiting for the conversation to end. She hadn't wanted to go to the service but Mali had insisted. "We don't want anybody asking where you are, do we? Put on your loose coat and keep away from prying eyes."

Twm walked over to her and squeezed her hand. She looked up at him. Seeing the sympathy in his eyes, she whispered, "You know, don't you?"

"Yes, but why didn't you tell me?"

"I couldn't Twm. I just couldn't. I didn't know how to tell you. I didn't tell Mam and Tad. The doctor did. What could you have done anyway?"

"I don't know Caron, I don't know." He paused. "Nothing, is the honest answer but I could've listened."

She nodded. Tears started to her eyes. His kindness affected her more than Mali's scathing comments.

Caron flushed. "Oh, Twm, what am I going to do?"

"You're going to have a baby. And I hear from Tad that Mam will sort out what's going to happen."

"I'm glad he's told you. It saves me having to explain."

"Caron how did it happen?" Twm paused and laughed despite their serious exchange. Well, I know how it happened but I don't know who and where."

"Oh, Twm. I wish I could tell you but I can't. Dr. Owen said it was best if no-one knew and I know he's right. If Mam even suspected that you knew who it was, she'd make your life a torment until you told her. If you don't know it's easier for you."

Twm nodded. "But Dr. Owen knows. Why did you tell him?"

"I had to Twm. I had to explain how it happened. I trust him. He won't tell anyone."

"And you don't trust me?" Twm's hurt was evident in his voice.

"Of course I do Twm. But I think it's better for you not to know."

Twm sensed a different Caron. In the past he would've been able to persuade her. With this new Caron he felt he would be unable to change her mind.

Though Caron meant every word, she was aware that she had another reason for not telling Twm. She couldn't bear that he thought badly of her. And she couldn't conceive of any way of revealing the truth without making herself sound like that word her Mam called her. 'Slut'. 'Slut'. If she could make Twm understand that she and Abram loved each other then perhaps he might not think of her in that way. But she knew it wasn't possible to explain her emotions. How could she describe the way in which Abram had filled her head to the exclusion of all else, how her mind trembled when he touched her, how he mattered to her more than anyone else, even Twm? As far as she was aware Twm had not been in love so how could he even begin to understand how she found herself in chaos.

"What are you two talking about?" Twm and Caron, lost in conversation, had failed to notice Mali approaching.

"Nothing." Caron's response was instinctive.

"I don't believe that. I could hear you keeping your voices low. And there would only be one reason for that. Sharing a secret with each other."

Twm, seeing Caron's agitation, made light of the matter. "Mam, there are no secrets. Caron tripped just outside the chapel door, that's all. I'm surprised you didn't notice. I was just checking that she hadn't hurt herself. I had a quick look at her ankle; the doctor showed me how."

Mali, distracted by the mention of Richard Owen, turned her attention elsewhere. Uncharacteristically whispering but not wanting to draw the attention of other chapel goers, she proceeded with, "That man. Don't even mention his name to me. Interfering in our family matters. I used to think he was worthy of respect but now I'm not so sure."

"He's a fine doctor Mam and a fine man. He would only have been trying to help."

Mali hissed, "Maybe so but I don't like anyone knowing what goes on in our family, not even him."

Later, with it being a Sunday, Twm, using the excuse of checking the sheep, gave himself some time to think about the situation. As he walked, he berated himself. In worrying about Gwyn's fate, he had neglected his younger sister. It wasn't possible. She couldn't have kept it secret. Someone would've seen them. Secrets didn't stay secrets long in Carreg-y-Bedd. Then it struck him.

What was it Cadoc had said all those months ago? He'd asked him, in a sarcastic kind of way, if he'd been looking after his sister. And he hadn't been. He hadn't given her a thought. He'd just dismissed it and put the comment down to Cadoc being Cadoc. And then Cadoc had gone on to talk about Gwyn and Bronwen and that had seemed to have more than a seed of truth in it so he'd deemed it more important. What else had Cadoc said? Oh yes. 'Pretty as a picture,' some disgusting words about Caron's figure and, 'She might like what I've got in mind'.

Then recently when Cadoc had 'put 'im right' he'd mentioned Caron's looks yet again. Certainly, Cadoc had seemed to find Caron appealing but surely Caron wouldn't be attracted to Cadoc would she? Women did find Cadoc handsome though, he knew. He'd heard Nain talking about how Cadoc Morgan could have had the pick of the neighbourhood if he'd been honest as well as handsome. Maybe Caron had been taken in by him. She was so young and so naïve. Then another thought surfaced.

What if...? Twm could barely bring himself to think it. Surely even Cadoc would stop short of forcing her. And when would he have had the opportunity to do that?

Considering the situation, Twm came to the conclusion that it was at the very least a feasible option. Caron walked to and fro to the village by herself. Everyone did. Carreg-y-Bedd was as safe as houses. He corrected himself. Carreg-y-Bedd had always been safe in the past but in the last year there had been Gwyn's unexplained death and a couple of thefts of livestock and implements. Times were changing. Outsiders were blamed. "Neighbours wouldn't steal from neighbours," Emyr had said, "and it certainly wouldn't be Moses and his family. He's straight as a die. More likely to be tinkers." But if Cadoc had forced Caron, surely she would have told him or told Tad at least. He tried to work out how she would behave in such a situation.

Any girl would be frightened and upset but Twm knew his sister. She was impulsive and likely to panic. Would that make her run to Tad? Possibly but

Cadoc would likely have threatened her to keep quiet. Caron would not want either Twm or Tad to tackle the Morgans. She'd be scared they'd get hurt. Griff Morgan and his two sons together were a formidable force.

And she would be just as intimidated about going to the police. Cadoc would undoubtedly lie and say she was willing. He would cast doubt on her story. And there would be some who would believe him. He could hear it now. "No smoke without fire." Mali would blame her for causing tittle-tattle. He knew just what she'd say. "We're the talk of the neighbourhood. We'll never live this down. How could you let this happen Caron? Are you sure you didn't lead him on?"

No, if Cadoc had forced Caron, the easiest option for her was just not to tell anyone and pretend nothing had happened. No-one would ever have known if there hadn't been a pregnancy. Suddenly he remembered Caron's reluctance to go to chapel the previous summer. That would be about the right time. What was it she had said? That she'd been 'wicked'. The poor girl must've blamed herself when in reality it was all Cadoc's fault.

Twm's anger rose as he worked out what had happened. It more than explained Caron's questions about the rutting. He had no doubt now about what had taken place. No wonder Cadoc had concocted that story about seeing Caron with a boy. He'd been trying to put Twm off the scent.

Now that he had discovered the truth of the matter, planning what to do about it was another question. He asked himself what Evan would do. That was easy. Evan would make straight for Lane End and smash Cadoc's face in. Just as quickly Twm dismissed Evan's course of action. Evan never had stopped to think before he acted. Twm knew he could hardly knock on the Morgans' door and accuse Cadoc. They'd beat him to a pulp. In any case he'd heard Mali proclaim that it was 'paramount' that the truth of Caron's condition was hidden from the world at large. If he accused Cadoc, then every inhabitant of Carreg-y-Bedd would know within the hour. He didn't often agree with Mali but on this occasion, he could see that secrecy made sense, not only for Caron but also for her siblings.

Twm at last understood why Caron wasn't telling them the father's name. The last thing Caron would want was to be associated with Cadoc Morgan. And when she had the baby, she wouldn't want it to know or see its father, for sure.

Having solved the mystery to his satisfaction, Twm searched out Caron the very next morning. He found her in the back kitchen, red faced and with her sleeves rolled up. The water in the copper was already boiling so the heat in the room was intense. Tablecloths and towels were on the line swinging in a cold breeze. Caron, wrestling with sheets weighted down with water, manoeuvred them towards the mangle. Now that he knew, Twm couldn't understand how he hadn't seen it before. Because of the heat she had divested herself of her ubiquitous grey jumper and he could see clearly that his sister's body, normally slender, had thickened considerably; her fine jawline replaced by puffy roundness.

"Let me help you."

She looked up at him gratefully. "Oh, Twm, thank you. I am finding it hard."

"You shouldn't be doing it," Twm replied grimly. "But I don't suppose Mam'll listen."

They worked together in silence feeding the sheets through the rollers until every drop of water was extracted, flattening them into linen pancakes.

After they'd hung them outside, Caron asked. "What are you doing here Twm?"

Twm grinned. "Helping you!"

"And I'm grateful but shouldn't you be out with Tad and Brad?"

"I came to see you Caron. I wanted to tell you that I know what happened and I know it wasn't your fault. You have nothing to blame yourself for."

Caron stood stock still. "But you can't Twm. You just can't know. I haven't told anyone."

"No and I understand why. But I worked it out."

For a moment Caron was silent. Then, "Well in a way Twm that's a relief. I don't know how you did it but it means I don't have to explain. You are the one person I know I can trust never to tell anyone, other than Dr. Owen of course. But I must ask you, do you think badly of me?"

Twm put a rough arm round her shoulders. "No sis, of course I don't think badly of you. You mustn't worry about that. It's too late for me to do much about it but I want you to know that I understand. That's the main thing."

"Caron, Caron are those sheets on the line yet?" Mali, immediately suspicious, appeared in the garden. "Twm, what are you doing here? Haven't you got enough to do helping your father?"

Giving his sister a squeeze on the arm, Twm replied, "I'm just going Mam. Came in for a drink and helped Caron put the sheets on the line."

"She doesn't need any help Twm. You've got enough to do. This is women's work. I hope she didn't ask you to help. I thought your Tad had asked you to plough ready for sowing the oats next month."

"No, Mam, Caron didn't ask for help. I just saw what she was doing and thought it would speed up the drying. I'm not starting the ploughing until later."

"Well, the job's done now. You get off back to your Tad. Caron, if you've told your brother anything you've not told me, you're going to bitterly regret it!"

Tŵm obediently followed Mali's direction. Working out what to do about Cadoc Morgan was going to be no easy task.

Month of the Wind

Caron was informed on St. David's Day what her future would be.

Envelopes had been arriving with an unknown post mark and feathery handwriting in bright green ink. One morning Caron had picked up a bulky letter only to have it snatched by Mali. "Give that here, Caron. It's nothing to do with you."

Caron had stayed resolutely silent about the fathering of her child. This had been less than easy. She had been subjected to an endless torrent from Mali. Her mother had tried everything: cajoling, threatening, bullying, persuading, even on one memorable occasion, subterfuge. Mali, placing her hand on Caron's shoulder, had said softly, "Now Caron love, Tad and I are only trying to help you." Worn down by the barrage, this had nearly worked. Caron's generosity of spirit instinctively responded to the unfamiliar gentleness. Fortunately for Caron, Mali couldn't resist following her first comment with, "I'll find a way to make sure he and his family pay for what he's done." The threat gave Caron fresh courage and she remained silent. She clung on to the thought that however bad her life became, it was never going to be as bad as it had been for Dee.

If Mali discovered Caron's secret then Moses and his family could expect no more work from the Tudors or even from other local farmers. Mali would see to that. She would undoubtedly try to hound them out of the area. Caron wouldn't put it past her to accuse the Gypsies of stealing. Anything to get her own back. It would also mean Caron had no chance of ever seeing Abram again. She was already a prisoner in Cwyn-y-Gwynt. Mali wouldn't allow her out of the house. Her every movement was subject to scrutiny. Mali watched her like the hawk that hovered over the ancient moorland of Hiraethog. Too ungainly now to ride Jac, Caron ached to go out for a walk, just to get away from the unrelenting scrutiny.

Mali's keen observation meant that Caron and Twm could not enjoy any privacy. Deeply distrustful after finding them doing the laundry together, she made sure they had no opportunity for further conversation. Caron, relieved that she had an ally, was troubled by Twm admitting his agony of uncertainty about Gwyn. He had reassured her of his understanding but, much as she wanted to reciprocate, she had little chance.

Mali was adamant. "You have forfeited the right to any independence." This was not too great a change since, with the exception of jaunts on Jac, Caron had not enjoyed any previous freedoms, other than an occasional walk to the village. She was not keen on venturing out in any case since she was so anxious that someone would recognise her delicate condition.

Caron was summoned by Mali early one Saturday. Mali had chosen her moment well. The Tudor men were all occupied. March was a busy month for them with the oats needing to be sown before April began. Emyr was dealing with a difficult calving while Brad and Twm were separating the sheep into groups ready for lambing. Siôn had been ordered to barrow manure to the vegetable patch. Once the lambing season got into full swing there would be little time for other tasks.

"Sit there Caron," Mali began, pointing to one of the kitchen chairs. "Next to Nain. You have her to thank for sorting out what is to be done."

"It's the only thing to do Caron. Best for you, best for the family and best for your baby." Nain smiled at her sympathetically.

Caron awaited an explanation.

Mali was not a woman to waste words. She came straight to the point. "You are going to pack a case Caron and take the train to South Wales to stay with Nain's cousin, Mair. She's a single lady, living alone, and has kindly agreed to take you in. You will bear the child in her home and she will make all the arrangements. You don't know how lucky you are. Most girls in your situation would go into a home but I don't trust those nuns. Catholic they are. No good will come of exposing you to mumbo jumbo, incense and plaster saints. You'll end up in a worse state than you already are."

Caron spoke up. "I didn't know you had a cousin in South Wales, Nain."

Nain responded. "I haven't seen her for donkey's years Caron but we write occasionally. Second cousin once removed she is. My great-uncle Lloyd's great grand-daughter. All the rest of the family stayed in North Wales but Lloyd, he had to go off to Cardiff. I always remember my Nain saying he was never satisfied, always had to move to somewhere different. Didn't work out for him. Went into a tannery, got married late in life and had three girls but only one, Lili, survived. Only ever had girls in that line of the family they did. Mair is Lili's granddaughter."

Mali interrupted. "Alright Mam, that's enough. Caron doesn't need to know all the family history."

Nain pressed on undeterred. "Lil, as they called her, had five girls. Two were old maids and three got married but two of those three went off to America in one of those big liners. Their men said it was the land of opportunity. Never heard how they got on. But the other one stayed in Wales. Did well for herself Lyn did. Married a shopkeeper by all accounts. An ironmonger. Sold all sorts. Goldmine it was. Left her well off. Anyway, Mair is Lyn's daughter. Only child. Think Lyn had some sort of medical problem. She had a terrible time when Mair was born by all accounts. Three days in labour. Nearly died. Purple fever I think it was called or something like that."

"Puerperal," corrected Mali.

Nain, lost in her reminiscing, suddenly remembered Caron and added hastily, "Most women of course don't have any problem. I didn't. My births were straightforward and so were yours weren't they Mali?"

"I don't think we need discuss anything like that Mam. It's not an appropriate subject for conversation."

Caron was looking terrified. "Am I going to die Nain?"

Mali leapt in. "Of course not, Caron. Don't be so ridiculous. Women have babies all the time and you're from good strong stock. Not that it wouldn't be better if you did. Better dead than live in shame. Reputation is to be valued more than life itself."

"Mam, will I be able to come back?"

"Not for a while. I've agreed with Mair that she'll keep you there for a short time after the birth. Then you'll come home and no-one will be any the wiser. We'll say you've been to visit a cousin in... where is it she lives Mam?"

"Aberporth. Lyn left her daughter very well off. Sold the business when Mair's father died. Can't remember his name. Mair looked after her mother till she passed on and then moved out of Cardiff. Bought a house she did. Aberporth is by the sea on the Cardigan coast. Mair says it's a very pretty place. Of course, she's got plenty of time to enjoy it. Doesn't need to work."

Mali sniffed. "The devil finds work for idle hands. I just hope Mair proves to be a suitable person for Caron to associate with. We don't want any further trouble."

"Well Mali, she has to go somewhere and quickly if you want to hide what's happened."

"True Mam." She turned to Caron. "At least we're not telling an untruth Caron. You are going to stay with a cousin. No-one needs to know any more than that."

"What do I tell people about why I'm going there Mam?"

"I've thought about that. Mair lives alone. So you can say that you're going to keep her company for a while."

Caron was puzzled. "Isn't that an untruth Mam?"

"Not really Caron. More an embellishment of the truth. I can't have you ruining Bethan's future. It's very important that we all stick to the same story."

A thought struck Caron. "Mam what's going to happen to the baby?"

Mali was definite. "It'll be adopted of course. After about six weeks. I don't quite know how Mair's going to organise it but she says she will. Thousands of women have lost husbands and sons in the war. The child will find a good home. From her letters Mair seems a very competent person." She turned to Caron. "And I hope you realise, young woman, just what trouble and expense you've caused. Sorting this out has taken a lot of time. We've got to pay for your train tickets and we've got to pay Mair for your keep. Not that she needs it. But it's a matter of pride. The Tudors don't take free hand-outs. And don't you eat her out of house and home. I don't want her asking me for extra money."

"Mam, how is Mair going to explain to her friends in Aberporth why I have arrived at her home to have my baby? Won't they think it's odd?"

"Auntie Mair to you Caron. Have some respect for your elders! From what Mair writes, she will say that you married an ex-soldier who returned to Carreg after the war. You will need to have a story ready in case people ask you about him."

"Mam, what will I say?"

Nain interrupted; her eyes became dreamy. "You can make up a romantic story. You can say he was older than you, had been wounded in the war in 1918 and sent to hospital. When he eventually returned to the village, you were only sixteen. Your mother died when you were a baby and then your father was killed in the war. His experience on the battle fields of France led him to ask you to marry him despite your age. He thought that you should both seize your happiness and not waste time. And he was right because he never fully recovered from his wounds and died leaving you alone and with child. With no family to look after you and not wanting to give birth alone, you wrote to your cousin and asked if you could stay with her for a while. It's a plausible story. It's happened to many poor women as a result of that terrible conflict. You'll have to give him a name of course."

Caron looked horrified. "It's a big lie Nain and I'm not good at lying. I could make mistakes and forget what I've said."

Mali was stern. "Caron, you will not forget and you will get your story straight. I don't approve of lies but in this case the means justifies the end. You have dragged the whole family down into a deep hole and it's up to you to get them out of it. You can call him Rhys. That's a good Welsh name."

"She'll need a wedding ring, Mali."

For a moment Mali was discomfited. "I hadn't thought about that. Haven't you got your Mam's wedding ring in a box upstairs?"

"I have. I was going to give it to Bethan for her wedding day but I haven't told her that, fortunately. Now Daniel Ellis will have to buy her one. It's only right that he does anyway. This is more important. Mam would understand that."

By the time Emyr came in to be told about the arrangements, Caron was already in her room sorting things to pack into a bag. She was to leave in two weeks.

Emyr, soon back outside helping Twm deliver an early lamb, was non-committal. "Your sister's going to be leaving us for a while Twm. Best thing, I expect." Explaining to Twm exactly what would take place, he added, "Always better to let the women sort out these matters."

Emyr's divulgence of information meant that Twm had even more to mull over. Gwyn had, for once, receded in importance. Caron's persecution came to the fore. Through no fault of her own, she was being turned out by her own family. Before being allowed back she would have to endure a frightening, painful experience amongst strangers and then separation from her child. It was all Cadoc's fault. He couldn't be allowed to think he had got away with it and that nobody knew.

But it would be of no use simply accusing Cadoc without thinking carefully what to say. Cadoc would just deny all knowledge and be itching for a fight. And Twm had to be careful. Under no circumstances could he let slip that Caron was having a child. Much as he disagreed with his Mam's treatment of his younger sister, he could see that Carreg-y-Bedd's discovery of a Tudor bastard would cause mayhem. Twm's imagination did not extend to visualising a Morgan offspring living at Cwyn-y-Gwynt. Not only would Caron's future be ruined but Bethan's marriage would certainly not take place and the Tudor reputation would be destroyed. Twm was not naïve enough to think that enjoying the respect of the community did not matter. Not only would the shame taint all their lives but their family would be forever bound in blood to the Morgans. That didn't bear thinking about.

Then there was no point either in questioning Cadoc. Cadoc would just deny everything and then give Twm a beating. No, Twm had to be cleverer than that. He resolved to give Cadoc no room for manoeuvre. But then what? Tŵm was no fighter, firmly believing violence was never a solution. His intellect always allowed him to stay well in control. So much as he fantasised about giving Cadoc a punch in the jaw, he knew he wouldn't do it. All he wanted was for Cadoc to know that he knew. That in itself should prevent Cadoc from ever interfering with Caron again. With the situation thought through, he determined to visit Cadoc and sort matters out.

Once he'd made the decision, Tŵm doggedly pursued his course of action. It was not a matter that could wait. Waiting would only mean worrying. He couldn't rely on simply bumping into Cadoc by chance. That may take some time and Cadoc may well have Gethin or Griff with him. No, there was no option but to beard the lion in his den.

Late Thursday afternoon saw Tŵm knocking on the door of Lane End. He had been forced to wait a few days. His absence from farming duties required a plausible explanation. Feeling guilty about using Ruth Parry as an excuse, he had nevertheless decided it was the only possible course of action. "I must visit Mrs. Parry. It will soon be a year since Gwyn's death. It's only a month till Easter."

"Then you could leave it until April. You know how busy we are at the moment." Mali didn't care for her offspring reminding her of her duty.

"It's a while since I've been. She's bound to need some jobs doing. I feel I should go."

Emyr interrupted. "Let the lad go, Mali. You should be pleased you have a dutiful son."

Mali, never one to miss an opportunity and seeing Caron approach the table with some fresh butter, countered with, "More than can be said for his sister."

Honesty compelled Tŵm to go first to Ruth Parry's house. As always, she gave him a warm welcome, a drink and a cake. He spent an hour weeding the vegetable garden in preparation for sowing seeds before saying, "I'm afraid I can't stay as long as usual, Mrs. Parry. I have errands to do."

"Then you must get on with them Tŵm. It's very generous of you to come and help me at all. Don't worry that you have to leave. I understand."

Tŵm thought, not for the first time, what a kind, caring person Ruth Parry was. A genuine Christian. No wonder that Gwyn had been such a gentle, loyal friend.

Feeling another pang of guilt at his lack of progress in solving the mystery of Gwyn's death, Tŵm made his way to Lane End, a tyddyn, which supported a couple of cows, four Welsh pigs, three Welsh Mountain ponies, a goat and some poultry. It had been years since he visited the place. It hadn't improved. He was greeted by an old sheep dog with a matted coat that sneaked up behind him and snapped at his ankles. A ginger and white cat with one eye, peered at him from the top of a rotting barrel. Twm wondered if the blind eye was the result of an air rifle fired by Gethin or Cadoc. With difficulty he pushed open the wooden gate which, reluctant to open, had embedded itself into the soil, slats chewed by, no doubt, aggressive curs. Its purpose seemed to be to keep visitors out rather than welcoming them in. Treading warily around the heaps of nondescript rusting metal that littered what passed for a path, he cursed under his breath as he felt the squelch of chicken mess. Shooing a couple of skinny hens away he trekked round to the gable end. For some unknown reason, the Morgans' door did not greet visitors at the front of the house as any self-respecting door would do. There had clearly been a front door at some point since there was a bricked up door shape between the downstairs windows. But someone had decided that the actual entrance would be best placed round the side of the house away from prying eyes. Accordingly, a hole had been knocked through straight into the room where the Morgan family spent their daily lives and the space filled with a door of dubious origins that had seen better days in some local barn. Made of pitch pine and riddled with worm, its most obvious feature was a crudely cut oblong in the upper half, in which glass had been so roughly puttied in that it shook insecurely when the door was opened. Its purpose was to enable the Morgans to check who was outside the door before deciding whether it was advisable to open it.

This was precisely what happened to Twm. Violet eyes inspected him through the glass and then the door opened to reveal Bronwen Morgan.

"Well, fancy that! Twm Tudor! Deignin' to visit us. Honoured I'm sure." Bronwen gave a mock curtsey.

Bronwen cut an incongruous figure in the Morgan kitchen. Silhouetted against a background of old newspapers stacked up on the floor, rotting apples laid out on window sills and a mass of unidentifiable rubbish completely covering the surface of a table, she was ready to go out in a mushroom-coloured slim fitting dress, her hair swept upwards and pinned neatly.

There's no doubt about it, she truly is beautiful thought Twm. He had some sense of why Gwyn would be smitten.

As though she'd read his thoughts, Bronwen followed up her previous comment with, "Come to ask me out 'ave ya? I wanna go to the pictures in Denbigh. Showin' 'The Deadlier Sex' they are. Only sixpence to see it. Well, it'll 'ave to be another day. Ya're too late today. I'm already meetin' someone."

"So I see Bronwen."

"D'ya think I look nice?" Bronwen twirled around to allow Twm to admire her figure.

Twm ignored the question. "Bronwen, is Cadoc in?"

"Oh, it's Cadoc ya want is it? Think 'e's outside somewhere. Follow me."

Stepping outside she led Twm round the back of the house, carefully circling the rubbish that was lying around. "Don' want to spoil me shoes, do I?" she said by way of explanation, pointing at her grey leather footwear with fashionable low heel and ankle strap.

Twm, realising that Bronwen's outfit had cost a pretty penny, wondered where she got her money. Better not to ask. To his surprise, he saw that the rear of the Morgan household was very different from the front public view. Cadoc was working in a weed free, freshly dug vegetable garden. This must be the very same garden where Gwyn had hidden behind the blackcurrant bushes that Twm could see at one end, to draw his picture of Bronwen. Twm could see Cadoc was harvesting the last of the carrots and swede and had seeds in a wooden box ready to sow. Probably cabbage, Twm thought. Perhaps it's not so strange that the patch is tidy, he reasoned. Everyone in the village was reliant on a well manured vegetable garden that produced year-long supplies.

Bronwen called to her brother. "'ey Cadoc, ya got a visitor."

To say Cadoc was surprised at Twm's unexpected appearance was an understatement. He was shocked beyond belief; so shocked that initially he was uncharacteristically silent. Now he was there, Twm didn't know what to say. The words he had so carefully rehearsed dissipated like Welsh mist in strong sunshine.

Bronwen looked from one to the other. "I'll leave ya two alone then. I mus' be off." She turned on her heel. They heard the gate scraping the ground as she left.

Cadoc, on home territory, recovered first. "I won't ask ya in. Wot ya doin' 'ere?"

Twm desperately tried to remember how he had decided to open the conversation. Confronting Cadoc had seemed such a good idea when he was safely back home at Cwyn-y-Gwynt. He decided to first assess how much of a threat the Morgans posed. "Are your Mam and Tad in?"

"No, they're visitin' me Nain, tho' wot it's gotta do with ya, I don' know."

"And Gethin?" Twm had not forgotten Gethin's threat to pay him back for the blow across his arm all those months ago. He was sure Gethin had a long memory.

"'e's gone with 'em."

Tŵm, relieved that he wasn't going to encounter the wrath of collective Morgans, tried to take some control. Thinking it would be wiser to tackle Cadoc in a public place, he said, "Fancy a walk into the village Cadoc?" Even Cadoc couldn't thrash him within an inch of his life if there were people watching. They would surely intervene.

Cadoc was immediately suspicious. "Ya 'ave to be kiddin'."

"No, I would just like to talk to you."

"Ya can talk to me 'ere."

Tŵm resorted to bribery. "I'll buy you a beer in the 'Lamb and Lion'." Considering what Cadoc had done, buying him a drink was the very last thing in the world Tŵm wanted to do, but the means justified the end, he told himself.

The bribe didn't have the desired effect. Cadoc was even more suspicious. "Buy me a beer! When 'as Tŵm Tudor ever bought me a beer?"

"There's a first time for everything Cadoc."

"Ya mus' be desp'rate t' speak t' me." He thought for a minute. The lure of the beer proved too strong. "I've nearly finished 'ere. Thirsty work it is. A'right I'll do ya a favour an' come with ya."

Tŵm heaved a sigh of relief. Cadoc wiped his filthy hands on his trousers and irritatingly slapped Tŵm across the back. "Well, come on then."

"You've got a lot of old stuff here Cadoc," Tŵm remarked as he made his way past heaps of broken wheels, rotting carts and miscellaneous, aging tools."

"Like scroungin' don' I," answered Cadoc.

Pinching more like, thought Tŵm but thought better of voicing it. No point in antagonising Cadoc just at the moment. He may change his mind about their beer drinking excursion.

The two of them walked in silence for the ten minutes it took to reach the 'Lamb and Lion'. Tŵm did not want to open the conversation about Caron until he'd got Cadoc comfortably settled. If he began with an argument, Cadoc may thump him and go back to Lane End but he wasn't likely to walk away from a free beer. Cadoc, though still wary, was curious enough to go along with the novel concept of Tŵm Tudor as a drinking pal.

The collective eyes of Carreg-y-Bedd were taken aback by the extraordinary spectacle of Cadoc Morgan and Tŵm Tudor entering the 'Lamb and Lion' to have a drink together. Tŵm, whose invitation to Cadoc had been a spur of the moment notion, hadn't legislated for such interest. He just hoped the uncommon event did not reach Mali's ears. Doing as promised, he bought two beers and carried them over to the corner table where Cadoc had seated himself.

"Thought ya might wan' a bit of privacy," Cadoc grinned at him.

Uncomfortable with this new intimacy, Tŵm drew a chair to sit across from Cadoc, rather than right next to him. This at least meant the table provided a barrier between them.

"So? I'm waitin'."

Though Tŵm felt more secure, he was still at a loss as to how to start. He cleared his throat. "Do you remember our last conversation Cadoc?"

"Ya mean when ya was carryin' a lethal weapon?" Cadoc laughed.

"Yes. When you put me right on a few things."

"Ya're not goin' to bring up that Parry lad again are ya?"

"No, Cadoc, I'm not."

"Then wot d' ya want?"

"You mentioned Caron. You said she was pretty."

"Well, she is i'nt she? So, wot?"

"And you'd mentioned her before to me. Once when I was riding Jac and again back in September, I think it was. I'd been to see Ruth Parry and we ran into each other." Tŵm was beginning to find his flow. "You did more than mention her to me. Said you'd like to do things to her."

Cadoc's face creased into a leer. "An' I still would. Don' tell me ya sister 'as a likin' fer me an' 'as sent ya to tell me."

Tŵm hadn't been expecting this. He paused. "You have got to be joking Cadoc. Of course not. I just want you to know that I know."

Cadoc looked bewildered. "Know wot?"

Tŵm was firm. "Know what you did."

"I dunna know what ya'r talkin' 'bout. This *is* 'bout that Parry lad again. I told ya, I didna push 'im in the pond."

"No, it's not about Gwyn. I'm talking about Caron."

Cadoc stared at Tŵm. "'as she said anythin' to ya? If she 'as she's makin' it up. I've done nuffin. Wot d'ya think I've done?"

This put Tŵm on the spot. He knew for certain he was right but he had no proof. Caron hadn't named Cadoc. And if he wasn't careful it would be all round Carreg-y-Bedd that Tŵm Tudor had accused Cadoc Morgan of rape. Caron would be the focus of gossip which was exactly what Mali was trying to avoid.

"Don't come the innocent with me Cadoc. I know you of old. All I'm saying is that I want you to know that I know what you've done and I'll be watching you. Don't ever go near my sister again."

"I 'aven't bin anywhere near yar sister. Tho' I wish I 'ad. Someone 'as though. Told ya before, I saw 'er with a lad in the f'rest. Too far away to be sure who it were but 'e looked a bit like that gyppo, Moses' lad."

Tŵm was dumbfounded, then furious. "Cadoc, that's a filthy lie. Don't ever say that to anyone because it's not true."

Eyes swivelled in his direction and Tŵm realised he had to keep his voice down.

Cadoc, accustomed to maddening self-control rather than outrage from Tŵm, was unsettled for once. "A'right, a'right, keep yar 'air on. I told ya I weren't sure."

"Then don't ever say it, Cadoc. I'm warning you, don't ever repeat what you just said to anyone else. Have you said that to Gethin or Bronwen?"

Cadoc was churlish. "No, I 'aven't. Why would they be int'rested in wot yar sister's doin'?"

"Remember Cadoc, I know what you've done. But I'm not going to do anything about it because Caron's more important than you. If it weren't for protecting her, I'd..."

"Ya'd wot?" Cadoc's usual aggressiveness was surfacing.

"I'd make sure you never did it to any girl again."

"I told ya. I 'aven't bin near 'er."

Tŵm resorted to sarcasm. "Yeah, yeah, Cadoc. As if I'm going to believe you. Keep away from Caron. Never go anywhere near her again. Is that clear?"

"I dunno why ya think I'm goin' to be scared of yar threats."

"Well, you need to be Cadoc. You need to be." Something in Tŵm's tone prevented Cadoc from goading Tŵm further as he usually delighted in doing. Tŵm continued. "Anyway, Caron will be out of your reach soon."

"Wot ya mean?"

"She's going away. She's going to stay with a cousin in South Wales."

"An' why's that?"

"Our cousin needs a bit of help and a companion."

"Well, ya won' 'ave to worry then will ya?"

Leaning forward and keeping his voice low, Tŵm continued, "Caron's only going for a few weeks. Till our cousin can find a permanent person. When she comes back, you remember what I've said to you."

Tŵm leant back and waited for his words to sink in. Looking around he realised that the two of them were the focus of intense interest to the regular drinkers in the 'Lamb and Lion'. Both he and Cadoc had been speaking quietly, even Cadoc realising that concealment was in his own interests.

Twˆm noticed Weyland Philpin, a little the worse for wear, several of the local farmers and some of his old school pals. He decided it was best to end his exchange with Cadoc as soon as possible. Pushing his chair back and not giving Cadoc a chance to reply, he said, "I'll be going then. I've said what I wanted to say."

Cadoc, not wanting to be seen at a disadvantage, raised his glass and, making sure everybody could hear, replied, "Thanks for the drink Twˆm. We'll 'ave t' do this again soon."

Twˆm trudged back to Cwyn-y-Gwynt. He'd gone as far as he could with Cadoc. To go any further would mean betraying Caron's secret and that was out of the question. At least he'd had his say. It couldn't do any harm since if Cadoc let slip what had been said, it would do him no good at all. And Cadoc always did what was in his best interests. Twˆm mulled over their conversation. He'd always had low expectations of Cadoc but even he was surprised at the depths to which Cadoc had sunk. To even suggest that Caron would go with that Gypsy lad, beggared belief!

As he pressed the latch on the back door, Twˆm sensed instantly that something was wrong. Entering the kitchen, he saw Nain knitting and Mali seated with her arms folded. She was waiting for him. "And where do you think you've been?"

"Mam I told you where I was going. I went to help Ruth Parry."

"And where else have you been?"

Twˆm was conscious of a flicker of fear. His mother was intimidating. Even at his age, he shied away from crossing her. Surely, she couldn't know where he'd been.

He was wrong. Mali did know. "Don't even think about lying to me Twˆm. You've been seen. At that public house, drinking with that Morgan lad, of all people."

Twˆm was beyond perplexed. Even though news travelled fast in Carreg-y-Bedd, this was well-nigh impossible. He was lost for words.

Mali didn't suffer the same problem. "How could you make such a spectacle of yourself Twˆm? With that... that common lad. Common as muck! And drinking! Beer! If you ask me, you're going the same way as your sister."

Nain interrupted. "Now Mali."

Mali ignored her. She was outraged. "How can I go to chapel on Sunday? Everyone will know. I'll be a laughing stock. And what about Mr. Ellis?"

"What about Mr. Ellis?" answered Twˆm unwisely.

"It was Mr. Ellis who saw you going in to the 'Lamb and Lion'. He'd been visiting Maggie Miles. Her rheumatism is terrible. She can't walk to chapel anymore."

"Good of him to come and tell you." Tŵm's sarcasm was lost on Mali.

"Yes, it was wasn't it? He came straight over here. Said that in his position he couldn't be associated with the consumption of alcohol and would I tell you not to go there again."

"Did he indeed? And who does Daniel Ellis think he is, telling me how to live my life. He's not even a member of our family yet." Tŵm was disliking the minister more and more with every passing minute.

"And he won't be either if you carry on like that. I'm disappointed in you Tŵm. I thought you had more sense than to fraternise with Cadoc Morgan. Did you arrange to see him and use Ruth Parry as an excuse? That would be shameful, to use the poor woman like that."

"No Mam, I hadn't arranged to see him." Tŵm was relieved to be able to state the truth.

"Well, that's something I suppose. But you still drank beer I'm sure. Come on, tell me if you did."

"Yes Mam, I drank beer but only one." Tŵm reasoned that if he tried to deny it, one of the other spectators at the 'Lamb and Lion' would be bound to tell Mali.

"Only one! You shouldn't be drinking any."

Nain interrupted again. "Mali, he's young. He's bound to try things out."

"Try things out! Bethan's future is hanging in the balance and you make excuses for him. Tŵm, I want your solemn promise that you won't go drinking again and that you certainly won't meet that rogue of a Morgan."

Fortunately, Tŵm escaped having to answer since Mali was stopped in mid-flow with Emyr and Brad coming in for supper. Mali, distracted into recounting Tŵm's sins to Emyr, began, "You'll never guess what your son's been up to Emyr." Tŵm took the opportunity to slip outside. He did not want to be interrogated further.

Just two days before Caron was due to leave for Aberporth, Mali suddenly realised Siôn wasn't in the kitchen as usual wanting his breakfast. "Where's Siôn?" she asked.

"I don't know," Nain answered. "Maybe he's gone outside with Brad."

"I don't think so. Brad's moving one of the rams. He won't want Siôn there while he does that. I'll just check upstairs. Surely, he can't still be asleep."

She re-appeared shortly afterwards looking unusually flustered.

"Anything the matter Mali?" Nain asked.

"It's Siôn. He's not well. Very sleepy and a high fever."

Nain was reassuring. "Probably just a chill. You know what youngsters are like. I caught him outside in just a shirt only yesterday."

"You may well be right Mam but I don't like the look of him. I've told him to stay in bed. Caron get yourself upstairs and light a fire in the boys' bedroom."

Caron did as she was asked. Her brothers all slept in the same room, the three beds barely separated with Siôn's narrowly wedged against one wall. She was out of breath by the time she'd carried up sticks, paper and coal. A spurt of soot landed softly on the newspaper as she laid the kindling in a criss-cross pattern over the tightly rolled up balls. Striking a match, she lit the paper from underneath and held a double page of the 'North Wales Chronicle' across the front of the fireplace to draw the fire. Flame licked at one corner, then spread upwards. Undeterred she waited until the heat scorching her hands became uncomfortable, then pushed the paper inwards and watched as it was sucked up the chimney.

Siôn murmured. Wiping her sooty hands on her pinny, Caron made her way over to him. Mali was right. Siôn was not himself. His face was pink. Caron could feel the heat from his body even without touching him. She smoothed his hair back from his forehead and Siôn opened his eyes. "Caron," he smiled weakly. "I feel sick. My throat hurts and my head aches."

"Would you like a drink and some breakfast?"

"No food. Just some cold water please."

By late afternoon it was clear that Siôn was not improving. "I'll see what a good night's sleep does but if he's no better in the morning, I might have to call that doctor." Mali spat out 'that doctor' as though it were a term of abuse.

Bethan, Mali and Caron took turns sitting with Siôn. Nain had offered but Mali had been clear, "We don't know what's wrong with him yet Mam. It's not wise to take risks at your age."

"I don't think Caron should sit with him either," Nain answered.

Mali was definite in her reply. "Caron will take her turn like everyone else."

"It's alright Nain," Caron replied. "I want to sit with Siôn and he wants me to be there."

"You've always mothered that boy Caron. He thinks the world of you," Nain responded.

Mali was quick to retort. "Made a namby-pamby of him more like! He needs to spend more time with Brad, learning how to help on the farm rather than reading stories with Caron. No good will come of that. Anyway, what sort of example is she to him now?"

Siôn slept most of that day and all through the next night but the hours of rest did not help. By the next morning his neck and face were covered in an itchy rash.

Mali was worried. "I don't know which way to turn," she said to Nain. "You bring children into the world and all they do is cause you trouble. Siôn's not well and as for that hussy..."

The hussy chose that moment to walk through the kitchen door. Mali turned her attention to her. "Have you packed everything on that list I wrote for you?"

"I've done what I can Mam but I don't have everything I'll need."

"Well, I can't have Mair going out to buy you things. We'll check what's missing and you can go to the village and get them. I've got enough on my plate with Siôn and I haven't got the time or the inclination to go running around after you. There'll be no talking to anybody mind. Just get over there, get what I say and come straight back."

Much as she wanted to go out, Caron was apprehensive. "But Mam, somebody might guess at my state. I'm pretty big now."

"You may think so but in fact you're very small thankfully. Often the case with a first child. In your loose coat no-one will be able to tell."

Unexpected freedom lifted Caron's spirits. It felt good to be out in the crisp March air. A chill easterly breeze was tempered by a touch of spring warmth. Though unaccustomed to her own heaviness, Caron strode out, enjoying the normality of buds bursting with leaf growth, burgeoning nettles, docks not yet big enough to stifle early celandines and pungent cow parsley overwhelming late snowdrops.

Mali had supervised Caron's packing. "You'll have to manage with the clothes you've got. I'm not spending anything on you if I can help it. All you'll need is undergarments, socks, two skirts so one can be in the wash, a couple of buttoned shirts as you'll have to feed it at first, a jersey and a coat. You'll be wearing your boots to travel in."

Mali had bought one wool vest on her last trip to Ruthin but only because one of Caron's had a hole in the front. "I begrudge the money but you have to be decent and it's too soon not to wear them. 'Ne'er cast a clout till May is out'." Her other purchase was towels. The new ones were to be used in Cwyn-y Gwynt. "You needn't think I'm giving you new towels to take," Mali had said. "You can cut up the old ones into decent sized pieces, then you can use them as diapers. You know how to change them because you did Siôn's when he was a baby. They'll need to be washed every day." This meant that most of the space in Caron's two battered carpet bags was filled up with towelling. Mali was blunt. "You'll need pads for yourself too. You'll be losing for weeks."

Caron was sent to Carreg-y-Bedd for a new hairbrush, soap, a toothbrush and dental cream. Both her hairbrush and toothbrush had missing bristles so were not deemed suitable for public view. "The shop'll have everything you need. You can buy Sunlight soap," Mali instructed, "as it will do to wash you and your clothes. You can't expect Mair to do them for you. You can use it to wash your hair too, not that it'll need doing very often." The dental cream was a luxury. "Salt is plenty good enough," Mali told her, "but I don't want Mair to think we're backward."

Rhian Hughes was startled at Caron's purchases. "Your Mam spring cleaning?" she asked as she handed over the soap. Caron nodded. The last thing she wanted to do was start a conversation about going away to visit relatives. Rhian, always curious, would ask never-ending questions. "Splashing out, aren't you?" Rhian added when she saw the new brushes. Caron smiled and nodded again. Seeing that Caron was determined to be uncommunicative, Rhian gave up. "Unfriendly, that Tudor girl," she said to Sam Lloyd, the gamekeeper, who had nipped in for a newspaper just after Caron had left.

Caron dawdled on the way back to the farm. The errand had provided respite from Mali's relentless carping. Ground down, Caron was mentally exhausted. She didn't know how much longer she could withstand the onslaught. Though scared of leaving home, she was also looking forward to the relief it would bring. She had given little thought to Mair. However critical she was, she couldn't possibly be as judgemental as Mali.

Rounding a corner close to where the fields gave way to forest, the hedge topped a steep bank. Caron, lost in thought, was conscious of a rustling sound behind the hawthorn. She put it down to young ewes trying to push their way through a non-existent gap. They were often troublesome at this time of year. The hedgerow finished just before the track along which Caron had so often cantered Jac. The noise increased and so did Caron's anxiety. Well used to rambling about the countryside by herself, she had never had reason to fear for her safety. But this time she was sure someone was behind the hedge, following her.

"Who's there?" she called out. With a crashing of branches and snapping of twigs, a figure pushed its way through onto the lane.

"Abram! How... what are you doing here?"

"Come t' see yer 'aven't I."

"But how did you know I'd be here?"

"I didn't know. I were just 'angin' around 'opin I'd get t' chance t' see yer. An' 'ere yer are."

"Where are the caravans and Moses?" Caron was finding it difficult to understand Abram's appearance.

"On their way t' Carreg. We're early this yeer. It's been a warm month. I came on ahead. Brân's be'ind thet 'edge." As if in response to hearing his name, Brân nickered.

Caron smiled. "If he's expecting Jac then he's going to be disappointed."

Abram strode toward her and gripping both sides of the coat she was clasping around her, he opened it wide.

"T' doctor didn't mek a mistake t'en. When's it due? A month?"

"Two weeks."

"Thet soon... 'ow did yer Ma an' Da tek it?"

Caron's voice broke. "Not well. Oh, Abram, I'm being sent away."

"When?"

"Tomorrow. I'm going on a train to South Wales. Aberporth. It's on the sea."

Abram responded to the new information. "Been there. As a child. Wen' t' visit family in t' area. Nice place. Played in t' rock pools."

"Abram. This child. It is yours you know. I was telling you the truth. I haven't been with anyone else."

"I 'ave t'ought about what yer said. 'tis possible I s'pose."

Caron sighed with relief. Abram believed her at last. There was a pause.

"So yer goin' away? T' 'ave t' babby?"

"Yes."

"T'en what?"

"The baby's being adopted. I'm staying with a cousin and she's organising it."

Light dawned. "Oh, I see. Yer Ma's kept it quiet. She's not lettin' yer brin' t' child back!"

Caron was incredulous. "Letting me bring the child back! Of course not. It's out of the question. The disgrace... the neighbours..."

Abram nodded. "'tis not t' same wi' us."

"How is it with you?"

"If t'is sort o' thing 'appens t'en it's not shameful. Just nat'ral. 'as t' be put right of course."

"And how do you do that?"

"In t' old days all yer 'ad t' do were jump over t' broom."

"Abram, what on earth do you mean?"

"Me Da would 'old out a branch of broom, bright yellow wi' flowers, an' yer an' me would jump over it. Me first, then yer, then both together 'oldin' 'ands."

"Why?"

"T' get married of course. If yer 'aven't got any broom, yer can use a besom made of birch."

"Married Abram? Are you suggesting we get married? If so I'm not jumping over any broomsticks whatever they're made of. I want to get married properly."

"Oh, that's jus' what used to 'appen. Much easier if yer ask me. An' yes, I'll marry yer. Wasn't what I planned but since yer 'avin me child..."

"Abram, what do you mean? Not what you planned. Don't you want to marry me?"

"Yer a Gajo. Me Ma an' Da won' be wantin' me to marry a Gajo."

Caron's confusion grew. "What's a Gajo?"

"Someone who's not a Romany. Yer an outsider. They'll t'ink yer not good enough fer me. Ma an' Da wan' me t' marry me cousin, Ellen."

Despite herself Caron smiled. "Then it seems we're in the same situation. My Mam would think you're not good enough for me either."

'Cept me people'll get used t' it. From what yer say, don' think yers will."

Caron could only agree. She nodded. "You're right Abram. They'll never accept it."

"Me Ma an' Da would never give a babby away."

"It'll go to a good home with a Mam and Tad who want it."

"Is thet what t'ey told yer? Makes it sound as t'ough it's a 'orse not a babby."

"I have no choice Abram. My Mam won't allow me to keep the baby and I have nowhere else to live and no money to keep myself."

"Yer could work."

"Doing what? No-one will take me on as a domestic with a baby. Anyway, I couldn't work if I was looking after a child."

"Thet leaves one thing t' do t'en. Come an' live wi' me. As a Gajo yer'll 'ave t' stay in camp. Yer won't be allowed t' leave but I don' s'pose yer'll be wantin' people t' see yer anyway. Yer'll 'ave to do as Seraphina tells yer, mind."

For a few moments Caron allowed herself to imagine being part of Abram's family. Sleeping in one of the gaily painted wagons, harnessing the horses, cuddling her baby, dipping hunks of bread into rabbit stew, dancing to the music of the fiddle. Her silence caused Abram to add, "Mebbe yer Tad'd let yer bring Jac."

Caron turned to him. "Oh Abram, I don't think they'd let me have Jac." The reaction of her Mam and Tad to her moving in with the Gypsies did not bear thinking about. It would be the last straw. It couldn't be kept a secret. Someone would see her and then everyone would know. Caron knew Mali was right about Bethan's wedding. It would be called off. The minister couldn't associate himself with such sinful behaviour. Then there was Twm to consider. His reputation would be tarnished through association.

Yet she wanted to be with Abram more than anything and if she was with him, she could keep her baby. What was she to do?

"Abram, if I live with you and your family, what we've done won't be a secret any more. Your family travels in North Wales. My sister is going to marry the minister. He'll call off the wedding if he finds out I've had a baby out of wedlock. My Mam and Tad'll never be able to hold up their heads in Carreg again. I can't come to live with you all. Don't you see?"

Abram did see. "T'en what we'll do is elope. Me cousins are in South Wales. I told yer. T'ey'll tek us in. We can travel wi' t'em. No-one'll know where yer are or who yer with. Yer Mam can say yer've gone t' live wi' thet cousin yer mentioned. She can say yer've got a job t'ere. No-one'll know t'en, thet yer've 'ad a babby."

Caron could see that it was a more feasible plan. Her spirits rose. "Do you think that would work Abram? Could we really?"

It took another ten minutes to make the final arrangements. Caron was to meet Abram that very night at eleven o'clock where the bridle path met the lane that led to Cwyn-y-Gwynt.

"Yer can't go wanderin' about by yerself in t' dark in yer condition," Abram told her. "Jus' bring a few t'ings as we can't carry much. T'en we'll walk t' Ruthin station an' catch t' earliest train we can. We'll be long gone by t' time t'ey realise we're missin'. Leave a note to tell yer Ma that yer elopin' an' thet yer safe. Tell 'er t' say yer've gone t' yer cousin. She won' try t' find yer will she?"

Caron grimaced. "No. I shouldn't think so. She'll be glad to see the back of me. It's only the same story as she was going to tell everyone anyway. The only differences are that I leave sooner and that I don't come back. How are you going to get out of the caravan without anybody seeing you? It's easier for me. All I've got to do is wait for Bethan to go to sleep."

"Yer leave thet t' me. Pro'bly tell them I'm goin' rabbitin'."

"I'd best be going Abram. I've been much longer than I should've been. I don't want Mam to come looking for me."

He gave her hand a quick squeeze and disappeared back through the hedge. She heard the sound of hooves as Brân trotted away.

Caron needn't have worried. When she arrived back at Cwyn-y-Gwynt, Siôn's condition had worsened and the last thing on Mali's mind was Caron's whereabouts.

"His fever hasn't lessened," Bethan told her. "His sore throat is worse. I've been trying to get him to gargle with vinegar and salt water but he can't do it. Keeps swallowing it and that makes him sick. I can see Mam's worried though she's not saying so."

"Is he still asking for me?" Caron enquired.

"Yes, he is, when he wakes up enough to realise who's there."

"Then I'll sit with him for a while. It might keep him calm. I'll go up there now."

"I'll come with you. His sheets are damp from the fever. They need changing and it will be easier with two."

Caron and Bethan made their way up the stairs together, passing Mali who was on her way down. She spoke to Nain as soon as she got to the kitchen. "I've looked at Siôn's tongue. It's like a strawberry. You know what that means."

"Scarlet fever," Nain replied anxiously. "We'll have to get the doctor."

"We can't do that Mam."

"Why not?"

"Because he'll put us in quarantine. Caron's going away tomorrow. By the time the quarantine period's over the baby will be due to arrive. Caron can't have the baby here. The trouble that girl's caused..."

"But Mali you can't risk Siôn."

"I'm not. There's no treatment for scarlet fever. We know what to do. Keep him cool and give him lots of water to drink. I'll let the fire go out. We can't get the doctor until Caron's safely out of the way. I don't want that man near the place if we can possibly help it, interfering busybody that he is. If Siôn improves quickly, we may not need to call him at all. Some children only get a mild bout of it."

"But Mali, Caron herself might have caught it. We can't have her taking it to Aberporth. Mair might catch it. Then the cat's out of the bag. We'll get into trouble for not reporting it."

"Not if we tell the doctor we didn't recognise any scarlet fever symptoms until after Caron had left."

Nain stared at her daughter. "You have it all planned out don't you?"

"I've been thinking about it while I've been sitting with Siôn. He's been sleeping. All we've got to do is to make sure everyone says that Siôn started with the symptoms tomorrow. I'll tell them at supper. They'll see the sense of it I'm sure."

"You'd better keep Caron away from Siôn," Nain told her. Less chance of her catching it."

"Yes, you're right. I'll go and fetch her down now. Bethan can stay with him."

When Mali made her way upstairs, she found that her daughters were talking on the landing. They hadn't changed the sheets as Siôn was asleep. Beckoning Caron and telling Bethan to stay, she told her younger daughter that she was not to go into Siôn's room.

"But..."

"No buts. You're not to go in and that's that."

After supper, Mali sent Brad to feed the stock and then revealed her plan to the rest of the family. There was shocked silence.

"I can see the reasoning behind it," proffered Emyr, "but are you sure we don't need the doctor straight away?"

Mali reply was steely. "Quite sure. I know how to deal with scarlatina. It's not always serious and a fever with it is quite normal."

The strongest opposition came from Twm. He was appalled. "Mam, you simply can't do this. It's wrong. You're taking a chance with Siôn's life and you may be risking the lives of others by not quarantining us all. I can't lie about this. It's too serious a matter."

"Twm, you will do as you're told. You don't have to lie. You just have to stay quiet. One day won't make any difference to Siôn."

"It might Mam, it might."

"And we can isolate ourselves anyway. We just won't go out. It's only a few hours."

"We'll have to not get too close to people," advised Twm, "and not touch things that they might touch otherwise we could pass the bacteria on to others and of course we can't see bacteria."

"Bacteria, bacteria. I don't believe in things I can't see." Mali was dismissive.

"What about God then?" retorted Twm.

"That's entirely different Twm as you well know." Mali turned towards

Caron. "This is all your fault. You know that don't you? All these problems you've caused."

"It's not my fault that Siôn's ill, Mam."

"But it is your fault that we can't call the doctor. If anything happens to him, you will bear the responsibility."

Caron looked horrified.

Emyr was placatory. "Now, now Mali. Leave the girl alone. She's not to blame for this."

"She certainly is." Mali turned her attention to Tŵm. "Get the mattresses off the beds and out of your room. Move them on to the parlour floor. You'll have to sleep there tonight. Tŵm you had scarlet fever as a baby and so did Bethan so you two are unlikely to catch it. Better that Siôn is alone. We need to prevent Brad and Caron catching it, if we possibly can. Brad's bed is further away from Siôn's than Tŵm's so with God's grace Brad will be fine. Even if he does get it, he's such a strapping lad, he should throw it off quickly. And I want all of you to remember that we tell the outside world that there were no scarlet fever symptoms today. Siôn just had a fever. None of us knew what the illness was until the doctor visited and that will be late tomorrow morning after Caron has left."

Tŵm was astonished. "I didn't know I'd had scarlet fever. Or that Bethan had."

"You were babies Tŵm. You won't remember. And I've never thought to mention it before, it was so insignificant."

"Tŵm, you and Bethan had a really mild dose of it, from what I remember," added Emyr. "Hopefully it'll be the same for Siôn."

Later that evening, Bethan emerged from Siôn's room looking tired and worn. "He's no better," she said to Mali. "If anything, he's worse."

Caron, checking her bag to make sure she had packed everything, had purposely left the bedroom door open so that she could hear what was happening. She was to meet Abram at eleven. She knew she should feel excited but she didn't. Instead, she felt torn. She didn't want to leave Siôn while he was so ill but told herself that she had to leave in the morning anyway. A few hours wouldn't make any difference.

She heard Bethan speak again. "Siôn's constantly asking for Caron. He's getting really upset."

Mali was firm. "Well, he'll have to ask. She's not going in to him."

That evening Caron, ensconced in her bedroom, this time with the door firmly closed, could hear a great deal of activity. She kept herself occupied checking and rechecking her bags. She did not want to forget anything. The door to Siôn's room kept opening and closing, there were muttered voices and much fetching and carrying with footsteps up and down the stairs. Bethan's and Caron's room was in the gable end of the house and as soon as it started to go dark, Caron opened the window latch, lowered her bags, one at a time, as far as she could reach and then dropped them into the garden. They landed on grass next to the lilac tree. It would be so much easier to slip out without bags. If she was caught going downstairs with her possessions, she would be questioned; without them she could say she was getting a drink.

Caron calculated that it would take her about three quarters of an hour to walk to the spot where she was meeting Abram, perhaps a little longer since she was carrying bags. To make sure she was there in time, she must leave by ten.

As the evening wore on, she could hear Siôn calling. He was shouting. Perhaps his fever's worse and he's delirious, Caron thought. She opened her door.

"Caron, Caron. I want Caron." Siôn's voice was uncharacteristically husky.

"You can't have Caron," she heard Mali reply. "Now stop thrashing around and just lie still. You're making yourself even hotter. Bethan, he's sweating. Go and get some more cool water so we can sponge him down. At least he's not coughing much yet. When he starts that he's at his most contagious."

Peeping through the door, Caron saw Bethan scurry downstairs with a bowl and quickly reappear.

"I want Caron to do it! Not you! Caron..."

Mali was firm. "Siôn you may be ill but you'll still do as you're told. Strip him off Bethan. Let's get him cooled down."

Siôn's objections continued but Caron could hear that Mali was carrying on with cold sponging.

"Now, lie still Siôn. What we've done should make you more comfortable. Try to go back to sleep."

"I want Caron to sit with me while I go to sleep. I'm scared."

Mali lost her temper. "Siôn, I've told you. Caron can't come."

She spoke to Bethan. "Bethan, I'm going to get some sleep. I was up and down most of last night. I'll take over from you in a few hours."

Caron heard her mother leave and go to the bedroom across the landing that she shared with Emyr. With Mali gone, Siôn started to cry. Racking great sobs which only resulted in Bethan pleading with him. "Siôn, please stop it or Mam'll come back and scold you for keeping everyone awake."

Her plea had some effect and Siôn's tears diminished. Bethan, ragged with tiredness, just wanted Siôn to settle. All went quiet but every so often Caron could make out the sound of Siôn whimpering. She wished he would stop. His misery just made her feel guilty. Though she had only been eight when he was born, Mali had left him very much to her when he was a baby. "I've got so many jobs to get on with, I can't always be picking him up," she had often said. Caron didn't like to leave him to cry and so Siôn enjoyed many a cuddle when he was distressed. "Such a proper little mother," Nain was fond of saying.

Another louder whimper proved the final straw. Caron stole down the landing and peeped through Siôn's door. The first sound she heard was rhythmic breathing. Bethan had fallen asleep in her chair. Anxiously keeping an eye on her sister, she crept towards the bed. Siôn's eyes were open. As soon as he saw her, he smiled wanly and reached out his hand for hers. It felt hot and dry. Caron put her finger to her lips warning him to be quiet.

"Stay with me Caron," he whispered.

Caron knelt down beside him, taking care that he didn't breathe on her. She wanted to rest her cheek against his and stroke his hair but common sense prevailed. It would help no-one, let alone her baby, if she were to be taken ill.

"Siôn, I have to go away for a short time," she murmured.

Siôn looked panic stricken.

"Siôn, I have to. But I promise I'll be back soon and when I come back, I want to see you better. Don't get upset about me. Just get better."

"Why do you have to go?" he asked weakly.

Caron put her finger to her lips and then pointed towards Bethan, warning him again to keep his voice down. She had no illusions about where Bethan's loyalties lay. If she realised Caron had disobeyed instructions, Mali would be the first to learn of it. "I just do. Now I want you to go to sleep as it'll help you get better."

"Stay with me until then."

"I'll stay a while."

Siôn closed his eyes. After a few minutes, Caron, conscious of the time, tried to withdraw her hand. Siôn opened his eyes and grasped on to it tightly. She allowed him to keep his hold. It was alright. She could afford to stay a little longer. Twice more she tried to spirit herself away and twice more Siôn gripped her tightly. Finally, his even breathing told her he had drifted off. Glancing at Bethan, relieved that she too was still asleep, Caron tiptoed out.

Pleased that she had had the foresight to drop her bags into the garden, she slipped downstairs. Nain was dozing in her cushioned chair. Impulsively Caron gave her a hug. Nain, startled, said, "And what's that for?"

"I'll miss you Nain when I leave."

"I'll miss you too cariad but I'm sure everything will turn out for the best. Mair will help get you out of your trouble. Now you need to get a good night's sleep before catching that train tomorrow."

Caron tried to be casual. "I will Nain but I'm just going to get a breath of fresh air before I go up to bed."

"Then put on a warm coat before you go out. You don't want to catch a chill. The evenings are still cold. Are you sure you need to go out? It's getting late. I'm just off to bed myself."

Caron glanced up at the brass face of Nain's heirloom. The oak long case clock was Nain's pride and joy. The hands indicated half past ten. She was late! She must have been longer with Siôn than she thought.

"I will put a coat on Nain."

Nain came to stand in front of her, tears filling her eyes. "Caron are you alright? I'm very worried about you. This is for the best you know. It will be hard, harder than you yet know but it will give you the chance to find happiness again." She placed her index finger under Caron's chin and tilted it upwards so she could look directly into her eyes. "I want you to know that I do understand. I will be thinking of you."

Caron, desperate to leave because of the time, only partly took in what Nain was saying. "Thank you, Nain. But please let me get some air. I feel faint again." Of all people she hated telling an untruth to Nain, but she was already late.

Grabbing her bulky, navy blue coat, Caron emerged into the yard. Emyr, Brad and Twm were occupied with a couple of ewes who had decided to lamb a little early. She could see them in the barn silhouetted against the glow of lanterns. They must have brought some sheep inside for some reason. She wished she could have said goodbye to Twm. Brad wouldn't even notice her absence. Making her way silently round the house, keeping close to the wall so that she was less likely to be seen, she slipped into the back garden, retrieved her bags and was soon off down the track that led from the farm. Her meagre possessions were heavier than she anticipated while her bulk made her ungainly and uncoordinated. Until her eyes became accustomed to the darkness, she tripped over cart ruts and stones. Stumbling over a large rock, she grazed her knee. Blood trickled down into her wool stockings. It was impossible to run and every so often she had to stop to put down her bags and ease her aching arms. Breathing heavily, she eventually made it to the rendezvous.

Abram was not there.

Caron knew she was late. As much as half an hour late. Maybe more. Surely, she hadn't missed him? Surely, he would have waited for her? She sat down on damp grass, leaning back against a tree trunk and waited. Used to the countryside, she wasn't usually anxious about nocturnal creatures making rustling noises in the hedgerows but tonight, they made her uneasy. Every time a hedgehog or rabbit followed a private trail through hawthorn and hazel, she thought it might be Abram and looked up in anticipation. But Abram still didn't arrive. She waited and waited until the grey light of dawn began to streak the sky.

He wasn't coming. Or he'd been and gone.

Caron had realised that fact hours ago but despair rendered her incapable of action. As the cold, dark night faded to flint grey, she knew she had no choice but to go back to Cwyn-y-Gwynt. Strangely the return journey, even with the burden of the bags, seemed much quicker than her frenzied dash through the night. As she approached the stack-yard, she scanned the barns for any sign of life. It was alright, Emyr was not yet out.

Caron opened the back door slowly to minimise the creaking. The Tudors never locked it. No-one in Carreg-y-Bedd ever did. Secreting her coat in the small porch, she managed to make it up the stairs and into her room. Bethan's bed was empty. She must still be with Siôn. Relieved, Caron thrust her bags under the bed, divested herself of her outer garments and slipped into bed. Within minutes she heard the morning stirrings. Her Tad and her brothers were on their way out. She'd had a lucky escape.

Emyr was to take Caron, complete with wedding ring, to Ruthin station. The train was leaving at 9.10am. "You'll get to Corwen at 9.48," he told Caron. "Remember you'll have to change trains there for Barmouth. And you'll have to keep your wits about you all day." He knew his daughter too well. "No dozing off or not paying attention or you'll end up goodness knows where. You've got to change trains again in Barmouth. It'll be a long day but Mair will meet you off the train in Camarthen." Emyr, noticing that Caron looked worried, was quick to add, "I'm sure it'll be fine. Sounds more complicated than it is."

"How will I know Auntie Mair, Tad?"

"She'll find you. There won't be many young girls with baggage, travelling alone. Your Mam said she'd sent her a photograph. The family one we had taken at Helsby's in Ruthin last year."

After a very early breakfast Caron had exchanged a short, and in her view, rather strange conversation with Tŵm. She had gone out to search for him so that she could say a proper goodbye. She found him grooming Beauty.

Stroking Beauty's nose, Caron remarked, "She's a lovely horse, though I do miss Cariad."

"Beauty's got a much better temperament, Caron. Don't fret over Cariad. Tad told you she went to a good home."

His words only served to remind Caron of Abram's opinion of what Mali had said about her baby.

Tŵm broached the subject of Caron's departure a little awkwardly. It wasn't after all a situation he had dealt with before. "Good luck Caron. I hope you'll be alright and I'm sure you will. Thousands of women have babies every day of the week."

She smiled wanly at him. "Tŵm, I'm frightened. But it's no use saying that to Mam because she'll just say it's my own fault. I've never been away from home before, I'm going to stay with someone I haven't even met and I'm going to have a baby, which, from the little I know, is going to be very painful. I wish you could come with me."

"I wish I could too, but it's impossible. Cousin Mair is never going to give me bed and board as well as you."

"I know Tŵm. I know you can't but I was just wishing... I'm worried sick about Siôn too. Do you think he'll be alright?"

"I hope so. I think Mam's wrong not to call the doctor until after you've gone. She's taking a risk not only with Siôn but with you. You could've caught it and you might give it to Cousin Mair. She's right of course that if you stay, you'll be quarantined and you'll have to have the baby here." Seeing Caron's face stricken with anxiety, Tŵm added, "Siôn's a real fighter. I'm sure it'll take more than a dose of scarlet fever to knock him out. You've got enough to worry about without worrying about Siôn as well."

"I just hope you're right Tŵm. I hate leaving him but I know I've got no choice in the matter."

"No, you haven't. Just look after yourself. As soon as you're safely on the train, Mam will call the doctor."

Tŵm, realising time was pressing, changed tack. "Caron, I've sorted out your other problem too. Well, at least I've done as much as I can without causing further trouble."

Caron looked puzzled. "I'm not sure what you mean Tŵm. What other problem?"

"I told you I worked out what happened. You don't have to worry about..." Tŵm hesitated, "about it happening to you again. It won't. I've seen to that."

"I don't see how..." But further exchange proved impossible.

Emyr had come looking for his daughter. "Caron, we must leave if we're going to catch that train. Come and say your goodbyes."

Nain was the only one to give her a hug. Caron suddenly remembered Dee's letter, her upset when her parents couldn't hug her in hospital. Dee had been used to parental affection; Caron couldn't ever recall Mali giving any of her children a cuddle. Physical contact was deemed unnecessary. At the same time, Nain took Caron's left hand in hers and slipped a wedding ring on her finger. "Your Hen Nain's ring, Caron. Take good care of it."

"I will Nain."

Bethan's parting gesture was a frosty, "Make sure you don't come back with it."

Mali was more vocal. "Make sure as well that you don't cause any more trouble for Mair than you have already. Make yourself useful with the housework and don't spend any more money than you can help."

At the station, with the train ready to go and shrouded in steam, Emyr just stood there unsure how to react to this novel circumstance in his life. In the end he simply shook Caron's hand and said, "You have let us down Caron. But you are my daughter and we have a responsibility to look after our own. When you come back, we will put this behind us and never mention it again."

He stood there with his hands by his sides as Caron responded by throwing her arms round his shoulders.

Caron, huddled in the corner of an empty compartment, thought back to Tŵm's words but it was no use. They didn't make any kind of sense. In the end she dismissed them as unimportant, putting them down to Tŵm just trying to reassure her. She hugged her stomach with her hands. The baby was active today, kicking vigorously. Once again despite her misery, she enjoyed a moment of excitement. She was going to have a daughter or maybe a son. She couldn't wait to find out which.

Mali was proven right. It took Richard Owen just a few minutes to confirm the diagnosis. As soon as Emyr returned from the station and Caron was safely on her way, Mali had sent Brad to fetch Richard Owen. After examining the patient and not wanting to speak in front of him, the doctor came downstairs into the kitchen where all the remaining female members of the Tudor family were gathered.

"It's scarlet fever Mrs. Tudor. Siôn is really very ill. Wipe him with cool sponges to keep the fever down and give him as much buttermilk as he'll drink. Some nourishing soup wouldn't come amiss either."

"We have made cawl doctor so I'll fetch him some as soon as you leave." Bethan's anxiety was evident in her voice.

"There's more you can do too," the doctor went on. "You need to keep the room scrupulously clean."

Mali took umbrage. "My room is already spotless."

Richard stayed calm. "I'm sure it is Mrs. Tudor but I mean more than ordinary cleanliness. I want you to take everything out of the room that isn't strictly necessary. Then wipe down everywhere with carbolic soap. Siôn will soon start to cough and he'll bring up a lot of mucous. Burn any rags you use that have mucous on them. When you change his bed clothes you will need to soak them in disinfectant for a good twenty minutes. And do keep washing your hands after you have been with him. Scarlet fever is highly contagious. Have any of the family had it before?"

"My Mam, Emyr and I all had it as very young children," answered Mali. A lot of people got it in those days. But none of the younger three have had it before. They weren't born when Twm and Bethan had a mild bout as babies. They barely had any symptoms." Disingenuously, she added, "That's why I didn't realise what it was."

"You can catch scarlet fever more than once but it's less likely if you've already had it. Children are more susceptible especially those under ten years old so with a bit of luck Brad and Caron will not be affected. However, it would be wise for Brad and Twm to move out of the room and sleep somewhere else," continued Richard.

"They slept in the parlour last night doctor. I got them to move their mattresses out of the bedroom for the night."

Richard Owen looked at her suspiciously. "Last night? Was Siôn ill yesterday? Why didn't you call me then?"

"Well, you know what children are like doctor. Up and down. Siôn wasn't well but we didn't know what was wrong with him and I thought he might improve overnight. I put Twm and Brad in the parlour to save disturbing Siôn when they got up in the morning. What a good job that I did."

"Very fortuitous Mrs. Tudor. But early diagnosis is important. You're sure he didn't have the scarlet fever symptoms yesterday?"

Mali prevaricated. "He may have done doctor but if he did, I didn't recognise them."

"When did the rash appear?"

"During last night, I think. He was covered in spots this morning."

"Yes, I can see that. But you're sure he didn't have them yesterday?"

Mali stuck to her story. "If he did doctor, I didn't see them."

"Well, hopefully we've caught it in time. It's at its most contagious when the patient is coughing and bringing up mucous but from what you say Brad and Tŵm moved out before Siôn started to cough. They should escape it." The doctor repeated his earlier warnings. "Remember what I said. Wash your hands well every time you see to him and disinfect them too. Keep your mother away from him even though she's caught it before. At her age we don't want to take any risks."

Mail nodded. "Just what I told her." Despite her new antagonism towards Richard Owen, she had to admit he seemed to know what he was talking about.

"One more thing," the doctor went on.

"Yes."

"Caron. In her condition it would be best if she didn't look after Siôn. If she catches scarlet fever, she may have to give birth while she's very ill. That will put her in real danger."

Mali's face took on a look of triumph. "Oh, Caron's left, doctor. She's gone."

Richard was disconcerted. "Left? Gone where?"

"To Cardiganshire, to stay with a cousin."

"When did she go?"

"Just this morning. Emyr took her to the station. Unfortunately, I didn't notice Siôn's spots until after they'd left. We were more concerned with getting her to the station on time and Siôn was asleep. We didn't want to wake him."

"She shouldn't have left the house. You should all be in quarantine. We must fetch her back. You don't want to spread the disease elsewhere."

Mali looked aghast at the thought of Caron returning. "Of course not doctor but Caron hasn't been anywhere near Siôn. I thought it best that she stayed away from him. We can't reach her now anyway. The train has left."

Richard Owen was furious. He struggled to compose himself. "That means she'll already have shared a compartment with other people. We'll just have to hope she's not carrying the disease. I must telephone the doctor in wherever it is she's gone and warn him that Caron may be in grave danger if she contracts scarlet fever before giving birth. What's the name of the place?"

"Aberporth, doctor, but I'm sure it isn't necessary to do that."

Unusually brusque, Richard responded with, "I will make that decision Mrs. Tudor, not you. I must ask the doctor to visit Caron, examine her and tell her that she must stay indoors. If she doesn't display symptoms within a week then she has probably escaped it. However, your cousin must be told that if Caron has any symptoms at all then she must see a doctor immediately."

Mali was placatory. "I will write to her today doctor."

"No need. I will find out who is the doctor there and contact him. He can visit and explain. I would be grateful if you could supply me with the address of your cousin. Why has Caron gone away? Her baby is due very soon."

Mali looked shocked. "Surely it's self-evident doctor. I can't possibly have it born here. The scandal! The child will be adopted and no-one outside the family need ever know."

Richard Owen looked grave. "Separation from her baby could have a significant impact on Caron. It's likely to make her very unhappy."

"Not as unhappy as having to cope with the shame of it doctor."

"We may have to disagree there Mrs. Tudor."

Mali ignored him.

"You will all have to be quarantined for seven days Mrs. Tudor so no going to the village or even to chapel. If no-one else has developed the fever by then, you can go out again. There are a couple of other cases in the village. Young Dilwyn Evans and his friend Dai Stephens. Siôn probably caught it from them. I'm going to recommend closing the school until the outbreak is over."

Bethan spoke up. "Siôn will be alright won't he doctor?"

"I hope so. It's an unpredictable disease. Some people just have a sore throat and barely know they've got it." He decided unprofessionalism was called for. Looking directly at Mali, he added, "Others don't make it through because there's a risk of infection. Siôn has a very high fever and his tonsils are enlarged and inflamed. We need the fever to break. When that happens, the rash should start peeling and he will be less contagious."

"And what if it doesn't break doctor?" asked Bethan.

Richard Owen became even more serious. "We don't want to linger on that possibility."

Richard Owen visited Cwyn-y-Gwynt every day for three days before Siôn finally turned a corner, the fever broke and he started to improve.

"He's had a very bad bout of it," Richard told Mali and Emyr. "It will take him some time to recover. You've been very lucky. Yesterday, I felt it was touch and go. He could've gone the other way."

Emyr looked shamefaced; Mali was as resilient as always. "But he didn't doctor, did he? The Tudors are strong stock."

"Remember you are all still in quarantine. The one to watch is Bethan, even though she's had it before and will have some immunity. She's nursed him night and day."

"So have I doctor; so have I."

Richard Owen decided flattery was needed even though it was obvious to him that Mali had passed the burden of care largely to Bethan. "Yes, I'm sure you have but you have such a strong constitution Mrs. Tudor. Bethan looks exhausted and that exhaustion will make her vulnerable. Just keep an eye on her that's all."

"Well, we've done everything you said doctor. Disinfected everything and burnt the rags Siôn used for coughing. Bethan's hands are red raw from washing and disinfecting them."

"I hope luck is on your side Mrs. Tudor. It has been so far."

On his way out, Richard Owen spotted Twm carting straw. "Getting ready for more lambs Twm?"

"Yes. It's a busy time." Twm cursed under his breath. He'd been trying to stay away from Richard Owen, uneasy that the doctor might ask him about when Siôn's symptoms started. But he'd mistimed leaving the cover of the barn. It turned out that his concern was well founded.

"Twm can you spare a moment?" the doctor asked.

Twm sighed. He guessed what was coming.

"I want to ask you about Siôn's symptoms. When I first saw him, he wasn't in the initial stages of scarlet fever. I'm sure he'd had it for a couple of days. I've seen too many cases to get it wrong. Yet your Mam said he didn't have the spots the day before I visited."

Twm found himself on the horns of a dilemma. Mali had said he must do as he was told. She had said he didn't have to lie. Just stay quiet. But he couldn't stay quiet since the doctor had asked him a direct question. He required an answer and he was looking him right in the eyes. Richard Owen had always trusted him and he had always been worthy of that trust. How could he let him down? But if he told him the truth, he'd be letting Mali down. Despite his disapproval of her actions, she was his Mam and family loyalty had been instilled into him from birth. The silence lengthened. He had to say something.

"I... I..." Tŵm tailed off. Then he made his choice. "You're quite right doctor. Siôn did have the spots the day before you were called out. He'd been quite ill for two days. Mam knew it was scarlet fever but she was more concerned with getting Caron out of the way than she was of calling you to examine Siôn."

"Thank you Tŵm, that's exactly what I thought." Richard Owen's mouth was set in a stern line.

"What are you going to do doctor?"

"There's nothing I can do Tŵm. Caron has already left and Siôn, thankfully, is recovering. Everybody except Caron is in quarantine. Hopefully Caron won't catch it and then all's well that ends well. If Caron does spread the disease your Mam is going to have some tricky questions to answer. I hope that doesn't happen for Caron's sake. It could bring the whole sorry tale out in the open. I'm pleased you told me the truth Tŵm. It was the right thing to do. Your Mam was in the wrong. She put your brother's life in jeopardy."

"She'd say she was protecting Caron and Bethan. She's said before that Caron's life will be ruined if anyone knows about the baby. Even Brad and Siôn don't know. And of course, Daniel Ellis won't marry Bethan if he finds out about illegitimacy in the family."

Richard Owen was blunt. "Tŵm, your Mam may well be right about the minister and I don't deny either that Caron would be the subject of gossip. But I don't believe for one moment that her actions are driven by concern for her daughters. There'd be more than a few who'd be happy to see your Mam fall from her high horse. The person she's protecting is herself."

Month of the Rain

Caron's son arrived with the lambs at the beginning of April. He was born four days after Easter Sunday, delivered safely by a midwife called Dilys. Caron named him Arthur.

Thankfully Caron had not gone down with scarlet fever. Richard Owen had been as good as his word and a Dr. Bartlett had arrived one afternoon to inform Mair of the jeopardy she was in. It was a rare visit indeed. Mair was never ill; she saw sickness as sheer self-indulgence.

She was not best pleased with the news. "The least Mali Tudor could have done is written to let me know. Caron told me her young brother was ill but said she didn't know what illness he had. The doctor didn't visit until after she left home," she told John Bartlett.

Caron had obeyed Mali's instructions to the letter and kept her silence. Mali had a long reach.

To Dr. Bartlett, Caron's condition was unexpected; he had not been informed of the reason for her visit. "Have you made arrangements for the birth?" he asked Mair.

"I most certainly have. She will be attended by an experienced midwife. If there are any complications then you are not far away and neither is the Memorial Hospital. I have an automobile so I can take her there."

Mair had an Austin 7, one of only two cars in Aberporth and an indication of her considerable wealth.

"Why is she staying with you? Where is her husband?"

"Doctor, I am grateful for your visit but I really don't think you need concern yourself with our family business."

Dr. Bartlett, unused to such lack of concurrence, left abruptly.

As he left, Mair said to Caron, "These doctors are all the same. Don't trust them. Prying into family matters! When she wrote, your Mam said your doctor in Carreg is always meddling in village affairs."

Caron had been surprised by Mair. Straight talking, frank and direct, she brooked no evasion. She greeted Caron at Carmarthen station with, "You can call me Miss Pritchard. None of this Auntie nonsense. I'm not your Auntie. Got yourself in a right mess, haven't you?" Not expecting an answer, she carried on with, "And you're wanting me to get you out of it! Well, family's family so I'll do my best. You should be grateful. Saved you from the workhouse, or even worse, I have. Don't believe in this nonsense about pregnant single women having a mental defect. As far as I'm concerned, it's quite simple. They're just immoral. And that applies to you too."

Overflowing with energy, Mair had certainly done her best. The whole process was organised. "When you start getting pains, I'll run down to Dilys. She lives in the village. Delivered 236 babies she has." Mair spoke in a kind of verbal shorthand as though full sentences were a waste of her time. Her gunmetal grey hair was as wiry and strong as her staccato speech.

As it happened neither the Austin 7 or the doctor were needed. Young and strong, Caron had a straightforward labour lasting just over eight hours. "Wish all my births were as easy as this one," Dilys said to Mair who had assisted with towels and hot water. Caron did not consider it 'easy'. Shocked to the core at the intensity of the pain, the birth had seemed to her to be never-ending agony. However, once she held Arthur in her arms all memories of birth cramps disappeared. She was infatuated. He had a shock of black hair. 'Just like Abram's,' she thought.

"His father must've been dark," Dilys commented. She looked at Caron enquiringly.

Caron stayed silent.

The time passed in a blur of changing diapers and incessant feeding. Caron took to suckling like the proverbial duck to water. She loved it. Never had she felt so close to another being. It was as though Arthur was as much a part of her as her own heart or her own limbs. Overflowing with milk, she couldn't wait for his next lusty cry so that she could hold him skin on skin. She tried not to think about what would happen in six weeks' time.

About a fortnight after Arthur's arrival, Mair sent her out early one morning on some errands. "I want you to go to the post office to buy some stamps and post my letters, then walk to the bakery for fresh bread and to the general store for potatoes and carrots to go with the fresh herrings I have for today's dinner. The sea air will do you good. You've been cooped up way too long."

Caron was unused to buying vegetables. At Cwyn-y-Gwynt vegetables surfaced from the soil of the kitchen garden. The thought of going out was appealing though. Much as she loved Arthur, he was very demanding and a short spell of freedom was more than attractive. She wavered, "But Miss Pritchard, though it'd be nice to go out and see the village, I can't leave Arthur. He'll want another feed."

"Nonsense. He's just been fed and he'll probably sleep till you get back. If he does wake up, I'll rock him in my arms. It won't take you long to walk down the hill. You'll see the beach in front of you. Traeth-y-Plas it's called. You'll have plenty of time to take a walk on it before you go to the post office."

"I've only seen the sea a couple of times before coming here," Caron told Mair. "Chapel outings to Rhyl but it wasn't the same. There, children were playing in the sand and paddling in the sea but here people are working. The sea is full of fishing boats. I can see them from your windows."

"Fishing's an industry here though it's well past its heyday," Mair replied. "It's not too fanciful to say that Aberporth's fortune was built on herring. It was a busy little port when Queen Victoria was on the throne and well before that too. In the old days, mariners would ship in coal, slate and limestone. Thriving little industry in slaked lime there was. You'll see lots of kilns around here. Folks would bring in coal dust and mix it with clay to burn on house fires. But Aberporth's not just a working port. We get day trippers and families coming on holiday and have splendid regattas when we're overrun with people. On those days I stay in and watch from here. Don't like jostling crowds."

Despite worrying about Arthur, Caron was curious. She'd hardly ever been outside Carreg-y-Bedd so this was a new world. "Do you think I'll have time to watch for a while?"

"Of course." Then Mair was unexpectedly sympathetic. "You go and get some fresh sea air. If you go back home looking sickly your Nain'll have something to say to me! You'll find the post office on your right just after the 'Ship Inn'. Then you need to take the path round the second beach, Traeth Dyffryn, to the upper village. Ask Hannah in the post office. She'll explain to you which way to go. When the path merges into a street, the bakery is in the first cottage on the left and the store is further on. You can't miss them."

It was a crisp, spring day, suffused with weak sunshine. Caron enjoyed the novel experience of being at the seaside, despite it feeling strange to be separated from Arthur for the first time. Licking her lips, she could taste the salt almost as soon as she left the house. She made her way down the hill, past the sign that said Rhiw-y-Rofft and could soon see the beach. Crossing the bridge over the stream, she could see the water's edge was thronged with fishermen loading up carts harnessed to placid horses, prospective buyers inspecting the catch, crewmen washing down the decks of the smacks, mariners shouting greetings to mates on shore and a diverse mix of locals who had wandered down to share in the bustle of the day's activities.

Caron patted a strawberry roan horse, standing patiently waiting for its owner's return. He reminded her of Jac and she felt a momentary pang. She missed him. Taking Mair's advice, she made her way down the path that zig-zagged its way down to the sands, skirted the tangle of nets, rowing boats, barrels and ropes and wandered on to the beach itself, allowing herself to enjoy the moment, the urgent calls of the gulls, the fresh smell of the sea, the green sliminess of the seaweed. Walking away from the hustle and bustle she made her way towards the headland. Above her she could see the chimneys and bedroom windows of Mair's house peeping out above the trees. A man with his cap well pulled down over his eyes was walking back towards her, accompanied by two long haired corgis. When she reached the rocks and feeling daring, she sat down on the damp sand, took off her boots and socks and paddled in the waves, just as she had done in Rhyl with her friends. Laughing with sheer pleasure, she jumped every seventh wave, holding up her long, thick skirt which nevertheless got covered in spray. For a few moments she forgot her worries, Mali evaporated into the sea air and letting herself go, she simply played.

She was disturbed by a dog barking. Expecting to see the corgis again she looked back at the lane to the beach. It was a sheep dog, minus its owner, running towards her expectantly with a piece of driftwood in his mouth. Leaping the waves, he joined her in the water. "Oh, you're just like Jono," she said to him. As she thought of home, her mood changed and she became conscious of fear churning deep in her stomach. The dog dropped the wood into the sea. She picked it up and flung it towards the rocks. He chased after it and was immediately back where he'd started. "This could go on all day, couldn't it?" she said to him.

Not knowing how much time had passed, she carried on her conversation with the unknown dog. "I must go to get the groceries. I don't want to be away from Arthur for too long. He'll need his feed." She threw the stick for him several times as she walked back up the beach towards the boats. He stood looking at her longingly as she climbed the path up to the street.

Caron found the post office, as Mair had said, just after 'The Ship'. A kindly woman, who Caron guessed must be Hannah, her face wreathed in smiles, greeted her. "Bore Da. You must be Miss Pritchard's cousin. It's nice to meet you. What can I do for you today?"

After sorting the stamps and posting the letters, Caron asked Hannah to direct her to the bakery. The shaded walk was more than pleasant though, not fully recovered after the birth, the hill caused her to be slightly out of breath. Stopping for a rest, she was now able to view the whole cove with its two beaches separated by a jutting tongue of rocks and behind them a scattering of cottages nestling on the folds of the hills that ran down to the clifftops. The waves were much stronger on Traeth Dyffryn. She wouldn't have wanted to paddle there, she thought. She would've got soaked.

The smell of the baking bread reached her nostrils well before she could see the cottage. As Hannah had told her, she "couldn't miss it". Joining a queue, she found she had to wait a good ten minutes before paying over her pennies. She couldn't help but notice the curious glances the other women gave her but, not wanting to enter into conversation, she kept her head down and was careful not to meet their eyes. As in Carreg-y-Bedd, clearly a newcomer was a source of intense curiosity.

Clutching her still warm bread, Caron made her way to her final destination. Opening the door, a bell announced her arrival and a wizened little woman, her cheeks studded with broken veins, emerged from a room at the back. She proved to be chatty. "Staying with Miss Pritchard, are you?"

Caron became anxious. Villages were the same throughout Wales. Everybody minded everybody else's business.

"Yes, I am."

"From what she told me, you've had a tough time. So sorry to hear about your husband."

Caron was shocked. What had Mair told everyone? What should she say? What name had Mali given her husband? Rhys? She wasn't sure. She'd better not say anything.

"What happened to him exactly?" The shopkeeper was not just sympathetic; she was nosy.

Not knowing what explanation Mair had given, Caron prevaricated. "I don't like to talk about it."

The woman grunted her assent. "Upsets you I expect. Understandable."

Caron stuffed the vegetables into her basket, counted out seven pennies and left hurriedly before she could be asked any more questions. As she walked back, she stopped again to admire the view. If circumstances had been different, she could have enjoyed living here for a while she thought to herself. A tingling in her breasts reminded her of the need to get back. She had been much longer than she'd expected.

Trudging up the steep hill, she was relieved to get back to Mair's handsome Victorian villa. Not as pretty as the whitewashed stone cottages, it stood proud in its lofty position with its twin gables and bay windows overlooking the bay. "More modern, spacious and a lot more practical than the cottages of the local fishermen, picturesque though they are," Mair had told Caron. "Plenty of room for my books." Mair was an avid reader, preferring to explore political issues rather than waste time on social chit-chat. Currently engrossed in, 'Suffragette: My Own Story', she regaled Caron with her opinions. "Emmeline Pankhurst. To be admired of course. We women should've had the vote years ago. Even those who live Down Under got it before us. Women have a damn sight more common sense than men. Never approved of the suffragettes' damn silly tactics though. Don't know why they thought smashing windows, burning down churches, going on hunger strikes and hurling themselves in front of galloping horses would help the cause. As far as I can see, all it did was confirm male suspicions that they were emotional and unstable. Germany did women a favour. Had more effect than the Pankhursts. The war allowed men to see that women could do men's jobs. Dangerous jobs, heavy jobs. Munitions, farming, education. You name it. They did it. And often made a better job of it. So, I have Germany to thank that I can put that cross on a ballot paper now. Still some way to go though. A travesty that men over twenty-one can vote but only women over thirty. It'll change though. It'll change. And I don't think it'll be that long either."

Caron, with other matters on her mind, had not entered into a discussion. She knew very little about the suffragettes. Women's votes had never been a major issue in Carreg-y-Bedd. Of more concern were the harvest, the stock and the weather. They left little time for anything else.

Caron arrived back with the intention of asking Mair what story had been concocted for the benefit of her neighbours. Clearly, she needed to stick to the same one. A chill struck her as she went through the back door. Something was wrong. The house felt different. What was it? There was a stillness about the place. A heavy silence that bore down upon her like a dead weight.

Dropping her basket, she raced upstairs to her bedroom where she had left Arthur safely tucked up in his crib. He must have slept for longer than she thought. She had expected to find him crying for milk, being consoled by Mair who, when Caron was exhausted, often helped by walking up and down and cuddling him. At the thought of feeding him Caron's milk started to leak through her shirt, stinging her nipples.

The crib wasn't there. Mair must have taken it downstairs. Caron searched every room and the garden. But there was no sign of the crib, Arthur or Mair. She was being silly, she told herself. Mali had said it would be six weeks before Arthur was adopted. It had all seemed so eminently sensible before he was born. But then Arthur had just been an unknown baby. He hadn't been

Arthur. He hadn't been real. Since he'd been born, she hadn't allowed herself to think about what would happen at the end of six weeks. But it was only two weeks. Mair must just have taken him for an outing. She sat down on a mahogany chair; the central bar, carved in a fan shape, dug into her back.

The wait for Mair to return seemed interminable as Caron swung between the anticipated ecstasy of Arthur's return and the agony of fearing he wouldn't. Finally, she heard the noise of the Austin 7 arriving. She hadn't thought to check whether the car had been taken out. This was followed by Mair pushing hard on the front door. It stuck at the bottom and required a heave to open enough to allow entry.

"It's the rain," Mair said as she came in. "The wet has caused the wood to swell. I must get it fixed."

Caron looked at her. There was no sign of Arthur. "Where's Arthur?" she began.

"Sit down Caron. I'll get you a cup of tea."

"No, I don't want a drink. Where's Arthur?"

"He's in a safe place Caron. A loving place. You mustn't worry about him."

Caron, stricken, began to sob. "You don't mean to say he's gone for adoption already. It's only two weeks since he was born. Not six weeks. Mam told me six weeks. And he needs feeding. He'll be hungry."

"He'll be fed Caron and looked after properly. Believe me he has an excellent home and will be well looked after."

"But no-one can look after him like I do. I'm his Mam."

Mair decided to utilise briskness as a suitable salve on the wound. "Caron, you knew this was going to happen. It's the best thing. Everybody decided it was the best thing."

"Everybody except me." Caron clung on to what she'd been told. "And it's only two weeks anyway, not six."

Mair decided the truth was the best option. "Caron, it was never going to be six weeks. You were just told that to make it easier for you. It was always going to be two weeks. Once you'd fed the baby with his first milk and I could see he was thriving, then he could go to his new home. Your Nain thought it best that you didn't have several weeks to become fond of the baby. And I agreed with her. We both thought that the sooner the separation happened, the easier it would be for you."

Caron snapped. "Easier! Easier! How could either of you have possibly thought that taking my baby away would be easy. I didn't know. I didn't know it would feel like this."

"Caron, I realise it must be hard but you only have yourself to blame. You can't blame your Mam or me. You got yourself into this situation and you have to accept the consequences."

"I want him back. I want him back now. Where is he?"

"Caron, Arthur has gone. He is never coming back. And you won't be able to find him. I've told you it's for the best. You will look back on this and see that I am right."

"How is it for the best? I haven't got my baby. How is that best? I want him back and I want to take him home." Caron's voice rose to a primeval scream.

"Caron, you're hysterical. You know that's not possible. Your Mam will not take in that baby and neither can I. We have to be practical. There is no other solution. There is nothing you can do. I took Arthur in his crib and packed up his clothes and took them with him. Now I'm going to make us a pot of tea."

Mair went off into the kitchen. Caron continued to sit, still as the flint on the fields of Cwyn-y-Gwynt. She drank the tea she was offered, without tasting it or even noticing that she was drinking it. Then she drifted upstairs with no sense of purpose. Her purpose in life had disappeared along with the crib and the clothes. The room was empty. It had been stripped. There was no indication that there had ever been a baby in the room. It was as though Arthur had never existed. With a flash of insight, she realised that she now shared the same pain as Ruth Parry and Nerys Philpin. She felt as though she were bleeding from her heart rather than her loins.

That night as Caron lay wide awake in the same bed where she had greeted Arthur for the first time, she could hear the mournful screams of the gulls as they swooped over the rock faces surrounding the beach. To her they sounded like lost souls searching for their loved ones. When she finally slept, their cries haunted her dreams.

The next morning Caron awoke to a leaden dread inhabiting her body. Then she remembered. Arthur had gone.

When Caron, with dark circles beneath her eyes, appeared in the kitchen, Mair, putting a boiled egg in front of her, said, "Well, it's time for us to bid each other farewell today. My job's done. And a good job I've made of it even if I do say it myself."

Caron looked at her questioningly.

"You're going home today. I'll take you to Carmarthen station in the Austin."

Caron began to cry. "But I can't. I can't go. Arthur's down here somewhere. He can't be that far away. I didn't even get the chance to say good bye to him."

"And a good thing too. The last thing we would want is a scene. Eat your egg and then go and pack your things."

Caron obediently followed Mair's instructions. What else was there to be done?

Emyr collected her from the station. It was drizzling and he was late. Caron pressed herself up against the wall of the station under the protection of the canopy that faced the road. About half an hour after the train arrived, Emyr came rolling up in the trap. It was good to see Jac and Caron immediately put her arms round the horse's neck, then stroked his muzzle. He breathed at her gently. "He recognises me," she said to Emyr.

"Of course he does. Horses are intelligent creatures."

They drove home in an awkward silence. "I take it you're well?" was the extent of the information Emyr had asked for. Caron had nodded her assent. She assumed that Mair had passed on news of the birth of a baby boy but didn't know for sure whether her Mam and Tad knew she had been safely delivered of a son.

It was no use asking her Tad for help, she knew. Mali's word was law. He would not be able to persuade Mali to take in their grandchild even if he wanted to himself, which was doubtful. He too would be concerned about the impact on the rest of the family. Emyr's boundaries extended to the fields, barns and stack yard. They stopped abruptly at the back door.

The only question she asked Emyr was, "How's Siôn? Is he better?" She had not been sent any messages about his health and hoped that no news was good news.

"He's much better now but it was a close-run thing. He'll be pleased to see you."

"And what about quarantine?"

"We're out of that now. It was only seven days and nobody else caught it. A miracle, your Mam called it. Said it showed God was on her side. Bethan nursed him night and day. Careful she was though. Did what the doctor said to the letter. Disinfected everything and kept washing her hands. Good thing Bethan had the fever as a baby though; otherwise, I'm sure she would've caught it once he started coughing."

"Did anybody else catch it in the village?"

"Two of Siôn's friends had already got it when the doctor visited us. Dilwyn Evans and Dai Stephens. The doctor reckoned Siôn probably caught it from them. Dilwyn was very ill and they nearly lost him but Dai only got a mild dose. The doctor closed the school so the fever didn't spread. A wise move. I remember an outbreak when I was a lad. Seven deaths there were. Lost one of my school friends. A lad called Islwyn. Can see him now. Fair, wavy hair and sticking out ears. Lost his two front teeth when he fell down the ladder that led to his hay loft."

After that exchange Caron did not speak again. Once relieved of her worries about Siôn, she nursed her own distress. Tad would not want to share in it.

Caron arrived home to no welcome. Nain was resting upstairs; Bethan was out and her brothers were working somewhere on the farm. No-one seemed to know Mali's whereabouts. Caron was just relieved her Mam wasn't there.

It had been a long journey to undertake on a boiled egg and despite her misery, Caron was hungry. Scouring the empty kitchen, Caron cut herself a chunk of bread and spread it with butter and damson jam. In Cwyn-y-Gwynt permission had to be given to eat jam but Caron's sins were so great that she judged stealing jam would count as a minor misdemeanour and therefore worth the risk.

It was Siôn who was first to discover that his sister was back. He had been watching Brad dealing with some ewes that were a little late with their lambing and had come in to rest, accompanied by Brad who only acknowledged Caron with a nod. Still pale and wan from his brush with mortality, Siôn ran up to her, threw his arms round her middle and blurted, "Caron, Caron. I'm so glad you're back. Did you have a good holiday with Cousin Mair?" Clearly Mali's narrative had convinced her youngest son.

"I did Siôn but no matter about that. How are you? Are you better?"

"The doctor says I need to rest a lot and I'm still sleepy at times but I'm going to be fine he says."

"Must be nice to have a holiday while the rest of us are working ourselves to the bone," Brad interrupted. It seemed that he too had not questioned Mali's version of events. Soon after this conversation Nain appeared and sent the boys out. She hugged her granddaughter. "What was it? A boy or a girl?"

"You don't know? I thought Miss Pritchard would have written. I couldn't write. I didn't know what to say and I didn't think Mam would want a letter from me."

"You're right there. She wouldn't. Mair did write but your Mam didn't even open the envelope. Tore it in half and threw it in the fire. Said it was of no consequence and we didn't need to know. Then the day before yesterday we got a telegram to say that you were coming home today."

"I had a boy Nain. I called him Arthur."

"A noble name, Caron."

The back door opened. Mali was back, talking to Nain as she came into the kitchen. "I've been to see Ruth Parry," she said to Nain. "I decided to go after you went upstairs. I can't believe it's a year since Gwyn died. Should've gone last Monday really on the day itself but I was helping Bethan to make her wedding gown and forgot the time. Poor woman has to endure two anniversaries. The date itself and Easter Sunday." Suddenly, she spotted Caron seated by the fire. "Oh, you're back are you? Well, you can help me get the supper. Bethan's gone to see Daniel Ellis. They're choosing the hymns and prayers for their wedding service."

"Mam, don't you want to know..."

Mali held up her hand. "Caron, I shall say this once and once only. The matter to which you are trying to refer is closed for ever. It is never to be mentioned in this family again. No-one will ever speak of it. As far as I'm concerned it has never happened."

Later that night, Caron lay awake in bed. A long journey and utter despair had contributed to her falling asleep the moment she went to bed. But then she woke up in the small hours. She couldn't get what Mali had said out of her head. "It has never happened." "It has never happened." Like an echo, it reverberated. Arthur had never happened. But he had happened. She remembered the warmth of his breath, the way his hand clutched her little finger, the softness of his skin, his mouth on her breast. As if in response, milk seeped through her flannel nightgown and on to the sheets. Her rock-hard breasts were more than uncomfortable, they were painful. But nowhere near as torturous as the agony in her mind. "Lactating heavily are you? You'll dry up eventually," Mair had said to her. "Just pad yourself with towelling squares." It seemed towelling was the answer to everything. She felt as though her whole body was crying in anguish, shedding tears of milk and blood that connected her to Arthur. It was more than she could bear to be separated from him. The years stretched ahead joyless and barren. Arthur filled her mind. There was no room for anything or anyone else. She realised she hadn't given Abram more than a passing thought since Arthur had been born. Abram. Abram. It was April. Moses and his family were likely to still be here as they were last year. She would be able to see him. He had offered to marry her. Was it really only four weeks ago? It seemed an eternity.

Wide awake now, Caron started to plan. She must go to Carreg-y-Bedd.

It was likely Moses had chosen the same campsite as last year, next to the 'Lamb and Lion'. Once she told Abram about Arthur, he would marry her, they would go to find the baby together and all would be well. Her solution planned, she slept at last.

The next morning Caron awoke along with a new found resolution. All she had to do was find Abram and speak to him. It was her fault that she'd been late meeting him, not his. He would've been there waiting, not knowing why she didn't arrive.

At breakfast, Twm was startled at Caron's more cheerful aspect. He'd been seriously worried about her when he saw her at supper. He hadn't known she was going to be back so soon. No-one had told him. He'd strode over to hug her despite Mali's disapproving gaze. A night's sleep has made the world of difference to her, he thought. Perhaps she's relieved that her life is back to normal.

Life was certainly back to normal. Once the men had gone outside, Mali issued instructions for the day. "I have to help Bethan," she announced, "so Caron you can cook the meals today." Bethan was to be married to Daniel Ellis in Ebenezer on May 19th and preparations were well under way. "More or less the whole village will be in the chapel to watch them getting married," she told Caron. "Such an occasion it will be, with the minister himself getting married. Nathaniel Lang, the famous preacher, is travelling to Carreg especially to marry them. Then everyone is invited back to Cwyn-y-Gwynt to share in Bethan's day. Today I want to make lists of the food we need. Then we're going to have the dress fitted with Haf Watkins. Getting on she is but she's exceptional with a needle. Ruth Parry has said she'll cook potatoes, Olwen Griffiths is making the cake, Nia Bowen and Nerys Philpin are roasting chickens and preparing vegetables. Next week I think I'll go to Bradley's of Ruthin to buy a dress."

Despite herself, Caron was interested. "What's Bethan's dress like?"

"You'll see it on the day like everyone else. All I'll say is that she will be covered up. Long dress, high neck and long sleeves. Disgusting it is, the modern trend for exposing arms on your wedding day or any other time for that matter! It says in the papers that some women are even showing their calves. Their calves indeed! I don't know what the world's coming to. Women smoking, drinking, dancing, wearing make-up like street whores and worst of all taking men's jobs! Men who have families to keep! Bethan will be the model of modesty in cream silk and lace. Cream's so much more subtle than stark white. Not that you'll ever be able to wear either Caron. The materials cost a bit but Haf isn't charging me much for making it. Owes me a few favours. We've more or less kept her in potatoes, vegetables and apples over the years ever since Joshua died. And it's not every day your daughter gets married, especially to a minister. What a lucky girl she is!"

"What about my dress? Am I going to be bridesmaid?"

"Unfortunately, yes. People will question it otherwise. And while we're on the topic, I don't want you eating much between now and then. You need to get rid of all that weight you've put on. I'm going to make your dress. It'll save money and I can't take you to Haf. She'll realise how fat you are. I've bought the material. Pale blue it is. We need to cover you up as much as we can so your dress won't be as slim fitting as Bethan's."

"Bethan's dress is slim fitting?"

"Of course. What's the matter with that? She wants to be fashionable as long as she's still demure."

Caron, deeming it best to stay quiet on the subject, wondered what Bethan's square, solid frame would look like in such a garment.

Mali spotted her chance to twist the knife. "Your...," she hesitated, "your mistake means that no decent man will ever marry you. He's not going to want spoilt goods. Doomed to spinsterhood you are and it's all your own fault."

Nain interrupted. "But Mali, he wouldn't know."

"I suppose that's a chance she could take but no good marriage was ever founded on deceit and lies."

Caron allowed Mali's words to wash over her. She was going to marry Abram and Mali didn't know.

The day passed, as many such days had passed before in Cwyn-y-Gwynt, with Caron making mutton stew and scouring pans. Her life was falling back into the same pattern that it had taken before Arthur. It was as Mali had decided it would be; as though Arthur had never happened. That was the hardest to bear. The fact that there was no recognition of his existence, that he was of so little importance that he could be easily dismissed. That was even worse than the festering wound of separation.

When the Sabbath arrived, Caron didn't argue about renewing her acquaintance with Ebenezer. It was a way to see if Abram was in the village. She didn't want to draw attention to herself by asking about the Gypsies.

Sunday dawned clear and bright. "We're in for some heavy showers if I'm not mistaken. You'd best stay home Eira," Emyr announced to his family just before they left. "Better take some umbrellas."

Caron hadn't been to chapel in weeks. It wasn't an activity in which Mair indulged. "Better things to do with my Sundays than waste time with people who are no better than me but think that they are," she had said to Caron. "I'd rather spend time in the garden or going out for a brisk walk. You see far more of God in the cold starlight of a frosty night than you do inside a chapel."

Caron missed Mair despite her spiriting Arthur away. It was not that she'd been kind or understanding or even sympathetic. She'd been none of those things. But it was refreshing to hear thoughts voiced. Nothing remained in the shadows with Mair. Whatever the matter that had arisen, it was subjected to the full glare of a bright sun. Her goodbye to Caron was typical. "Got you all sorted now. Time to go back home. You're young enough to start all over again if you ask me." And with a wave of her hand, she was gone and Caron heard the Austin chugging its way back up the road.

Emyr was proven right. They were subjected to a sharp shower on the way and then again black clouds loomed as they neared Carreg-y-Bedd. As usual, Emyr drew Jac to a halt to allow his family to alight. "I'll just take Jac over to Moses. He'll unharness and tether him while the service is on."

Caron had her opening. "Oh, are the Gypsies back?"

Emyr nodded. "Early they were this year."

"I'll just help Tad," she told Mali by way of explanation as she led Jac down the side of Ebenezer. Fortunately, Mali, occupied with regaling Ruth Parry with news of Bethan's preparations for the big day, took scant account of her daughter's movements. Caron could hear her Mam saying, "I haven't decided yet whether to buy a new dress or a costume. I'll go to Dicks in Ruthin for shoes and Emyr can buy a new suit at Evans."

Handing Jac over, Caron stood while Emyr passed the time of day with Moses. She could see Abram relighting a camp fire that must have been put out by a heavy shower. Caron could tell that he knew she was there. He was taking sidelong glances as he knelt before the charred sticks trying to blow them into life. Good, that was what she wanted. To let him know she was back. She was sure he'd find a way to see her.

Chapel was less religious solace, more compulsive purgatory. The last time she'd been there she hadn't been a mother. Now she was. Unaccountably Arthur had cleansed her previous guilt far more successfully than the absolution ever had. How could she feel guilty about bringing Arthur into the world when he was so innocent, so endearing? She stared back at the deacons as if daring them to make an accusation.

Time passed slowly. Caron continually felt as though she was waiting for something. She did everything she could to avoid being alone with Mali. She didn't know what to say to her. She felt that, to her Mam, her presence was uncomfortable, embarrassing. Fortunately, Mali was embroiled with wedding business but she was not so occupied that she didn't check Caron's whereabouts. She was particularly concerned about keeping her away from Tŵm. She continued to be wary of their closeness, suspecting that if Caron was to divulge her secret, it would be to Tŵm. Eager to know what had happened, he tried to speak to his sister alone, but Mali governed Caron's movements too well, making sure that she was always with Bethan or Nain and safely out of Tŵm's reach. He didn't dare to even ask her how she was in case the question alone drew down Mali's wrath on Caron's head.

As far as Mali was concerned, the problem had been solved and was over. It was now dismissed. The one time they were forced into each other's company was for Caron's dress fitting and Mali's comments were limited by the mouthful of pins she was using to make the necessary adjustments. All she managed was, "I'll make it tighter than it should be to allow for the weight you're going to lose over the next couple of weeks." Mali was keeping a strict eye on Caron's food intake, so that nagging physical hunger accompanied the ravenous longing for Arthur's milky softness.

Caron did all she could to bring about an accidental meeting with Abram, offering to walk into the village on errands and riding Jac around the lanes and along the forest tracks. But for a couple of days there was no sign of him. He must be busy she thought. Moses must have him working on one of the farms and he wouldn't be able to get away.

Then mid-week fortune favoured her. She was out on Jac. Mali had not made her usual objections. Any exercise meant more weight loss. Caron wasn't actually expecting to see Abram. Since it was afternoon, she guessed he would be planting potatoes somewhere. It was more than unusual to be out on Jac at such a time but, oppressed by the weight of her thoughts, she had needed to escape. As always, the rhythm of Jac's movement soothed her tortured spirit. She cantered down a mossy track, stopped to admire a drift of primroses on a bank under some ash trees and then dismounted to give Jac a rest. Realising she was very near the clearing where she had first encountered Abram, she decided to rub salt into her wound and led Jac forwards until she reached the pool. The glade was as beautiful as ever. How could it be just the same when she felt so different? Was it really nearly a year since she had met Abram there? So much had happened. The spring still bubbled, the bluebells and the primroses grew as thickly as always but somehow the beauty of the place no longer touched her soul. She felt apart from it rather than part of it, as she had in the past. Keeping her arm through Jac's rein, she took off her stockings and lowered her feet into the coolness of the pool. Last year, though she was unaware, Abram had been watching. She turned round; the memory so real that she half expected to see him there. But she was alone.

Caron didn't know how long she sat there in her green space, absorbing the heady pungency of wild garlic, the delicate perfume of the primroses, the heavy odour of moist, sticky earth and the sunlit scent of new, unfurled leaves. She felt leaden, languorous, strangely in limbo. For these few moments she could suspend pain. All she had to do was just be.

She was brought back to reality by Jac nudging her shoulder. He had finished grazing his patch of grass and wanted to move on. "Alright lad," she said. "Let's be getting back." Before long she was rounding a corner on the lane that led past the Bowen farm when Jac shied sideways. Someone was digging behind some trees. Stroking his neck to calm him, Caron peered through a gap in the hawthorn. Abram looked back at her.

Shocked, she blurted out, "Abram. I'm so glad to see you."

He didn't reply so she continued, "I thought you might be trying to see me."

"An' why would yer t'ink thet?"

Startled by his response she answered, "Well last time we spoke we arranged to go away together."

"Yer didn't turn up."

"Abram, I couldn't get there in time. Siôn was very ill with scarlet fever and I couldn't get away."

"I waited fer yer but yer didn't come. So, I went back to t' camp."

"I thought that must've happened. I did come Abram but I was late."

"Too late. Mebbe 'twas fer t' best."

"What do you mean?"

"Well, lookin' at yer, yer trouble's gone away."

Caron changed tack. "Abram, don't you want to know what happened. Whether you had a son or a daughter."

"If yer wan' t' tell me, I'm 'appy to 'ear it."

"You have a son Abram. His name is Arthur."

"Where is 'e?"

"I don't know. He was taken from me." Caron explained to him what had happened.

"Well, what're yer expectin' me t' do about it?"

"Abram, you said we could elope to your cousins in South Wales. Arthur is somewhere in South Wales. We could look for him together."

There was a long pause. Caron waited.

"What's t' point in thet?"

"To find Arthur of course."

"We wouldn't know where t' start lookin'. From what yer say, thet cousin o' yours isn't goin' t' tell yer. I reckon it'd be impossible t' find 'im."

Caron looked at him in disbelief. "But Abram we could try. And we could still elope and get married."

This time Abram responded speedily. "I don't see t' point of thet either. As I said, yer trouble's gone away. Best t' let sleepin' dogs lie. 'Twas different before. T'en we had a problem but yer cousin's sorted thet fer yer. I'm too young t' get married. Yer a Gajo. Me family won't like it. Better we go back t' life as it were before."

"But Abram don't you love me? I thought you did."

Abram spelt it out. "Yer a pretty girl an' we had fun. Thet's all. Now go back t' yer family an' I'll go back t' mine. Let me get on wi' me plantin'."

He turned his back and Caron, glad she was on Jac and could get away quickly, trotted down the lane. How could she have got it so wrong?

That evening after she had taken advantage of a moment alone to hurl her rush ring into the depths of the fire, Caron didn't speak either during or after supper. Mali interpreted her silence as envy of Bethan.

Caron had been banking on Abram providing her with a means of getting Arthur back. While the Tudors were eating, she rolled over in her mind the conversation with Abram. He wasn't going to help her. He wasn't going to marry her. He had no interest in finding his son. The hope she had nursed to her was extinguished. Arthur was gone.

After yet another largely sleepless night Caron was aroused by Mali. "Get up, you lazy girl. I called you half an hour ago. I'm not here to wait on you hand and foot."

"Sorry Mam, I didn't sleep well and I must've dozed back off."

Once breakfast was over, Caron and Bethan were sent out to plant parsnips, carrots and broad beans in the sheltered kitchen garden. Bethan, full of her wedding plans and uncharacteristically garrulous, prattled on about clothes and food and visitors and how she would be mistress of her own house. "Fancy! The Duke of York is getting married today, just over three weeks before me. That must be a good omen. I can't wait to see the pictures of what the new Duchess is wearing." Caron, relieved not to have to make conversation, just murmured assent at intervals.

After about an hour, Mali came out bearing beetroot seeds. Bethan, in full flow, simply carried on. "And then of course, in God's time, we'll start a family. I wonder how many I'll have. Three, maybe even four or five like you

Mam. I'd like a mixture of boys and girls but I hope the first one will be a son. Every man wants a son to carry on the family name."

It was the last straw. "Bethan, how could you be so insensitive? Going on and on about your wedding and children. You know I had a son. You know I had Arthur. Nain must've told you."

Bethan looked at her sister in astonishment. "Well, she didn't. Of course, I knew you'd had an illegitimate child Caron but I didn't know you had a boy or that it was called Arthur. Why did you give it a name when you weren't going to keep it? Its new parents will do that."

Mali intervened. "Caron, I've warned you. You are not to mention that... that incident. It is never to be spoken of in Cwyn-y-Gwynt. You seem to have no shame. Fancy attacking Bethan like that. Of course she's excited about getting married. Any girl would be, marrying such a fine man as Daniel Ellis."

But the floodgates had opened as far as Caron was concerned. "I don't think he's a fine man. He's odd, distant and cold."

Bethan confronted her. "Take that back."

"I won't. It's true. How you're going to share a bed with him I just don't understand."

The argument escalated. Nain, drawn from inside the kitchen by the shouting, could only watch helplessly as Caron's pent-up anger was released.

Bethan retaliated. "Well, you would know all about that wouldn't you, you little slut."

"I'm not a slut. You don't understand what happened. I thought he loved me and I didn't..." She tailed off. It was impossible to explain.

Mali moved to stand face to face with her daughter.

"Love, love." She spat the words out sarcastically. "What sort of nonsense is that? I've told you before. Marriage has nothing to do with love. It's about shared moral values, financial stability and social standing. And Bethan's right, you are a slut. Fancy giving that bastard boy of yours a name! He'll have inherited your bad blood. You're lucky you're not going to see him grow up. Bound to be a common thief or worse."

Caron stared at her mother. Insulting her was bad enough but to abuse Arthur...

She waited a full ten seconds, then, "Mam, I may be a slut but you are... you are... a bitch!"

Caron was prevented from saying more by a stinging slap across her face.

"Don't you dare speak to me like that! After all I've done for you as well. Giving you a fresh start."

"A fresh start! A fresh start! What sort of start can it be for me without Arthur? I've had enough. I'm not staying here one moment longer. I'm going to look for him."

"And just how are you going to do that? You've no money and no job. Without us you'd be out on the streets with the other trollops." Mali finished with a triumphant flourish. "And you won't find that baby. We've seen to that."

Nain, shocked at what she had witnessed came forward. "That's enough," she said. "From all of you. Caron, come inside. I want to speak to you." She ushered Caron into the kitchen. "Wait here." She was back within a few moments with a tightly rolled wad of pound notes. "I've been keeping this for a rainy day," she told Caron. "I think this counts as a thunderstorm. You can't stay here. Not after this. Your Mam'll never let it go. I thought it was for the best that your baby went to a proper home. I thought you could find yourself a good man in Carreg and start again. But I was wrong. Caron, don't think I don't understand what it's like to lose a baby, because I do."

Caron was confused. "What do you mean Nain?"

"You know those bootees you found in the attic. Well, they belonged to your Mam's twin brother."

"Mam's twin? But she's an only child."

"No, cariad. She was the second born twin. My first born died two weeks after he was born, two weeks in which I learnt to love him. I called him Geraint."

"Two weeks Nain! The same time I had with Arthur. And Geraint is one of King Arthur's knights too."

"A strange coincidence cariad. So, you can see I do know how you feel. I still miss him now; I have his scent in my soul."

"So, Nain why did you let them take Arthur away when you knew that it would break my heart."

"I had little choice Caron. I couldn't see any other way out. It seemed best for everyone. Your Mam would never have allowed you to stay here with your baby. Your brothers and sister would've had their lives ruined. And you're only eighteen. You need the chance to start again. I take it your young man wants nothing more to do with you?"

Caron nodded. Her eyes filled with tears.

"Thought so. Happens to too many lasses. Taken in they are."

"Nain, do you know where Arthur is?"

"I don't cariad. I wish I did. But Mair saw to all that. Now go and pack some things and get yourself to the station. It's a long walk but that doesn't matter. There are five trains a day. Save your money and go third class. Do you remember where you changed trains? Get yourself to Corwen, change there... well you know the way; you've done it before. I don't know what you'll do then. Mair won't be best pleased to see you but she may take pity on you and put you up for a night. To get a job you may need to go to Cardiff or Swansea. You should get a domestic position if Mair will speak for you. You're not qualified for anything else."

"I want to find Arthur."

"I doubt you'll be able to do that from what I know of Mair. But you will be able to make a life of your own, find a good man and have a family. And if you take my advice you won't tell him about Arthur. You're an honest girl and you'll want to tell him but, trust me, some secrets are best staying secrets. Life has taught me that. Allowing skeletons to rattle their way out of cupboards can cause a lot more harm than keeping the door firmly locked, hard though that may be."

"Thank you, Nain. I'll write."

Mali, who had been venting her spleen to Bethan, came into the kitchen. "What's going on?"

"Caron's going, Mali."

"Going where?"

"Away."

"But she can't. She's got to be bridesmaid for Bethan."

"You should've thought of that before you came out with words that should never have been spoken."

It took Caron only a short time to pack her meagre belongings, just a few clothes and the sparkling stone Tŵm had given her. She paused. She needed to say goodbye to Tŵm, to explain. But there was no time. She had to get away. Hastily she found a pencil, scribbled a note and pressed it into Nain's hand, whispering, "Give it to Tŵm."

Three hours later, she was huddled in the corner of a compartment on a train bound for South Wales. Cwyn-y-Gwynt lay behind her; only God knew what lay in front of her. Her only certainty was that she was going to search for Arthur.

Tŵm, shocked at Caron's sudden departure, fully understood. Nain told him what had happened. Since Caron had returned, he could see that life was going to be impossible for her. She was stricken. He could see that.

Cwyn-y-Gwynt provided bleak comfort. Mali's vitriol showed no sign of lessening and Bethan's forthcoming nuptials only served as a reminder of what might have been. Siôn, distraught at his sister's second disappearance, was inconsolable. Nain spent many hours trying to calm him by reading the stories Caron used to read. It was going to take some time before he adjusted to Caron's absence. Brad, immersing himself in the farm, was largely indifferent to Caron's whereabouts but Caron's flight caused a predicament for Bethan and Mali who concerned themselves with providing a believable explanation.

"We'll tell everyone that she was offered an opportunity that was too good to turn down. That should do it," Mali suggested.

"But most employers would allow her to attend her sister's wedding," Bethan objected.

"Then we'll say she's got a position as a companion to a sick old lady, whose only son has just emigrated. All will be well Bethan. People will have no reason to question what we say."

Without Caron, Tŵm felt as though he didn't belong any more. Like new boots trying to mould themselves to their owner's feet, he had tried to fit into farm life. But it was no use; he was still uncomfortable, his spirit rubbed raw by the misfit. He determined to visit Olwen Griffiths and Dr. Owen. He needed to sort out his life.

The evening of the next day saw him opening the gate and walking up the same path trodden by his sister when she too was in need of counsel. His brief visit to Tan-y-Graig that morning had started the ball rolling; he now needed to increase the pace.

Richard Owen opened the door himself. "Nos da Tŵm. Come in. What a pleasant surprise." Calling Glenda to make tea and bring some cake, he took Tŵm into his study and seated himself in the brown leather chair, crazed with age, which was his favourite spot for a late night whisky and a chance to ponder over the day's events.

Tŵm came directly to the point. Now he had made the decision, he wanted to make it happen as soon as possible. "Dr. Owen, it's no use. I've tried but I can't farm with Tad any longer. It's not what I want to do with my life. Can you help me get to medical school as soon as possible?"

Richard Owen leant forward. His gaze was intense. Well as he knew him, Tŵm found it disconcerting. "It's late to apply for this year Tŵm but I'll see what I can do. Is it still Liverpool that you want to go to?"

"It is. It's not too far away so travelling is easier. Then there's the Welsh connection. A lot of Welsh people have gone to find work in Liverpool. They've built chapels too and they hold eisteddfods. I'll feel at home there though I doubt I'll have the time or the inclination to be part of chapel society. Also, I had an idea. As you know, I've been thinking about my career for a while so a few weeks ago I visited Tan-y-Graig. You remember Catrin Griffiths, Evan's sister. Well, she lives in Liverpool so I asked Mrs. Griffiths if she'd write to Catrin to see whether she'd put me up for a while, if I were fortunate enough to get a place in medical school. Catrin wrote back by return and immediately offered me a home with her and her husband, Charles."

"That's excellent news Twm. It removes a major obstacle from your path."

"So, doctor, what do I need to do to get a place studying Medicine?"

"You already have enough qualifications Twm but they'll want to know that you are a promising candidate. I'll write you a testimonial fully recommending you and explaining that you have been my highly satisfactory assistant for several years, that I have tutored you and that you already have considerable knowledge. Then, as it happens, my father knows the Dean quite well. They studied together. I'm sure he'll be pleased to vouch for you. They get together on occasion for a sherry and to put the world to rights. I believe there is an entrance examination but with both my father and I speaking up for you, they may decide to forego it in your case. If not, I'll arrange for you to sit it. You won't have any problems passing it, I'm very sure."

He paused and was just about to begin again when Glenda knocked on the door and entered with the refreshments on a tray. As soon as she had poured the tea, Richard Owen settled back down in his chair.

"Twm I want to talk to you very seriously. You remember when I asked you about Siôn's symptoms?"

Twm nodded.

"You told me the truth."

"I did Doctor. I really did. I wasn't lying."

Richard Owen smiled. "I'm not questioning that Twm. I know you told me the truth. What I want you to know is that if you'd lied to me about Siôn, I wouldn't be writing you a testimonial for Liverpool. Doctors have well-nigh impossible decisions to make on occasion. They need a moral compass. You have the right instincts Twm. Never forget to follow them."

"I won't doctor. And my instinct tells me to leave Cwyn-y-Gwynt and go to medical school. I'm not meant to be a farmer. I know that. I have to be a doctor. There's a compulsion in me that means I can't let it go. I just can't, no matter how much trouble it causes back home or how many obstacles are put in my way."

"Then you must follow that direction Twm. You don't have a choice. If you stay in Cwyn-y-Gwynt, you'll never be happy. I'm sure of that."

"Doctor Owen, Mam is dead set against me being a doctor. She says it's my duty to take over Cwyn-y-Gwynt. I'm sure she won't let Tad pay for me as a way to stop me going."

"Now don't you worry about that Twm. You can find yourself a part-time job in Liverpool. There's plenty of work there. It won't be easy with studying as well but others have done it before you and you can do it too. You've already worked on the farm and studied at the same time so you know what it's like. You still passed your exams. You'll have to balance it though. You'll have to leave enough time for your studying and you'll need to watch the shillings. But you're a sensible lad and you'll be able to do that. Then there is something else Twm..."

"Yes, doctor?"

"I am prepared to sponsor you. To help fund your course. You will still have to work but not as hard or as long."

"Doctor Owen. I'm very grateful but I can't take your money."

"Twm you can and you will. I am comfortably off. Just like my brother, I inherited a trust fund from my grandparents. It wasn't huge but it provides me with another income. You would be doing me a favour. I have wondered how best to spend my extra funds and nothing would give me greater pleasure than to see you succeed and go on to heal others, like my friend, Henry, who was a doctor at the Front. Countless soldiers were saved by his skills."

"What happened to him? Where is he now?"

"He was killed Twm. The Germans shelled a field hospital and his medical team took a direct hit. They couldn't even find a body to bury."

Twm stayed silent. There was nothing to say.

Richard Owen continued. "He left behind a wife and two daughters back in Newborough. I visit them when I can and my father and I help them out financially too. I didn't want Henry to join up but he said his skills were needed and of course he was right. I should've gone instead Twm. I didn't have dependants. You asked me once before why I didn't go and I told you that doctors were still needed at home. But you've been honest with me Twm and I will return the compliment. The truth is I was frightened. Given my profession, I didn't have to go. It gave me a way out. And to my eternal shame I took it. I'm not a brave man Twm. That's the truth of it. And to make matters worse I was shown up by my younger brother who answered Kitchener's call. Huw's injuries only serve to rub salt into what will always be an open wound."

Tŵm paused, then spoke. "Doctor Owen. You are the finest man I know. You've saved lives right here in Carreg-y-Bedd. We can't all be fighting men. If you'd gone instead of your friend who's to say what would've happened? You might've been sent somewhere else entirely, rather than where he was sent. Those men whose lives he saved, may well have died."

Richard Owen's reply was simply, "Thank you Tŵm." Then he abruptly changed the subject. "Now tell me how's that sister of yours? Now she's returned from South Wales, has she settled? I'm concerned about her. It's very hard for a young mother to be separated from her baby. Think of how the ewes call out if their lamb has died. You will need to look out for her Tŵm. She isn't in, how shall I say it, a sympathetic environment, is she?"

"No, that's for sure. Mam's been very hard on her. Hasn't let up at all. But Caron's not there, doctor. She had a blazing row with Mam, packed a bag and left. Nain told me what happened. Mam's telling everyone she's got a job as companion to an old lady but she hasn't of course."

Richard Owen frowned. "But where has she gone Tŵm?"

"I simply don't know. She left me a note though." Tŵm drew a crumpled scrap of paper from his pocket. Nowhere in Cwyn-y-Gwynt escaped Mali's scrutiny and the last thing Tŵm wanted was for his Mam to read it. He handed it to Richard Owen. He knew it off by heart.

Tŵm

I know you must want to know how I am and I haven't been able to speak to you. Mam has been watching me all the time.

I had a baby boy and called him Arthur.

I have to go. I can't stay. Mam's making my life wretched and I must look for Arthur. I'll go to see Cousin Mair first and then find a job. Don't worry about me. I'll write to you.

Love Caron

Richard handed it back to Tŵm. Tŵm pushed the doctor's hand away. "I'd be grateful if you could keep it for me doctor. Mam might find it and she'll burn it if she does."

The doctor nodded. "Of course. I'd be happy to. But this is distressing Tŵm. Caron's very young and she's led a sheltered life. I don't like to think of her on her own with no-one to help her."

"I agree doctor. But I can't see what to do. I don't know where she is. She said she'd write and I'm sure she will. Then when I know where she is, I'll go to see her."

"This is what I feared. Separating mother and child is brutal in my view. The anguish Caron must have suffered does not bear thinking about. I'm sorry Tŵm but your Mam has a lot to answer for."

"Don't apologise doctor. I can only agree with you." Tŵm felt profound relief. Previously, guilt about family disloyalty had prevented him from criticising Mali but choosing to tell Richard Owen the truth about Siôn seemed to have released him from his familial obligations.

Tŵm returned to Cwyn-y-Gwynt in a changed mood. Now that he had determined his course it was as though his winter fleece had been shorn. He wore a lightness of spirit and had fire in his belly. Nothing could stop him now. Caron had chosen her own way and he was going to do the same. If his younger sister could do it, then he could too.

Things were certainly going to change at Cwyn-y-Gwynt. Bethan would soon be leaving and Mali would be left with an all-male household, except for Nain. She would have to do all the housework, cooking and gardening herself, with only Nain to help. She wasn't going to like that, Tŵm guessed. Caron had narrowly escaped a life of slavery and drudgery.

The day after Tŵm had visited the doctor, the prospective new regime at Cwyn-y-Gwynt caused Mali to raise the topic. "I'm going to find it difficult to manage the house and garden all by myself. We can't expect Nain to do more. I was thinking of asking Ruth Parry to help. God knows she needs the money and she only works two days at Bryn-y-Castell."

"Good idea," Emyr replied. He approved of anything that helped Ruth.

"As I've said many times, none of us are getting any younger. It won't be long Tŵm before you're going to have to take over more work from your father. Remember the farm will be yours one day and you need to start taking more responsibility."

Emyr intervened. "I'm not on the scrapheap yet, Mali. Don't write me off too soon."

"I know you're not Emyr but farming is hard, especially when the weather is cold or wet. You are fortunate in having two strong sons and another growing fast. They need to pull their weight."

Tŵm was aware of his future being mapped out for him. He could see it lying in front of him like a wasteland which must be endured, traversed, but with never any possibility of reaching the comfort of fertile richness. If he hadn't already organised his escape route, his future would be bleak indeed.

Like a fox in a trap, he fought his way out. "Mam, you know I don't want to farm. I've told you before."

Mali was uncompromising. "And as I've told you before, Twm you have no choice. I have decided that Cwyn-y-Gwynt will be yours. We'll look for another farm for Brad. You'll need to be thinking too about finding yourself a wife in the next few years. There's no hurry. Men don't need to marry as young as women."

"But I want to be a doctor. I was speaking to Doctor Owen. I have the qualifications to go to Liverpool to train to be a doctor. He said he would give me a testimonial."

"That damn doctor! I never swear but his name has forced me into it. He interferes far too much in our family affairs. First your sister and now this! How do you think you would afford it? Your Tad and I are not going to pay."

Emyr had had enough. "Mali, Mali. If the lad's set his heart on Medicine, why can't he do it? We're not wealthy but we're fortunate enough to be able to afford to help him and it's an honourable profession."

"Twm will do as he's told and that's the end of the matter."

The next morning proved to be a fine, sunny April day. After chapel, Twm, sent out to check the stock, couldn't get the previous night's conversation out of his head. Mali wasn't going to budge. That much was clear. But Tad was a different matter. He could be persuaded. Perhaps the way forward was to enlist Emyr's support. Twm was well aware that this was not going to be a straightforward task. Emyr did not like fighting with Mali. He preferred an easy life.

But this was too important to give up now. The past year had changed many lives. Gwyn's death, Caron's troubles. Nothing was the same.

Twm realised that he hadn't even been looking at the sheep, let alone checking that all was well with them. The world inside his head had taken precedence. He couldn't even remember which way he had walked. He looked around him. His long strides had taken him much further than he meant to go. He was right on the boundary of the farm. On an impulse he climbed the stone wall that bordered the large field, Dol Fawr, making a mental note of the repair needed as he did so.

It was a very long time since he'd been there. How many years must it be? Possibly ten. The three of them had been exploring one day when they found slabs of rock, camouflaged by ancient trees, both oak and yew. Climbing up the limestone, they discovered a well disguised fissure, impossible to see until they were directly facing it. Excitedly, and led by Evan, they edged themselves sidewards through the crack and to their delight found themselves in a cave. Waiting until their eyes became accustomed to the gloom, they felt their way around the small space.

"It's not very big," remarked Gwyn.

"No, but it's secret and it's ours," replied Evan. "I don't suppose anyone has ever been here before, or not for millions of years anyway!"

"We could do with some light," added the ever-practical Tŵm. "We need to bring candles next time."

They had returned again and again, making a den that no-one else knew anything about, lighting a campfire so that shadows flickered up the rock walls. One memorable day they had pretended Evan was Tŵm Siôn Cati, the Robin Hood of Wales, robbing Tŵm and Gwyn of all the money and jewels they were carrying. Bright, sparkling pebbles they found in a nearby quarry were ideal rubies, sapphires and emeralds while acorns made perfectly satisfactory coins. The cave became the bandit's hideaway.

"Tŵm Siôn Cati was even better than Robin Hood," Evan announced. "I'm going to be him."

"Well, it's debatable," answered Tŵm. "I read that he took from the rich and gave to Tŵm Siôn Cati, rather than giving to the poor. Anyway, I should be him, I have the same name."

"Oh, you can't be him Tŵm."

"Why not?"

As always, Evan had an answer for everything. "Because you've never learnt to fire an arrow. That's why. Tŵm Siôn Cati was an expert marksman. He used to pin his victims to the saddle with an arrow."

"Then I don't want to be him anyway," retorted Tŵm. "He sounds cruel."

"No, you're wrong. He was famous for not killing or hurting people too badly."

Tŵm, sarcastic, answered, "No, of course not Evan. It really doesn't hurt much at all to be pierced by an arrow!"

Evan ignored him. "You know Tad made me a bow and arrow when I was five and showed me how to use it, so I have to be Tŵm Siôn Cati." Evan, triumphant in victory, had dealt the final blow.

Tŵm knew when he was beaten. He gave in. "Well, alright then. You can rob me and Gwyn."

Gwyn, hadn't taken part in the argument, content to wait for his role. But once Evan had cut down some yew branches and shown them how to make crude bows and arrows, sharpening the tips with a penknife, he threw himself into the game. Tŵm had brought the string.

"In the old days, archers poisoned the tips with red yew berries," Evan informed them. "Then their enemies died a long and lingering death." He drew out the words with relish.

Gwyn shuddered. "I don't think we should touch the berries. We don't want poison on our hands."

Tŵm agreed. "No, Evan we don't. I've known cattle die from eating yew."

Evan, intent on shaving off wood peelings, didn't even look up. He just shrugged. "Alright, no berries then."

They had played the highwayman game all that day. It must've been autumn mused Tŵm if the berries were on the yews. Strange that childhood days seemed never-ending while now the days simply flew past. Evan, enjoying his role as expert, had taught them to shoot. "Look at your target, stand sideways, keep one finger above the arrow and two below, draw the string back to your nose and fire."

Gwyn's arrow had flown straight and true, only stopping when it hit the trunk of a tree. Tŵm's arrow had fallen to the ground just missing his feet. He pulled a face. "I thought I'd be better at this than you," he told Gwyn.

Gwyn, ignoring the insult, laughed. "I'm older than you and I've done it before. We visited a cousin and he'd been given a bow and arrow for his birthday. We played with it all afternoon. It just takes practice that's all."

By the end of the day, they were all reasonably successful gentlemen of the road, well able to fire arrows over a short distance. Tŵm smiled at the memory. It hadn't crossed their minds that one day two of them would have to shoot for real. Not arrows of course; conflict had moved on. But still...

Tŵm wondered if anyone else had discovered their hideout. "For old times' sake," he muttered to himself. Climbing up through the trees, the slope seemed steeper than he remembered. He scrambled up, determined to reach his goal, his feet slipping on loose stones. Grabbing at a tuft of grass, he finally hauled himself up the base of the rocks. Squeezing himself through and around the fissure proved a little tricky. Of course, I'm much bigger than I was, he told himself. The cave smelt familiar, damp and mossy. Tŵm tripped over something. Bending down to feel what it was, he realised it was the remains of what had once been a campfire, their campfire. It didn't seem that anyone else had succeeded them; the sticks, now turned to charcoal, were in exactly the position they had set them down all those years ago. Tŵm felt his way around just as his ten-year-old self had done. As his eyes adjusted to the darkness, he could make out a shape against the far wall. Gingerly he made his way across the uneven floor, hands outstretched. If only he had a candle. Touching whatever was there, he used his fingers to identify it. It seemed to be made of some sort of material. Then his fingers touched something cold. Tracing the edges, Twm identified a metal tin of some sort. Alongside it was another object, bottle shaped but covered in what felt like serge, with straps attached to it. Carefully Twm gathered them all up and made his way out into the daylight, blinking against the sunshine. He slithered back down the slope until he reached the flat grassy bank at the base. Sitting down, he examined what he had found. In the clear light of day, he could see immediately that what he had laid out in front of him was a filthy webbing haversack, held together with straps and rusty buckles and an enamel water bottle, covered in felt, encased in hard, cracked leather straps, presumably to fasten it to a belt. Levering the stopper off the bottle, he turned it upside down. It was quite empty. He smelt it. There was no smell at all. Must've been for water he thought. Certainly, no-one had kept alcohol in it.

Twm turned his attention to the haversack. It took some time to undo the straps which had seized on to the buckles. Even Twm's hardened fingers struggled to cope. He swore under his breath as a rusty buckle pin pierced his finger. Eventually he won the battle and lifted the flap. A thick sheaf of pictures spilt out. Gwyn's deft, firm lines were unmistakeable.

Clearing the sheep droppings out of the way with his foot, he spread the drawings out on the flat ground. He noticed the numbering almost immediately. Each picture had a number neatly imprinted in the top left-hand corner. Twm began putting them in order. There were more than he thought. By the time he had finished, fifty sheets of paper lay stacked before him.

Twm began to investigate the detail one by one. As he did so, a cold chill spread up his spine and froze his spirit. He was a voyeur with harlot's wares flaunted in front of his fascinated gaze. He tried and failed to avert his eyes. Drawn ever inwards, he became a part of a world he did not want to enter.

Gwyn had used his skill to portray his journey; a journey that began in the hills of Wales and wound its way to the battlefields of France. Gwyn's inimitable style, more graphic than words, allowed the story to unfold. The sequence began innocuously with no hint of what was to come. Gwyn with his serious, intent expression and Evan, all floppy hair and lop-sided grin, training at what must be Kinmel Camp: fixing bayonets; firing pistols; wiping rifles with oily rags; marching stripped to the waist; cleaning boots; resting on one elbow while eating a sandwich and smiling as if having a photograph taken. Next came the station: steam billowing from the engine, enveloping a mother in a wide brimmed straw hat; a young woman, her head nestled into the neck of her lover like a dove with its head under its wing. The men, on their way to the Front, leaned out of carriage windows, waving their hats, women thrusting photos into their hands. A little girl, in a frilled dress, clutched a hanky and a dog barked madly in the midst of the mêlée. Farewell shouts, love's whispers, cries of, 'Keep safe,' or 'God bless,' echoed from every stroke of the pencil. Tŵm marvelled at Gwyn's God-given talent. Emotional vibrancy throbbed from every line; apprehension camouflaged by excitement, expectation, patriotism and, above all, pride.

He moved on. The detail was astounding. While his friends were at the Front, Tŵm had pored over every news story, anxiety fuelling his attention. He had no difficulty in recognising the sordid images of warfare. A soldier, flat on his belly, aiming a twin legged Lewis gun at who knows what; horses and mules, with staring eyes, piled high ready for burial; a pigeon being flung aloft bearing its military message; marching soldiers in heavy overcoats, bent double with the weight of gas masks, rifles, ammunition, water bottles, trench tools; a group of lads carrying reels of telephone cable; blast-defying sandbags stacked on top of trench parapets; floating observation balloons; field guns protected with sandbag walls and shrouded in camouflage netting; trophy rats hung on a line; a tank teetering drunkenly on the brink of a shell hole; a tri-plane in a dog fight with a Focker.

Then there were the operating instruments essential for this orchestrated theatre: rifle grenades standing stiffly to attention; the exploding canisters of trench mortars; hand bombs; rifles complete with bayonets; machine guns; wooden clubs made deadly with horse shoe nails; sharpened daggers; automatic pistols.

On occasion, paradoxically beautiful images sliced through the nightmare. 17, 21, 26, unlike the others, were in colour. God only knows where Gwyn had found crayons and chalks but he had. Perhaps he had smuggled them in himself, sewing them in to the lining of his jacket. Tŵm wouldn't put it past him. He remembered that in school Gwyn sometimes forgot his lunch but never his pencils and crayons. 17 portrayed an explosion, perhaps a mine. A swelling mound of yellow-brown smoke, supported by an underbelly of orange-pink clouds, lit up the night sky; silhouetted figures in dug outs inhabited the foreground while a sole sniper guarded his post. In 21, stars glittered like steel in an icy, ashen sky, while in 26, a coppice of trees glowed green through soft swirls of mist.

Some of the saddest images were those that reminded Tŵm of the soldiers' attempts to retain a semblance of normality: two comrades using the water in a shell hole to shave; a lone recruit reading a post card from home; men sleeping half upright in a narrow trench, using a pack as a pillow; a bearded officer sucking at a pipe; a sergeant prising open a can of bully beef. Then in 28, a rare moment of humour, with a smirking Tommy wearing a souvenir German coalscuttle helmet at a jaunty angle. Tŵm paused over 31 and 32. Gwyn had captured rare shreds of humanity among the sickening, grisly degradation: a British soldier offering food to a German prisoner; a mud-soaked rifleman covering what remained of a face with a bloodstained cape.

Then the images changed. Each one bore the face of despair, the grim mask of suffering. Stretcher bearers bore a young boy, one lacerated arm hanging slack over the side, a gaping hole where once there had been a nose, while in the background a battle-scarred veteran tossed a Mills bomb with practised ease. Two men struggled to free a comrade held fast by wire gouging deep into his flesh; another four, dodging shells in No Man's Land, were dragging a young lad towards a trench, shreds of a handkerchief tourniquet flapping round a protruding shard of bone where his thigh used to be. He stopped momentarily at 37. The paper had been divided into two halves, a ghastly cause and effect. On the left side, clouds of gas were enveloping the men; on the right, soldiers were vomiting and coughing, tearing at blistered skin, clawing at inflamed eyes; three had managed to don hideous masks that made them look like devils emerging from the smoke of hell.

The next few drawings compounded the nauseating sights: soldiers digging a grave for a fly blown corpse; a medic dressing blackened and rotting feet; a young German soldier sinking into the filth of a mine crater, eyes flashing white with panic; a young lad pissing into a Boche helmet with bloated rats, big as otters, floating in the filthy scum that surrounded him; a stretchered body covered with a Union Jack.

Tŵm, gripped and unable to draw his eyes away from the horror that was unfolding, inexorably crawled towards number 42.

At first Tŵm did not realise what had changed. Then, like a splinter of shrapnel, it struck him. *He recognised the faces.* All the other pictures had been simply faces; anguished faces, terrified faces, stoical faces. But all just faces. Number 42 was different. For one thing it had a date on it: *23rd March 1918.* It also had a place: *Morchies.*

A bright moon lit up the darkness above swirling fog. Tŵm could see a patrol of five soldiers, creeping across shell blasted ground towards what appeared to be an enemy stronghold. Two of the group were clearly identifiable as Gwyn and Evan. He could make out a lone machine gun in the distance but it didn't seem to have anyone firing it. They must be using the cover of night to launch a surprise attack, thought Tŵm. He picked up the next picture and realised there was a sequence. He was following a story.

Upturned faces of astonished, alarmed Germans greeted him in Number 43. This time the machine gun was in the foreground with the enemy hunkered down in a foxhole behind it. Two of Evan's and Gwyn's comrades had leapt into the hollow and started to grapple with the enemy. One fusilier, halted abruptly in mid-air, was impaled on a Boche bayonet, mouth agape, tongue lolling. Gwyn was hesitating on the brink; Evan behind him, mouth open, was urging on his friend. Tŵm could only guess at the words he was using.

44 came as a shock. A pitched battle was taking place. One of the enemy was falling backwards hit by a well-aimed pistol shot. Evan was in the thick of it, wielding a club, wound round with barbed wire, in one hand and a combat knife in the other. He had a look of intense determination, was parrying a blow with the club and thrusting the knife forward. Tŵm did not give much for the German's chances. One of Evan's mates was using a trench spade to slice the throat of a soldier who was trying vainly to free his bayonet from its case. His companion was pushing away a burly Hun who was attempting to throttle him. Gwyn was looking down on them seemingly frozen with horror.

Tŵm picked up 45 with a sick feeling in his stomach. Evan's victim was clutching a chest wound which looked to be close to his heart; an enemy soldier, throat gaping open, had fallen backwards and lay against the bank of the fox hole; a fallen fusilier, head askew, had likely had his neck broken while the remaining Tommy was clinging to the back of the Hun who had been choking his friend, stabbing his side with a knife. Gwyn, solitary, stood in the same place. The only difference was that he had fixed his bayonet. At least he's thinking of action, Tŵm thought.

46 provided a brief respite from the bloodshed. The page had been divided into two, just like 37. On the left side, six callow members of the Kaiser's army, grey with dread, stood with their hands in the air, clearly with no taste for engaging in further combat with Evan and his hostile companions. The unknown victor stood guard over them with a pistol; on the right side, the six Germans could be seen, under direction from the sole fusilier, being forced to carry the machine gun back towards British lines. Tŵm sighed with relief. It was over. He picked up 47.

His heart lurched. It wasn't over. Another German soldier who must have been hiding, awaiting his chance, had climbed out of the hole and was confronting Gwyn, the point of his bayonet almost touching Gwyn's throat.

Gwyn's expression registered trepidation. He was going to have to use his own bayonet thought Twm and he was going to have to use it quickly before the German made his move. Indecision was stamped on Gwyn's features. Twm could not imagine Gwyn thrusting a bayonet into living flesh. He remembered the time Gwyn slowly and carefully released a terrified hare from a trap laid by poachers. Killing was not in his nature. Would he be able to fight in self-defence?

The answer lay in 48. The sketch showed Evan, now out of the foxhole. He had thrown the club and knife to one side and was now equipped with a pistol in his left hand. Realising Gwyn was incapable of action, he had placed himself in between Gwyn and the enemy.

Number 49 unveiled the stark truth. The German soldier's action had clearly been deflected by Evan's swift intervention because the German was lying askew in the trench, his head caved in, presumably by the pistol butt Evan had been wielding. But using the 'unnatural' hand had left Evan's body unprotected. Before the German died, he must have thrust with his bayonet, skewering it deep into Evan, for Evan's bowels lay in a steaming grey heap alongside his body. Evan, anguish etched on his face, was pointing at Gwyn's bayonet. His eyes said it all. There was no question as to what he wanted.

Twm turned to 50. There it was, clearly numbered like the rest. But it was completely blank. Clearly Gwyn couldn't bring himself to outline what had happened. Faced with a white sheet of paper, Twm drew a mental picture. Evan was still alive in 49. It was impossible for him to survive. He was in unspeakable agony. What else could his best friend do?

On the very last day of April 1923, Twm, satisfied that he had uncovered the truth at last, took spring daffodils to Gwyn's grave. "You certainly weren't 'yella' Gwyn," he told his friend, "you were braver than all of us. I understand now why you did what you did. You were carrying an unbearable burden and none of us knew."

What was it Gwyn had told him in a rare moment of intimacy? That he didn't speak about the war because he didn't want to share the pictures that haunted his head. Twm realised now that Gwyn had been trying to protect his friend. He had told Twm that once there, the images were there forever. And he was right. Twm could not unsee the pictures he had found. He had to learn to live with the images that Gwyn only managed to erase in the depths of Pwll Berw. He was only thankful Number 50 was not inhabiting his mind as it must have dwelt in Gwyn's.

On reaching home, Tŵm sought out Mali. He found her weeding in between the broad beans and early peas.

"Oh, Tŵm there you are. If you're not doing anything for Tad, you can help me with this."

"Mam I want to speak to you and Tad. Nain's making a pot of tea and Tad's just gone in for a drink."

Mali, resenting being directed by her son, answered, "No, Tŵm. I want to finish this first."

Feigning courage, he didn't really possess, Tŵm took a deep breath and continued. "Mam, this is important. I want to speak to you both but if you don't want to come in then so be it. I'll just talk to Tad." He turned his back and walked into the house.

Mali, nettled but intrigued, not wanting Emyr and Nain to know something before she did herself, put down her tools and made her way into the kitchen. She found, what remained of her family, seated around the table. Siôn was in school, Brad was mending a gap in a stone wall and Bethan was visiting a friend in the village.

Mali decided to take charge. "What's the matter? Why the serious faces?"

Tŵm took the plunge. "Mam, Tad, I have made a decision. I'm not going to take over the farm. I'm going to become a doctor. I have the qualifications for entry and I'm going to do it."

Mali didn't allow him to go any further. "Tŵm I won't have it. I've told you before, you have a duty to run this farm and run it you will."

"No, Mam I'm not going to do that. Nothing you can say will make me do it. I helped on the farm during and after the war but I'm not going to do it anymore."

"And where do you think you're going to go?" Mali, tight lipped, was clearly seething.

"Liverpool. I'm going to Liverpool."

"Oh, so you've got it all sorted have you? I suppose that doctor's at the bottom of this."

Tŵm stayed calm. "He has helped me, yes. I asked him to. I will leave in September. Up until then I will help on the farm."

"Tŵm, Cwyn-y-Gwynt is your inheritance. If you do this you will be struck out of my will."

"Mali!" Emyr was aghast. "You've lost one child and you're going the right way to lose another."

"Tad, it's fine. I don't mind. Let her cut me out of her will if she wants. Leave the farm to Brad. That's the best thing to do. If Brad wasn't here, the situation might be more difficult. But he is. He's a born farmer. I'm not. Then there's Siôn. He will grow into a fine young man. You won't be short of helping hands. We're in a much better position than the Griffiths' and many others besides."

Mali, expert at playing the martyr, retorted, "Twm, I don't know how you could do this to me."

Twm was not going to go out of his way to antagonise Mali further but he continued to run on his chosen rails. "I'm not doing it to upset you Mam; I'm doing it for me. Evan and Gwyn had their lives cruelly cut short. I'm making sure that I live mine the way I want to. I'll feel I've wasted my life otherwise and I can't carry on feeling that. It's no use arguing with me. I won't change my mind."

"Then there's no more to be said," contributed Nain. Knowing exactly how to placate her daughter, she continued, "I think being a doctor is an admirable career. You should be proud of him Mali. No-one else in the chapel has a son training to be a doctor."

"No-one cares what you think Mam. Owning land is what matters. Gives a man real standing in the community."

Nain was not to be silenced. "So does being a doctor. It's not as though Twm's announced he wants to be a burglar is it?"

"Mam, now you're being ridiculous."

At last, Emyr spoke up. "You'll be twenty-one this year Twm. Able to make your own decisions. We can't stop you even if we wanted to, which I don't."

Mali flushed, unused to not having Emyr's support. She tried again.

"And precisely how are you going to pay for the training Twm?"

"I've thought of that Mam. Liverpool's a big city. There's plenty of work there. I'll work as well as study. It'll be tough but I know I can do it." Twm had decided beforehand that it wasn't wise to tell Mali of the doctor's generosity. She didn't need to know.

"You'll have to find somewhere to stay. That'll be expensive."

"I've already got somewhere Mam."

"You can't have. Where is it?"

"I'm going to stay with Evans' sister, Catrin and her husband, Charles. They said they'd be pleased to have me and they're only going to charge me my keep so I've no rent to pay."

Even Nain was surprised at that. "But you've never liked Catrin, Twm. You've always said she's stuck-up and only interested in money."

"Well, maybe I was too hasty. Perhaps Evan's death has made her see things differently. Mrs. Griffiths wrote to her to ask if could just stay while I looked for somewhere. But Catrin wouldn't hear of it me looking elsewhere. She replied by return of post to say that they have plenty of room and I must live with them. She wrote that she was more than happy to help me, as Evan's friend."

Mali couldn't contain herself. "Twm, you spoke to Olwen Griffiths about this before you spoke to me! How could you? I didn't think my eldest son, of all people, could be so deceitful and underhand! I'm going to give Olwen Griffiths a piece of my mind. Going behind my back like that!"

"You'll do no such thing Mali." Emyr's voice was unexpectedly firm. "That poor woman has suffered enough without you causing her more trouble. I won't allow it."

Twm joined in. "Mam, it's not her fault. She was only trying to help. I asked her to write to Catrin. Mrs. Griffiths actually asked me if I'd spoken to you about it first but I said there was no point unless Catrin had got room for me. I knew you might not be pleased about it."

"Oh, so you did realise I would be upset," Mali sniffed.

"I knew you wouldn't be in favour of my plans."

"Well, Twm, if you decide to abandon your family and your duty, you needn't think you will find a welcome here. You will have made your bed and you'll have to lie in it."

"I didn't expect to Mam. But I've got to go my own way."

Emyr was quick to respond. "Mali, Twm is my first-born son and there will always be a home for him at Cwyn-y-Gwynt. I am not losing a second child."

Unused to being contradicted, Mali's anger intensified. "And as for you Emyr Tudor. All I can say is that there must be bad blood in your family. First, Caron; now Twm. Thank goodness for Brad and Bethan. Maddock they are, through and through."

Emyr was not for backing down. "You cannot compare the two Mali. Caron did wrong. I don't deny that. But she's young. She's not the first to be led astray and she won't be the last. Twm's not doing anything wrong. He's simply choosing his path and it's different from the one you mapped out for him. That's all."

"That's all! That's all! Cwyn-y-Gwynt is not a path and it's not a choice.

It's our lifeblood. It runs in our veins. For Twm to turn his back on it is to be nothing less than a traitor to his forbears."

Seeing that Mali was not going to move from her position, Emyr took control. "Mali, I should never have allowed you to bring pressure to bear on Twm this last year. It's his life and he's entitled to do what he wants with it. I'm proud he's going to be a doctor and you should be as well. It's about time someone told you that you're wrong, very wrong and that someone is me. I'm only sorry I haven't done it before. And that is the end of the matter." He turned to his son. "Twm have you finished your tea? I need a hand in the cowshed."

Listening to Emyr, Nain felt like applauding. Emyr was right. It was about time Mali was put firmly in her place, though how long she would stay there was open to question.

At the minister's house, Daniel Ellis pondered his future. In less than three weeks he would be a married man. He could look forward to a settled life, respect from God's community, a wife to look after him, upright sons and caring daughters. He heaved a satisfied sigh. What a blessing he'd done the right thing.

He shuddered at the thought of how close he'd come to humiliation, personal rejection and public exposure. After all the sacrifices he'd made; sharing his time, his soul and his God. He'd more or less offered himself on a plate. Only to be rebuffed, to be called, 'Disgusting!' 'Repellant!' 'Depraved!' He hadn't meant to strike out but the abuse was the final straw. He couldn't be expected to turn the other cheek.

No, he'd had no choice.

The Parry boy would have spoilt everything.

Acknowledgements

I would like to thank:

Dr. John Krijnen MD, whose encyclopaedic knowledge of WW1 and the Royal Welch Fusiliers allowed me to embed fictional events within historical fact. John, one of the first members of the Western Front Association, in fact, member number 70, generously gave his time as a guide in Belgium and France. This enabled me to visit the war cemeteries in Cambrin and Morchies and museums such as Passchendaele, to see for myself the locations referred to in the War Diaries. The book has benefited from his unparalleled expertise and unquestioned authority.

Brian Owen AMA, Curator of the Royal Welch Fusiliers Museum. Endlessly helpful and enthusiastic, it was Brian who unearthed the War Diaries on my visit to the museum so that I could research the movements of the 2nd and 9th Battalions in 1916 and 1918 respectively. He also provided me with the format of official letters to the bereaved families of those soldiers who had been killed. He sadly passed away in 2019.

Mr. Michael Crumplin FRCS, retired general surgeon and expert on battlefield injuries and surgery. I am indebted for his advice on medical matters, his patience in answering my, often naïve, questions and his ability to explain complex physiological changes with clarity.

Ifor Roberts, farmer and friend, whose historical and contemporary experience of agriculture in North Wales allowed me to reflect the seasonal rhythms of the farming year. I'm grateful for his cheerful good humour in response to my many queries and his help with my use of the Welsh language.

Gill Frances, retired English lecturer, ex-colleague and friend. Her skills in analysing narrative have meant that 'Bread and Buttermilk' is a better novel than it would have been without her critical eye. She provided motivation and encouragement when I needed it most.

Above all my love and thanks go to my husband, Paul. I am so grateful to him for his understanding of my tendency to inhabit a different world, his patience with a grumpy writer who hates being disturbed, and his willingness to cook meals so that I could continue to write.

Appendix 1

Welsh Translation

Mam	Mother
Tad	Father
Taid	Grandfather
Nain	Grandmother
Hen Nain	Great-grandmother
Hen Tad	Great-grandfather
bore da	good morning
pnawn da	good afternoon
nos da	good night
fawr	big
bechgyn mawr	big boys
carthenni	blankets
cariad	darling
cau dy geg	shut up
diolch	thank you
ffridd	mountain pasture
heol isaf	lower road
heol uchaf	higher road
hiraeth	yearning for home
tyddyn	smallholding
tâs sopyn	corn ricks
traeth	beach
Dwi'n dy garu di	I love you
Pam fi Dyw?	Why me God?

Meaning of Place Names

Cae Hir	Long Field
Cae Glas Uchaf	Higher Green Field
Dol Fawr	Big Field
Carreg-y-Bedd	Rocky Grave
Hiraethog	Upland region in Conwy and Denbighshire between Snowdonia and the Clwydian Range. It includes the Clocaenog Forest.
Cwyn-y-Gwynt	Lament of the Wind
Banc-y-Defaid	Hillside of the Sheep
Bryn-y-Castell	Castle on the Hill
Ffynnon Ddu	Black Well
Tŷ Faenor	Stone House of the Chieftain
Tŷ Capel	Chapel House
Hendreforgan	Home of the Morgans
Moelfre	Bare Hill
Pwll Berw	Seething Pool
Tan-y-Graig	Under the Rock
Tan-y-Waun	Under the Moorland
Tŷ Celyn	Holly House
Y Betws	House of Prayer
Yr Efail	The Smithy
Pen-coed	Head of the Wood
Pen Rhiw Bach	Small Top of the Hillside

Anthem and Festivals

Mae Hen Wlad Fy Nhadau	Land of my Fathers (Welsh National Anthem)
Nos Calan Gaeaf	Winter's Eve/Spirit Night October 31st
Calennig	New Year
Cymanfa Ganu	Hymn Festival
Plygain	Traditional Christmas service between 3am and 6am Christmas morning
Dydd Santes Dwynwen	St. Dwynwen's Day 25th January; Valentine's Day in Wales

Appendix 2

Villagers in Carreg-y-Bedd

Ieuwan Benyon (farmer, Moelfre); Marc Benyon (Ieuwan's son, farmer/ shearer); Gareth Bevan (young organist); Sarah Bevan (Gareth's sister); Glenda Davies (doctor's housekeeper); Samuel Davis (vet); Alun Edwards (police sergeant); Dilwyn Evans (school friend of Sion); Idwal Edwards (odd job boy); John and Rhian Hughes (shop owners); Anwen Hughes (their daughter); Dylan Jenkins (farm labourer); Idris Jones (farmer, Tan-y-Waun); Merfyn Kendrick (farm labourer); Robert Lewis (police constable); Sam Lloyd (gamekeeper); Maggie Miles (old lady); Hywel Morris (school friend of Twm); Aled Owen (schoolfriend of Caron); Alis Phillips (older organist); Bryn Powell (publican, Lamb and Lion); Maldwyn Price (butcher); Manon Price (Maldwyn's daughter); John Pritchard (ex-soldier); Lowri Pritchard (John's daughter); Cadog Roberts (farmer, Banc-y-Defaid); Dafydd Roberts (schoolfriend of Caron); Dewi Rogers (musician); Llinos Rowlands (housemaid); Dai Stephens (schoolfriend of Sion); Jane Turner (Post Office); Haf Watkins (needlewoman); Luned Williams (schoolfriend of Twm).

Printed in Great Britain
by Amazon

13167643R00210